Following two ye[ars in the]
Australian Army, [he attended the]
University of Tasmania, graduating in political science and winning the university's prize in international relations. Later, as an Australia–Japan Business Cooperation Committee Scholar, he carried out research on Japan's relations with China and the rest of Asia in the Law Faculty of Tokyo University. He then worked for an Australian resources company in Japan, before being recruited into the Australian Secret Intelligence Service (ASIS). After training with MI6 in London, he served as an intelligence officer for ten years in Asia and the Middle East. Later, he worked as a consultant to Australian firms operating in Asia, published a number of books on the region and also worked for three years as chief operating officer of the Committee for Economic Development of Australia. More recently, he has been occupied in writing and commenting in the media on intelligence and security matters.

Also by Warren Reed

Plunging Point: Intelligence Failures, Cover-ups and Consequences (with Lance Collins)

CODE CICADA

蝉暗号

WARREN REED

HarperCollinsPublishers

HarperCollins*Publishers*

First published in Australia in 2004
This edition published in 2006
by HarperCollins*Publishers* Australia Pty Limited
ABN 36 009 913 517
www.harpercollins.com.au

Copyright © Warren Reed 2004

The right of Warren Reed to be identified as the author of this work has been asserted by him under the *Copyright Amendment (Moral Rights) Act 2000*.

This work is copyright. Apart from any use as permitted under the *Copyright Act 1968*, no part may be reproduced, copied, scanned, stored in a retrieval system, recorded, or transmitted, in any form or by any means, without the prior written permission of the publisher.

HarperCollins*Publishers*
25 Ryde Road, Pymble, Sydney, NSW 2073, Australia
31 View Road, Glenfield, Auckland 10, New Zealand
77–85 Fulham Palace Road, London W6 8JB, United Kingdom
2 Bloor Street East, 20th floor, Toronto, Ontario M4W 1A8, Canada
10 East 53rd Street, New York NY 10022, USA

National Library of Australia Cataloguing-in-Publication data:

Reed, Warren.
　Code Cicada.
　ISBN 0 7322 7964 X.
　1. Spies – Australia – Fiction. 2. Secret service –
　Australia – Fiction. 3. Diplomatic and consular service,
　Chinese – Australia – Fiction. I. Title.
A823.3

Cover design by Heiko Meins
Internal design by Mark Gowing Design
Typeset in BaskervilleBerthQA 10.5/13 by Kirby Jones
Printed and bound in Australia by Griffin Press on 50gsm Bulky News

6 5 4 3 2 1　　06 07 08 09

This book is dedicated to the vast majority of loyal Australians who work to better themselves and their country. It is a story about how easily so many can be betrayed by so few.

AUTHOR'S NOTE

None of the characters in this book resembles, or is intended to resemble, any person, living or dead.

The story was inspired by a report in May 1995. This involved an ABC-TV and *Sydney Morning Herald* account of the alleged bugging of the Embassy of the People's Republic of China in Canberra and the subsequent, unsuccessful efforts of the Australian Government to stifle publication of the details of that alleged operation. Although the sequence of publicly disclosed events occurred more or less as set forth, each of the characters and the non-public events are fictitious.

CODE CICADA
蝉暗号

ONE

Sydney: 12 April 1995

'Thank you for coming, Ms Fenton,' Zhang said, smiling warmly at the software executive.

He moved on to another guest, an Indian–Australian businessman who was already extending his hand. Zhang glanced at the man's name-tag. 'Oh, Mr Gupta,' he said, 'I'm so pleased to see you.'

Zhang was in full diplomatic mode, though he was working the room 'on automatic'. It was his fifth such function this week and he was tired as well as bored.

There was a reasonably good crowd at the cocktail party he had organised for the trade delegation from Fujian Province, but as usual things had gone wrong. The evening was heavy and the air-conditioning had broken down again at the Sydney Consulate of the People's Republic of China. With luck, no one would linger beyond eight and he would get home in time for something he wanted to watch on television.

Zhang Wendao was a 'straight' trade official – meaning that he had no links with intelligence – and worked with MOFTEC, China's Ministry of Foreign Trade and Economic Cooperation. Originally a student of anthropology, and later of economics, he was a social animal who drew a lot from people around him.

A middle-aged Australian, smartly dressed in a lightweight business suit and green tie, now came up to him. They had met a number of times before. Although Peter Phillips claimed to be a fellow trade officer, Zhang suspected he might be some sort of spy. But they both liked kung fu movies – Zhang had been a champion in the sport – and Phillips always had something interesting to talk about, whatever the topic.

The Australian handed Zhang a small package. 'Here's the video you wanted.'

Zhang smiled, touched by the gift – a new digital three-hour version of the 1968 kung fu classic, *A Touch of Zen*, wide-screen and very hard to get. He offered his thanks.

'Look,' Phillips went on, 'I've got something to tell you.'

Zhang could see from his expression that, whatever it was, it was more serious than a discussion of movies. 'If you can hang on for a moment,' he said, 'I might be able to slip away.' The television would have to wait.

Phillips nodded. 'Take your time. I'll be waiting outside.'

– – –

Zhang felt his tiredness drain away as a gentle flush of cool air from the restaurant's overhead fan dried the sweat under his shirt. Round-faced and with short, straight black hair that stuck up on the crown of his head like a boy's, the 44-year-old Chinese was both solid and agile. He was on his second posting to Australia, knew the country well, and felt at ease with its people.

Phillips was in good form. There were the inevitable comparisons between Jackie Chan and Bruce Lee, a spirited defence of Hong Kong director King Hu's *The Fate of Lee Khan*, and rhapsodies about Angela Mao.

'Oh, those high kicks – pure poetry!' he proclaimed.

Zhang had no reason to disagree, but he was keen to know what it was that the Australian wished to raise with him. A quick glance at his watch did the trick, bringing Phillips back on track as they reached their main course, having almost finished a bottle of wine. Phillips began by suddenly asking about a consular report that Zhang was writing on Australia–China trade – a report that was meant to be secret.

Zhang's annoyance showed, but Phillips smiled placatingly. 'Don't get mad,' he said. 'You'll understand when I explain.'

Zhang frowned again. 'As for my report,' he said, 'it's coming along fine, but with all due respect that's hardly *your* business.' He paused. 'Look, what I need to know is how you know about it.'

Phillips took a deep breath, then sighed. 'Your embassy in Canberra is bugged,' he said quietly.

'But it's checked every few weeks, I think,' Zhang said, realising he had no choice but to acknowledge reality.

'I know it is, but it's still bugged.'

'Are you sure?'

'Too right I am.'

Two thoughts flashed through Zhang's mind: one, that Phillips was a genuine 'walk in' with vital information; and the other, that he was an *agent provocateur* out to trick Zhang into identifying the real intelligence operatives in the consulate in Sydney.

'You see, there's a whole story to this,' Phillips said. 'ASIO's been helping with a huge bugging job on your new building in Canberra. It all started when it went up a few years ago.'

Zhen de, Zhang thought, studying Phillips intently: this sounds horribly true.

Although a genuine trade official, Zhang had long ago been obliged to complete basic espionage training with the Chinese Ministry of State Security. This had honed his senses and taught him the importance of keeping his face and hands under control so they could not be read like a book. Now his instincts told him that Phillips was not fooling around.

'Virtually the whole of your embassy's been rigged with optical fibre.' Phillips hesitated over the technical term, raising his eyebrows for confirmation that Zhang knew what it meant. Zhang nodded.

'The NSA in America provided all the hardware, all cutting-edge stuff.'

Zhang smiled politely.

'We couldn't have done a job like this ourselves,' Phillips said, 'so it's been a joint operation all the way, and still is.'

Zhang chose to say nothing. He was keen to hear the rest of Phillips's story. Other thoughts were racing through his mind, but they would have to wait until later.

The Australian kept his voice down. 'Actually, in an earlier position in intelligence I was involved in the project myself.' A subtle but confident smile crossed his face.

He must think that's a plus of some kind, Zhang thought. It's also an admission that he's in the spying game.

'But the operation's a bit of a failure,' Phillips said. 'It's been nowhere near as successful as the Americans hoped.' He grinned mischieviously. 'Of course, things broke down when you moved into the place and made those modifications. All that structural mucking around played havoc with the NSA's setup, but bits and pieces worked and we're still pulling in some pretty useful material.'

Zhang was now prepared to believe that what he was hearing was true. Phillips went on to reveal other dimensions of the story, all of which begged more detail, but that could wait. For now, Zhang was more interested in knowing where Phillips himself fitted into the picture.

'So you work for ASIO, then?' he asked.

'Oh no, I'm with ASIS – the Australian Secret Intelligence Service. That's our external outfit – our CIA.'

'But the name-tag you were wearing at the consulate ...' Zhang said, keen to see what Phillips would say.

'Oh, the Austrade thing? That's just a cover I use for diplomatic functions like yours. Not meaning any offence, of course.'

'Naturally.'

Zhang had a strong urge to ask why Phillips was telling the Chinese – in particular Zhang himself – this incredibly sensitive story. But he bided his time. His philosophy, let alone his training and experience, told him that silence was usually a sharper interrogatory scalpel. However, puzzlement must have shown on his face, for Phillips picked it up and it prompted him to reinforce his own *bona fides*.

'Your ambassador Mr Li,' he said, 'obviously values your work on energy matters. He loves your idea of linking Australia and China in some kind of long-term arrangement. And he really liked the way you spoke about it passionately at last Thursday's meeting.'

Zhang was amazed. This was the most delicate matter he was handling for Beijing at the moment. *Ta ma de*, he thought: damn it. Is there anything this man doesn't know?

'And he expects your draft dispatch on the subject by the end of the week.'

Zhang smiled wryly. The point was well made. But Phillips had yet to finish.

'Before, that is, you get locked in to the visit of your ambassador's younger brother, Li Yanbin, and his family. You know, the one in the People's

Liberation Army, the one who wants to carve out a slice of the Australia–China wool trade for himself.'

Zhang knew that this information had not been extracted from bugged phone conversations. It had come from a particular discussion he remembered quite well, one that had taken place some ten days back, when he visited the embassy in Canberra. He had talked for more than an hour with one of his trade colleagues in that man's office, following an earlier meeting they had had with Ambassador Li.

Now a momentary silence hung over the two men as they sat in the restaurant.

Phillips broke it, staring at Zhang. 'Do you still doubt who I am and the story I'm telling?'

'No, I don't. I believe you.'

Phillips smiled. His gaze softened, confirming to Zhang that this was what the Australian had been seeking. His eyes spoke with greater force than his words. Zhang again felt the man's charm, which somehow belied the seriousness of what he was saying.

Phillips sat forward in his chair and talked on with some animation. To Zhang he seemed almost lighthearted, as though by revealing such secrets he was unburdening himself of a terrible guilt. He provided his own explanation for his actions. Zhang listened intently but refrained from comment. More could be learnt from letting things flow and reading between the lines. It was a technique he recalled from a witty handout – *An Intelligence Officer's Guide to Reverse*

Engineering – given to him as part of his basic espionage training. Point one had been: if you want answers, don't necessarily ask questions.

'You see, what really disturbs me about this eavesdropping thing,' Phillips went on, 'is our obsequiousness. I mean, without a care in the world we've allowed the Yanks to take control of every bit of intelligence we get. And it's supposed to be a "joint" operation. Well, that's plain ridiculous. All we see is what they bother to pass back.'

Zhang nodded sympathetically, which seemed to spur Phillips on.

'That cuts across Australia's national interest, but you won't see anyone high up in the system raising objections.'

Up to this point Zhang had thought Phillips's argument quite rational – if anything, too predictably so. Now he wondered how the Australian could possibly reconcile his concern for his country's wellbeing with the broader betrayal in which he himself was engaged. Zhang had long suspected that the minds of people willing to sell their soul in this way were somehow uniquely equipped to accommodate such stark contradictions. Personally, he abhorred betrayal in any form, but was fascinated by the psychology of it and the factors in both a person's past and their present that drove them to break from the group, in terms of loyalty, while continuing to function as part of it.

Phillips began to explain his longstanding belief that China would, within twenty years, become the dominant power in the region. Then he added: 'Australia's playing with fire when it gets mixed up in a bugging operation like this. We risk being seen in Asia as an American lackey. And God knows, if we get stuck with a label like that, it could take generations to make up lost ground.'

Obviously, Zhang thought, he can't see any contradiction between what he says and what he does. His own act of betrayal, if it ever gets out, is going to show Australia up as a lackey like nothing else could.

Later in the evening, when both were mellow from a second bottle of the Lacrima Christi, Zhang allowed himself a few questions. He had assiduously filled Phillips's glass, while limiting himself.

'Can I ask you, Peter, why you chose *me* as the person to approach?'

Phillips casually pulled off his tie and slung it across the back of the chair.

'Well, if you want a straight answer, I'll tell you. It's because I felt I needed someone in your outfit I could trust. It's as simple as that. What I'm doing, you know, is no easy thing.'

He smiled ruefully, looking Zhang in the eye, as if to challenge him to deny the merit of what he had said. It was indeed a point that Zhang wanted to pursue, but instinct told him to leave it alone — at least for the moment.

'Thanks.'

Phillips seemed content with that response. 'You see,' he said, 'the most important thing in classical spy work is communication and sensitivity. You have to be acutely aware of the wavelength that people are broadcasting on, otherwise there's little hope of transmitting messages. That's what it's all about. After all, it's an intensely human exercise.'

No doubt it is, Zhang thought, as the traumas that had swept over him and his family during the Maoist Terror of the Cultural Revolution in the 1960s and 1970s flashed through his mind. Phillips's experiences would no doubt pale into insignificance compared to that.

Talk of the human side of intelligence caused Zhang to wonder what the ASIS man wanted in return for his favours. But he knew that broaching the matter might lead to commitments he was unable to make. Perhaps it was better to leave it untouched. Besides, he felt that their conversation had run its full course. Phillips, he sensed, probably felt the same. Zhang glanced at his watch.

'Yes, I think we'd better be going,' the Australian observed.

'To be honest,' Zhang replied, smiling, 'it's been a pretty long day.' He reached down for his satchel, which he had placed on the floor, and pulled out the *Touch of Zen* video that Phillips had given him earlier. 'Peter, I must thank you for this. I've tried a number of times to get it from home, but with no success.'

'Oh, don't mention it. It was no trouble at all.' In reality, Phillips had ordered ASIS subordinates in Hong Kong to pick up a copy, however they did it.

Zhang caught the eye of the waiter and asked for the bill. Phillips made no attempt to share the cost.

While they waited, Zhang said: 'Peter, how's your interest in ... didn't you tell me once you were a fish collector or something? Or was it frogs?'

'Well, actually,' Phillips said, his eyes lighting up, 'it's insects. They're one of the great loves of my life, and have been since I was a kid. Especially beetles, cicadas, butterflies – things like that.'

Zhang nodded. *Shenme ren, zheige?* he thought: what sort of person is this? He's like an onion with endless skins. You never feel you'll get to the inner heart.

'Peter, look, as you'd imagine, I'll have to talk to my ambassador. I'm sure I'll catch him first thing in the morning, when he passes through here from Melbourne. Maybe you and I could meet up again later in the day, so I can pass on to you his thoughts on what we might be able to do together.'

'That's fine with me, but be careful, won't you. Please don't pass on any of this information by phone.'

'Of course not. Believe me, I have your interests at heart. Have no doubt about that.'

A time and a place were set – a restaurant in Sydney's Chinatown which they both knew.

With the meeting over, Zhang felt excited, confused, even apprehensive. Phillips was a man of contrasts. He was sharp, quickwitted and calculating, yet there was a warmth that was immediately attractive. But *other* people, Zhang kept telling himself, would judge why Phillips was doing what he was doing and what he wanted in return.

Zhang still had much to do that night.

It was already 10.20 by the time he arrived back at the consulate. He had done a lot of thinking in the taxi on the way, and his priorities were clear. First, stay cool, don't rush, and be methodical; second, let the most important people know that something's come up – the ambassador, the consul-general in Sydney, and Gao Chun, the local intelligence chief; and third, do all this with an eye to security and discretion.

He had handled emergencies before, though nothing like this. As he slipped inside the building, he thought: full marks to the Ministry of State Security for that basic spy course.

Despite the pressure on him now, he was revelling in the adventure that Phillips had brought into his life. Never had he imagined that this sort of thing could be so much fun.

TWO

Tokyo: Mid-April

Greg Mason sat quietly in his room, gazing at the photograph in his hand. It showed him and his wife Prue, who had died of breast cancer a few years before. Taken one spring in Kyoto, the shot had the Kiyomizu Temple looming large in the background. The huge wooden structure stood high on a ridge across the valley, floating like a ship on the sea of cherry blossom that covered the slopes below. Both Mason and Prue were laughing. An elderly Japanese man, asked to take their photo, had quipped: 'I won't say "cheese", because I can't stand the stuff!'

It had been a happy stay in the ancient capital, where a friend of Mason's had put them up for a few days in his family's very traditional home. Prue was transfixed by the age of the place and by the magnificent artworks the house contained. Kyoto as a whole had affected her like no other city. Now, as Mason studied her face, he found himself mesmerised again by the lively blue eyes and blonde Nordic features of this woman of solid British stock.

How healthy she was then, he thought, before she was slowly eaten away. How could we have known that all that was just around the corner? What a gaunt, bony shadow of herself she was at the end. It still tore his heart to pieces.

Though Mason had visited Tokyo on business many times since her death, on this occasion something had compelled him to take the same room in the Okura Hotel that they had stayed in on their last trip there together.

He checked the time on the clock in the bedside console. It was still only 10 a.m., so he had plenty of time before leaving for his meeting at the Matsutomo Corporation nearby. At 41, Greg Mason was a Sydney-based energy and resources consultant, a job he had taken on after leaving ASIS seven years before. The Service had originally snapped him up because of his background. He had been born in Kobe, where his father, a former World War II Australian Army interrogator and Japanese linguist, had run a metals import business. Mason's mother was an American, and she too had been born in Japan, where her father was a doctor to the foreign community in Yokohama. During the Pacific War she had worked in Hawaii on US propaganda leaflets to be dropped across Japan. Young Mason had been schooled in Japan and had graduated from the Law Faculty of Tokyo University.

Later he spent a few years in Taipei running a

branch of his father's business. With a flair for languages, he soon became as proficient in Mandarin as he was in written and spoken Japanese. Eventually he settled in his father's home city of Sydney, where he found himself to be more mature than most Australians his age. He was self-assured, though respectful of others. At first he thought Australia a puzzling and undisciplined place, but soon adjusted. Despite being born outside the country, his loyalty to it was strong. Japan had endowed him with a powerful sense of duty and obligation. Aware of this, and valuing his knowledge of Asia, ASIS had wasted no time in recruiting him. His dark hair and olive skin also made it easier for him to blend in than it was for most foreigners in the region.

His time in the Service had been enjoyable and productive and he was well regarded for his accomplishments in the field. In Jakarta, however, things had gone badly awry. His station commander there, Martin Clarke, had been jealous of the younger man and had done whatever he could to spike Mason's career. For one thing, he had stolen his wife, though Prue had been quickly discarded when her illness set in. Professionally, Clarke had dogged Mason at every turn, including thwarting what would have been his crowning achievement on the post.

As he stared at Prue's photograph now, another vivid image from his days in the Indonesian capital flashed up in Greg's mind.

– – –

He had sensed that something was wrong when he saw the front gate half open. The guard was nowhere to be seen. He was never far up the driveway at that time of night.

Mason slipped inside. The porch light was shining through the oleander bushes that blocked out the view from the street. Crossing the lawn, he spotted the guard lying prostrate on the front steps. As he rushed over, the man groaned. He was semi-conscious and had an ugly gash on the back of his head. It was useless asking him what had happened.

The door was open and Mason could hear a woman's cries of pain at the back of the house.

'*Di mana? Di mana?*' a male voice was shouting in Bahasa: where is it? Where is it?

Mason knew what 'it' was.

He slipped quietly but quickly down the passage. Flattening himself against the wall at the end, he peered into the room. It was a large space where the Malaysian family spent most of its time. He could see Mustafa's wife being held down on the floor. A stocky, black-clad Indonesian sat on her back, twisting her arms. Another man, thin but muscular, had grasped her by the hair with one hand, and was holding her head off the floor. He held a knife to her throat with the other.

'*Di mana?*' he snarled, intent on an answer.

'*Tidak ada,*' the woman said, crying as he threatened to kill her: there isn't any.

Mustafa's eight-year-old son lunged at the man with the knife, pushing him off balance. Mason saw his chance and moved in fast.

The man straddling the wife picked up the motion out of the corner of his eye, but Mason's swift and powerful chop to the back of his neck disabled him instantly. He fell to one side. The man with the knife released his grip on the woman and thrust the blade at Mason, an arm's length away. Mason rolled with the action, thumping the man's shoulder and spinning him around. At the same time, he struck him hard in the temple with his knuckles. The assailant dropped the knife in mid-flight and fell limp to the floor.

It was all over in a matter of seconds.

'Uncle Greg!' Mustafa's son called out in English, relieved that the violent trauma was over.

'Tell me quickly,' Mason cut across him. 'Were there only *two* men?'

'Yes, only two. But Greg, look at Papa. They've killed him.'

Mustafa was slumped at one end of a sofa, bleeding from a deep gash in the head and from another, far more severe, in the forearm. He had been slashed from elbow to wrist, and the tendons and arteries were exposed. Blood was oozing from the wound.

'Your Daddy's still alive. But quick, you help your mother, and I'll take care of him.'

Mason ripped off his shirt and bound the arm tightly. He stemmed the flow, but wondered how long the first aid might last.

Mustafa stirred when he heard the Australian's voice. 'Greg, have they gone?' he said feebly. His eyes were clogged with blood.

'Well, they're not going to cause any more trouble. Let's put it that way.'

Mustafa sighed with relief.

'What should we do, Greg?' his wife asked, getting herself up off the floor.

'Call the ambulance first, and the police after that. I'll tie these blokes up so they can't get away.' He turned back to the boy. 'And you, my little friend, you run out to the front and see if Yousef's OK.'

'They were after the money, Greg,' Mustafa said, whispering to Mason when his wife was out of earshot. 'That's why I told you "ten" on the phone. They wanted ten thousand dollars US tonight. I should've mentioned they'd said they'd kill us if they didn't get it.'

'I know, mate. But let's clean you up first, before we get into that.'

'Oh, Greg, am I glad to see you! I thought we were finished.'

'Well, I just wish I'd got here faster.'

Mustafa was a spy with the Malaysian external service. He had been operating in Jakarta for three years and had recently agreed to pass on secret intelligence to Mason if ASIS would cover his gambling debts, which had got out of control. This was a potential coup for the Service, which placed a high priority on 'turning' any South-East Asian intelligence officer. Mason had gained approval from his station commander, Martin Clarke, to hand over the cash from station funds but, unbelievably, was told at the last minute not to proceed. And this despite a deal having been struck with Mustafa.

But Mason was a man of his word. He had promised the money and he would deliver it. He had reached the bank only minutes before the shutters went down and had haggled for more than an hour over an advance from his personal account. His bank in Australia had already closed for the day, but with his track record of friendliness and some pleading in Bahasa, he had won half of the amount he needed. The remainder had come from his friend, Elizabeth Cantrell, a CIA officer with whom he worked closely on energy matters.

The $US10 000 was in his bag when he arrived at Mustafa's front gate.

All that, as well as the thoughts of Prue, were far from Mason's mind as he sat in an office on the twentieth floor of the Matsutomo Corporation, a block away from his Tokyo hotel. There was a powerful sense of *deja vu* about what was happening to him. It was disturbingly like his old days in ASIS, though this time *he* was not asking the questions. It was the Japanese executive sitting in front of him who was pumping him for sensitive information. As an intelligence officer, Mason had cultivated new agents in just the same way.

It reminded him of what one warped bastard, Bass Morgandale, had told him years before: 'Nobody in the spy game is in it for the national interest. Those who are get out fast. Those who stay look after themselves. But it's a honeypot, Greg. If you ever get out, never touch it again. You'll be sucked back in before you know it.'

That was nice, coming from one of the most senior men in the Service.

Mason's eyes moved around the corner office, taking in the minimalist furnishings, the vase of purple Turkish poppies on the shelf near the window, and the low grey cloud outside. The usual view over the palace moat was all but obliterated, which was uncommon for this time of the morning. But then, it was unseasonal weather for mid-April in Tokyo.

He looked again at the steely Nobuyuki Kiriyama and wondered why the man was so averse to telling him more. Normally in Mason's consultancy work he could expect a detailed briefing on a project like this. He would also be given some idea of how his advice was to be used. Instead, the only thing this Japanese businessman seemed to want was information – intelligence information.

'You see,' Kiriyama said in the subtlest Japanese, 'we need a – how can I put it? – a distinctively *Australian* perspective.'

His turn of phrase was polite, though, appreciating as he did Mason's feel for Japanese thinking, it also contained a hint of condescension. A little more should be revealed perhaps. But then, the charter was there if Mason wanted it.

An Australian perspective? Mason thought. That confirms it. It's classified material he's after. But where's he coming from? Maybe his

Japanese colleagues in Australia have learnt that I once worked with ASIS and they've tipped him off. Hard to say. I might be able to patch something together for him, but I certainly won't be ferreting out state secrets.

Kiriyama was head of the general affairs division of the Corporation at its Tokyo headquarters. He knew it was best not to push Mason on a matter like this. The two had known each other for five years and, while not close personal friends, enjoyed a rapport that extended beyond the professional arena. Oddly, the greater the effort that Kiriyama made to conceal the truth, the more evident was the existence of some other dimension. As a former spy, Mason picked these things up quicker than most. He was the younger of the two by a significant margin, but he had mixed enough with senior Japanese to know that this man was under pressure. And before he left Tokyo he intended to find out what was driving it.

'*Yappari*,' Kiriyama said, using a colloquialism that suggested more was about to emerge, 'all I'm asking for, Mason San, is that you inject into your report your own strategic thoughts. If you can add those of experts you talk to, so much the better, especially if they know where all this is heading. Naturally, Matsutomo has its own views on how your country fits into the oil and liquefied natural gas scene, but they're often contradicted by news from our branches in Perth, Melbourne and Sydney. So, if you could, say, flesh it out a bit – round it off – add your own twist – then we'd be extremely grateful.'

Nakagawa, a friend of Mason's in Matsutomo's Sydney office, came readily to mind. For a Japanese, Nakagawa was remarkably outspoken, often throwing up dimensions of an issue that his colleagues would never have thought of. In fact, his intellectual and cross-cultural reach sometimes embarrassed Japanese around him, leading to the sort of friction that Mason understood only too well.

Now Mason found himself in an odd position, one he had not experienced since hanging out his shingle.

The Corporation liked his style. The people he knew there believed that his sense of courtesy militated against unexpected losses of face. And face was important to the firm, which was one of the grand old trading houses of Japan. It had a long history in the development of Australia's wool industry and had made significant contributions to the bilateral resources trade. The firm had contracted Mason for a number of lucrative projects, but none had ever been pressed upon him in the way Kiriyama was doing now.

'You see, Mason San, I need a clear and informed picture. Who's going to fund future energy growth and development in Australia? How much capital can you throw in yourselves? What sort of cooperation are you seeking from overseas interests? Who will be your key partners? And above all, as I said, what role is gas going to play in all this?'

'*Wakarimashita*,' Mason replied: I understand.

The reference again to gas had let the cat out of the bag and set Mason's mind racing.

'Thirty thousand dollars Australian,' Kiriyama said. 'How does that sound? And I'd want your report within a month.'

Mason gazed out over the mirror-like waters of the moat after Kiriyama had farewelled him at the front entrance. They were just visible through the mist. Dark green pines and a whitewashed turret of the Imperial Palace were reflected there, as if frozen in time. It was a quintessentially Japanese scene and one that matched the delicacy of the decision with which he had been confronted. There was no way he would spy out secret information – governmental or commercial – for any Japanese cause. It was a subject he felt strongly about, if in an old-fashioned way.

But, yes, he had thought, I'll stitch something together to satisfy this corporate animal. If he's so willing to pay for my insights, that's what he'll get. God only knows how many other Australians have been engaged by Matsutomo for the task. It's possible I'm only one of a few. But it must be urgency that's jacked up the price. And I could certainly do with the money. Hard to say where I fit in overall, but gas is clearly the name of the game – and with luck, I'll find out why.

First, he thought, he would contact a former colleague, now working in ASIS's Tokyo station, to ascertain privately what the Service might know. Next, and most importantly, he would seek to meet up with one of his oldest Japanese friends. This man, Kenichi Fujisawa, was very well placed and if anyone knew what was going on it would be him. Hopefully, he would not be too busy for them to get together.

A revolving perspex stage dominated the scene. It was brightly lit from above and below, with the rest of the place in darkness. The stage was fifteen tiers of seats below where the two men stood. They had just entered through a curtained door at the top.

It was a small amphitheatre-like establishment, packed out as usual on a week night with a hundred or more patrons. All were male and most were drinking beer from cans. A Michael Jackson hit tune rang out from overhead speakers.

Performing on stage was a young woman – foreign and strawberry-blonde – who lay naked on an inflatable mattress. A stocky, brown-skinned Japanese executive in his thirties had stripped off and was mounted on top of her. He had been pumping away for a while but, as everyone knew, was not making much progress. The thickness of his member was adequate to the task – all had seen it at the start, when a pink condom was slipped over it by the blonde – but its length was letting him down. The more frustrated he grew, the more vigorous his action became. But it kept slipping out. Sweat glistened on his back.

Minutes ticked by and the man's half dozen colleagues were becoming restless. The comments they were making threatened him with a loss of face from which he might never recover.

Mason and Fujisawa, a friend from university days, moved down closer to the stage. They stood leaning against the wall at the side, waiting for someone to leave. Before long, two seats in the front row became vacant.

Overhearing the new arrivals using Japanese, a young man behind them tapped Mason on the shoulder. In quite a loud voice he cheekily observed that he hoped the woman on stage was not the foreigner's sister. This drew raucous laughter from people around, to which Mason responded with a smile and a slight bow of the head.

'Actually, she *is*,' he said, 'and I get half her earnings!'

This set the group off again, but their mirth only worsened the plight of the man on stage. Sweat now dripped from his brow. The woman lifted her hand to wipe it away with a small pink towel. That was the last thing he needed.

'Give the poor *yatsu* a drink,' someone shouted, using the colloquial word for 'bloke'.

This made things even more desperate.

Known as a *nudo gekijo*, or nude theatre, this sort of live-sex joint in Japan made Mason wonder about Japanese sexuality. Why was there this strong voyeuristic streak in the men, and why the subliminal need to debase women? He found the former trait questionable and the latter one downright disgusting.

Meanwhile, the executive on stage persisted stubbornly, though his efforts went unrewarded. For a moment there was a glimmer of hope when he let out a pleasurable cry. The woman responded with an orgasmic moan that was meant to be helpful. The spectators cheered. Headway at last!

But nothing happened, and the couple slipped back into their earlier torpor.

'*Honto ni, Jiro Kun, ashita wa, hayaku!*' a colleague pleaded: for God's sake, we have to go to work in the morning!

Mason shared the man's sentiment, though for different reasons entirely. He had already told his friend that he wanted to talk, confidentially, about gas deals, and Fujisawa had agreed. Yes, he knew a lot. But first, he insisted, they should enjoy the entertainment, at least for old time's sake. Mason could hardly object, though he wasted no chance to broach the subject. He knew how frantic his friend's life was: his beeper might go off at any moment and he would be called back to the office, even at this hour.

Fujisawa was an analyst in the Cabinet Research Office, inside the Japanese Prime Minister's Department. The CRO acted as a coordinatory body for the country's sprawling intelligence community. Wiry and tough, Fujisawa was married, with twin daughters. Like most Japanese men he was also largely indifferent to the fact that his only meaningful contact with his family was at the weekend. The rest of the time he was out drinking with friends in the evening in small bars or frequenting sex clubs with them. Male bonding – the excuse that allowed a man to spend less time with women –

was the fuel that kept much of Japanese society functioning.

What Mason was counting on was a key fragment or two of information from Fujisawa that would give him a sense of what was driving the Matsutomo executive's request. Instinct told him he was on to a story of no mean proportions. But Fujisawa had been busy with briefings for ministers and high level bureaucrats, all wanting ideas on how to handle American demands for increased market access. Therefore he could only see Mason on his last night in Tokyo. Could they meet at the east entrance of Tsurumi Station, to the south of the city, at ten? After dropping into a nearby *gekijo*, they could have a late snack, and there would be plenty of time to discuss gas.

Fujisawa had a zest for life and a tenacity that Mason had admired since they first met at a martial arts tournament on campus. They hit it off from the start. Scuba diving was a great passion they shared. Mason had also learnt a lot about friendship from this Japanese man, especially that it was unnecessary to like all of the person all of the time. Instead, that core of goodness inside was what mattered, regardless of the wrapping. He could never forget that it was this friend who had made a quick trip to Sydney to bolster his spirits when his wife Prue had finally died. It was a rare gesture and one he knew many would never experience.

'Actually, Greg,' Fujisawa now said, 'there's something huge happening on the gas front at the moment, which is what I gather your bloodhound nose has got you on to. It's strictly secret, but, as you obviously already know . . . '

Distracted, his words petered out.

The revolving stage had brought with it much puffing and panting as the blonde and her suitor headed their way. The executive's work had still not been done. No longer bothering to feign interest, boredom drove the woman to scan the dimly lit audience for something to focus on.

'And where are you from?' she said in English, spotting Mason's foreign features in the front row.

'Same place as you, if I'm not mistaken,' he replied, recognising her broad Australian accent.

'Married?' she said, nearly abreast of him now.

'Widowed.'

'Kids?'

'None.'

'Been in Tokyo long?' she persisted, as though these questions had to be asked.

'Off to Sydney tomorrow.'

'Typical! Every dinkum bloke I meet in this place comes and goes in a flash.'

Mason's eyes fell upon her struggling companion, which she noticed, and they both laughed at the pun.

'Well, they *do* eventually,' she said, as the stage carried her off on its circuit. 'Unless they bloody die on the job.'

Fujisawa understood the exchange and was trapped between the comic humour of the situation and his sense of embarrassment for a fellow Japanese in such a thankless position.

After the couple's umpteenth revolution, he grew tired of Mason's spasmodic remarks. Mixed with their own dialogue on energy matters, he found it confusing. It was then that he decided to haul his friend off to a watering hole up the road.

As they climbed the stairs to the exit, Fujisawa mused to himself over certain qualities unique to this Australian. For Mason, the chat with the woman was something quite genuine. But for a Japanese overseas, in a similar scenario, it would be shameful to talk as an equal to a compatriot in such a lowly position. Most would only think of putting her down. Mason did the opposite — he lifted her up. This was something Fujisawa esteemed.

Outside the theatre, the road was narrow and wet. It was lined with strip-joints and small noodle bars. Each eatery had a distinctive shop-curtain over the door. A few sported large, round, red lanterns with lights burning inside. That, and flashing neons, made it a colourful scene.

Who'd have guessed this gas thing was so big, Mason thought, as Fujisawa fended off another spruiker trying to lure them inside a club.

And more was to come, but even the bits of the jigsaw he had picked up so far left for dead anything Kiriyama had told him. The huge undersea discovery that the Japanese had made to their north would have enormous consequences. It could do for Japan what North Sea oil had once done for Great Britain. And it had implications much further afield, especially in Australia.

'So, do the Russians know what you've found in their waters?' Mason said.

'Well, no. At least, not yet. That's the problem. You see, we only have a few weeks left before we're obliged to hand over all the data, and if we can't put an attractive development package together soon — one that they'll be unable to resist — they'll end up throwing it open to the highest international bidder the minute they get all the details. And Japan won't get a look in.'

'So the pressure's on?'

'You can say that again!' Fujisawa replied. 'The Government sees this as a matter of national importance. We just *can't* let this one slip out of our hands.'

'What the hell do you mean, "he couldn't get Mason to talk"?'

Sebastian Morgandale was angry. As ASIS's deputy chief, and a confidant of the Foreign Minister, he constantly used his authority to pry into matters that were outside his jurisdiction. Commonly known as 'Bass', he was middle-aged and a stickler for hierarchy.

'For God's sake,' he went on, 'how can a serving officer fail to get the lowdown from a former colleague — and *friend* — who set up the meeting in the first place?'

Martin Clarke was left squirming, which was what Morgandale wanted. The two contemporaries hated each other. Clarke had known it would be something like this from the moment Bass shouted down the phone line: 'Come by my room as soon as you can, and bring your offsider with you.'

As the Service's director of operations for North Asia, Clarke was unaccustomed to being addressed like a schoolboy. And to have to take along with him Todd Lambert, his own deputy, made it all the more galling.

Morgandale had sighted a copy of a cable just in from the Tokyo station, which reported on a private meeting with Greg Mason, who had been visiting Japan. But all it revealed was that Mason had suggested that 'something big might be happening in the energy arena'. The station knew of nothing in the offing, and anyway, all Mason seemed to be going on was a hunch.

'Hunch!' Clarke scoffed, hoping that by matching Morgandale's ridicule he might somehow lessen his own embarrassment. 'I have the station on a standing brief to track Mason closely whenever he's in town, but to have *him* initiate contact and then ask questions like this is a dead giveaway. It's bloody obvious he already knows what's going on. What he's trying to do is find out whether we're up to speed.'

'And we're not!' Morgandale shot back.

Clarke had told the deputy chief nothing he had not already worked out for himself, but Morgandale knew that his colleague had walked into a trap and that was just fine. Clarke had effectively admitted that his ops branch needed to do better. A point-scorer, Morgandale loved playing games, and was not finished yet.

Dismissively, he turned to Lambert, who was in his thirties and a fast-rising star in the Service. A former SAS officer, he was typical of a new breed of experienced recruits taken in by ASIS in recent years. Though he was known to be a friend of Mason's, he rarely talked within the Service about meetings the pair had. Others like Lambert did the same, often consulting Mason for an independent, outside view. It was a liaison that riled 'oldtimers' such as Clarke and Morgandale, which was the reason Bass sought now to turn it back against Clarke.

'So, if *you* were running the show, Todd, what would you do?' he said, exuding the sort of charm he could switch on and off like a light.

'Well,' Lambert replied, aware of his ticklish position, 'I think the best we can do is to get the station to pull its finger out and work its stable of agents much harder. I mean, target them specifically on oil, gas and coal – the things that always take Greg to Tokyo. He's not there for the cherry blossoms.'

Morgandale nodded, as though the younger man had come up with some startling new angle. All the better to make Clarke squirm again, which he was already doing, though he was careful not to let it show. Morgandale, however, could read the signs accurately, no matter how subtle.

'Not that we don't *drive* the station anyway,' Lambert added, in a half-hearted attempt to assuage his own boss.

Tough and husky, Lambert had an intellect as sharp as his tongue, both of which Morgandale feared, which was why he treated him with respect. Though Morgandale himself was experienced in the field, he had achieved little of credit. He had simply 'done time' on postings in Bangkok, Jakarta, Hong Kong and in other parts of Asia. He had also had stints in London with MI6 and in Canada, which was where he had first become chummy with Australia's current Foreign Minister, then doing a PhD in Town Planning before later going into politics. While he was a China buff, among other things, there was no great depth to Morgandale's knowledge of that country's history or culture – only his love of its art and its portrayal of nature. He was fascinated with scrolls depicting bamboo leaves in rain or a solitary frog on a lotus stalk, and likewise with carved ink seals featuring the same kinds of theme. The minister read much more into this than he should have.

But if there was one thing that Morgandale had learnt in his career it was the importance to his own preservation of keeping the brightest young officers on side. Clarke had learned the value of that, too – the hard way, and a little too late. Both men were similar and shared wide-ranging interests, which each generally kept separate from his work. Their mutual antagonism, however, precluded any meaningful exchange.

Clarke returned to his office furious.

That bloody Mason's got contacts all over the place, he thought, seething inside. I can tell a mile off that he and his mate in our Tokyo station talked in detail about this energy scoop, whatever it is. And Mason's told *my* officer to keep it to himself. How dare my man not report back fully, as ordered!

One thing that had long haunted Clarke was the way in which Mason – who had starred in the energy field as an ASIS spy in Jakarta and been forced out by Clarke's intransigence – had gone on to thrive in that area in the private sector. What he feared most was that, with the high demand in Canberra for secret reporting on key energy developments, Mason would get on to a big story first. He would tip off close contacts in the capital, many of whom were regular readers of ASIS's product, and they in turn would oblige the Service to show why it had not informed the Government earlier.

Gilbert needs a stern warning, Clarke thought. He has to know I won't stand for this any longer.

He got to work on his keyboard. A sharp rebuke to that officer's boss in Tokyo would put the entire station, as well as others, on notice.

Priority: For Station Commander, Tokyo
Copy to: All Station Commanders, North Asia

You will recall that on my visit to your post a few months ago, I highlighted the importance of closely tracking the movements of Gregory Mason whenever he is in your bailiwick. It is essential that no former officer, trained at the Service's expense, be able to draw upon its resources while travelling overseas. It is well known that Mason also liaises with former American, British and Canadian deep cover colleagues while in your area.

I will not tolerate any circumstance in which Mason privately tips off the Service's Canberra customers, or business or the media, to a major energy development, where Mason has either discussed the matter with an officer on your station or with a local agent for whom he has previously acted as case officer.

I urge you and your station colleagues to find out, without delay, the precise nature of the energy 'scoop' that Mason claims to have got on to during his visit to your area. Liaise with whoever you need to, but leave no stone unturned.

Director Ops/North Asia

THREE

Sydney: Mid-April

When the group was seated, Ambassador Li reached across for a white marble ashtray in the centre of the table and dragged it close, as though it were a treasured possession. He pulled out his cigarettes – Hongta, or Red Pagoda, China's favourite – and lit one with his antiquated lighter. Drawing heavily, he blew the tart-smelling smoke up towards the ceiling and sat back relaxed. It was Li's customary signal that proceedings could begin. He was powerful in the Chinese system, but used his influence sparingly. In his early seventies, he was lean, bald and laconic. There were shades of the Confucian gentleman about him, except perhaps for his earthy sense of humour.

Li had arrived at the offices of Stephen Wu & Associates, accompanied by his colleagues from the consulate, at 8.30 a.m. A long-established group of Chinese–Australian solicitors, the firm occupied two floors of a small building near Sydney's Chinatown. Its senior partner had readily made his meeting room available when requested by Gao Chun, the local intelligence chief. After all, the ageing lawyer was a personal friend of the ambassador and was always willing to help. He was trusted and never asked questions.

The air in the room was musty and laced with the smell of stale tobacco and food. Another staff member from the consulate was already waiting there for them. She was the wife of one of Zhang's fellow trade officers and was a trained psychologist as well as head of the consulate's visa section. Ambassador Li had called her on the way in from the airport. He was anxious to have her assessment of Zhang Wendao's encounter with Peter Phillips and of the conclusions he and the others had already reached.

'The first thing that has to be considered,' Li said, 'is a damage assessment within the embassy. If what this walk-in is saying is true, substantial leaks might have occurred already. Where does that leave the security of our mission? Well, that's a process I'll be triggering off as soon as I return to Canberra.'

The others nodded. It was indeed a matter of prime concern. Gao had thoughts of his own, but preferred to wait until he had heard more of what Zhang had to say about the Australian involved. The ambassador, as though reading Gao's mind, turned to Zhang and invited him to describe the spy he had encountered.

Zhang began by giving a realistic picture of Phillips. Having listened carefully to him for hours and closely observed his mannerisms, he sounded almost as if Phillips were speaking through him now – as though he, Zhang, were a mere interpreter.

'He's certainly focused and tries hard to give the impression he's very much in control, but when he moves from subject to subject, which he does quite often, you don't feel that what he's saying is underpinned by any great depth of understanding. He's like the expert dilettante who knows something about everything. The only exceptions I picked out were his personal interests – things like his love of nature, particularly insects, and of kung fu movies. In those he really shines. Yet on broader topics, like Asia and its varied cultures and histories, I didn't sense a lot of depth at all. Maybe the kung fu thing's just a cover for what he lacks. Even so, he bills himself as the total, all-round Asia hand, but conveniently ignores the fact that fingers are missing.'

This drew a laugh.

'For example, I offered to get him a copy of an English-language booklet we have in the consulate on the thoughts of Lao Zi, and when I told him it was full of pithy observations on life and was easy to read, he jumped at it. He said he reads mainly military history – I gather that means Western – and claims he can't handle anything heavy from other cultures. If it's small and manageable though, he said he wouldn't mind having a look.'

'And he seems unaware of this contradiction?' Li said.

'Exactly, but that's not all. In a more general sense, you get the impression his perception of the world around him, and where he fits into it, lacks any firm anchor. I think when any of us meets someone for the first time we always try to get a fix on that person's centre of gravity, on where they're coming from, on what motivates them and how they see their purpose in life. Well, after a lengthy session with Phillips, helped along by a good deal of drink, I must say I still have no idea what makes him tick. He's – how can I put it? – just *floating*, not firmly fixed.'

Gao was nodding in a way that told Zhang and the others that this might be a not uncommon feature in traitors. After all, Gao was a professional and had recruited and run many such people.

'But don't get me wrong,' Zhang said. 'He's still an enormously engaging person to be with – full of charm and very interesting. In fact, his charm's so effective it even sucked me in. I think I got so involved in trying to gauge the extent of his knowledge that I clean forgot to ask about basic things we need to know. Like what position he holds in ASIS. Though whatever that is, it clearly gives him good access. I learnt nothing about his private life – whether he's married, divorced or whatever. It didn't even occur to me to ask him whether the name he uses is his or just an alias.'

'Oh, you can be sure it's the latter,' Gao said.

Ambassador Li lit a fresh cigarette and offered the packet around, but as usual everyone politely refused.

'I must say,' Zhang continued, 'when I thought about it this morning I felt quite ashamed. I mean, the fundamental question is why he's offering us such sensitive information. All I ended up settling for was what he volunteered – that he doesn't want Australia to be seen in Asia as a lackey of the Americans. And when I think about it, even that's probably a false justification for what he's doing. What's really motivated him to do this, I must confess, I have no idea.'

He looked at the consulate's resident psychologist as he spoke.

Zhou Chaoying was a kindly and dignified woman. She bowed her head slightly to acknowledge the gesture.

Ambassador Li invited her to provide her analysis. 'So, what do you think we have on our hands?' he said.

'Well, it sounds to me,' she replied softly, 'as though he's a very calculating type. Certainly that, rather than someone who's simply disgruntled and trying to get even with the system. Zhang's perception of the lack of an "anchor" tells me a lot. I think if Phillips is genuine, and not just trailing his coat, his gesture is a desperate attempt to drive a stake into reality – in effect, to create the fixed point of reference that's missing. And of course a desire for money will no doubt be pivotal to this whole process. But look, there's just so much more we need to know. All I can say at this stage is that he'll be driven by a combination of factors, some dictated by his past and some by his current circumstances. We have to learn a lot more about both.'

The others were listening intently.

'If there's one thing we can safely assume, he has to be bright. If he weren't, he surely wouldn't have lasted long in intelligence, let alone have risen to a senior position. So at least that's something we have going in our favour.'

She paused, seemingly hesitant to add more.

'Then again,' she ventured, 'it could perhaps be the nature of the profession that produces people like him, that distorts the personality of weaker types. Not that I'm pointing the finger, of course.'

She smiled at Gao across the table, as though saying: 'Now this hot potato's all yours.' Both were mindful that Ambassador Li had to make a speedy decision.

Solidly built and square-jawed, Gao was one of her closest friends. The two often joked about how each would like to be equipped with the professional skills of the other. Gao, who was in his early fifties, was a tough but moderate man and very successful. He had short, bristly hair, the face of an ex-boxer and a hearty laugh that was infectious.

'You're closer to the truth,' he said, 'than you think.'

From Zhou's experience, she had no doubt he was right. That was why she had raised the issue. She believed it was important for it to be lodged in Li's mind, and it was not something that Gao would have highlighted of his own accord.

'In short,' Gao went on, 'Phillips is a well-known type in my craft, whether you're dealing with them as fellow operatives or as recruited agents from the other side. Inevitably, they're damaged goods before they're drawn into the game, but it's true, once they're in, the pressure certainly makes things worse. As for what this means with Phillips and any danger he might pose to us, is hard to say at this stage, but I suspect he might be manageable if he's handled the right way. I think it's well worth a try. After all, if he can tell us about the embassy bugging, he's just as likely to give us information on other US intelligence operations on China. By any measure, it's an opportunity too good to miss.'

Li nodded. He took a quick look at his watch then turned back to Zhou, the psychologist.

'In essence,' he said, 'how do you rate the risks?'

'Well, reasonably high, but as long as we're all aware of the flexibility it'll take on the part of whoever runs him, it could, as Gao says, be worth the effort — especially in the hands of a professional. There's no doubt it'll be a rollercoaster ride. As quickly as he's come, he might go, and that's why we'll need to glean as much information *on* him, as we attempt to get *from* him. Every insight will help. But, of course, I realise that's easier said than done.'

The ambassador seemed happy with that.

'Right,' he said, putting his cigarettes away, 'this is what I'll do. I'll recommend to Beijing that a second meeting between Zhang and Phillips – which is at what, four this afternoon? – go ahead as scheduled. Now, Gao should be there too, with the aim of taking over the case as soon as he can. As I see it, Phillips should be given one main task for the time being. That's to get as much detail as possible on the bugging operation, as well as samples of what the Americans have been extracting from it.'

'Do you agree?' he said, looking at Gao.

'I do.'

The ambassador outlined the rest of his thinking. The others, he knew, were aware of a secure, cypher-protected back-line, via the embassy in Canberra, to the Ministry of State Security in Beijing. He hoped that the link remained uncompromised by the optical fibre net the Americans and Australians had thrown over his mission.

'Let's get a message off quickly,' he said. 'We may blow the fact that we know what's happening – as well as Phillips's identity – in the process, but that's a risk I'm willing to take. With luck, we should have an answer back in an hour or two.'

He lapsed into silence, lost in thought. The others waited deferentially.

Then he glanced across at Zhang and smiled, certain that the younger man knew what it was. He was right: they were both thinking of energy matters and the tedious negotiations they were engaged in with the Australian Government. Yes, there was more than one way this new development could be leveraged.

– – –

Zhang and Gao were already seated in the Golden Orchid Seafood Restaurant when 'Chang Zhe Chan' strode in just after four.

It was Gao who had suggested the operational code-name for Phillips. It meant 'Singing Cicada' – an insect that the Han people were fond of and often kept in small, box-like cages. The Australian would have no knowledge of the name, though he himself had given rise to it by describing to Zhang how he had treasured a cicada collection in his formative years.

The Chinese rose to greet Phillips, who seemed slightly ill at ease from the moment he spotted another person with Zhang. When he shook Zhang's hand he displayed considerable warmth, even giving him an affectionate slap on the back. But when Gao moved forward to be introduced, Phillips appeared hesitant. Both Chinese were conscious, almost telepathically, of what was in the other's mind. Had Gao's clandestine work been uncovered by Australian intelligence? Might Phillips, as a senior ASIS officer, already have seen Gao's mugshot and file? Or was it mere apprehension over someone new being in on the act? Was Phillips having second thoughts, perhaps, about what he was doing?

Gao was not unduly alarmed. He had had this experience before and was confident that whatever Zhang chose to do next would be appropriate.

'Peter,' Zhang launched in with his customary verve, 'Mr Gao here is one of my closest personal friends in the consulate. He's much more senior than me, but always keeps an eye on what I'm doing. He's what I think you call, in English, a mentor.'

This struck a note of some kind with Phillips, who turned and looked at Gao.

'I'm not going to tell you,' Zhang continued, watching for the Australian's reaction, 'that he's a so-called political officer, or something like that. But I do know he can help us with what we were discussing last night.'

Phillips wavered briefly. Then, with a grin, he reached into his pocket and pulled out a business card. He handed it to Gao, who studied the green and gold Austrade insignia and the designation, Adviser, International Trade Agreements.

Smiling, Gao did the same.

Phillips noted the other man's position: Consul, Science and Technology. A broader grin broke out on his face.

This formal acknowledgment of Gao's cover rank seemed to give the Cicada the assurance he wanted. He extended his hand. Gao shook it firmly and the three men sat down at the table. Some sort of compact had been sealed. But before they were settled the Australian complained about a gurgling noise coming from a large fish-tank nearby. It was stacked with lobsters and fish and had live abalone sticking to the glass.

'For some reason,' Phillips said, 'the sound of water makes me feel queasy, though I'm addicted to seafood.'

As they moved to a table further away, the two Chinese caught each other's eye. Hardly the sort of admission you'd expect from a spy.

Phillips removed his jacket as they made themselves comfortable.

'I say, I like your tie,' Gao said. 'It reminds me of my childhood in China.'

'Oh, really? How come?' Phillips responded.

He glanced down at the red feathers adorning the dark green material. Gao's comment had hooked him immediately. A neat dresser, this was Phillips's favourite piece of neckwear and one thing in his wardrobe that always attracted attention.

'They're duck feathers,' Gao said. 'You know, in my village I had to stuff pillows with those bloody things every day after school!'

Zhang was quietly amused at his colleague's capacity to draw on his agricultural heritage. Whether the stories were true or not was irrelevant. Gao also had a reputation for the ruthless prosecution of his craft. Not the least of the weapons in his arsenal was his own ability to exude inordinate charm, and of a type much cleverer than the Cicada's. It was that, Zhang understood, which would now be subtly employed against this priority target.

Phillips found Gao's use of the Australian vernacular engaging and laughed freely. The ice had been broken. But both Chinese knew this was merely one humble step on a long journey. This ASIS officer was no ordinary person.

Phillips said he had no time for a meal. He was due to catch a 6.20 flight back to Canberra. But yes, when the restaurant manager assured him the cook could produce his favourite dish in only ten minutes, he agreed. The three would share that, along with a few bottles of beer – Tsingtao – one of Phillips's favourites.

It was Zhang who then steered the conversation where Gao wanted it to go. In so doing, he was mindful of instructions received from Beijing just an hour before: Gao was to take over the case as soon as possible. Thereafter, Zhang was to put in only occasional appearances as an understudy in the event that his services were later required. Monetary reward or payment in kind could be offered to whatever extent necessary. Ambassador Li's priorities were fully endorsed.

'To get to the point,' Zhang said, 'we've discussed with our boss – who's been in Sydney today – what you've told us and he's asked us to thank you. It may sound simple to put it like that, but he knows you appreciate what your help means on something like this.'

Phillips nodded, clearly pleased.

Zhang went on to explain how the Canberra embassy's primary task was to gauge the extent and effectiveness of the bugging operation. Next would be to gain an idea of the yield derived from it. What, he wondered, might Phillips be able to do in that regard?

'That's no problem,' Phillips replied, appearing to draw confidence from the way things were going. A gleam of excitement showed in his eyes. 'It might be tricky getting the actual drawings and plans,' he said, 'but I'll do what I can.'

He spoke in a businesslike manner, his concern for Gao's presence now a thing of the past.

'In the meantime, let me give you a pen sketch of what Canberra's up to and how far the penetration's reached. In short, those modifications you made to the building stuffed up much of the optical fibre network.'

Phillips grinned cheekily as he looked at Zhang and Gao. They smiled in return, unwittingly swept up by the Australian's sudden enthusiasm.

He went on to outline areas that were safe and those that were not. For the Chinese this was gold.

'I have to tell you that, in general, you're extremely vulnerable. Virtually every sensitive matter talked about in one room gets repeated somewhere else. You're going to have to restrict yourselves – religiously – to the secure spots I've mentioned. But be careful how you spread word of this, otherwise it'll stand out that you've been tipped off.'

The Chinese nodded.

'You know, we're very grateful for this, Peter,' Gao said, 'and we'll heed your warning, for sure.'

The Cicada smiled, knowing the Chinese undoubtedly would. This seemed to be what he wanted: to be in charge, and getting results.

There was a pause when the waiter brought the beer. He filled their glasses methodically, then sauntered back to the kitchen.

'Other areas, too,' Phillips said, 'pose a serious risk.' Now his facial expression was sombre, matching his words.

Gao raised his glass in a silent toast and the other two followed.

'For example, the room where your drivers sit around chatting – that's where real gems they pick up while driving their cars come right out. And the sexier the topic, the greater the stress they put on it. Then there's communications. Wow, that's something you're going to have to watch closely.'

The Chinese listened carefully. Not only were they engrossed in what Phillips was saying; they were equally engaged by his delivery, which again was animated.

'Frankly, your most highly classified transmissions – Top Secret and upwards – haven't been accessed. Not as yet, anyway. But that's not for want of trying on the Americans' part. Let me tell you, it frustrates their technical people no end, especially with Washington so rapt about the take from that earlier op. You know, the one our Defence Signals Directorate and ASIO did on your old embassy in Canberra. They bugged the shit out of it for years. The one in that converted motel.'

Gao flashed the Cicada a mischievous grin and received a wry smile in return. Whatever passed between them, it was enough to tell the Chinese that Gao was now in on the game. A professional rapport had been established.

'You'll also have to be careful with content,' Phillips said, reverting to his earlier theme. 'If you make even the slightest change, they'll pick it up fast.'

'I wonder,' Gao asked cautiously, 'if you might get us a few samples of what this eavesdropping operation's producing? We'd be interested to see some of the – what do you say? – the hottest reporting, especially if it had comments attached.'

'Oh, that's no trouble.' Phillips exuded a confidence they found quite surprising.

Gao glanced at his watch. 'Perhaps we should move on to tradecraft,' he said, buoyed by the Cicada's positive manner. 'If you keep on helping us this way, Peter, we'll have to make sure our meetings and contacts are safe – for your sake, as well as ours.'

'Naturally.'

Phillips suggested five venues in Sydney, in order of priority. Gao agreed, proposing a slightly different sequence along geographic lines. This described a rough circle. By moving around it in a clockwise direction and by alluding only to the name of the suburb involved, a venue could be pinpointed with ease and security.

'An old trick of the game, eh?' Phillips said, with a glint in his eye.

No meetings, they agreed, would take place in Canberra. Sydney was best by far. And Phillips, anyway, visited regularly to look after his 86-year-old father, who was widowed and living alone.

Phillips's approach to these housekeeping matters, as he called them, was so professional –

if not starkly procedural – that Gao found himself briefly thrown off balance.

'I don't think *we'll* have any difficulty,' Phillips said, addressing his comment to Gao. 'After all, you and I are trained to the hilt, aren't we? Plus we're too old and wise to make those sorts of mistakes.'

Gao reacted with the same confident laugh. His private thoughts, however, were focused on something quite different. He was trying to reconcile what he was experiencing with this traitor and the kind of instructions he normally gave to recruited agents. While all were in the business of selling secrets, the Cicada was in a category of his own. Never before had Gao dealt with an agent who had come in from the other side, one who was himself a fully trained and practising spy, let alone a manipulator of the first order.

It's uncanny how smooth it all is, he mused. You'd think we were engineers in a new Coca-Cola bottling plant. But then, he obviously has a need and he wants it satisfied quickly. Whatever's driven him to this, it'll only partly have to do with flaws in his character. In the main, I bet it's because of some situation he's got himself into inside the Service.

A series of dates was set for future meetings and matched with venues. There would be minimal contact in between, and then only to confirm arrangements, rather than for dialogue. Gao gave Phillips a mobile phone and two numbers to ring for this purpose.

'Well, I must say,' Phillips said, 'I'm looking forward to you and me working together. And maybe sometimes the three of us can meet, too.' He smiled at Zhang as he spoke.

'Can't see why not,' Gao replied, though he knew he would be keeping such meetings to a minimum.

The Cicada seemed pleased with himself. He took a quick look at his watch, just as the waiter arrived with the spicy fish they had ordered. It filled the air with a fragrance of ginger and chilli. After their bowls had been filled with rice, Zhang dismissed the waiter and spooned out a serving for each.

'I'll have to be off in fifteen minutes,' Phillips said.

He paused as though something else of importance remained to be broached. Sitting forward in his chair, he picked up his chopsticks and took a small mouthful of food. He was silent as he chewed, as if the dish had lost all its flavour.

He's waiting for something, Zhang thought – something he thinks should be coming his way, and that *we're* meant to raise. I've got it. Yes, that's what it is.

Gao's mind was on the same track. It was the question of payment. Gao made the first move.

'You know, Peter, the help you're giving us is going to put the Australia–China relationship on a much sounder footing. That's not to say my colleagues and I are "anti-American". Not at all. But let's be frank, the games Washington plays aren't going to help Australia be accepted as part of the region. So your contribution will go a long way to bringing things back into balance. Maybe what I'm trying to say isn't coming across well in English, but . . . '

'Far from it,' the Cicada cut in. 'I understand clearly.'

'Anyhow, it's no secret to us,' Gao said, 'that there are certain stresses and strains involved in what you're doing.'

The Cicada smiled. He saw what was coming.

'Look, I'd like to give you five thousand dollars a week,' Gao said. 'Let's say, to cover expenses. And on top of that a lump sum of, say, one million, in a Hong Kong account, after three months of continuing help.'

The Cicada's face was expressionless. Then he grinned sheepishly. 'It couldn't be just a *little* higher, could it?' he said.

Shenme ren, Gao thought: he certainly knows what he's worth.

'What about one and a half million?' Gao replied, leaving the other figure untouched.

'It's a deal,' the Cicada said in a flash.

There was a pause, then his attention moved back to the food. He took another mouthful of fish, silently savouring its taste.

Gao slipped a blue Qantas ticket pouch over the table.

'Your first weekly instalment,' he said.

The Cicada's eyes fixed upon the red kangaroo on the front. He seemed distracted by this, but quickly gathered his thoughts.

'You won't need a receipt?' he said, parodying the routine that dogged any spy in the field.

Once recruited, agents usually received monthly payments in cash, for which they were expected to sign.

'Well, not for the time being, at least,' Gao said with a laugh.

The Cicada casually tucked the pouch into his jacket as he pulled it off the back of the chair.

He checked the time again. 'You'll have to excuse me,' he said, standing. 'If I don't make a move, I'll miss my plane.' He shook Gao's hand with vigour, as though the two were firm friends. 'It's hardly goodbye,' he said.

'It's just the beginning,' Gao responded.

'And you, my friend,' the Cicada said, turning to Zhang, 'I'll be seeing you soon enough, I trust.'

'No doubt you will,' the Chinese replied. 'In the meantime, read this when you have a spare minute.' He handed over a booklet called *The Thoughts of Lao Zi*.

'Now that's a size I can manage,' the Cicada said, touched by the gesture. 'I'll let you know what I think.'

He gave Zhang a friendly slap on the back and left.

'Well, let's not push it too far,' David Farnsworth, the Prime Minister, said, 'just because we have the upper hand. OK, *we* have the gas, and *they* want it. But we also need the deal. Sales like that would improve our current account deficit overnight.'

'Granted,' one of the departmental heads responded politely, 'but we can't afford to be seen as a pushover.'

'True,' Farnsworth said. 'Clearly, that's something we have to factor in.'

Nevertheless, he was concerned that the point Canberra was trying to make to the Chinese might destroy the ultimate goal. The two governments had been in talks for over a year on a long-term energy agreement, the centrepiece of which was a major Chinese involvement in the development of new gas-fields in Australia. A review of progress in the negotiations was at the top of today's agenda for the weekly departmental heads' meeting with the PM.

'Look,' Farnsworth said, 'whoever the Chinese do business with, they always have a wish-list as long as your bloody arm, and they usually expect a government like ours to back private enterprise to the hilt. OK, it's important we let them know they can't have everything they ask for, but at the end of the day it's no secret between them and us that we're far and away the most reliable supplier in this part of the world. Indonesia's not within a bull's roar of us in terms of political stability. So let's be careful not to overdo the foreplay and lose out on the sex.'

The message was clear, and conveyed with the humour for which the PM was known.

FOUR

Sydney: Mid-April

Rain from the night before had pockmarked the sand on the beach. A soft autumn sun, though warm, was too weak to dry it out at that time of the morning, even with a mild breeze wafting in from the Pacific.

Greg Mason and Zhang Wendao were ready to set off on their run in the bayside Sydney suburb of Balmoral. It was their custom to meet there on Sundays at eight, regardless of the season.

'Bloody oath, have I got a story for you,' Mason said, 'but I'll leave it until we've finished. You'll need to sit down to hear this one, I tell you.'

Zhang smiled to himself as his friend moved off ahead. Mason was teasing him, knowing how he hated having to wait for something he sensed was significant.

Mason had thought long and hard about whether to broach the subject at all. But it was best to tip off the Chinese, he resolved, if indeed they did not already know. Australia's interests would suffer for sure if the Japanese had their way.

His first instinct had been to report Tokyo's plans directly to Canberra. Then the chilling realisation came, that anything he passed on would go straight back to ASIS. That would lead to his own currency being immediately debased, if not also that of the report itself, at least in the short term. The Service's management was not to be trusted. Instead, he had tipped off the management of Australia's major liquefied natural gas producer, via a friend working with the firm. They were grateful for inside information that allowed them to rejig their package on offer to China. Nothing would be mentioned to Canberra, for the time being at least. 'Too many nervous Nellies there,' the executive had said, 'to dare go against anything Japan wants to do.'

The wet sand was crisp underfoot as the two men ran on abreast, enjoying the open air and space. This was not a feat of endurance for either of them. It was a daily ritual for Mason, whose apartment was close by in Cremorne. But for Zhang, who lived with his family in Kirribilli, near the Bridge, once a week was the best he could do. Both men were fit, with the Chinese as lean as kung fu types usually were. Mason, too, regularly scuba-dived and occasionally played golf. Companionship was what really brought them to this place.

The two had originally met on Zhang's first posting to Australia, when he was an economic attaché at the Chinese Embassy in Canberra. Mason was with ASIS then and was back in the capital between stints in Bangkok and Jakarta. He had been given the task of making Zhang's acquaintance in order to assess whether he might be a target for recruitment. Mason's opinion, however, was that he would be unlikely to succumb to the blandishments of any intelligence operative. He was not that sort of person. He had a message of 'not for hire' writ large across his soul.

Instead, the pair had become friends, partly brought together by the sea. Zhang was a history buff and an expert on Ming Dynasty voyages, such as those to the east coast of Africa. He was fascinated by Mason's experiences diving on wrecks. The two men had a meeting of minds, especially on matters of knowledge and learning, and felt easy in each other's company. Mason had once described their bond to Zhang with memorable precision, when their ways temporarily parted after Canberra. He recounted a meeting he'd had with an elderly Indian official on a visit to New Delhi some years before. They'd been talking of friendship when the old man pointed out that friends were never actually 'made'. 'Rather,' he said, 'they're kindred spirits who recognise each other and decide to travel the path of life together.'

Now, after one full lap of the beach, they were back at the spot where they'd left their gear. A lone cormorant stood with its wings outstretched in the breeze, as though guarding their possessions, but departed when they plunged into the water to cool off. When that was over, they grabbed their towels and looked out to sea. Clouds billowed over the horizon, losing their tinges of gold as the sun climbed higher.

'What a sight!' Zhang said, in Mandarin.

'What a city,' Mason replied, his voice as clear and strong in Chinese as it was in his native tongue.

'OK, Greg, what's this tale I have to sit down to hear?'

'Well, sit down and I'll tell you.'

They spread their towels on the sand, then Mason outlined Matsutomo Corporation's request to him for information on gas. He explained how he had followed it up with contacts in Tokyo just a few days ago, though he kept their identities to himself. As expected, there was more to it than Kiriyama had let on. And Australia had nothing to gain. Quite the opposite: it had much to lose.

'For a few months now,' he said, 'Moscow's had a Japanese gas exploration team working in Russian waters on contract. What they've found is a massive new field off the island of Sakhalin. It's high quality stuff. Not a word's leaked out yet, because the Japanese are playing their cards close to their chest. They've even kept the news from the Russians themselves and won't come clean until Tokyo's ready to put a proposal to Moscow. It's going to be something the Russians won't want to knock back. But first the Japanese have to lock other things into place if they're to have any hope of keeping the upper hand.'

Zhang listened intently. He had known nothing of this.

'Strategically, the discovery's of enormous importance. It's right on Japan's doorstep. Therefore the Japanese Government is giving it the highest priority. They've got this small, secret team of bureaucrats working flat out on a national plan that will grab for Japan as much of the action as possible. And that means putting together a consortium of top Japanese firms to develop the field. *If* Moscow agrees, that is, to let Japan take the lead. And the assumption is that they will.

'In the meantime, they've called in Matsutomo to help out on a number of fronts. One thing they have to do is find out how competitive Australia's likely to be *vis-a-vis* a development like this – commercially, strategically, as well as politically. After all, we're a major exporter of gas, and they need to know what direction we're heading in. They've also been given the task of dampening down any interest Canberra might have in China opening up new gas-fields here.'

Zhang groaned in dismay. Energy matters were close to his heart and this threatened the major project on which he was spending much of his time: a long-term deal with Australia. It was a task of which Mason was aware, as he was of China's determination not to become as reliant on Middle Eastern energy as had Japan when its economy took off.

'Anyway,' the Australian said, 'the Japanese think they've got the Sakhalin thing all sewn up. Tokyo plans to cough up the funding to develop the field, in return for exclusive sales rights to the gas for the next twenty-five years. And here's the bit you'll love. They can only make it all work if two major purchasers come on board, in addition to Japanese buyers. The two would have to commit themselves, long term, to take two-thirds of the yield. Now, Korea's already signed up, but without China as the number one buyer the project simply won't go ahead. Do you see what I mean?'

Zhang was left wagging his head. But clearly Mason had more of the story to tell.

'What's got Tokyo excited is the idea of linking up economic development in North Asia to the signing of a peace treaty between Russia and Japan. They'll lock the North Koreans in too. And, of course, you Chinese will become so dependent on this new energy grid that you won't let anything threaten it. Anyhow, as you'd imagine, Tokyo's desperate to keep all this hushed up until they've got a viable deal to put to the Russians. They're scared witless that if word leaks out to the global oil and gas industry, the likes of Exxon and Shell will be bashing on Moscow's door with offers the Russians won't be able to resist. So, for Tokyo . . . '

'. . . time is of the essence,' Zhang said, reading Mason's thoughts.

'Exactly! So there you are. That's it. What do you think? Do you want me to run through it again?'

For a while Zhang was lost in thoughts of his own. Then he looked up. 'Greg, you realise what those bloody *guizi* are up to?' His pejorative term for the Japanese likened them to devils of the very worst kind. 'They want us Chinese right out of the energy field in Australia. No Chinese investment here in gas – no long-term contracts – nothing at all. It's as simple as that.'

'You've got it. And that's precisely where Matsutomo fits in.'

'*Ta ma de!*' Zhang ripped out the expletive in earthy Chinese, punching the sand with his fist.

Mason had seen him angry before, though it was not a common occurrence. He had no doubt that the Japanese would get a good run for their money if Zhang were to have any say in the matter.

Beijing was pushing for local business – with government support – to open up two new fields. They were adjacent to the North West Shelf gas project offshore from Western Australia, which was the nation's largest resource development. China's aim was to be the driving force behind the project's expansion, as part of its quest to guarantee future energy requirements. But Beijing needed concessional funding and, while Canberra wanted the exports, the Australian Government's dilemma was whether such a huge outlay of public money could be justified upfront.

Ambassador Li had entrusted Zhang with the job of overseeing China's endeavour to bring Canberra onside.

Mason welcomed Chinese involvement,

regarding it as vital to his country's interests. A heavy dependence on the commodity trade with Japan had long worried him – as it did many Australians – and it was primarily for this reason that Mason had decided to convey to Zhang the gist of what he had gleaned in Japan. He was determined to see Australia come out on top, which had not always been the case in the resources area over the past quarter century.

'So Matsutomo's role, then,' Zhang said, 'is to slow down any agreement between Australia and China – if not stop it dead in its tracks – through peddling their influence and money.'

'Precisely.'

'Greg, I'm really grateful for this. And let me tell you, I'll work as hard as I can to get Australia the best possible deal.'

'I know you will.'

Zhang rose and stretched his arms. He breathed in deeply, savouring the fresh salty air.

A young migrant couple of Middle Eastern descent sauntered past. Their toddler had just begun walking. Zhang waved and the child beamed back. It was a side of his friend that Mason relished and had seen on many occasions. Zhang loved children and animals and could create instant rapport where others would not bother to try.

'Shit, I'll need another dip after that,' Zhang said. 'It's the only way I'll cool down.'

Mason watched as he ran back into the water, contemplating the things that bound the two of them together.

Both had a keen interest in human complexity. They had been pummelled by life and this had sharpened their instinct for the better things that people had to offer. To them, trust, loyalty and integrity, as well as wit and fun, were important. Both had a lot to give. Zhang, some said, was too trusting, while Mason was slow to bestow that upon anyone. He also didn't suffer fools lightly, often battling to keep feelings of disdain to himself. Zhang, in contrast, was more contained.

Soon after they had met up again, this time in Sydney, Zhang asked the Australian straight out if he worked for his country's intelligence service. Mason confirmed that he had, though he refrained from explaining why he'd left. All he said was that along the way he had worked with some pretty fine people, but for a variety of reasons had found it time to move on.

'*You de shihou* . . . ' Zhang had said, with a bit of a laugh. 'One of these days I'd love to hear why you chose to get out. I guess there's a great story behind that.'

'Maybe you're right,' Mason replied. 'And one of these days, you never know, I might tell you why I never really fitted in in that place. Anyway, why do you ask?'

'Oh, I suppose for a number of reasons. There's a certain . . . *presence* you have, like a strong sense of awareness of things around you, things the average person doesn't pick up.'

Mason had thanked him for the compliment.

― ― ―

Later, driving home from the beach, Prue was in his thoughts again. She had loved the sea and was a diver like him.

Martin Clarke had seduced Mason's wife only a few months before the blow-up in Jakarta over Mustafa. Mason was close and loyal to Prue, but that had not been enough and he realised too late. Long nights were devoted to his intelligence work, with frequent travel to other parts of the country. Essentially she felt she was no longer a major part of his life.

'Just three more recruitments,' he said, 'and I'll pull back. I'll have made my mark in this place.'

But Prue was unwilling to wait and had succumbed to Clarke's magnetism. Like most women, she had found him physically attractive and, as ever, Clarke had known how to fill a vacuum in someone else's life. The pair moved in together. Mason was shattered, and Clarke made things worse than they needed to be. But it was the Malaysian case that was the last straw. In essence, ASIS management in Canberra had betrayed him. Challenged by Clarke's unyielding stance, it had shown itself weak and ineffectual, meekly accepting the consequences of the station commander's repudiation of his colleague. Only when Mason returned to headquarters did he learn what Clarke had been feeding back all the while.

Mason had given full vent to his feelings in a meeting with William Hestercombe, the Service's chief – a former diplomat with no experience in intelligence – and Morgandale, who was then director of operations. The exchange was as fresh in Mason's mind, now, as when it took place.

'What you've got in Indonesia,' he told them baldly, 'is a commander from the Service's old school – that group that went into Asia early on with little knowledge of the region. Then new recruits like me came into ASIS, with languages and hands-on experience. But Martin found that hard to accept. He's typical, in that when he came back from his first few postings he saw himself – and the Service, understandably, did as well – as an instant Asia hand. There simply weren't others around who were more qualified. Yet, with the new breed, people like Martin couldn't bring themselves to acknowledge that the newcomers were the real McCoy. Granted, they had a lot to learn about intelligence, but most were already streetwise in Asia. Regrettably, that only fuelled the jealousy of Martin and his cohorts.'

'Utter rot!' Morgandale said. 'You don't know what you're talking about.'

'Well, that's where you're wrong, Bass, and you know it. You're just as bad as Martin. Neither of you has ever tried to roll with the times. You want reality frozen so it doesn't threaten your own bloody comfort zone. OK, your input might've meant something once, but it's stunting the growth of the Service right now.'

Hestercombe, who was left in a flap, sought safety in supporting Morgandale's stance.

'Look, Greg, if you want to stay in the Service,' he snapped, 'you'll just have to toe the line.'

'Not with people of your ilk running the place. I'd rather be out on the street.'

Mason resigned that day.

Now, as he slowed to a snail's pace in the Sunday morning beach traffic, he felt Prue's presence. It was as if she were sitting alongside him, listening to him explain.

'I'm *so* sorry, Prue. Obviously I was blinded by what I was doing for that bunch in Canberra, and couldn't see you moving away. It was my fault, nobody else's.'

He missed her like never before, wondering how things might be now if she were still around.

The two men dashed for cover as a sudden squall swept across Canberra. Martin Clarke and Todd Lambert had thought the walk from ASIS headquarters in the nearby Foreign Affairs building might be therapeutic, especially as they'd worked through the lunch break. There had been just a fine drizzle and no wind when they left. And with the capital awash with autumn tints, Lambert, whose rural upbringing made him nostalgic for such things, suggested they try it on foot.

Clarke was feeling testy. He was looking forward to the afternoon's meeting with relish, intrigued to see how Canberra's bureaucrats would handle something like this. Morgandale had planned to attend, but was closeted with the minister over some tricky evidence to a Senate committee. Instead he had asked Clarke to stand in for him and to take his offsider as notetaker.

The two were the first to arrive at the low-slung government building, and were dripping wet when they reached the entrance. While Clarke was generally very controlled, any disturbance to his clothing unsettled him. His concern for his appearance always amused his 36-year-old deputy, though the younger man never let it show. It was not the sort of thing that Lambert himself, as a former SAS officer, ever worried about. His short fair hair and square jaw fitted well with his build and spoke clearly of his toughness.

Upstairs, the tall and distinguished-looking deputy secretary of the Attorney-General's Department ushered them into the meeting room. He fetched a tea towel from a small kitchen nearby and handed it perfunctorily to Clarke, a man by whom he was quietly detested for his confident urbanity.

'You look like drowned rats,' he said to them, his voice heavily nasal from a bout of the flu. 'I'm afraid I can't help you with a bath towel.'

Others now began to arrive. The 17 April meeting had been called at short notice to address a disturbing development in the bugging operation on the Chinese Embassy. Once everyone was seated at the long, rectangular table, the deputy secretary launched into proceedings.

'For those who haven't already heard,' he said, 'it seems that a newspaper might be on to the story.'

A silence came over the room.

Clarke took the chance to scan the others attending. They were all people he knew. The only woman in the room – Alexandra Templeton – was the representative of ONA, the Office of National Assessments, with whom he had a hot-and-cold relationship, both professionally as well as personally. Those from ASIO, the Defence Signals Directorate and Foreign Affairs all required careful handling, too. As Clarke had learnt from experience, they would challenge any statement he made if he could not fully support it. All had serious looks on their faces.

'What's happened,' their host said, 'is that Adrian McKinnon, that investigative journalist from the *Sydney Daily Courier*, has been sniffing around Canberra. It looks as if he's come up with a few pieces of the jigsaw, though seemingly not enough to give him a clear picture of what's going on. Somebody recently overheard him asking questions and reported it, which set alarm bells off all over the place.'

Some of those listening coughed nervously. This was the type of thing the bureaucracy dreaded, if indeed the matter turned into a fully fledged leak. Not only would political masters be running for cover, they would also be looking for scapegoats. And that was before the reaction of a powerful ally like the United States had been factored in.

'To be on the safe side,' the deputy secretary continued, 'we've pulled out all stops. We've been monitoring McKinnon's phone calls, as well as electronic communications, and this morning something interesting cropped up. You see, we've intercepted a call he made from Sydney to the *Courier*'s bureau chief – Jeremy Torrens – up in Beijing. Now Torrens, it appears, had received a couriered letter from McKinnon a week or so ago, which tipped him off to something.'

The deputy secretary flicked through a transcript of the phone call. 'Yes, here it is,' he said, preparing to read aloud.

> It's a fascinating story, mate, but it's one that'll need a lot more investigation before the paper could risk touching it.

'McKinnon,' he went on, 'must have asked Torrens which of his contacts in Australia might be able to help with a deeper probe. The pair had a pretty guarded conversation, which included mention of a few architectural terms. Then we heard the following ... '

> I tell you, if this gets out, it'll have diplomatic repercussions for sure – if, of course, it proves to be true. At this stage, it looks like one of those notoriously difficult nuts to crack.

'Now, while they didn't actually name names,' the deputy said, 'they did manage to identify three 'people in Canberra – in the "defence and security system and likely to be in the know on things Chinese" – who might be worth chatting to.'

He explained that the Government's National Security Committee had already met to consider this development and the risk that it posed. As a result, he had been instructed to establish a working group of officials presently in the bugging 'loop' to monitor the situation.

'Under no circumstances,' he stressed, 'are the Americans to be told, which means we're going to have to take particular care with those two US eavesdropping technicians stationed here to oversee the operation.'

He cleared his throat in a theatrical way, suggesting that an impersonation of someone was imminent. 'For God's sake, don't frighten the fucking horses unless we're sure the stable's on fire!'

This portrayal of the Foreign Minister's reaction to the news made everyone chuckle. The deputy proffered a deferential apology to Templeton, who was the top China analyst at ONA, but it had nothing to do with his use of the expletive. Rather it was because of her status as Canberra's best-known mimic. She was a bright and attractive woman, as well as an outstanding linguist, and frequently had people in stitches with impersonations of public figures. Her brick-red jacket and cream blouse added a welcome touch to the dour greys and white of the men.

'I've heard much worse than that from him,' Templeton said, referring to the minister's use of profanity.

The deputy nodded. 'Anyhow,' he said, '*we're* it. We're the watchdog until this damn thing's put to rest. So, to start with, I'd like you all to read the transcript.'

The Defence Signals Directorate representative handed out copies. It was a lengthy document, thanks to the twenty-minute phone conversation involved.

'I suggest you study it carefully,' their host said, 'because what's written there is probably just the tip of the iceberg. It's what they both *already* know – what they're *not* talking about – that we have to deduce. You'll notice we've left the juicy bits in because they illustrate how well these two know each other.'

Once more the room fell silent. This was briefly interrupted a few moments later when the deputy secretary had coffee brought in. Its aroma softened the sterile smell of the room.

Templeton visibly squirmed when she turned to the fourth page, though she was not a fainthearted person. So did some of the others. They had entered into the privacy of an intimate conversation, an act that hauntingly questioned their right to intrude. The early part of the dialogue related to Torrens's wife, who had had a difficult time with the birth of their second child eight months earlier. The couple's sex life had still not resumed. Justified or not, the ethics of what DSD had done were laid bare.

Templeton was shaking her head. Others paused, then returned to the task, but most realised it was not a proud moment.

Todd Lambert, the youngest in the room, was first to finish. Clarke perfunctorily skimmed the last few pages in order to keep up with his offsider. The host sat contemplatively at the head of the table, obviously keen to discuss the matter.

'It's McKinnon's apparent determination to persist with his enquiries that concerns me,' he said, ruminating aloud. 'I just can't get these images out of my mind of the damage that'll be done if this is what we think it is.'

Sensing that Lambert was watching him, he looked up and smiled warmly. He was the sort of man who respected intellect and zeal in someone younger, for which reason he was keen to hear what construction Lambert put on the development. Admittedly Clarke's colleague could be a tad arrogant, but at least he knew what he was talking about.

'With Martin's agreement, of course,' the deputy secretary said when the others had finished, 'I'd like Todd to tell us what he makes of all this.'

Clarke nodded his approval. He didn't mind in the least, he decided. He could sit back and work on a magisterial observation to make later – which no doubt would grow out of something Todd said. Todd never failed him in this and always looked as though his thinking had been nurtured under his boss's tutelage.

'Thank you,' Lambert said, exuding his customary ease. His voice was confident and had a husky tone that added weight to his manner. 'Well, while we can't prove one hundred per cent that it's the Chinese Embassy these Charlies are talking about, I must say I'm convinced that it is.'

The others either nodded or mumbled something to indicate agreement.

'Actually, I'd hazard a guess,' he continued, 'and say the *Courier* chap in Sydney *doesn't* know the Americans are involved in the bugging, but *does* know about the method used to wire up the building.'

'You mean, the optical fibre stuff?' someone queried.

'Yes.'

'No, I don't see it that way at all,' the Foreign Affairs representative said. 'I really don't think that's inherent in what they're saying. In fact, I feel he knows the whole bloody lot.'

There was a clear consensus that the Foreign Affairs man was wrong. But Lambert let the matter rest, reasoning that most around the table would assume that an intelligence officer had a greater capacity to elicit truth from the words of others. A barely disguised sigh from the ASIO representative said as much. Clarke stirred in his chair, but had nothing to add.

Oh, how delightful, he thought. There's a real fight brewing here.

'So,' Lambert said, summing up and ignoring the Foreign Affairs official sitting opposite, 'I think our interpretation has to be that they're not on to the American angle yet. Not for the time being at least.'

Clarke quietly approved of this tack. Both he and Lambert appreciated that their DSD colleague would want to report a clearcut view back to the interception team to provide it with guidance on what to look out for. A multifaceted outcome, which was often the product of Canberra meetings, was never helpful.

'Yes,' came the response, like an affirmative tide washing round the table.

Only the Foreign Affairs man was silent.

'Well, let's hope we're correct,' the deputy secretary said, taking charge once again, 'but how long that might apply for is anybody's guess.'

He hated handling intelligence cases. They tended to be messy and awkward. What was needed here was clear thinking, decisiveness and effective coordination.

'Of course, if this gets out,' Clarke said, 'it'll be the last straw to the Americans. Washington's wrath could be worse than that of an aggrieved Beijing. Let's face it, it's no secret that the CIA believes we've got moles in our system.'

A quiet fell over the room as the group contemplated what might happen with Uncle Sam on the warpath. A sudden squall outside lashed the windows, accentuating the image most had of Washington rampant.

No one had anything to offer, so the deputy moved on with his agenda. He raised ASIO's plans for a more detailed pursuit of the journalists, DSD's ongoing alert, and the likely nature of Chinese retaliation if the bugging operation were to blow wide open. The latter, after all, would be top priority for the next meeting of the National Security Committee.

It turned out to be a long and tedious discussion, highlighting the fact that nothing could be decided until much more was known.

Hold tight, Clarke mused to himself, things are shaping up nicely. There's a smell of opportunity in the air – to play a few games with these people.

Joe Pellegrini, the nuggety and balding ASIO officer, made a suggestion. 'At the end of the day,' he said, 'we could always hit the *Courier* with a D Notice and stop the thing dead in its tracks.'

A government device, the D Notice was a warning to newspaper editors and others in the media to desist from publishing a story that could harm the national interest. It had no legal standing in its own right, but inherent in its use was the hint that criminal charges could be preferred under the *Crimes Act*. Traditionally, the media obeyed such notices.

'Well, that's easier said than done,' the deputy noted. 'Frankly, it's a procedure with little of the clout it had in Cold War days.'

'What about an injunction, then?' Templeton said.

'Now, on that legal note . . . '

The deputy secretary, in whose territory this question obviously fell, was cut short by the Foreign Affairs man, who seemed bent on regaining lost ground.

'Oh, come off it. What's an injunction ever achieved?' he said rashly, looking Templeton in the eye. 'It's just a lawyer's plaything, *dearie*, and one that'll pour petrol on a fire like this and make it much worse. Not put it out!'

As was often the case with this man, he had hit the nail on the head, though his manner of doing so diminished the merit of his observation.

Here's a chance, Clarke thought. 'So, what are you recommending?' he joined in, knowing that the deputy would be worried that such condescension might get Templeton's hackles up.

'I'm not recommending *anything*,' the other man said, with a vehemence verging on rudeness.

Never a fan of Clarke's, he detested any display of superiority on ASIS's part, especially in light of the heavy dependence the Service had on Foreign Affairs for diplomatic cover for its spies.

'What I'm saying is that no court will allow itself to get snagged on Canberra's narrow interests. It'll be looking at what the public needs to know, and whether any of us should have been mixed up in a harebrained scheme like this in the first place.'

Again, the point was valid.

Lambert's instincts warned him that Clarke was spoiling for a fight. He had an unsavoury habit of baiting Foreign Affairs types, though usually to score points for himself.

'Frankly,' the deputy said, treading warily, 'an injunction's simply a device – a tool. It's not necessarily a plaything.'

He glanced at Clarke as he spoke, hinting that he would not want to see the issue blown out of proportion.

'You see, nothing in our arsenal is perfect,' he added, 'but *nothing*, by itself, is less than good.'

His eloquence and the calm way in which he spoke summed up the situation adequately, as was his custom. And that might have put paid to it if Clarke had not chosen to drive the point home.

'Look, mate,' he said to the Foreign Affairs man politely, though leaving no doubt he sought an honest answer, 'come clean and tell us what you're *really* getting at?'

Well, look what's happening, he thought, deliberately looking away from the deputy secretary. They're not listening to you, you pompous bastard. They're more interested in where I'm taking the discussion.

To the Foreign Affairs man, the question was patronising in the extreme.

'Let's face it,' Clarke added tersely, 'you yourself were *gung ho* when this bugging job was first mooted. You were all for us sticking it up the Chinese. Yet now you bucket it.'

'So?' the Foreign Affairs official responded, shrugging, as if to disown the process he had started. His neck had gone red, contrasting with the white collar of his shirt.

'So whose side are you on, then?' Clarke persisted.

The other man missed the simple thrust of the question and took umbrage before Clarke's words were all out.

'What the hell do you mean by that?' he barked, pointing his finger threateningly across the table.

'Come now,' the deputy pleaded, attempting to regain control.

But Clarke was unwilling to let go. 'Well, it sounds like you've gone soft on Beijing,' he said, half laughing in atonement.

The diplomat scowled, as the others watched in dismay. It was obvious that he had overreacted, but the comment stung deeply.

'What do you reckon, Joe?' Clarke said, looking at the ASIO man.

When you're on a run, he thought, go with it!

Joe Pellegrini also had a well-known antipathy to Foreign Affairs, but the stern look on their host's face warned him not to be drawn into Clarke's game.

The room was tense and many were counting the seconds before the ASIS man's target walked out. Lambert knew better than the others what was going on. He had seen Clarke use this tactic before, but thought it cruel and unnecessary.

'Look, I think there's an easy way around this,' Clarke said, suddenly changing his tone. 'See, I happen to know McKinnon, so I'll give him a call. He sounds me out on things from time to time. You never know, he might . . .'

'Oh, Martin,' the deputy cut across him. 'I really don't think that'd be proper. Certainly not at this stage.' He glanced around the table, seeking support.

Pellegrini shrugged. Templeton was stonefaced.

'Well, it was just an idea,' Clarke said, grinning.

Lambert could see clearly what had happened, though the others were still distracted by the nature of Clarke's suggestion. The man had helped whip up a firestorm, then doused it by changing the subject and making himself the focus of attention. If there was one art at which he was adept, it was that of manipulation.

But why now? Lambert thought, glancing at his colleague and noticing the look of contentment on his face. What can he possibly hope to gain from all this?

The three-member Chinese 'inventory team' worked smoothly and efficiently. Their personal banter disguised a deeper professional dialogue, with the superficial task of moving pieces of furniture and attaching labels, providing the cover they needed for the sophisticated electronic sweeping exercise in which they were engaged. The weekend had been chosen for the job as it made it easier to empty the embassy of people.

Zhang, though not formally part of the team, was following its progress with interest. A silent partner, he was under instructions not to utter a word. Nor would the others acknowledge his presence.

The technician in charge reached up high and ran a long detection arm gently across the upper part of the wall, careful not to make contact. The other two – a young Mongolian and a middle-aged woman – studied his every move. They chatted away casually, as was intended. A weak but distinct signal came through on the equipment they had positioned above the political counsellor's desk. It was well that he was not there. A fastidious type, he would not have been amused by this violation of his space.

'I'm afraid I can't understand the number on this picture,' the technician with the detector said, using his free hand to lift a scroll painting out from the wall. Putting it back, he lowered the scanning arm and laid it gently across the counsellor's chair. Rubbing the stubble on his chin, he pondered for a while.

'Shenme le?' the woman asked: what is it? 'Has someone replaced things with fakes?'

For a moment, it appeared he was going to say something, but instead he broke into a rasping, tubercular cough. This unsettled his companions, who knew that his spasms sometimes rendered him useless for days.

Zhang stood quietly by.

'Shi, shi, shi,' the technician replied, regaining his composure: yes, that may be the case.

'Fake' was the team's codeword for a find that would have to be discussed later in the embassy's secure room. Mention of aberrations with the furniture signalled that they were close to key parts of the optical fibre network they were tracking.

He scribbled a quick note on a clipboard, which the younger man held up for him: 'Probably a computerised transmission control box for mikes at this end of the building. It fits in with the drawings we have.'

The Mongolian showed the note to both the woman and Zhang.

'Hao le,' the woman said: right.

She responded to the technician's written message on one plane while, on another, indicating that she thought they should move on. 'Let's do the rooms on the other side of the passage,' she said. 'I've spotted chairs over there that aren't even on the inventory.'

Beijing's dispatch of the technical team to Australia came one week after Peter Phillips appeared on the scene. Shortly before the group left China, he had had his first one-on-one meeting with Gao. It had been an easy and productive encounter, with the Australian providing a range of material so diverse and relevant that the Chinese authorities were left bewildered. Included were detailed plans of the optical fibre network.

The Chinese team had travelled under the guise of a roving inventory and auditing squad. Only the ambassador and two others in Canberra – and Gao, Zhang and the psychologist in Sydney – were privy to what was occurring. Gao himself had planned to take part in the exercise, but had had to attend to an agent's urgent requirements in Queensland. Ambassador Li had therefore suggested that Zhang take his place. It would be good, he thought, for at least one of them to see how far the attack on the mission had reached.

The embassy staff had been told to stay away, though all relevant keys and combinations were made available to the team.

Now, working their way methodically round the premises, the Mongolian entered each room first.

His garlic breath left a trail wherever he went. Using a simpler hand-held device, he declared each office clear before the others came in.

'These diplomatic yokels think inventories are a joke!' he said, scoffing in his heavily accented Mandarin.

He had just exited the room used by Ambassador Li's secretary. His colleagues, who were waiting outside in the passage, were alarmed. The message inherent in his words was that something quite unexpected had arisen. Now it was the technician who was holding the clipboard.

'There's a small bug,' the Mongolian scribbled in characters, 'under one of the chairs. There's only a mike – no transmitter.'

The others went in to take a look. It was a small Japanese device which could be quickly and easily placed and which bore no distinctive manufacturer's marks. The Chinese nevertheless were well acquainted with its origins. They had on occasion used the same make in their own operations. One had been fixed under a chair used by visitors waiting to enter Li's room.

The group stood in silence after each had examined the bug. It was the woman who reached for the clipboard, penning a note: 'Last sweep here was nine days ago. There's a chance this device might have been placed by the Japanese themselves. Suggest we remove it now.'

Her colleagues nodded, chatting about the furniture as the Mongolian turned the chair upside down. He prised the mike loose from its adhesive base with a screwdriver. The team realised the bug had nothing to do with the US–Australian operation. It was something freshly planted, put there by somebody with shorter-term interests. Unquestionably, it would be one of a number in that part of the building, locked into a network with its own transmitter. Signals from that would be monitored by a listening post close to the embassy.

The next thing to check would be the rooms in which the rest of the bugs were likely to be. There was little doubt that Li's secretary's office would be peripheral to the main target area – and the team was certain what that was.

Later, when all the devices had been found and the remainder of the area thoroughly checked, a search of a different kind could begin. That was the quest to identify the owner. And the obvious place to start would be a list of official visitors over the previous nine days. Who, for example, might have paid a call from the Embassy of Japan? Had Li's counterpart dropped in for a friendly chat and to apologise for the Rape of Nanking? If there had been a visit, how many flunkies had accompanied him and what were their rankings? It should not be too hard to pick those with technical training. After all, Beijing's holdings on Japanese diplomats – whether genuine or spies under cover – were unrivalled.

The team moved on to the ambassador's suite.

Except for Zhang, they did not quite know how Li would use this new information, but they were sure he would employ it with all the deftness and elegance he applied to calligraphy – one of his great pleasures in life. Some of his finest works hung on the walls of his office.

'Really, Bass, the pair of you test my patience,' the ASIS chief said with a grin. 'It's either a case of one of you annoying other people, or you and Martin at each other's throats. Just give me a break, will you?'

Hestercombe and Morgandale were reasonably close friends, in addition to being professional colleagues, which accounted for the deputy's laidback attitude as well as the slovenly manner in which he sat in front of his chief's desk. His arm had already knocked out of place a carved ebony inkstand from one of Hestercombe's diplomatic postings in Africa. It was an act of no consequence in itself, but one that rankled with the director-general, who was someone who liked things in perfect alignment. For him, a bookish and careful type, order was supreme.

Morgandale had heard about Clarke's savaging of the Foreign Affairs representative on the bugging committee and had chipped him over his abrasive manner. 'Really, Martin, we should be able to trust that you can control yourself at all times.' That had occurred just prior to a meeting of senior officers in the Service, at which antagonism between the pair had flared yet again. On this occasion, it was the topic of discussion that had triggered it off: new operational activity in China.

That was something clearly residing in Clarke's jurisdiction. But Morgandale – who had a strong view on everything, especially if it involved the Chinese – had persistently interjected, questioning not only the judgement of Clarke and Lambert but also that of other officers from ops branch. Hestercombe had quietened them down, and Clarke – appropriately – had come out on top.

'I just wish you wouldn't goad him, Bass,' the chief said. 'If you feel that strongly about something, tell me, and I'll broach it. And anyway, ultimately it's you who chats to the minister – not Martin.'

Hestercombe had long had to tread a fine line in his relationship with Morgandale. While his deputy generally backed him to the hilt on whatever he wanted to do, the director-general was also close to Clarke, and had been for years. He could not afford to have either man offside, especially after the recent sudden resignation of two long-serving officers, Poulson from ops and Imlach from ASIS's security branch. The pair had already moved to Jakarta, where they had established a consultancy. Clarke and Hestercombe were deeply shocked by this, partly for reasons they chose to keep to themselves, while Morgandale described it as 'outright treachery'.

'I must say, Bill, I'm rather concerned about Martin's balance – his sense of proportion – and most of all on anything to do with China.'

Hestercombe's ears pricked up, as Morgandale expected they would. It was a delicate matter for the Service's deputy to raise, but he was a past master at the art of disinformation. A few years with MI6 in London had only served to polish this skill.

'It's got that way with him, Bill, where no one else can proffer anything useful on the subject without having their head bitten off. I don't like that at all. It destroys the idea of checks and balances, especially in working out how best to proceed with a huge and complex country like that. Hell, if we put one foot wrong there, we're stuffed for all time. Admittedly, Martin's rarely wrong on China, but we can't assume he'll always be right.'

The chief shook his head, more out of confusion than because he disagreed. Morgandale sat quietly, as was his want after planting a seed of doubt.

'Look, with that bugging committee,' Hestercombe said, retreating to safer ground, 'make sure you get along to the next meeting yourself. And if you can't make it, let me know and I'll try to divert Martin so that Lambert can attend. Nobody seems to have any quibble with him, plus he presents a "new face" of the Service.'

Morgandale smiled.

FIVE

Western Australia: Late April

A school of sharks homed in on the bait as soon as it hit the water under the rig. Several of them were large, but one, paler than the others, was huge.

The sea glinted under a strong sun as the creature threshed its tail to ward off contenders. A flock of gulls, waiting patiently for their share of scraps, panicked and flew around noisily.

A bulky piece of meat had been lowered on a crane hook, which was customarily used to winch up the twice-weekly provisions delivered by boat to this offshore gas production platform far from the coast.

A stiff sea breeze blew across the rig, warm and sharp with tangy salt.

'Holy shit, he'll take it!' The Honourable Dr Michael O'Sullivan called out excitedly, doing a little jig.

China's Ambassador Li, who stood alongside him, smiled politely. But a few of the workers who had gathered around sniggered. It was the first time they had seen their Foreign Minister up close, but they were aware from media reports of the image that his two years in office had served to consolidate rather than improve. Tall, skinny and in his late forties, O'Sullivan had unusual attributes for the position he held. But the Prime Minister as well as the Party owed him a number of favours, even though no one expected the tolerance of his parliamentary colleagues to extend beyond the next general election.

Ambassador Li noted the workers' slight to the minister and acted quickly to help him. He had his own reasons for wanting to keep the Australian onside. If the country's top diplomat was inept enough to make himself the subject of derision, then this was an opportunity to be exploited. In a way it also saddened him, though he was not one for sentimentality. Li had met O'Sullivan on many occasions and liked him. The minister was intelligent, witty and eternally curious. But something was missing: it was called common sense. Many said that not much could be expected anyway from a celebrated town planner who had gone into politics to 'liven things up'. He had certainly brought flair and energy, along with colourful bow ties, but none of the subtlety that his new profession demanded. Often he would become so engrossed in something that he lost sight of the impact his actions had on others around him.

Now was just such a moment. The 'affliction', as Li chose to call it, reminded him of tunnel vision: focusing on one minute point to the exclusion of all else around. He had seen it often in the Japanese, but not so much in educated Anglo-Saxons.

'You know, I could sell that monster for big money in China,' he said in English, peering down at the shark that had them all mesmerised.

'Well, would you like to take it with you?' the production engineer said.

He knew that the ambassador was attempting to save O'Sullivan's face and was keen to lend a hand. No one wanted to see the minister openly ridiculed. It would mar the visit entirely.

'*Xie xie*,' Li replied, switching to Mandarin: thank you. 'But maybe only one bit of it.'

He turned to Zhang to interpret and added more, even though his own command of English was adequate. But he was ever mindful of the capacity of his younger colleague to squeeze humour out of such situations.

'Mr Li says if you fillet it carefully, he'll take it – and the fin – back to Canberra to sell in the embassy. He could do with a top-up to the pittance he gets as a salary.'

The twenty-odd men in orange overalls who surrounded them roared with laughter. It was rare for a foreign VIP visitor to break the ice as fast as this one had done. Word of the ambassador's gift of cartons of fruit for the crew had spread within minutes of the party's helicopter touching down.

O'Sullivan's long, wavy grey hair blew about in the wind, exposing a bald spot on the top of his head. It was something he was sensitive about, and even now kept trying to cover. He chortled to himself for some time after the mirth of the others had died down.

The long flight out from the Western Australian coast had been uneventful, except for a deluge of technical information. The rig's production engineer had accompanied the party to the platform, which was perched precariously in the sea atop giant metal pylons. After landing, O'Sullivan, his senior adviser and the Chinese had been given a briefing, then taken on a tour of the facility. This was followed by a smorgasbord lunch. Time was set aside to take in the air before heading back. It was out on the main deck, after a group photograph with the rig's crew, that the production engineer mentioned sharks. He had explained how they gathered to feast on rubbish thrown overboard from the galley. If the cook had meat that was 'off', it was sometimes lowered on the crane hook to catch one of the pack. Li had expressed an interest in seeing this done and that was what the group was watching now.

'What often happens,' the engineer said, 'is that we lose them. When they're hoisted out of the water, they thresh and break free before we get them to the top.'

The winch had just lifted the shark clear of the swell. Writhing wildly, it rose a metre or two, then slipped off the hook. Like a whale breaching, its white underbelly flashed in the sun as it hit the water with an impact they could hear up above.

'Bugger!' O'Sullivan said. 'It's always the big ones that get away, isn't it?'

Nobody reacted. They kept watching until the shark had swum out of sight.

When the excitement died down, Ambassador Li saw his chance. Taking the minister by the arm, in a manner only someone of his years would attempt to do, he strolled with him across to the guardrail on the other side of the deck. It was obvious to those looking on that the two should be left alone. Zhang, in particular, was pleased that Li's mission was now under way. If anyone could get inside O'Sullivan's head, it would be this wily old man.

The minister spoke first. 'So, what do you think of our rigs, Mr Ambassador? I'm told they're some of the best in the world.'

'Oh, very impressive. What more can I say?' Li replied, leaving it to his host to add something if he wished.

O'Sullivan, who was disarmed by the silence that followed, turned and looked out to sea. He scanned the flat, rolling swell in search of a topic. A large ocean tern glided up and hovered only metres away. Somehow it provided O'Sullivan with the inspiration he needed.

'I must say, Mr Li, many of us in Canberra are keen to strike a deal on this gas thing.'

'No doubt you are,' Li replied with a smile.

The old man's English was stilted and slow, but easy to follow. He made each word count. Now he was quiet again, knowing that O'Sullivan was uncomfortable with silence.

The minister kept brushing his hair back, though it blew about endlessly. His effort was pointless, but it was something to do.

'So, what do you think the chances are,' he said, 'of signing something fairly soon?'

'Oh, I'd say they're pretty good. Actually, they couldn't be better.'

O'Sullivan warmed to this, grinning as though a date was about to be set.

'For *us*, though,' Li said in a more intimate way, 'it's all a matter of finance.'

The minister nodded. He must mean budgetary problems they're having in China, he thought.

'You see,' Li went on, going in for the kill, 'if you Australians can't offer attractive concessional terms — and I mean, with respect, *really* attractive — then Beijing won't be able to come to the party. It's as simple as that. And to put it bluntly, none of the numbers your side's presented so far comes anywhere close.'

O'Sullivan fought back by regurgitating the figures Canberra had offered.

'Quite frankly, Mr Li, these add up to huge loans — and at give-away rates.'

Li was unmoved. He merely shrugged and waited for O'Sullivan to continue, which he was clearly eager to do.

'So, with respect, you can't really say that Canberra's not making an effort.'

This was a valid point and Li knew that the sums were correct, but he was working on something quite different. O'Sullivan, whose Western mind was stuck in a rut, had no way of sensing that another game plan was about to engulf him.

In reality the ambassador had scored a hit, and this he found pleasing.

Hao le, he thought: great. He's obviously read his briefing paper and knows it well. So, let's probe its contents and see what's inside. Is he aware of what the *guizi* are plotting in Tokyo? I can't imagine he'd know nothing about that. If he does, then how much pressure will Japan's plan for the Sakhalin field put on Canberra? How much will these Australians give to make sure we opt in their favour and not place our money with the Nips, closer to home?

'Actually, it's the scale of your offer that's really at issue,' Li said. 'It's a – what do you call it in English? A stabbing block? A stubbing . . .'

'A stumbling block?' O'Sullivan said.

'Yes, that's it. You see, if you can't double or triple those terms, then I'm afraid China won't even think of a thirty-year deal. It would be out of the question – absolutely out of the question.'

O'Sullivan was thrown off balance.

Fucking oath! he thought. This is miles beyond the parameters Treasury's set. How the hell could any government back a commercial deal to that extent?

Li gauged with accuracy the impact his statement had had. Too much of what O'Sullivan was thinking showed on the outside. He was like a clock with its internal mechanism exposed. Much of the art of diplomacy had to do with keeping a straight face, and in dealing with Asians on matters like this, control was more important than anything else.

The minister was quiet, unsure what to say.

'Of course, the World Bank might come to our aid,' Li said, thinking aloud as he tried to draw O'Sullivan out, 'unless, that is, there's some other interested party with something to offer . . .'

'Well,' O'Sullivan cut across him, 'we all know the Japanese have money and that they're desperate for energy from reliable sources. So that might be a possibility . . .' He left his words hanging, wondering how Li would react.

'Yes, yes,' Li said, wiping a film of salt from his brow, 'that's certainly worth considering.'

Bu xiangxin, he thought, astonished: I can't believe it. He has no idea what the Nips are up to, nor of what they've discovered and what they're doing with Moscow. If he knew, he'd hardly suggest bringing them in.

'Maybe that's something your side could best follow up,' Li said, opting for one last try. 'You know, I envy the relationship you Australians have with Japan.'

'Yes,' O'Sullivan replied. 'It's unique. I'll look at sounding them out.'

Later, as the chopper cleared the rig and climbed away to the east, Li adjusted his life jacket and settled back in his seat. Zhang, who was alongside him, had been talking to the minister's adviser during liftoff. Free now, he turned to his boss.

'*Zenmeyang?*' he asked: how did you go?

'You wouldn't believe it. I don't think he knows anything about the plot the *guizi* are hatching. And you know what that means – the rest of their system's as much in the dark.'

Zhang was amazed, but took care not to let it show.

'Does the adviser know anything?' Li said.

'No, not a thing.'

Li nodded ever so slightly. He could read Zhang's mind: why hadn't Australian intelligence got on to the story? How long would it be before they did?

China's own operatives in Japan were working hard on the topic. After Zhang's tip-off from Greg Mason was passed to Beijing, word had come back quickly that something of that nature was known to be brewing, but details were sketchy.

Why, Zhang thought, didn't Greg pass it on to his colleagues in Canberra?

'Fascinating,' Todd Lambert said, 'but we've heard nothing from our Tokyo station on it. Nothing at all, which is driving Martin bananas. Nor is there any inkling from signals intelligence. All we know is that when you were sniffing around up there recently, you suggested there might be something big happening behind the scenes, but you "had no idea what it was". Bloody Bass gave Martin a real roasting over that, I can tell you. Then Martin blew shit out of everyone else.'

He sat with his back to the window, in the sunlight streaming into the café in Kingston, an inner suburb of Canberra.

Mason shook his head. The Sakhalin story was one that ASIS should have picked up. But then, he and Lambert knew the troubles the station was having. The commander had been caught making up intelligence reports from English-language newspaper articles and was warned by Clarke not to do it again. Implicit in his reprimand was headquarters' awareness of the fact that he had also fabricated the existence of the agent concerned and his payment. That had thrown the commander into a fit of depression, which in turn impacted on the station's activities.

'Anyhow, sit on it for a while,' Mason said. 'Let's not have Martin scoring free points off me. Not with all the crap that bastard's been spreading around lately. Actually, I had a call from a Foreign Affairs mate yesterday who gave me a firsthand account of what he's been saying. Pete overheard him telling his boss to let all his business contacts in Sydney know I was unbalanced and someone they should stay well away from.'

He sighed in disgust. He was only too aware that, coming from an authoritative Canberra source, this was the kind of mud that stuck.

'Of course,' he added, 'if you were doing his job, Todd, I'd have some faith in the system.'

Lambert grinned, then said: 'By the way, Greg, there's another battle raging here at the moment between the Indonesia lobby and the China lobby. I must say, there are a few people mixed up in that who wouldn't hesitate to use a story like this to kill off those overtures from Beijing. And that clearly wouldn't be in Australia's interests.'

Mason nodded. He was well acquainted with the power these factions had. Centred in Foreign Affairs, they had followers in Defence and much of the intelligence system.

While Mason had friends in the Service, it was only with Lambert that he would lay all his cards on the table. A few years Mason's junior, Lambert had transferred from the SAS Regiment to join ASIS well before Mason left. He was a man free of agendas, and one whose sense of duty was high. Both shared an interest in scuba diving and had visited sites in the Pacific with friends to dive on World War II wrecks. Mason had come to the capital to discuss with him and other contacts the report he was compiling for Matsutomo Corporation. But only with Lambert was he raising the discovery that the Japanese had made.

'There's yet another dimension to all this now,' Lambert said, as the waiter brought their cappuccinos, 'one that I've only just heard about.' He paused until the man had left. 'You see, when the PM was in Jakarta last week the President put a proposal to him on energy. Apparently it's all very informal at this stage. Nothing's been put in print and it hasn't been included in their notes of discussion.'

Mason wondered what it might be.

'In brief, Subroto's wondering whether the two countries shouldn't lock their gas grids into one. We'd share joint processing facilities – develop the Timor Sea gas-fields together – things like that. And have some sort of long-term agreement to cover it. All very neighbourly.'

'Really?' Mason said, curious. 'But why does he raise it now, just when the Japanese are busy with their plan?'

'Well, from what I'm told, it was broached – off the record – with our ambassador some six months back and he relayed a private note on it to Canberra. But it appears the PM's in two minds about it and doesn't want it placed on the record until he's had time to think. I hear he feels there's merit in it, but sees the Indons as too fickle. Anything could happen. Then there's this Chinese thing that everyone's busy with. Beijing's proposal for an energy deal is far more concrete, as well as promising – *if* we can get the financial side of it right.'

'I see,' Mason said. 'You can well imagine how the Indonesia lobby would run with the Timor Sea idea if they felt it had legs.'

'That, Greg, is why the PM's keeping it out of the system. In the meantime, he's told O'Sullivan and a few of the others to take a more serious look at China's proposal. He believes that's where our future lies. Plus, he's worried that the Government's already seen to have too many eggs in the Indonesian basket. So Jakarta's been put on the backburner for a while and Beijing brought forward.'

Mason was lost in thought.

'So where does this leave your Matsutomo report?' Lambert said.

'That's what I'm wondering. The more I look into it, the more I see dimensions I *won't* be raising. Which doesn't leave a lot of substance to play around with. But I said I'd do it, so I'll conjure up something. I knew I should've left this one alone. If it hadn't been for the mortgage, I wouldn't have touched it.'

Lambert nodded sympathetically, though he realised that that was hardly the only reason Mason had allowed himself to be drawn in. He loved the thrill that came from handling issues like this. He had thrived on his work with ASIS and had never let go. As one Service oldtimer put it, he was no different to many ex-officers: 'They're like air traffic controllers who carry their radar with them when they come down from the tower.'

Fifty-year-old President Stafford Dunbar sat back in his chair, pondering what the CIA chief had just said.

With four major bugging operations under way against foreign targets, he had asked to be informed of any significant developments. Besides, with so much at stake overseas it was a useful means of keeping the intelligence people on their toes by looking eagle-eyed.

'Another traitor in Canberra – this is definite, is it? We've always thought there were more.'

'We certainly have, Mr President.'

'But are you sure?'

'Well . . . '

'Come on, Johnny, tell it how it is. We all know the doubts you have about the Australians. But if *you're* convinced, that's good enough for me.'

This was the cue that John Sherrington wanted. Bearded, and with the Marine haircut of his Vietnam days, he was an ex-Corps officer of distinction. His voice and authoritative manner matched his background and position. As Director of Central Intelligence he had already been in office when, three years earlier, Dunbar won the top job. The President had quickly confirmed his older friend in his key intelligence post. The pair went back a long way, since before their law school days. Their professional relationship had been greatly enhanced by Dunbar's long fascination with what he called Sherrington's 'ancient craft of intrigue'.

The President was an impressive man. Tall, solidly built and good-looking, his wit and easygoing style served him well in politics. In his early morning PDB for 21 April – President's Daily Brief, compiled by the CIA – he had seen reference to the joint US–Australian eavesdropping operation in Canberra and the fear that the Chinese might have been tipped off to the fact that they were a target. He had asked for a personal briefing on the matter as soon as the relevant officials could be assembled. All five were with him now in the Oval Office.

Sherrington knew that a certain level of formality was called for, even if most were well known to each other. They sat in an arc around the President's desk, with Sherrington at the centre and his top China analyst alongside. Included in the group were a youngish woman – the newly appointed Assistant Secretary of State for East Asian Affairs – and the Director of the National Security Agency, who was a general.

One of his technical advisers was with him. The late morning light from a spring sky outside filtered into the room.

Out in Australia, the NSA technicians controlling the operation on the Chinese Embassy had been suspicious for a fortnight. The first hint that something was wrong had come well before the Chinese swept their premises. Of course, the elaborate cover for that had only served to confirm that Beijing was conscious of the fact that it was under attack. The inventory ruse was standard procedure, if cheeky, but who could blame them? A change in the embassy's transmission pattern to China, coupled with increased traffic on some other link between the embassy in Canberra and its outpost in Sydney – if not beyond – braced up the fact. Further, the quantity of intelligence customarily gleaned from the operation from day-to-day talk in the embassy had markedly decreased. Hardly anything had been picked up after the sweep. In effect a clamp appeared to have been placed on verbal exchanges of sensitive information inside the building. No matter how subtle, it showed.

The Americans' suspicions had not yet been communicated to the Australian side. Instead, the reduced yield from the bugging operation was attributed to technical glitches in the optical fibre and microphone net. But a US decision on what should be done could no longer wait.

'So Johnny, you're convinced there's another traitor, are you?'

'Sure as I'll ever be, Mr President.'

'I see,' Dunbar said, sighing. 'You know, I've always had a soft spot for our cousins Down Under. But it's sad to hear they've inherited more of those Brit genes than we thought, huh?'

This drew a laugh from the others. All were aware of the high leakage rate for intelligence shared with London.

'Come to think of it,' the President said, 'it might actually be the Brits who are stuffing things up. After all, the take from this operation goes through their embassy in Canberra, doesn't it?'

Dunbar caught the eye of the NSA Director. Did he have any thoughts?

'Mr President, I really don't think it's them. I'd wager the Brits aren't the problem in this case. They're simply providing a relay facility, as we often do for them. It's a tit-for-tat thing that's rarely been known to break down. Anyhow, the take from the Chinese operation comes through raw to the NSA and, for technical reasons, we know the Brits aren't tapping into that. We edit the material and remove what we don't want the Australians or British to see. Then we pass the rest back. No, it's the Aussies who have a bad smell about them on this one. And on that note, sir, I'd defer to John. Let's face it, the CIA's been determined on this front much longer than us.'

Dunbar nodded. It was rare to see senior officials working smoothly like this. Too often his attention was distracted by Washington's interminable and debilitating inter-service rivalries.

'That's certainly true,' Sherrington said, 'but the Aussies seem to think turncoats are a bit of a joke. It's not that they haven't got good people who take these things seriously. They have, and in no short supply. But their efforts seem to be constantly thwarted by cronyism at the top – too many intelligence managers willing to sell their professional souls to get into the big seat and stay there. I can't recall one resignation, at that level in Australia, where someone's taken a conscientious stand on the need to fix up the system.'

He left it at that. It was a sensitive subject, even in Washington terms, and there was always the risk that Dunbar might have a dig about the consciences of those seated before him. He loved that sort of irony.

The CIA's doubts, Sherrington explained, went back to Cold War days, but little had ever been done to get to the heart of the matter. It was always easier to stem the flow of US intelligence to the Australians than to track down the leak in Canberra and plug it. When it was in America's interests to share something with Canberra the Australians were told only as much as they needed to know. Overall, they had been on a reduced drip for longer than anyone cared to remember. They seemed unaware of their diminished position and still boasted that they were in the inner sanctum of the Western intelligence club.

'You see, Mr President,' Sherrington said, 'the Aussies have simply lost the capacity to cleanse themselves.'

He leaned forward. His dark gaze was intense and the President watched him with heightened interest.

'They can't catch one of their kind and deal with 'em properly. And to my mind that's gutless. We have bad apples in our box, too – occasionally – but we pull 'em out and they pay a high price. The Australians, though, seem to think they pack their fruit in different containers. Let's face it, they have the same incidence of murder, rape, arson and gluttony as any developed society, yet *no* traitors. Hell, if that were true, it'd outstrip the immaculate conception!'

Everybody smiled, but no one laughed.

Except for Dunbar and the Assistant Secretary of State, the others in the room knew what was likely to follow. Sherrington would not let the matter rest until he had milked it for all it was worth. This time he wanted action, and was determined to get it.

'I tell you, no spy *ever* gets caught in Australia,' he said.

'So?' the President responded.

'Well, sir, I think it's time we did something about that. You see, history's taught us that the longer it takes to find a turncoat, the higher up they'll be in the system. And with Canberra's track record, I'd say we've really got something to worry about.'

'What do we do, then?' Dunbar asked.

'This time, Mr President, I want to get someone in there fast – somebody who can tell us what's going on, who can go straight at it, who can sniff out the traitor and bring 'em to ground.'

Dunbar nodded. 'And how will that happen?'

'Well, to start with, we won't be discussing our suspicions with the Aussies. Not officially. Not this time round. And that's a decision I'm sure my NSA colleagues would fully endorse.

'Yes, we're with you on that,' the general said.

'It'll be a new tack altogether. One we haven't used in the past.'

Dunbar could see Sherrington meant business.

'You might remember Omega Blue,' the CIA Director added. 'That's what gave me the lead.'

A grin lit up the President's face. He devoured operational case studies like novels, and Omega Blue had been better than any spy thriller he had come across.

Adrian McKinnon slipped quietly into his boss's office at the *Sydney Daily Courier*, holding a raised finger to his mouth. He handed over a single sheet of paper with a brief, typed message on it. Under this he had written, 'If the above is true, we're bugged. Let's go outside to talk.' Minutes later the two men were clear of the building and free to chat. It was a fine Sydney day with a cloudless sky.

'I'd say it's genuine,' Don Hull, the lanky editor-in-chief said. 'Granted, a rational mind might throw up other possibilities, but instinct tells me it's real. Let's face it, it's not the first time we've seen tip-offs like this.'

A year before, McKinnon had been given an anonymous lead by someone inside the Office of

National Assessments who had heard about a foreign policy story he was working on. That sole snippet had helped him produce an award-winning article, one that had sorely tested the Foreign Minister's ability to backtrack gracefully in public.

A mixed group of office workers sauntered past them now on the Pyrmont Bridge, off to an early lunch.

'Frankly,' Hull said, 'what you're on to is one hell of a story. And believe me, I'll back you all the way.'

McKinnon extended his hand. He was grateful for his boss's support. As the long-serving chief of the *Courier*, this white-haired veteran was respected by journalists of all ages. To those who were younger, he was often both professional and personal mentor. Over his 40 years in the game he had been a correspondent in Europe and North America, as well as in Jakarta, Tokyo, Manila and Hong Kong. He was a newspaperman from a different era, whose experience gave him a rare capacity to see issues from inside, looking out, as well as from outside in. It was this 'extra sense' that the astute McKinnon valued most. The older man's eyes were as sharp as his mind. Quietly spoken, Hull had a loud laugh when excited. A hard upbringing had taught him to savour lighter moments in life and he rarely let one pass without making the most of it.

McKinnon, the *Courier*'s top investigative reporter, had similar attributes, which said much about the bond the two shared. Hull saw him as a younger version of himself. McKinnon had the same keen interest in history. His articles were solidly based, and educational as well as informative. Stocky, and with a mop of straight ginger hair, he and his boss could not have looked more different.

They rested their arms on the bridge's balustrade as they mused over what the next step should be. Three crews of Dragon Boat enthusiasts, out training in long, brightly coloured craft, streamed towards the arch below. Disappearing underneath, their chanting resonated in its tunnel-like space.

The Chinese Embassy case had occupied much of McKinnon's time over the past few months. He had exercised great care in questioning sources in a variety of places, inside and outside the capital, but suspected that sooner or later somebody in the system would get wind of what he was up to. To that extent, it was no surprise when this ASIO tip-off came his way. He knew he had friends in the system who valued the work he was doing.

The message had been dropped off at the *Courier*'s front desk. It was in a plain white envelope addressed to McKinnon and read: 'ASIO has crossed a fine line between the national interest and yours. All your communications are being monitored. No warrant has been issued.'

So McKinnon had taken the note straight to his chief's office. But right from the start he'd regularly briefed Hull and the *Courier*'s editor on the Chinese story. It was something he had first heard about from a friend in an engineering firm which had been contracted to build part of the new Chinese Embassy complex in Canberra. McKinnon's friend was site manager at the time. Further questioning in the capital confirmed that wide-scale bugging had taken place, and gradually McKinnon managed to piece together much of the picture. He knew how the embassy had been rigged with optical fibre and that outside assistance was crucial to getting the operation up and running. Until recently he had known nothing of the American involvement. Hurdles remained, however, before the story stood any chance of going to print, but McKinnon was not short of resolve.

"Allo, 'allo, 'allo!' a familiar voice called from behind, aping a London bobby's stereotyped greeting. It was one of the *Courier*'s senior journalists. Rotund and dressed in a worn corduroy jacket and lugging a bundle of papers under one arm, he was heading back from an interview on Asian organised crime.

'Pick up anything new?' Hull asked.

'Certainly did,' the journalist replied, still puffing, 'but I can see you two aren't just whiling away the time. I'll leave my little scoop until later.' Excusing himself, he shuffled off.

'As I mentioned before,' Hull said, 'now that Canberra's on to you they'll have a bloody D Notice ready – or at least an injunction – to wallop us with. You know, this'll have them shitting their pants.'

McKinnon knew that neither his chief nor his editor would have allowed him to go this far unless there was some dimension to the story that showed how Australia's interests could have been much better served. And as all on the *Courier* appreciated, Hull was not a man to shy away from a scrap when he knew he stood on firm ground. If it came to an out-and-out fight with the Government, he would assert that his paper had an obligation to disclose matters and to let the public make up its own mind.

Since learning of American involvement in the operation, McKinnon had raised that aspect with a number of contacts and had discerned a note of dissatisfaction in each over the question of access to the product. It was something that even the less reticent spoke about openly. All were loyal Australians and were appalled at such material being held back from the nation's top decision-makers.

'Of course, when the Canberra system's got its evil eye on you,' Hull said, 'which this note firmly establishes, there's a fair chance that physical surveillance will be part of it too.'

'That thought did cross my mind,' McKinnon responded. 'But really, what a farce all this is. If it's so bloody important, why can't the intelligence people just come round and see us? Put it to us directly. All this cat-and-mouse stuff only makes things worse.'

'I couldn't agree more. But Adrian, mate, let me tell you something. In my experience, these fellas are at their best when they're covering up their own failures. Call me a cynic, but over the years I've learnt that that mob have as many human foibles as anyone else, if not more. And they have a greater capacity than any other organ of government to cover them up.'

'In the national interest,' McKinnon said with a grin.

'Naturally!' Hull replied. 'Anyhow, the *Courier* has interests of its own to look after, which means we'll have to get a technical team in fast to check out our lines and to look for anything else that might've been planted. And I think I know just the people to handle the job. With luck, they might be able to trace some of it back.'

McKinnon's home phone, the chief reasoned, as well as his mobile and his private computer system, were all under threat. But Hull had high level contacts of his own in Canberra. If they were brought on stream to identify who had ordered such tactics, things might develop rapidly. Who, Hull pondered, would relish catching ASIO bugging a journalist without a warrant, and no doubt on the instruction of some pollie? This, he felt, could be more fun than you'd think.

'Of course, we can't sit on this story for ever,' he said, as they headed back to the office. 'So as soon as you show me beyond reasonable doubt that Australia's not fully in charge and it's in the public interest to know that it's not, we'll run with it.'

This bald challenge focused McKinnon's mind. And he knew that the *Courier*'s top legal advisers, who the chief had asked to drop by later in the day, would ensure that it stayed that way.

Hull looked at him. 'Adrian, I'm right behind you on this, but it's going to have to be rock solid for us to go out on a limb.'

'Oh, no! I'll explode if I eat any more,' the Cicada said, as the waiter brought yet another dish to the table.

Gao Chun had promised him a series of treats that were rarely served in Chinese restaurants, and they had come one after the other. The latest, featuring the leaves of the garlic plant, was likewise something the Australian had not seen before.

There were few diners in the Middle Kingdom Club on this evening; the hum of conversation blended nicely with the soft piped music that set the tone of the place. It was one of Sydney's leading establishments for the Chinese elite and only a select few non-members ever found their way onto its premises. Guests were expected to somehow enhance the standing of the Chinese community. The Cicada had been keen to try the food there, having heard Gao, and originally Zhang, refer to it more than once.

It was the beginning of May and three weeks had elapsed since the ASIS traitor walked in. Gao's meetings with him had all gone well – indeed, far beyond what he had dared to imagine. The man had become a steady performer and there had been nothing in his behaviour that threatened the viability of the alliance they were forming. Nevertheless, after each encounter, Gao held a wash-up with Zhou, the psychologist, and Zhang. Money, they now appreciated, was what the Australian craved.

The Cicada appeared to derive confidence of another kind too, from the path he was treading. While he gave no hint of how he justified the increasing scope of his betrayal, the delicate nature of the intelligence he was handing over seemed to endow him with a sense of purpose and power. It was recognisable to the Chinese, no matter how carefully it was disguised. As calculating as the Australian was, Gao had got his measure – at least to a significant degree – and felt he was often able to see behind the mask.

The motherfucker's thriving on this, Gao thought now, as he watched him.

When the waiter had gone, the Cicada perused the new dish. They had been discussing Washington's interest in the extent of Beijing's support for North Korea's armaments industry and nuclear weapons program. How high a priority did this issue have on both American and Australian intelligence lists? Gao was about to return to that topic when the Cicada cut across his thoughts.

'Hey, let me tell you something,' he said, dropping his voice. Leaning closer over the table, he moved his rice bowl to one side, then used both hands to flatten the white cloth in front of him.

Shenme? Tebie de yisi? Gao thought: what's he up to now? There must be some symbolism in this. He's getting ready to raise something big.

The Cicada flicked away a small piece of food. 'You see, there's been a major development. One that nobody saw coming.'

He was clearly on the alert for Gao's reaction.

'Oh, really?'

'Yes, a journalist with the *Courier* is on to the story.'

'Not *our* story?'

'I'm afraid so. The newspaper knows that your embassy's bugged.'

'But how? Who could've told them?'

'Well, that's the big question, and it seems that those in Canberra who pose it haven't got a bloody clue.'

'And you know who the "posers" are?'

'Oh, yes. And from what I hear, they're searching all over to find who's spilt the beans. But let me tell you, there'll be more than one person leaking this stuff.'

'Do you think the journalist knows exactly what's happening in Canberra?'

'No, not necessarily everything. Not as far as they know.'

'*They?*' Gao said, assuming the Cicada might be as much in on the matter as anyone.

What followed was pure gold.

The Australian said he had been briefed inside ASIS on meetings held in the Attorney-General's Department in Canberra, and proceeded to list the officials regularly participating and the roles played by each. In meticulous detail he described who thought the journalist knew this much and why, and who thought he didn't. The politicians had one set of priorities, he explained, while the bureaucrats had concerns of their own. No matter the question, the Cicada had the answer. Gao had only to ask.

Well, this *is* a first, the Chinese thought. I've had years in this game, but seen nothing like this. He spits out names like a pea-shooter.

It was as though Gao himself was on the AG's committee. He knew that no matter how amenable agents were, meetings with them were circumscribed by the notion that one side acted as a conduit through which secrets passed to the other. The case officer was remote from the nerve centre to which the agent had access. It had always been thus.

But it was different with this one, he thought – as though he'd broken through an impenetrable barrier and was now actually inside the Cicada's Service, sitting around chatting with him and his colleagues.

The man himself appeared buoyed by the fact that, as spies, both he and Gao could savour the contortions of a Government grappling with the eavesdropping debacle. Inside, Gao was rejoicing, while on the surface he showed nothing but measured gratitude for what the two were now sharing.

'And guess what! The bloody journalist himself has been bugged,' the Australian said, not knowing that his words put Gao into more of a spin. 'They're reading his emails and hacking into his hard drive, and they've whacked surveillance on him too.'

The Cicada considered this comical, as Gao also did in a way. But there were more pressing matters the Chinese wished to address.

'So, when will the *Courier* run with the story?' he said, as the Australian quietened down.

'I have no idea. Possibly in a month or two.'

'What's the hold-up, then?'

'Don't know. There must be pieces of the puzzle they still haven't got.'

'And *you'll* get to know when they're going to print?'

'I'd imagine so.'

Gao felt that the subject had run its full course. There was clearly something else on the Cicada's mind and he wanted to know what it was.

The waiter reappeared, asking whether they had finished and, if so, could he clear away the dishes. Gao jumped in quickly and ordered a pot of hot jasmine tea. Then once again the Cicada flattened the tablecloth. There was a vague look of despondency on his face now and he seemed to be searching for words. Moments of silence embraced them, which Gao left undisturbed.

'You know, when this story's had its full impact,' the Australian said, 'I suppose it'll mark the end of what you and I have going.'

'No, not at all. Why should that be the case?'

'Well, in the sense that there'll be nothing left for me to contribute.'

He's fishing for something, Gao thought, wondering what it was. He felt frustrated at knowing so little about the Cicada's life. The man was full of detail on so many things but there was still no good fix on his true identity. He hedges about his track record in ASIS. If there were anything there to boast about, surely he wouldn't hesitate to raise it. But he slips quickly into anecdotal stuff that doesn't boil down to much. Maybe that's the pivotal point, the root cause of his problem – that there's no great substance inside – inside him, let alone in his ASIS career.

Gao knew from experience that duds had an uncanny capacity to climb in the world of intelligence. One seemed to attract another on the way up the ladder, and before long the need for mutual protection drove those in high places – whether in the spying game, the bureaucracy or politics – to gloss over their failures. All the while they thrived on the talents of better operatives out in the field. That was often why such types were impossible to weed out of the system. Gao himself had twice fallen foul of these people and almost lost his career. The harder he fought back, the more the crony network rallied its forces against him. No one on the outside would believe the pettiness that spies were capable of, especially the deskbound variety. But for now Gao cast such thoughts from his mind.

'Don't worry, my friend, you'll have a lot to contribute,' he said, reaching across and giving the Cicada a supportive pat on the arm. 'This is just the beginning. Not the end. Besides, there are other ways you can be helpful to us.'

The Australian smiled. 'Good,' he said. 'I've been thinking about that myself. If it's useful to you, I do have other contacts who can put their finger on things you might want.'

Gao was enthralled by this positive news but contained his elation. It was the very subject he had considered broaching himself. A spy was always on the lookout for sub-agents who could 'grow' and take on grander roles in the future. As one of China's senior operatives in Australia, Gao's priority was industrial espionage. That was far more extensive in Australia than realised, and the Chinese were not the only ones playing the field. It was for this reason that Gao was keen to monitor the effectiveness of ASIO's procedures for detecting his type of activity.

'Others?' Gao said.

He wanted to know more about the extent and quality of the network to which the Cicada was alluding.

'Well, I have close contacts throughout the system.'

He listed a host of organisations, with Gao asking what he meant when he described each contact as 'well placed' or 'reliable'. These were common terms in the jargon of intelligence, but personal affinity could endow them with extra significance. It might also lead to distortion.

'They're mainly people who owe me favours. People who'll hand over virtually anything I need.'

'In return for . . . '

'Well, I usually give something back.'

'So money changes hands?'

'Oh, yes.'

The Cicada looked Gao in the eye. 'I mean, if you and I were after something special, I could certainly "oil the path", if that's what you're getting at.'

Gao nodded. That was indeed what he meant.

'And on my behalf, then,' the Chinese said, 'you could do the same thing with ASIO?'

'Of course.'

'Well, let's give it a try.'

'Why not?'

Coming as this did with the material the Cicada had handed over earlier in the evening – on US and British intelligence priorities on China – this final offering made the day one that Gao would never forget.

SIX

Sydney: Mid-May

Kenichiro Yoshida took a studied sip of his chilled riesling – a 1992 Brown Brothers.

He enjoyed displaying his skill in distinguishing the subtleties of flavour in fine wines and delighted in the attention it brought him on occasions like this. He was well able to ruin careers with a word dropped in the right place, and he wanted people to know it.

'I won't beat about the bush,' he said. 'There are certain things going on in Tokyo at the moment which are at – how can I put it? – *sugoku bimyo na dankai*: at a delicate stage. I'm sorry I'm not at liberty to give you the details. All I can say is that we need your help, and fast. Put simply, we have to kill any prospect of China clinching a long-term energy deal in Australia.'

Yoshida was standing with his compatriots on the rear deck of a luxury cruiser, sharing a quiet drink while the group's outdoor lunch was prepared. Lifting his glass to his nose again, he gave the riesling's bouquet a final appraisal. The speed with which he could jump from matters of high state to those of the palate served to heighten his air of authority.

'*Honto ni, oishii'n desu ne,*' he said, in a mellifluous tone: it really is a tasty little number.

'*So desu ne,*' the other Japanese agreed, in almost perfect unison, their reaction as much a matter of deference as of personal judgement.

The day was overcast and the still air bracing. A mid-May Sydney sun loitered above the cloud, keeping the cold at bay. Conditions were pleasant for a cruise on the harbour.

Yoshida was short, lean, and middle-aged. Of upper-class background, he exuded an overbearing confidence that most who worked alongside him found intimidating. New in the job of chief of the Cabinet Research Office, he had been hit with the bombshell in his first week in office: the secret Sakhalin gas discovery. But he thrived on this sort of thing, believing a gutsy national challenge with a touch of intrigue would give him a chance to prove his mettle. He had arrived in Sydney early that morning on an overnight flight. It was his first visit to Australia.

The quietest of the foursome on board was Japan's consul-general in Sydney. Senior in the bureaucratic way of things, he held a post that had slipped in status since the heady days of the 1960s and 1970s resource trade. Invited to sit in on the day's confidential talks, he knew that Yoshida would fly straight to Canberra after lunch to brief the ambassador there on what was brewing.

Another Japanese, Miyata, was his usual dapper self and the only one bold enough to have removed his jacket. He had headed the Australian operations of Matsutomo Corporation for three years and would see this gas affair through before winding up and returning to Japan. Tokyo's request had posed a moral dilemma for Miyata, who tried hard to stick to his principles in carrying on business. Old-fashioned he might be, but he had never liked the way the Corporation allowed itself to be drawn into political games. To his way of thinking, it was not what a trading house should be about. Nevertheless, he would do his best. Toshio Nakagawa, his next in command in Sydney, and a rising star, would make sure of that.

The son-in-law of the company chairman in Japan, Nakagawa bothered little about disguising his ambition. He was a qualified skiing instructor and horseman, and his tough features indicated a harsh disposition. His heavily oiled hair caused those who disliked him to joke that he must have *yakuza* – Japanese gangster – affiliations. The challenge of thwarting this Chinese energy deal with Australia was something he too realised could make his name. And as Miyata appreciated, if he stood in the younger man's way the slick Nakagawa would go through him like a *yakitori* skewer.

Now Yoshida was admiring the scenery on the foreshore, breathing in deeply. A rich marine smell laced the air. '*Do iu tokoro, kochi?*' he said, asking about the cove in which the cruiser lay at anchor.

Protocol gave him the right to choose what the group would discuss.

Shading his eyes from the glare, he scanned the low-slung buildings on the hillside a hundred metres away. It was one of many questions he had posed in the hour-long trip to the place, which was nestled inside the harbour's entrance. They had left the convict-built, stone Man o' War steps alongside the Opera House at 11.30 and first headed round under the bridge to the Sydney fish market. There the young Australian skipper had collected a large tray of fresh *sashimi* to supplement the smorgasbord meal already stowed away.

'Those structures,' Nakagawa studiously explained, 'are part of a quarantine station set up in the early nineteenth century.'

'*Haaaaaw*,' Yoshida reacted gutturally, in a typical Japanese response to something newly comprehended. A scholar–bureaucrat who soaked up facts avidly, he gave Nakagawa countless opportunities to display his erudition.

'Gentlemen, lunch is served,' the skipper suddenly announced from the door of the deckhouse. Looking smart in white naval attire he spoke polished Japanese.

Seated, and with a new wine poured, the guests were left to themselves. A Tamburlaine chardonnay and a fine Chateau Tahbilk marsanne had also been opened and sat in a silver ice bucket alongside their table. The young Australian made himself scarce in the galley below.

'*Kampai,*' Yoshida said, raising his glass in a toast. 'Long may we keep the Chinese dragon under control.'

'To success,' Nakagawa responded huskily.

The others repeated his words.

'*Shinajin, kochi ni hairanai yo ni,*' Yoshida said, raising his glass again: here's to keeping the cursed Chinese out of this place.

His companions nodded in deference, noting the derogatory term he had used for those who dwelt in the Central Kingdom.

What Yoshida had chosen not to reveal was that in late June – little more than a month away – Russian exploration crews would join their Japanese colleagues on vessels test-drilling off Sakhalin. Once on board, there would be no way of keeping the gas discoveries from the Russian engineers. The cat would be out of the bag. The challenge in Australia, therefore, was to halt any progress on China's drive to sign a bilateral deal. For Japan it was crucial that China's massive purchasing power be harnessed for the good of the Sakhalin project. But before entering into talks with Beijing, Tokyo wished to know for sure that China had no chance of succeeding with the Australians. Yoshida's role in this was clearly defined and failure would not treat him kindly.

'Something else I can tell you,' he said, with an air of confidentiality, 'is that our embassy in Canberra has cleverly managed to bug the

Chinese ambassador's office . . .' He paused for effect. 'But unfortunately that's all come unstuck.'

The consul-general coughed nervously, but quickly regained his composure before his slip attracted attention.

'I'm told that the Chinese discovered the device and rendered it inoperative,' Yoshida said.

He shook his head in disdain, hinting strongly of unexpected amateurism on Japan's part. Then he leaned forward in his seat, readying himself for another pronouncement.

'Look, what we have to achieve here,' he said with force, 'is to get these Australian *inakamono* to pull back. They have to be made to convince the Chinese that they really can't make up their minds.'

His use of the pejorative 'bumpkins' was unkind, but he meant it.

'Beijing's talks here have been dragging on for over a year,' Nakagawa said, ever alert for a chance to contribute, 'so it shouldn't be too hard to swing it our way. Not if we hit the right buttons.'

He deliberately left his words hanging. Miyata could see what was coming and was unamused, though no one could tell from his face.

'By which you mean?' Yoshida said. His stern demeanour left no doubt that the answer would have to be good.

'Well, you see, we've been "making friends" in this country for ages,' Nakagawa replied, revealing nothing new, except his own sordid capacity to flaunt the truth, 'so if we can't go straight to the people who'll swing things our way, and get the results we want, then the laugh's on us. Not on the locals.'

'Good point,' Yoshida said, nodding. He was obviously eager to hear more and his stare warned Nakagawa that he was unaccustomed to waiting.

'Any decision on a big China deal here,' the younger man said, 'is inevitably centred on government. Private enterprise alone won't get this thing off the ground. Which means Canberra is the focal point, and all we're really interested in down there is procrastination. Now, that's not a lot to ask. And to get it, we just need to be sure that the money we dish out hits the target – accurately and fast. That's all we have to do.'

'So?' Yoshida said, wanting more.

'So we oil the wheels where they squeak.' Nakagawa's smirk exposed his Machiavellian side. 'You see, we've already mapped out twenty-odd people in the system who can slow things down to a snail's pace on anything like this. Come to think of it, we sent the details to your office in Tokyo some time back, but nobody's yet produced the funding we need. It seems they've never understood what we were getting at about having this sort of machinery in place and ready to go at the drop of a hat. Especially on matters of national importance to Japan.'

Yoshida acknowledged the point, but was clearly disgruntled.

Miyata was both horrified and pleased.

You've gone too far this time, Smart Arse, he thought. This arrogant toff might be new in the job, but teaching him how to suck eggs is the silliest thing you could do. He'll tear strips off you back in Japan. *Shikashi, yoku dekita naaaa*: anyhow, you've stuffed things up for yourself better than I could've hoped for, and hit him with the truth in the process.

Driven by the rationale of his case, Nakagawa persisted. Oddly, for a Japanese, he lacked some of the mechanisms that governed normal behaviour, which alerted his countrymen to the need to keep quiet.

'So, get to the point,' Yoshida said. 'What are you suggesting?'

'Well, if your colleagues in Tokyo could just get that money to us, we'll have a certain Australian on our staff here spread it around to maximum effect.'

The person concerned, he explained, had worked for Matsutomo for many years and was a past master at greasing the palms of people in power. Judicious in every way, his exploits never blew back on Japan.

'*Ah, so desu ka?*' Yoshida responded sarcastically: really? 'Well, that's definitely the kind of arrow I like to see in a quiver. It's good to have your Corporation as a buffer. Naturally, Tokyo's hand has to be protected at all costs. And of course, as you'd all appreciate, our ambassador in Canberra has his own ingenious ways of providing assistance.'

There was a needle in his words, which said: you're not the only person, lad, through whom we work in Australia.

The others smiled in acknowledgment, while Nakagawa was stung by the put-down.

'What we must make these Australians understand, gentlemen,' Yoshida said, 'is that it's far preferable for them to develop their gas reserves independently and lock China into a standard, short-term contract. That would certainly be easier and more reliable.'

'*So desho ne,*' the others agreed: there's no doubt about that.

Yoshida looked the chairman's son-in-law in the eye, long and hard.

'And let's pray, Nakagawa Kun,' he said, using a diminutive that further demeaned the younger man, 'that your Australian staffer who performs these wonders can deliver.'

Yoshida wielded the language like a sword. Its subtlety lent itself to drawing blood like no other could. His arrogance only heightened the impact.

Moments of silence passed as the boat swayed gently.

'I suppose you own a restaurant in Chinatown,' the muscular young worker said. He had overheard Mason and the Chinese talking about industrial gases before Mason had gone off to the toilet.

'I only wish I did,' Zhang replied with a grin.

Until he was sure what these Australians were about he would stay on alert.

'The way I'm going,' he added, 'I'm lucky to shout my family a *yum cha* at the weekend.'

The other man roared with laughter. His half dozen colleagues at the bar did the same. Beery breath hung thick in the air.

From a piano removals firm, and dressed in blue T-shirts and shorts, they had just delivered a Steinway grand. Returning to their depot on this warm Saturday morning, they had dropped in to the hotel for a drink. It was in a working-class district not far from the city, through which Mason and Zhang were also passing.

Mason had sensed there was something the Chinese wanted to get off his chest. A drink, he thought, might help things along. The two of them had just used Zhang's four-wheel-drive Toyota to collect an old wooden chest advertised in the *Courier*. Zhang and his wife were interested in early Australian furniture and picked up the odd small piece when the price was right.

'What do you do for a living, then?' the young man asked.

'Actually, I work in the Chinese consulate,' Zhang replied, touched by the fact that the group had bothered to strike up a conversation while he was standing alone. 'My friend and I were talking about liquefied natural gas, but nothing to do with kitchens.'

When Mason returned, he and Zhang chatted with the men for a while before going back to their earlier topic. They continued speaking in English, so as not to cause offence.

'By the way, Greg,' Zhang said, 'remember I'm putting together for you a file on China's energy procurements. It's not classified stuff, but it's pretty hard to come by unless you're inside the system. It should help you pad out your report for Matsutomo.'

'Thanks a million,' Mason responded, smiling.

'Talking of energy,' Zhang went on, 'I must say the intransigence we're seeing from Canberra on this Australia–China energy agreement is very confusing. "Hot and cold flushes", I think you call it. We know there have been doubts on the Australian side from the start, but the policy-makers who favour national development were expected to carry the day once the concept wound its way through the bureaucratic machine. But despite a bit of progress recently, the process has suddenly slowed down again for no obvious reason.'

'Well, there'll be something interesting driving that,' Mason said. 'Some rogue element, perhaps, that we're unaware of.'

'What do you think it could be?' Zhang replied. 'A few of my colleagues claim to know.'

'Oh, it's probably the Japanese. And if it is, they're certain to be working under some other guise, twisting arms inside the system. But it'll be done very shrewdly so the picture's fudged and no one will know what they're up to.'

Zhang was silent. The audacity of the joint US–Australian technical operation on his embassy in Canberra still had him reeling. And the Cicada had added another dimension to that, which even Beijing's wishful thinkers had not envisaged. But Mason was seemingly oblivious to these developments, and anyway, they were matters that the two could clearly never discuss.

'Let me tell you,' Mason said, 'I wouldn't put anything past the Japanese. They're determined to spike your Australia–China deal. Just the other day I dropped into Matsutomo to discuss my report. Well, did I get interrogated? The full treatment, it was: questions on this, questions on that. The local *bucho* – the executive I touch base with – is as slick as they come. I reckon he'd be up to his ears in something like this. Smart as a rat with a golden tooth.'

'How far do you think they'd go?'

'Frankly, I wouldn't be surprised if they target your lot, and when you least expect it.'

'What do you mean exactly?' Zhang said, intrigued by this allusion to a truth that only the Chinese were aware of.

'Well, your embassy for starters. They'd want to slip some sort of device in there to see what you're up to. They might try your consulate here in Sydney, too.'

Zhang was shocked and it showed.

'Look, mate, if you don't think they'd do it, you need your bloody head read. They've probably got you bugged from floor to ceiling already, as we speak – so to speak.'

Mason laughed at his own joke. But Zhang was quiet, though games with the language normally amused him. Mason sensed something coming, so left the silence undisturbed. Zhang, he suspected, was about to cross a line. The pair never talked of hard-core intelligence. Atmospherics, even the psychology and intellectual intricacies of the craft, were often canvassed. But more sensitive matters, like what the Australian, Chinese or other services might be doing, were, by tacit agreement, out of bounds. No exceptions were ever made to the rule. Mason's mention of Japanese tactics, however, had slightly changed the equation.

Zhang took a deep breath. 'Greg, the reality is, the *guizi* have already been up to their tricks, just as you've described. In fact, you've hit the nail on the head. You see, they've already had a go at our embassy.'

Mason feigned astonishment, but chose to say nothing.

'You see, they've bugged the ambassador's office and another room alongside. We got on to it a few weeks back during a sweep. I've heard that the things they planted were standard Japanese stuff. My colleagues checked out all of Mr Li's visitors and homed in on who committed the crime. And guess who it was? A technical officer – someone who's just appeared at the Japanese Embassy. Works under cover, it seems, as a "research assistant" and occasionally takes notes at meetings as well. He's the one who orchestrated the bugging. He accompanied the Japanese ambassador and two of their diplomats when they paid a call on my boss.'

Mason's eyebrows lifted.

'Anyhow, this bastard – by himself – called on Li's secretary a few days before the visit, saying he wanted to talk about a gift his ambassador was planning to present. He claimed it was similar to something Li had once admired in his counterpart's office. Well, the gift turned out to be quite expensive. It was one of those elaborate Kabuki dolls, about sixty centimetres high, with a shock of long red hair and an archer's bow. There were various bits and pieces, he said, which had to be fitted on at the time the presentation was made, so he was wondering where Ambassador Li was likely to put the doll in his office. Could he come and have a quick look in advance, so there wouldn't be something – like the bow – sticking out at the wrong angle?'

'Oh, how considerate,' Mason said. 'And you fell for it.'

'Well, yes. She let him drop round and showed him the shelf where it'd go. And, of course, later, what did we find? The bloody doll's head, which is this really intricately crafted ceramic thing, had an infra-red transmitting device inside. And not only that, but a microphone as well.'

Mason smiled. This came as no surprise.

'And why the positioning was important,' Zhang went on, '*and* the direction the face was pointing in, was because the infra-red beam that comes out of one eye had to pass through a window in Li's office at a – what do they call it? – a "predetermined angle". Apparently, the transmitter relays a message along the beam after picking up the signals from two separate mikes. One was stuck up under a chair in the secretary's room and the other was fixed inside the other eye of the doll. So, from what we know, the meeting with Li was built entirely around setting up this equipment. And right under our noses. That's the bit that hurts.'

They laughed at the brazenness of the Japanese and the complicity of Tokyo's envoy.

'Well, blow me down!' Mason said, in mock amazement. 'Who'd have thought the Japanese would stoop so low?'

'As you've often told me, Greg, spying's a dirty game,' Zhang observed, recognising an opportunity to raise Mason's inability to let go of the craft. It was something Zhang and his wife had often discussed – the fact that Mason was being drawn back in via commercial channels, while seemingly wishing to cut loose, once and for all.

'You know,' Zhang ventured tactfully, 'I've been thinking a lot lately about why you're so glad to be out of your old line of work. Actually, at the risk of sounding intrusive, I wonder if . . .'

'Pig's fuckin' arse!' someone shouted.

Newcomers had swaggered in off the street and their rowdiness stopped the chatter in the pub like a police raid on a backyard casino. There were half a dozen young men in their twenties who, though not drunk, were well on the way. Dressed in tight jeans and black leather jackets, they were on the prowl and looking for trouble.

Zhang's muscular removalist friend, his animal instincts aroused, picked up their vibes from the start. Mason spotted him tracking their path as they focused on the Chinese man, the sole Asian enjoying the place.

Abreast of Zhang now, the thickest-set lout sidled up close. He deliberately bumped into Zhang, with the obvious aim of provoking him. 'What are you lookin' at, slope-head?' he snarled.

'He's *not* looking for trouble,' Mason said, stepping in front to protect his friend. Strong at the best of times, his voice now carried even more weight.

Zhang knew how Mason's temper could flare and feared an all-out fight might ensue. If it did, then one of the attackers – if not more – would likely be dead before they realised what had hit them. Mason had had that sort of killer training. The fact that he was marginally shorter than the assailant made no difference at all.

'So what's it to you, Chink-lover?' the lout growled at Mason, as his mates gathered around.

His words were barely out when two huge meaty arms locked around his neck. 'Don't you talk to my mates like that,' the young removalist yelled at his victim. His air of authority perfectly matched his vice-like grip.

'Say you're sorry or I'll break your fuckin' head off!'

'OK, I didn't mean it,' the newcomer gasped, choking.

'I told you to say you're sorry,' Zhang's new friend demanded, squeezing the man's neck even tighter.

Mason glanced at the victim's accomplices and saw their adrenalin rising. He sensed that the removalist's colleagues had noticed it, too. They were closing in fast. Sturdy types, they had unquestionably weathered many a fight and were adept at reading the signals. They were ready for action and knew Mason was also. The tension in the place was electric.

'I'm sorry,' the lout spluttered.

'Again.'

'I'm sorry!'

Then one of the newcomers pulled a knife.

In a flash, Zhang grabbed him by the wrist and in a neat judo-like throw laid him flat out on the floor. Mason took hold of one of the others and did the same. The removalists tackled the rest, pinning them down.

'Time to make a dignified exit,' Mason said, rearranging his shirt as he turned back to Zhang.

'That's not a bad idea,' Zhang's friend chimed in, grinning. 'Let's face it, this is not really a diplomat's scene.'

'We'll give you a call,' Mason said as they left.

'Sure thing. Have a good day!'

Later, in the four-wheel-drive, Mason asked Zhang what it was he had been about to mention before the yobbos appeared on the scene.

'Ah, that?' Zhang said, caught off guard. 'It was nothing.'

He realised that all momentum had been lost for the issue. Instead, he thought of something else he had planned to tell Mason.

'Look, you won't believe this,' he said, breaking into Mandarin. 'Ambassador Li has this close *cukong* friend in Jakarta, an Overseas

Chinese who has the ear of the President. Evidently Tokyo's been pressuring Subroto to get into some joint gas arrangement with Australia. The Japanese want to capitalise on their investment in your Western Australian fields and leverage off that to exploit Timor Sea gas. They want Jakarta in on it, too. And now, with this Sakhalin thing driving them crazy, the *guizi* have doubled their efforts.'

'*Dizhen chiliangbiao*': a pocket seismograph, that's what I need.

The five Chinese men and two women in the room in Beijing looked baffled. They knew the speaker was jesting, though his polite language suggested there was more to it than that.

'It's like being on an intelligence faultline,' Gao went on. 'You never quite know where an agent like this might jump to on the Richter scale.'

The analogy had the desired effect, as indicated by the startled look on the face of the official from the State Council. It was he who had asked what Gao might usefully take back to Sydney to help with the case.

The same man glanced at his watch and then across to Wang Meijian, China's sprightly intelligence chief. In her sixties, and the most powerful woman in the country, she was chairing the meeting. Tough, she ruled her domain with a rod of iron. As much a stickler for fairness as discipline, however, Wang commanded wide respect and devotion among those who worked for her. Short in stature, and with trim white hair, she was dressed in her trademark grey slack-suit. An ivory silk blouse was one of Wang's few concessions to femininity, as was the small, fresh red flower she always had pinned to her lapel. On this day, it was a miniature rose.

Others in the room also checked their watches. It was just after noon.

The group sat around one end of a long conference table on the top floor of the Ministry of State Security. A low-slung Revolutionary building, it faced Tiananmen Square and had the Spartan appearance of the period. The room in which the eight had talked for more than an hour had a thick green carpet that at least softened the resonance, which the high ceilings amplified. A number of spittoons were strategically placed near the wall. Air-conditioning units set in the windows created a clatter that annoyingly competed with the dialogue in this most sterile of places. But nobody complained. The capital's ministries were a maze of vexations that defied all attempts at redress.

Wang, who was the ministry's permanent head, had called the meeting more as a political act than to enhance the knowledge of those attending. With Gao – one of her long-time favourites in the spy service – in town for only a few days, it was an opportunity too good to miss. She could give an assortment of key advisers at the top of the system a taste of the craft and keep them onside. Throughout, the identity of 'Chang Zhe Chan' as a senior ASIS officer was closely guarded. The Singing Cicada was described as a 'walk-in from the highest level in Canberra'. In addition to Wang and Gao, only one other person in the room knew who he was – or at least what his alias was.

Things had gone well in the meeting, with Wang's aim achieved. Gao was tough, polished and professional and had put on a consummate performance. Now he would be treated to an exchange of much greater substance – as soon as the others had left.

'Thank you for joining us,' Wang said, rising from her cumbersome chair with its white lace antimacassar. Her voice was distinct but not loud. It was confident, and pleasant to the ear. 'I trust we've not wasted your time.'

'No, not for a moment,' the State Council representative said, speaking up for the others. 'It's been a fascinating insight into the world of the spy.'

'We all wish you well, Mr Gao,' another member of the group added, 'and we hope your agent doesn't cause you too much trouble.'

The comment summed up their sentiment and confirmed that handling someone like 'Chang Zhe Chan' was seen as no easy task.

'Let me show you down to the entrance,' Wang said, refusing their offer to see themselves out. It was a considerate gesture, which a person of her rank did not need to make.

Gao hung back, as arranged. He was answering a last minute question from one of the visitors who waved to the others to go on ahead.

Xin Yushi, a corpulent man, was lingering for the very same reason. He was the other person who knew who 'Chang Zhe Chan' was. Wang, as Gao's mentor, had invited Xin, an old and trusted cohort, to join her and her Sydney-based colleague for lunch. He was an adviser in the President's Office. The same age as Wang, he carried more weight behind the scenes than most were privileged to know. Hailing from Sichuan Province in the south, he and Wang had maintained their childhood friendship through numerous bouts of ideological and factional change. Xin was a man of fortitude, renowned for his skill at survival. His face, however, in no way belied his strength and resilience. With delicate skin and double chins cascading over his collar, his features were more those of a Tang Dynasty princeling accustomed to a life of indulgence.

Gao shared the pair's Sichuan origins, though he had not met with this top adviser before.

Soon Wang returned. An attendant closed the high double doors behind her as she strode in from the passageway with a spring in her step.

'Come, my friends,' she said, rubbing her hands together with glee. 'Let's eat.'

They walked across to another set of doors at the end of the room, with a waiter opening them from inside as the threesome approached.

A cosier, carpeted chamber – much smaller in size – was revealed. A dining table, laid out in the Chinese manner, stood in the centre. The walls were freshly painted in yellowy-gold, with woodwork in white, and on a head-high stand in one corner sat a porcelain pot of blue morning glories on a bamboo frame. It was a comfortable room and one that Gao had not hitherto seen. The air was cool and obviously filtered, though no conditioner was to be seen, let alone heard. A tantalising aroma of hot Chinese food wafted about.

'Take a look at the view,' Gao's chief said, patting him warmly on the shoulder.

It was a gesture that told Xin this was a man to be trusted. The grey tiled roof of the Tartar Gate, back behind Mao's mausoleum, loomed large through the polluted haze outside the window.

Gao's attention was only briefly distracted.

'You know, Wang collects anything that's not bolted down,' Xin said, observing Gao's interest in the objects adorning the walls and the shelves.

Among a selection of old Western landscapes and photographs of eminent people were framed pieces of calligraphy from Asian dignitaries who valued a shared Chinese heritage. One boldly brushed piece from the classics stood out from the rest. Gao examined its signature closely and recognised the name of a right-wing Japanese prime minister from an earlier decade. The other two merely smiled as they noticed his look of surprise. Nothing was said.

When they were seated, a waiter unfurled their starched white napkins. The table was uncluttered with glasses, for Wang was a strict abstainer during working hours and expected the same of her guests. Almost immediately, the first of the dishes came in from the kitchen.

'Shades of our birthplace, hmmm?' Wang said.

It was Sichuan fare for sure, which meant that her personal chef also shared their origins.

'I'm overwhelmed by the honour you afford me, Zhuren,' Gao said, formally addressing his chief as he always did in the company of others.

It had to be so, until reversed by the grand lady herself.

'Listen, my friend,' she said, 'don't stand on ceremony with us. We're here to talk business – not to engage in ritual.'

Gao was relieved that the stage had been set.

'You see,' Wang said, 'Xin and I are off to Zhongnanhai first thing in the morning.'

Gao nodded, knowing that the Chinese leadership compound next door to the Forbidden City was where all major decisions were made.

'We want to sharpen up our proposal and get the green light to make our next move,' Wang explained, picking at one of the dishes with her chopsticks.

Gao smiled, though he had no idea what she meant.

'It's virtually ready to go,' Xin added, 'but with the polish you'll bring we can put just the right gloss on it. One we know will get it over the line.'

'Look, what it boils down to,' Wang cut in, swallowing a mouthful of food, 'is the question of how far we can push this Australian agent of yours? That's our logical point of departure.'

'You see,' Xin said, 'there's something we'd like you to ask him to do, but obviously there'll be things he can and can't tackle.'

Xin's studied look told Gao that this high-ranking pair appreciated that only his judgement could give them the assessment they needed.

'Well,' Gao said, 'as long as he can handle it safely, whatever it is, it might be possible to push him a little further.'

He thought this response wise, as it left him with room to manoeuvre.

'Chang Zhe Chan' and his contacts, Gao went on to explain, were currently producing Top Secret material that most other agents in China's Australian stable would baulk at procuring.

'Why we ask,' Wang said, 'is because we're contemplating getting your friend to feed to that Sydney newspaper the bits of the story it hasn't already got. We want to give them everything they need in order to broadcast it as widely as possible. Put bluntly, we want the world to know how shoddily China's been treated.'

She gave a theatrical wave of the hand.

'Uncle Sam And Kid Brother Bug Chinese To Oblivion,' Xin said, mimicking the sort of headline that might appear.

'And while we're at it,' Wang added, 'we might get a chance to skin the cat twice.'

'You see,' Xin said, 'if we can get the story out in this way, suitably embellished, then we'll be in an ideal position to sell our silence to the Australians. For the right price, of course.'

Gao nodded.

'You take my point?' Xin said, smiling. 'With that sort of leverage, it shouldn't be too difficult to hustle the Australian Government into the long-term energy agreement we've been talking about. And on the terms China's been pushing for. Perhaps, dare I say, on terms even *better*. Either that – quietly and discreetly settled "behind the curtain" – or an irascible China stomping across the international stage, rubbing salt into the wound at every possible turn. The choice will be stark for the Australians, but unavoidable. After all, they got themselves into this mess. They can get themselves out.'

'But that's only stage one,' Wang broke in. 'Once we have a sealed agreement we'll move on to tackle the Japanese themselves. "No", we'll tell the *guizi*. China's participation in the Sakhalin gas project is not necessarily out of the question. But the terms and conditions will have to be highly attractive to China if it's to burden itself with *two* long-term commitments – one in Australia and the other much closer to home.'

'So, what do you think?' Xin said, looking Gao in the eye. 'Is this agent of yours up to the task?'

'Yes,' Gao replied, after a moment of quiet. 'I think he is.'

Wang and Xin were patently pleased.

Things couldn't be better, Xin thought. I'll trust Wang's faith in this fellow. I like a careful response to something like this, and that's just what he's given. Good to see someone under pressure at a point of decision. You get a glimpse inside, where all sorts of strengths and weaknesses are hidden. And this chap's not weak. You can feel he's on top of his job.

Wang, too, was convinced that Gao could carry

it off. His exploits in Australia, the nature of which she had earlier relayed to Xin, left her in no doubt. But he would have to watch his step. She knew only too well, as did Gao, that the Australians were no pushover. They had many good people.

As Wang glanced across at him now, she saw that Gao's attention had wandered. One of her most valued possessions had caught her visitor's eye.

'What do you think?' she said, as he studied the lines of the piece.

His interest intrigued her. What Gao had spotted was a fine antique clock. It sat on a polished rosewood cabinet, off to one side.

'Oh, it's classical,' Gao replied. 'Subdued and not too ornate.'

'*Yingguozuo*,' Wang enthused: it's English-made. Her eyes were alive. 'It's from around 1780, I'm led to believe. Tasteful on the outside and a top-class mechanism inside, but there's much more to the story than that.'

'You're not going to tell us it's the world's earliest bugging device,' Xin said.

'Don't worry, I've had it checked,' Wang replied, surprised that the quip was so close to the mark. 'You see, it was a personal gift from the head of MI6, the British Secret Intelligence Service. *C*, as they call my British counterpart, was here in Beijing. We had talks on London's offer of specialist intelligence training. The clock, I suspect, was meant to soften me up.'

'And no doubt it did,' Xin said, turning to Gao. 'Heaven knows what relic you'll need to find in

Australia to keep this intrepid woman quiet. I warn you, you'd better start looking.'

Gao already knew. As soon as he returned he would suggest to Ambassador Li that the Japanese Kabuki doll, with its high-tech ceramic head, be dispatched.

'Try the braised eggplant,' Xin said, gesturing to Gao and using a more intimate form of address. 'You won't find anything like this in . . .'

The shrill ring of a phone stopped him in midflight. It was from a dated, multi-line device which sat on a sideboard near the door to the kitchen. A waiter popped out and brought the phone over to Wang, who excused herself as she picked up the receiver.

She listened intently for a moment. '*Shi, shi, hao le. Yizhi dai lai.*' Yes, by all means. Bring it up straightaway.

Shortly the chief's offsider arrived with the news. It was a secret report on Japan's game plan for gas from Sakhalin, fresh in from China's spy station in Tokyo. Wang skimmed the pages, then dismissed her assistant.

A sensitive document, it had been obtained from a delicate Japanese source. She read aloud from the summary translation at its head.

> TOP SECRET
> Cabinet Research Office, Tokyo, May 15
> For: Prime Minister Sakamoto
> Kenichiro Yoshida's Visit to Australia:
> The Way Ahead

> Synopsis: This report details the outcome of discussions held by the CRO's Director-General with Sydney representatives of Matsutomo Corporation and with our ambassador in Canberra. Also included are the conclusions reached at a CRO coordinatory meeting held after the Director-General's return. Addressed herein are (1) likelihood of China's entry into Sakhalin Gas Project, (2) expected American reaction to announcement of discoveries in Russian waters, and (3) projected Russo–Japanese concessions to US demands for participation of American companies, especially in pipeline contracts for supplies to Eastern Russia, Korea and China.

'*Tai hao le,*' Wang said, passing the full 30-page report across the table to Xin: a nice piece of work. 'Even if I say so myself. Here we are, getting it from both ends of the spectrum. *Tatemae* from the Japanese Government, and now *honne* from our own people inside their system.'

This was a clever dig at the Japanese and their language. The propensity they had for two versions of the truth – one for official consumption and another for private – was not an attribute this woman admired, though the Chinese themselves were in no way devoid of the trait.

While the other two examined the report, Wang excused herself and sauntered off into the kitchen. She muttered something about checking on the Sichuan fruit for dessert.

'Cocky little shits, these Sons of Nippon,' Xin observed.

Gao laughed at the earthiness of the language used to fire off this shot. 'I've heard stronger terms used to describe them,' he replied.

Xin smiled wryly. 'I mean, a transmitting doll's head in our ambassador's office!' he said, slapping his leg, which seemed to be a habit he had when something tickled his fancy. 'That's a bit rich, in anyone's book.'

SEVEN

Sydney: Mid-May

'Hello.'

'*Selamat Pagi,*' the American woman's voice came down the line: good morning. '*Pak Mason, di sana?*' Is Mr Mason there, please?

'Yes, that's me.'

'How would you feel about a *nasi goreng* for lunch? One with a wobbly egg.'

Her words were like a beam of light. But they also had more than one meaning – one quite benign and the other possibly sinister. He had no idea which it might be.

It was a voice Greg Mason had not heard for some time. He and Elizabeth Cantrell had worked closely during his last posting with ASIS seven years back. Cantrell had been a spy in Jakarta and had attended regular briefings at the CIA station inside the US Embassy. It was through such meetings that ASIS operatives liaised on the ground with their American counterparts and shared political, economic and military reporting on Indonesia and the broader South East Asian region. Mason and Cantrell, however, had had a specific interest in energy and resource matters, on which their activities were carefully coordinated. An Asia hand from Cornell University, Cantrell was an Indonesia specialist. She had a solid fluency in the language and her contacts in government circles in Jakarta were unrivalled.

At a personal level, between the CIA and ASIS in Jakarta, trust had been high and much more was talked about at those meetings than most cared to put on paper. It was the one time of the week when Mason and Cantrell felt completely relaxed, professionally, within the confines of the American station. He had enjoyed the dialogue immensely. Martin Clarke had displayed little interest in contributing and had been content to let his deputy attend in his stead.

Images of Cantrell now flooded back into Mason's mind as he heard her on the other end of the line. He made a mental note of the fact that she would now be in her late thirties, a few years younger than him, and single again after a childless marriage.

But what game is she playing? he thought. Is it just for old time's sake, and perhaps a bit of a flirt? Or is it something much darker and more urgent?

Beth, as she was known, had been part of that bonhomie which Mason and his Jakarta colleagues – both American and Australian – remembered with fondness. Markedly taller than average, and lithe, she had natural blonde, shoulder-length hair.

Her dry sense of humour, and the laugh that went with it, matched the personality of this confident and highly qualified woman.

More than a few members of the Jakarta group to which she and Mason belonged had had a liking for *nasi goreng*, a popular fried rice dish available across the country. Some, however, had an aversion to the fried egg and its typically uncooked yolk, which commonly sat on top. Mason was in that category and was usually the first to send his back. But between him and Beth, the egg was also code language for one of two things, depending on tone: I need to see you fast to let off steam, or, for operational reasons, I must see you as quickly as possible.

'So, are you free or not?' she said.

'Well, it depends. I'm no longer in the game, you know.'

'Let's say, Greg, I've got something to tell you that you really must hear. And lunch with a wobbly yolk comes as part of the deal.'

'It's as *wobbly* as that?'

'It certainly is.'

She was deadly serious.

'OK, I'll come.'

Mason was aware that Cantrell was still with the 'Langley mob', as he called the CIA. The odd letter along the way and recently emailed jokes had filled him in on much of what had taken place in her life. She was aware of how Mason's former wife had died.

In Australia, Mason had cared for Prue in the final year of her life. In contrast to Clarke's callousness, his magnanimity was something Cantrell would never forget. But for him, her earlier friendship and intimacy with Clarke in Jakarta had left an indelible mark. Images of this now flooded his mind: Cantrell's fascination with Clarke's wide-ranging interests and his trips to remote parts of Indonesia, where he picked up from dealers exquisite pieces of Chinese porcelain looted from the graves of early Chinese traders. All this had been before Clarke teamed up with Mason's wife. Still, Cantrell was fun to be with and the prospect of spending time together again was something to relish.

He noted that she had not mentioned her name over the phone. This could only mean she was fearful that his line might be tapped.

But by whom? It could only be my old employers, he thought.

'Can you do the city?' she said, knowing he was at home. 'I'm at the Cremorne ferry wharf at the moment and there's a boat leaving for Circular Quay in twenty minutes. Can you make it?'

'*Bisa, bisa,*' he replied, his Bahasa springing from nowhere: indeed I can.

During the walk down to the ferry, Mason was preoccupied with thoughts of the dilemma that Cantrell had brought. She had obviously slept with Clarke, and that was no easy matter to accept. In ASIS's Jakarta station, Clarke had even boasted of his conquest to Mason and his five other colleagues.

She had virtually confirmed it herself, Mason thought, recalling a quip Cantrell had made at the time. They had been discussing Clarke's failure to win the attention of a high-ranking female technocrat in the Indonesian Industry Ministry. The woman concerned was someone he felt would readily succumb to his blandishments. But things had turned out quite differently.

'Well, that'll put a dent in his pride,' Mason had observed. 'No,' Cantrell said. 'Knowing him as I do, it won't impact on his manhood at all. Certainly not on his virility.' The wry smile that had accompanied this statement had told Mason more than enough: she had slept with his boss.

How could she get so close to a creep like that? he asked himself now, as he had many times in Jakarta. The thought still caused him to shake his head in disbelief.

Mason arrived at the wharf with minutes to spare. Dressed in a dark navy suit, he was ready for other meetings later in the day. He wore a gold silk tie with a matching pocket handkerchief. That was a colour Cantrell had told him long ago suited him best. After a morning's work at home on his computer, the placid waters of the harbour were refreshing. Deep, mirror-like reflections and foliage spilling down to the shoreline washed his mind clean. It was a sunny day, following earlier rain, and the lingering moisture added a lightness to the salty tang in the air.

Cantrell was standing twenty metres up ahead near a crowd of shoppers heading off to the city. She was clad in a beige Burberry coat, with a silk scarf of apricot and brown tossed around her shoulders. He noticed that her blonde hair was shorter than before, but otherwise she appeared unchanged. Though she had her back to him, images of her face were easy to recall.

Intuitively, she felt his presence. Turning, she spotted him standing off to one side. No signals passed between them, but it was as though they were speaking across the heads of the passengers. The ferry from the city, with its green hull and yellow superstructure pulled in right on schedule. As it reversed its engines and a surge of foam and bubbles rose, Mason felt that more than the boat had arrived.

A new bunch of passengers shuffled on board and within minutes the engines revved and the vessel was off. A wash of sea air blew into Mason's face as he stepped out of the cabin and onto the deck. Its full length was lined with seats in bright red. He spotted Cantrell up near the bow.

'What a pleasure,' he said, slipping into a vacant seat alongside her and giving her a kiss on the cheek. 'I can't believe this is happening.'

'That goes for me, too,' she responded.

They talked for some time about how neither had aged, until Mason decided to get to the point.

'Look, how much time have we got? Are you here for a week or just a few hours?'

'Greg, believe it or not, that depends upon you.'

'Uh, ha. So it's something like that.'

'Well, let's face it, there's not much I'd be able to hide from you.'

'Sock it to me, Beth. I know you can't wait.'

'Something really dirty's blown up in Canberra. That's what's happened.'

'So what else is new?'

'No, Greg. This is a big one. You see, a joint US–Australian tech op has been under way here for some years. The new Chinese Embassy is the target. The whole thing's run by the NSA out of Washington and they have two tech guys out here on the ground.'

Oh, shit! Mason thought. I've just told Zhang to make sure they sweep the place properly.

Cantrell described the optical fibre technology used in the bugging and the type of intelligence drawn from the exercise – until recent weeks, that was.

'Well, I can't say I'd heard about that,' he said.

Cantrell had expected as much.

'The NSA,' she went on, 'first noticed a change in comms patterns, then the conversations of the Chinese themselves dropped off drastically. In the space of a week, the yield turned to a trickle. Then, in the middle of all this, they picked up signals emitted from the ambassador's office that were plainly being monitored by the Japanese.'

Mason laughed. This was sounding awfully familiar. It was what Zhang had told him about at the pub.

'Anyhow, not long after that, the Chinese launched into a sweep of their premises. It was well beyond a routine check and in the course of it they seemed to stumble across the "plants" that the Japanese had put in.'

Mason listened carefully. He was reminded too much of his past. God, I hope they don't want me to get mixed up in this one, he thought.

'So, Greg, the upshot is that Langley and the NSA, as well as the FBI, have put their heads together urgently. And here's the conclusion. We believe the op on the Chinese Embassy's been betrayed. And from *inside* the Australian camp.'

Mason wagged his head, more in disgust than disbelief.

'Another vital piece of information,' Cantrell said, 'came in the other day, not long after Sherrington briefed the President and some other key people. He told them how he was going to clean up the Australian intelligence system once and for all. You see, Greg, the decision to send me out here had already been taken when Tokyo suddenly came up with something that sent Sherrington ballistic. You may not know, but at the moment the Japs are desperate for favours from the CIA. So much so, that as a sweetener they've handed over a transcript from one of the conversations they'd bugged in the Chinese ambassador's room in Canberra.'

Mason was silent.

'It was in Mandarin, and between the ambassador and three of his officials. Along the way, the ambo mentions a specific American report that the embassy's little "singing bird in Australian intelligence" has provided. That report, Greg, was one of ours. It was a CIA rundown on operational targets in China. And we'd sent it to ASIS at the Service's request, and *only* to ASIS. Next thing we know, the goddamn Chinese ambassador to Australia's passing judgement on it. I mean, it was as though we'd sent him a personal drop-copy.'

Mason was appalled, but refrained from commenting.

'Unfortunately, the bugged conversation doesn't identify the ASIS traitor, beyond referring to "him" a number of times as their "singing bird". So there you have it, Greg. That's the story.'

Mason was left shaking his head.

'We thought that Mitrokhin's warning a few years ago,' Cantrell added, 'about traitors in Canberra, would have led to a clean-up. But apparently it didn't, and now someone else is at it. You know how big Sherrington is on this. He can't stand allies who let their ships leak. He admires the work that many of your people do, but he's convinced you've got a few at the top who are sus.'

Mason nodded, appreciating the point only too well. Though he had never met the CIA Director, the man's stance on the matter was no secret, especially among Australians who understood what fuelled his suspicion. A CIA officer had once confided to Mason overseas that, 'until you Aussies have the guts to bring the lie detector in, you'll never really know who's on your team'.

'Anyhow, Greg, this time the boss has taken it all the way to the top. And the NSA has backed him to the hilt. I can tell you, he's not going to let go. He wants action fast and he's determined to get it. And now that the White House is involved, that lot's going to be panting for results. You know what they're like. In fact, if the CIA doesn't come up with something, Sherrington's detractors won't hesitate to use it against him, and mercilessly, too.'

In Mason's mind, cogs were rapidly engaging.

If the President of the United States is pushing for action, he thought, then it's going to be decisive and speedy. And Sherrington's going to have to make sure that it is. What Beth's trying to do is rope me into the witch-hunt, to get me to work against my old Service. I bet that's what this is all about.

Cantrell caught the half-quizzical look on his face. It spoke of a growing realisation of what was now thick in the air. She knew Mason well and could tell he had already picked up the scent.

'So, you want *me* to . . .'

'Precisely.'

'With . . .'

'With no one. Hopefully, just by yourself, being the resourceful guy you are. At least to start with, that is. Of course, we understand you might have to bring a few other Aussies in on the act if things evolve in the way we expect. And naturally, you'd have all the American help you need.'

He had no doubt Cantrell could provide it. She was a top-flight CIA officer who had cleverly identified more than one traitor inside her Agency. It was clear in his mind why she had been chosen for this job.

'But, it may be,' Mason mused aloud, 'that Australian and Chinese interests are more closely linked on this than Australian and US interests are. Such a situation could possibly arise, couldn't it?'

Cantrell chose not to react. It was not what she wanted to hear, but she understood what he was getting at.

'Even though we're friends and allies,' he said, 'my fundamental loyalty will always be to what I see as Australia's best interests.'

Cantrell nodded. It was a legitimate point, and if it were necessary for him to make it she had no objection. Her quick smile told him that his message had been received and registered. Politely, she returned to the matter in hand.

'When word went out in Langley, Greg, that an Australian – particularly somebody who knew the system intimately – would be the one to take on the job, a handful of names came up. And yours headed the list. You were way out in front.'

'Shit, don't tell me why.'

'Well, I *must*. You see, they've specifically asked me to let you know. They want you to be aware of exactly why they've decided on you. There's no end of reasons, Greg, but *trust* is a big one. I mean, the very fact that you've raised the issue of loyalty underlines your integrity. Now, on our side, that's crucial. Whoever we choose, we must know exactly where they're coming from. We also think you've got a strong sense of purpose, clarity of mind, reliability – those sorts of qualities. And of course, there's your intimate knowledge of ASIS and the main characters that staff it, topped off by the fact that you're no longer in it yourself. And when you left, you went on a point of principle.'

Mason shrugged. He had no disagreement with that.

'Then there's Omega Blue.'

This brought a smile to his face. Early in his intelligence career Mason had spent six months in Hong Kong running a delicate ASIS operation into mainland China. A top Chinese agent of the day, who was highly placed in the People's Liberation Army, had told Mason he had been offered – at a ridiculous price – secret state-of-the-art military technology 'soon to be available in Australia'. Careful investigation had shown this to be a sophisticated anti-missile system that Australian defence scientists were in the process of refining, in conjunction with a team from the Pentagon. The work was carried out at a sensitive Australian establishment on the outskirts of Melbourne.

Mason had discovered that a rogue French spy, operating under deep cover in Australia, had penetrated the program. It was this operative who was attempting to sell the product of the Australian–American collaboration to the Chinese Army via contacts he had in Beijing.

Mason reported this in detail to ASIS headquarters, but the matter was never taken seriously. He had then slipped the information, in full, to his local CIA colleague in Hong Kong. All hell had broken loose in Washington. The story proved to be true. Mason's tip-off led to the Americans uncovering additional French operatives in the US. Under the code-name Operation Omega Blue, the entire network was rooted out. ASIS management was furious, but there was nothing it could do to discipline Mason. He had broken no rule and, in fact, had displayed initiative in a way that many members of the Service openly praised. With time, the issue passed, though for some at the top – particularly Morgandale – Mason's 'maverick status' still hung over his head.

'So, with this in mind, Greg, Sherrington said: "Get that man if you can. That's the sort of doggedness we want." What it boils down to is this. You've helped us once. Can you pull it off again? It's as simple as that. The CIA's been given full charge of the hunt. And the first thing the boss decided on was that there'd be no direct approach to Canberra on this. Certainly no hint will be given to ASIS. "*God dammit to hell, we might end up talking to the very traitor we're trying to catch*,"' she said, aping her boss's words.

'Therefore, Greg, time is of the essence. Sherrington's intent on getting to the bottom of this. And if you're willing to help us you can have whatever you want for as long as it takes. If it plays havoc with your business, then we'll cover that too, and many times over. The question is, will you or won't you?'

Mason was already pondering the answer. Other things were stuck in his mind.

He was not at all keen about the idea of the Americans running the operation against the Chinese. From what Cantrell had said, it was a classic case of Big Brother having total control. It was not hard for him to imagine what Washington was picking up in the process. There would be material on how much wheat China was planning to buy from Australia. And the US was one of Australia's major competitors.

But then, he thought, I've staked out my boundaries – where I stand if there's a conflict of interest – so, if they're prepared to hire me on those terms, maybe I should suck it and see.

'You realise, Beth, that I've cut myself free from the spy game and I'm revelling in my simple, one-dimensional life. Then, here you are, asking me to step back in again.'

'You could put it that way.'

'And you expect me to turn my world upside-down to run with your baton?'

'Well, that's for you to decide, Greg. I didn't come here to push you – just to get your response.'

Images of his business being disrupted flashed through his mind, as did others of being sucked into a vortex from which there might be no escape. A powerful force deep in his gut urged him to stay clear. Even his friend, Zhang, had tried to broach this matter with him. But old professional instincts exploded, overriding everything else. They were like a bright light illuminating the path up ahead.

I've long wanted to see Canberra cleaned up, he thought. So if the traitor *is* caught – and hopefully some of the others mixed up in it, too – we might see some progress at last. Plus, the prospect of doing all this with the backing of the

President of the United States is too good to be true. That really *is* in Australia's interests.

The answer seemed obvious and almost leapt out to declare itself before he had reconciled it with other gravitational pulls.

'Well . . .'

'You mean, yes?'

'Well, yes.'

He felt that fate was answering for him, which he found unsettling. It had often served him well. But emotion masquerading as fate had sometimes stepped out in front and confused things no end.

'Thanks, Greg. And you know we mean it.'

Mason nodded.

He was still wrestling with the implications of the commitment he had made, knowing he should have asked for at least one night to sleep on it. But Cantrell was not that kind of person. For her, instinct was vital in these things. Hesitation on his part would be read in only one way – he was no longer up to it.

'Oh, and there's more,' Cantrell said, putting a stop to his thoughts. Her grin suggested something lighter.

The ferry was approaching Circular Quay and tall, glass tower blocks reared imposingly in front, peering down like sentinels checking each vessel.

'*More* – after that? OK, let me have it.'

'Well, there's this guy, Ben Jameson – a black American – who runs the Agency's setup here in Sydney. He'll be waiting to meet us outside. You might've seen him around.'

Mason indicated that he had. He recalled seeing Jameson dining with others at the American Club.

'He's keen to meet up with you. Ben's full of beans – a delightful person. Actually, I gave him a quick call on the cell phone after we spoke to let him know we were coming. If you'd knocked us back, Greg, the idea was that you and I would walk straight past him, out through the gate. But seeing as you've come on board, the three of us can have lunch together, if you can spare the time.'

'Sounds good to me.'

The ferry bumped heavily against the quayside, its engines reversing to kill the momentum.

'I must say, Beth, you ain't changed one little bit, have you?' he said, as they got up from their seats.

She smiled.

The metal gangway dropped with a clang, as passengers milled around to cross onto the wharf.

'You know,' he said, 'I wouldn't mind seeing a copy of that Japanese transcript. The one of the Chinese ambassador's bugged conversation.'

'Just ask Ben. He'll fix it up.'

Todd Lambert, Clarke's deputy in ASIS, listened intently to what his friend had to say. He was keen to hear what Mason had to report on his secret meeting with one of the grand old men of the Service, let alone more about his reasons for flying down from Sydney for these undercover talks.

Following Cantrell's appearance in mid-May, Mason had headed for Canberra to begin his search for the traitor. In the guarded way that former colleagues could talk, Mason had already conveyed by phone to Lambert – who he regarded as his smartest and most trusted friend in the Service, as well as a man unquestionably loyal to his country – the gist of what had come up. His first appointment had been with Alfie Trevelyan at the hobby farm the veteran and his wife ran not far from the capital. His last meeting for the day was with Lambert that evening at the latter's apartment.

'In typical Alfie style, Todd, he says: "Look, you tell me who you think it is, and we'll roll on from there." So I did, and that's when the old fella's instincts came to the fore.'

Lambert knew what Mason meant. Trevelyan, now in his seventies, was well known to both.

Long a mentor to the Service's Young Turks, Trevelyan had been a founding member of ASIS in the 1950s. He had risen to the position of deputy director-general and was in line for the top job, but with the prize within grasp, had unexpectedly retired. Originally, he had been recruited into Army Intelligence after Pearl Harbor in December 1941. Then in his twenties, he was the brightest of a group given intensive Japanese language and interrogation training. He had shared this with Mason's father, who was still a close friend. Both were members of the elite Z Force that operated behind enemy lines in Indonesia and New Guinea. Trevelyan's daring exploits were legendary in the Defence Force, even half a century later. Practical results and clear thinking had always been his benchmarks and in his time in ASIS he had backed any officer who approached the craft of spying in that way. Mason had served under him for a few years and a warm father–son relationship had developed, deepening after the old man's departure.

Lambert had crossed over from SAS to join ASIS after Trevelyan left, but had made the war hero's acquaintance through Mason.

Out at the farm, Trevelyan and Mason had talked for hours, with the younger man gaining the insights he needed. Now, at the end of the day, he and Lambert were cooking a meal for themselves. Lambert's wife, a nursing sister, was on duty. Mason had picked up some steak and an expensive bottle of wine on the way. He was cutting the meat into strips, while Lambert diced vegetables to stir-fry with it. A few spoons of *laksa* paste and they might have a reasonable dinner.

Lambert was not surprised to hear what Mason had to say. It had not taken long to recount Cantrell's story in detail, and Lambert's speedy and positive response buoyed Mason's spirits. Doubt though, lingered in his mind over whether he had bitten off more than he could chew.

'Altogether, I threw up seven people to Alfie,' he said. 'They're in order of both suspicion and likely access, whether or not they'd be officially aware of the Chinese operation. Of course, you're much better placed than I am to judge who might know what. Anyhow, to start with, I'm ruling out the DG because I don't think betrayal would be his type of thing.'

'I agree,' Lambert said.

'Now, in judging their likely motivation,' Mason went on, 'I've used one main yardstick and that's greed. I'm more or less discounting ideology, such as some warped admiration of China's political system. Instinct tells me it'll almost certainly be money that's the driving force behind this – which is Alfie's view, too.'

Lambert was nodding.

'OK, first off – Martin Clarke,' Mason said.

Lambert's eyebrows rose, but his expression was in no way dismissive. In recent months Mason had heard a lot from his friend about Clarke's various doings.

'I read you,' Lambert said. 'I know where you're coming from. He's definitely a candidate in terms of money.'

'Bass Morgandale,' Mason continued.

'Yes, he'd be in it for the dough. Absolutely.'

'Tim Wherret; Catherine Jacobson; Mark Corbett.'

Lambert wagged his head. 'Possibly. Anyway, we can check them out.'

Mason's other names drew a similar response.

Lambert added three suspects of his own, one officially aware of the operation and the others having come to know through Morgandale, who often talked out of shop with favourites.

'I'd say it's between Bass and Martin,' Lambert said, 'but let's not rule the others out yet. We'll need to look at them all pretty rigorously.'

He paused halfway through slicing an onion. 'You know, Greg, there's a real irony in this. See, a few weeks ago, DSD intercepted a phone call from McKinnon – that hotshot *Courier* journo – to Jeremy Torrens, their bureau chief in Beijing. And what they talked about revealed that they're also on to this Chinese Embassy story.'

'Oh, lovely!' Mason said. 'How the hell can you run an op like that if you can't keep it secret?'

'Exactly, but you know Canberra. Needless to say, the Government's in a flap over it. It's the Mother of All Leaks, as some wag's calling it. Anyhow, they've done what all good governments do in a panic – set up a committee. It's a working group inside AG's and it's meant to watch the situation closely until we have a clearer picture of who knows what and where they got it from. But the only thing they've achieved so far is to force ASIO to intercept *all* of McKinnon's comms. And that's something that Joe, who's part of the group, isn't too pleased about – nor me.'

Joe Pellegrini was the head of ASIO's technical operations unit and a person well known to both men. Mason was aware of his views on this sort of issue: focusing government resources on the person receiving the information, rather than on the likely source of the leak.

'You don't have to tell me what Joe thinks about this,' he said.

'I know, but that's not all, Greg. Bass himself is on the committee, though he rarely turns up for meetings. Martin's also attended, though he rubbed one of the Foreign Affairies up the wrong way and the poor bastard nearly walked out.'

Mason was left shaking his head.

'But no one's complaining,' Lambert said. 'You see, they're pushing me out front at the moment, as I'm apparently regarded as professionally sharper and far less likely to get caught up in personal feuds.'

'That wouldn't be hard.'

Lambert smiled. Mason understood the knack that Morgandale and Clarke had of gathering around them people who could help out in this way. Clearly, they were using Lambert as a proxy who would routinely report back, as part of his job, everything they needed to know.

'There's not a lot of talent in the group,' Lambert said. 'Apart from Joe, the only other two with their heads screwed on are Alexandra Templeton from ONA and the DSD chap.'

'Have the Americans been told about the leak?'

'No, not a word, which I think is looking for trouble. In fact, we're under strict instructions to say nothing about it. Not a word. Not until the "picture is clearer" and we – meaning the Government, and Canberra as a whole – have worked out a solution. As you'd expect, they're hoping to cover it all up so the Yanks never get to know.'

'But they already *do*,' Mason said.

'And no doubt for the better.'

Lambert poured some oil into the wok and turned on the gas.

'So what did Alfie think of all this?' he said.

'He was shocked. Not just because the op's been blown. More for the fact that the Americans feel it necessary to tackle it this way, using someone like me to suss it out clandestinely.'

'Yes, it'd be like a red flag to a bull for old Alfie,' Lambert said. 'After all, he worked bloody hard on relations with Washington.'

Trevelyan had advocated speedy action whenever hints from the Americans indicated that the loyalties of an Australian officer might be in question. But his efforts were regularly thwarted and little was ever done. 'An intelligence service is only as good as its ethics,' he used to say, often within earshot of those who needed to know. He had repeated this warning in full in his farewell speech to the staff.

'What's Alfie's view on your suspects?' Lambert said.

'Well, he went straight for Bass and Martin, but he agrees we should run an eye over the others. "Focus on those two for a start," he said. "They might both be involved, though I can't imagine them working together." If anything, he'd put Bass ahead of Martin in terms of suspicion, but after a few hours on the subject, he had them pretty much on par. Alfie sees Bass as someone who'd sell his soul out easily. He thinks that's the only reason he got into intelligence – in effect, to feather his own nest.'

Lambert nodded. He knew this was an allusion to a trauma that had once shaken the Service.

Trevelyan had resigned over the failure of ASIS management to keep Morgandale under control.

His habit of interfering in operational matters outside his area of responsibility cut across the need-to-know principle, which Trevelyan regarded as fundamental. Morgandale's guile, however, always carried the day. Eventually, he challenged the deputy director himself by interfering in an operation that Trevelyan had launched in China. Morgandale, via contacts in London, had drawn MI6 into the game, which led to confusion and also to the loss of valuable agents. Mason had been Trevelyan's team leader for the operation. In the end, it was Morgandale who survived and Trevelyan who left.

'Alfie thinks that if Bass is the traitor we're looking for,' Mason said, 'then the betrayal of the Chinese op would be part of a long chain of events. He doesn't see Bass as the type who'd do this on a whim. He's a schemer, so it'd be part of some grand plan to guarantee him the lifestyle he believes he's entitled to.'

'And Martin?'

'Well, Alfie sees a real difference between these two. He doesn't think Martin would blow ASIS secrets systematically. Not on a regular basis. Instead there'd be a number of things that weren't going well and the pressure would build up to a level where he couldn't hack it any more. He'd be so full of angst that he'd snap. Then he'd go for a king-hit – some one-off thing, big and nasty – to spite the Service. And money would be a major part of the deal.'

Lambert nodded. All this rang true.

'You and I know, Todd, that Alfie's always had serious doubts about Martin. We've both heard him say he shouldn't have been brought into the Service in the first place. Actually, he told me today that initially Martin was knocked back by the recruiting board, but strings were pulled and he was let in anyway. "All very fishy," as Alfie puts it. He still thinks Martin's whole reputation is based on a sham, which is why he's had run-ins with people like me. He believes that that Malaysian recruitment was just sheer luck. Martin happened to be in the right place at the right time. But those two Indons – no way.'

Early in Clarke's career, he had been posted to Malaysia where, in what some viewed as a dangerously short space of time, he recruited a senior figure in the Foreign Ministry. The agent produced top quality material for nearly a year, but was then suddenly dismissed and lost all access. Later, when Clarke was first sent to Jakarta – which had been as a deep-cover officer – he chalked up two star recruitments in the space of six months. One was a police general and the other a senior army officer. Trevelyan believed that both were linked and were double agents. In reality, *they* had hooked Clarke, rather than the other way round. Their product was in great demand in Canberra and ASIS management had thrived on the kudos it brought. Security checks, which Trevelyan and others urged, were blocked and, ultimately, never carried out.

'There's another streak in Martin that Alfie points to,' Mason said, 'and it's relevant here.

He's convinced that if he is the traitor, it'll be vindictiveness that's drawn him into the act. It'll be his past catching up with him. And once he's taken the plunge, he'll be in it up to his ears. There'd be no turning back.'

'Had Alfie heard about Martin's new job?' Lambert said. 'That fill-in role as an ops director?'

'Yes, and he thinks that might have been the last straw for Martin, especially coming on top of Bass's promotion over his head. Alfie thinks it was crazy making Morgandale Bill's deputy.'

Hestercombe, the Director-General, had a soft spot for Clarke and had been inclined to favour him for that position, but the minister had expressed a clear preference for Morgandale. Many in the Service had believed that the chief should stand up to his political master and make the decision himself, but Hestercombe was a bureaucratic *apparatchik* – not an old hand at intelligence who appreciated the finer points of the craft. So, when someone suggested a new role of Director – North Asia, Hestercombe had agreed to give it a go. A sliced-off portion of the overall ops branch, and one never previously handled separately, it was a makeshift arrangement and nothing more than a sop.

'Even the bloody tea-lady,' Lambert said, 'knew that Martin would hit the roof over a half-baked promotion. Shit, with Martin and Bass the fiercest of rivals, that was looking for trouble. Bill should have given him the Washington liaison posting he'd always been after, or some other glamorous thing overseas.'

'Which is why my instincts, Todd, like Alfie's, tell me Martin might be the main contender, with Bass a close second.'

A thought flashed through Mason's mind, but he chose not to share it with his friend. Not for the time being, at least. In an aside at the farm, Trevelyan had joked that he would like nothing better than to see Morgandale nailed as a traitor. 'You probably feel the same way about Martin, Greg, what with the shameful way he treated you in Jakarta.' But the pair had agreed that prejudice could not be allowed to intrude upon important matters like this.

'Well, you can count on me,' Lambert said. 'I'll help check all these people out. Then there's Joe. How about him? I'm sure he'd be only too willing.'

Mason had already considered Pellegrini, who he knew well and trusted. Having ASIO's head of tech ops on board would not go astray on a mission like this.

'Let me see what the Yanks have to offer,' he replied. 'I want to be on top of their side of things first.'

'As it happens, Greg, he and I are off to Victoria the day after tomorrow. There's a joint ASIS–ASIO exercise on, which we've been asked to assess. Let me know if you want me to sound him out while we're there.'

'Thanks.'

'In the meantime, mate,' Lambert said, giving Mason a slap on the back, 'pour some of that cheap plonk you brought.'

As Mason reached for the bottle, he pondered the fact that Lambert epitomised all that he himself had stood for in intelligence.

At the end of the day, he thought, it's all about trust and a strong sense of duty. At least with Todd around, and people like Joe – and maybe Alexandra as well – this job might be manageable after all. They're people who have long wanted to see the system cleaned up.

He recalled what Trevelyan had said when they parted: 'Work closely with Todd on this one and you'll crack it wide open. If you fail, the Americans will never trust us again.'

Lambert's support was reassuring to Mason, who was still wrestling with his radical re-entry into the murky world of espionage. Oddly, Zhang, on their latest Sunday morning run, had warned him – and movingly, too – to stay well away.

'Can I ask you something, Todd?' Mason said.

'Of course.'

Lambert sensed it was significant.

'You know, it means a lot to me to have your backing on this. To be sure that you think I'm doing the right thing.'

'Oh, I haven't any doubt about that. No doubt at all. And anyway, we're both in it now.'

What else could I say? Lambert thought. Besides, I believe it. Greg could hardly have knocked the Yanks back. And *I* certainly wouldn't have.

But Lambert knew this was the last thing Mason needed when he was still trying to close off on his past. It was going to set that process back years.

Mason held the opened bottle over the wok as Lambert stirred the food.

'Hey, not with a Bin 389!' Lambert shouted, pushing his friend's arm away.

'But who'd *drink* cheap stuff like this!' Mason quipped.

Lambert smiled. 'Look, make yourself useful,' he said. 'Go and set the table.'

As Mason wandered off into the dining room, images from his time in Jakarta flooded back. A particular incident, which he and Alfie had recalled at the farm, was most vivid. It was one of the closest shaves he had had in his intelligence career as a deep-cover operative.

'*Dari mana?*' the military policeman called out, beckoning Mason and his Indonesian friend across to the jeep: where are you from?

His driver cut the engine, which suggested the pair might be in for close scrutiny. Maybe they had been specifically targeted, otherwise there would be no logical reason to block the busy daytime traffic in this narrow back street.

It's no use throwing up a different nationality, Mason thought quickly. If they take us in, they'll check on that fast, then we'd be in deep shit.

'*Dari Australia,*' he replied, displaying enthusiasm over having been asked.

After all, the policeman had used a standard greeting in Bahasa, and the Indonesians –

overwhelmingly – were a friendly and outwardgoing people.

For the moment, Mason was grateful that his Indonesian 'friend' – Mochtar, one of ASIS's most sensitive agents – was quiet. The pair had already run through this scenario in case it occurred, but Mason had no experience of how the man performed under pressure.

The policeman nodded in a way that implied more serious questions were to follow. Mason had his story ready but if it were to come across as too thin, and be pursued all the way, then both he and the agent would be doomed. Mochtar, for certain, would end up with his throat cut – a common fate for traitors of any pedigree – while Mason would share the same end if Jakarta's anger overrode any fear of having to account to the Australian Government for his mysterious disappearance.

Mochtar was a defence attaché in the Indonesian Embassy in Beijing, and was distantly related to the President. Fluent in Mandarin, which was unusual for a Muslim Indonesian, his skills were commonly used for intimate, one-on-one dialogues with China's leaders, held away from formal meetings and their bevy of official interpreters. On this occasion, China's defence minister was paying a secret visit to Jakarta to discuss a possible missile development deal. What made the topic unusually sensitive was the direct involvement of Israel in any likely project. To avoid the risk of leakage, it had been agreed that Mochtar would fly down from Beijing to interpret.

With great care, he had managed to get a message through to Mason soon after arriving. The two had long shared a high level of trust, since Mason recruited him during Mochtar's intensive language course in Hong Kong.

Now, as Mason readied himself for the policeman's next question, his agent's alarming tale from their initial debrief the previous day flashed through his mind.

'The President, Greg, had me brought straight to his office from the airport, where he subjected me to something I'd never known before. You see, he handed me an unsealed envelope, which he asked me to open. It was full of crisp US dollar bills – $5000 in all. When I asked what the money was for, he simply said: "It's for you. I need to be absolutely certain you're *my* man. If you're not, you know what'll happen." He drew his finger across his throat. Of course, it was all wrapped up in matey Javanese, as though it was some kind of joke. And naturally I laughed, as I had to.'

The debrief had produced all the information that Canberra and Washington wanted on the missile deal, but Clarke had insisted that Mason go back for more detail. It was an irrational demand and Mason had protested vigorously, especially in light of the difficulty he and Mochtar had had in arranging just one meeting. He had considered outright refusal, but with Clarke in one of his 'control freak' moods that was unlikely to work. It was his station commander's threat to send him back on the next Qantas flight if he failed to act as instructed that had pushed him to go against his own professional judgement. He feared that if he did leave, Clarke would undoubtedly attempt to contact the agent himself – and that could be fatal, especially with Clarke's intelligence status declared to the Indonesians.

'So, what brings you two together?' the policeman asked, almost forensic in approach.

'We work in artificial insemination,' Mason said.

'In *what*?'

'We're vets on a cattle breeding project in Central Java.'

The policeman was nonplussed, seemingly as much by Mason's capacity to handle Bahasa as by what he had said.

'Fuck me!' he responded, guffawing as he turned to his driver. 'You never know what you'll hear next, do you?'

'Too right!' the other Indonesian said. 'I don't think we'd have much to ask them.'

The policeman agreed. 'Where are you off to, then?' he said, clearly just to be polite.

'Well,' Mason replied, 'my colleague's promised to show me the old Portuguese church out at Kota, but somehow I don't think we're going to get there. He's more interested in a bit of cheap sex.'

'Listen, you animal,' the policeman said to Mochtar, in jest, 'you treat your friend with respect. Now jump in, both of you, and I'll take you over there straight away!'

– – –

Back in Lambert's dining room, Mason found himself laughing, just as he and Mochtar had after the police jeep pulled away and they were safely inside the church. The sense of relief had been enormous. A small group of Italian tourists up near the altar had looked around, wondering what had triggered the pair off. Mason could see the looks on their faces now.

But his thoughts soon returned to Clarke. Just look where the pair of us have ended up, he mused. Bloody Martin's still in the Service and I'm out, but hot on his trail. Intelligence really sucked him in, then pushed him way out of his depth. Yet the clever turd's used charm all along to cover up his defects. If anyone's ever mastered the art of being two people, it's him, but for the very worst reasons.

Only Lambert's call from the kitchen brought Mason back to the task in hand.

EIGHT

Sydney: Mid-May

'There, that's it,' the Cicada said, pointing out a small cottage as he drove slowly past.

Zhang was pleased that 'Chang Zhe Chan' was relaxed in his company. Hopefully it would make it easier to pose the questions Gao and his colleagues had listed for him and which he had lodged in his memory. They wanted as much personal information as possible – and other things, too.

Money had obviously been spent on the house to bring its style and appearance into line with the classy tone of the area. Palm Beach was that sort of place. An hour north of the city, it was a multi-millionaire's playground, with lavish dwellings built into a steep hillside at one end. Most commanded enviable views of the Pacific, with prices to match. The beach itself was spectacular. It had rich golden sands, rows of stately Norfolk Island pines and, often as not, surfers riding the breakers.

They were driving along Ocean Road, which was down on the flat that skirted the beach.

It was a Friday morning and the weather was perfect: not a cloud in sight and a mild breeze washing over the coast. The sea shimmered all the way to the horizon, erasing any worries brought from the city. Casually dressed, both men had the windows down in the Cicada's old BMW. An aroma of freshly cut grass wafted in.

'You know, they've extended the place to double its size,' the Australian said, 'but it's still the same old shack to me.'

Set against an embankment, the cottage sported a fresh coat of paint. Its plain white contrasted with the purples and mauves of lasiandra bushes in full bloom in the garden.

'Of course, my wife virtually owned the place. Her parents bought it as a weekend retreat back before the war. But later the oldies lost interest and spent more time at their other house down beside the harbour.'

On the drive up through the northern beaches, the Cicada had explained to Zhang how he and his family had spent happy summer breaks at the cottage. That was, until overseas postings with ASIS disrupted their visits and other 'unfortunate events' pushed his marriage up on the rocks. This was a story Zhang had not heard before, for the Australian had steadfastly refused — since he walked in five weeks earlier — to discuss his personal life.

Perhaps we could check his identity from the ownership of the house, Zhang mused to himself, though Zhang's need to concentrate on what was being said stopped him from pursuing that line of speculation. Others could do so later.

Gao had had a number of sessions with the Cicada in the meantime, but Zhang had seen him only once, briefly and in the company of Gao. Gao had also paid a quick visit to Beijing, of which 'Chang Zhe Chan' was unaware, and after his return the Australian had agreed to the proposal that vital parts of the bugging story – which the *Sydney Daily Courier* appeared not to know of – be leaked. He had endorsed Gao's logic that if the story were destined to blow anyway, why not have its nature and timing orchestrated by the Chinese themselves?

Today's meeting between the Cicada and Zhang, however, had been arranged at the Australian's request. He was in Sydney for a series of ASIS appointments and had managed to keep a day clear for himself. Would Zhang like to get together? Yes, he would be honoured. And besides, Zhang had a few new kung fu movies to hand over. Gao and his colleagues thought it a good idea, describing it as a classical 'welfaring task'.

The Cicada decided that they should go for a drive and have a picnic. Zhang had no quibble with that. As Gao observed, the further they were from the city, the less likely they were to be spotted; and the more remote the place, the better.

'What I'd really like,' Zhang had said, 'is to get out on the water in, say, a dinghy. I haven't rowed a boat for years. Maybe we could go to some deserted beach and have a snack there. It's not the kind of thing you can ever do in China.'

The Cicada seemed pleased that he could treat Zhang to an experience like this.

The pair had met at eight in the morning. Zhang's wife had packed a hamper and the Australian had booked the boat. On the drive to Palm Beach the Cicada had been unusually open and easy. Early on in the trip he had started to talk about his early adult years: his first love affairs, university, and being recruited into ASIS. It was a turnabout that surprised Zhang, who had no idea why it should be so, beyond the fact that people often seemed to find solace in unburdening themselves to him. With Gao, the Cicada was far less forthcoming on personal matters.

Now the Australian's spirits were high and his sense of humour ran free, like a city dog off its leash. They parked the car and strolled to the southern tip of the beach. The Cicada's pace was casual and slow. Where the sand came to an end a large swimming pool was built into the rocks. Young mothers sat on a bench at its side, enjoying the quiet of the place. Chatting in the sun, they watched their toddlers intently as they played just back from the edge. The Cicada recounted to Zhang a rugby joke that was long and lewd, about a nun introduced to pornography on her first day out of a convent. The Chinese grasped the gist of it quickly, before the punch line was out.

They lingered for a while, looking out to sea and enjoying the breeze. The Cicada shielded his eyes as he spotted a tanker off in the distance. It was making its way down the coast and was too far out to be calling in at Sydney.

'Maybe,' he mused aloud, turning to Zhang and breaking a silence neither had noticed, '*you* should stay here in Australia and *I'll* take your place back in China. What do you reckon?'

'Oh, I don't know about that.'

Shenme yisi? Zhang thought: what the hell does he mean? Is it simply because I like Australia and this country's quality of life? Or is it something sinister, some veiled allusion perhaps to the devious game of treachery he's opted to play? Who knows?

Gao too, had spoken of this phenomenon, of these fleeting glimpses inside his mind. He had described the Cicada as a 'fractured opal': bright greens and blues most of the time, and streaks of black when demons stirred inside.

This is probably typical, Zhang thought, of the mind of a traitor.

'We'd better move on,' the Australian said, checking the time. 'I've booked the boat for ten.'

They ambled back to the car and drove off at a leisurely pace. The dinghy that the Cicada had arranged belonged to a boatshed at Newport, near the head of the inlet known as Pittwater. From Palm Beach, a scenic route round the foreshore would take them fifteen or twenty minutes.

'Say, when am I going to meet your family?' the Cicada suddenly asked, as they turned off the coast road. 'They sound like pretty nice people.'

'Well, I wouldn't argue with that,' Zhang said, rubbing his chin. 'Let me see if I can fix something up.'

It was a commitment he had no intention of keeping. There's no way, he thought, that I'd draw my wife and son into this. But what if Gao and Li say I have to? Where would work stop and privacy start?

'Kids,' the Cicada reflected aloud, 'are fun for a while, but take more than they give. Adults,' he said, 'offer enough of a challenge, without creating new ones to add to the burden.'

Zhang went along with this line, all the time retaining as much detail as possible in the knowledge that the smallest point might be useful to Gao and to Zhou, the psychologist. Gao had warned him that if Zhang himself were to become the topic of conversation, he would need to carefully craft the dialogue to shift the focus back onto the Cicada.

Earlier in the day the Australian had asked him what new experiences he had recently had. Zhang's natural inclination was to talk of his encounter with the piano removalists and the fight at the pub, but he stopped short of letting that out. The involvement of Mason, a former ASIS colleague of the Cicada's, would have to be disguised if he did. No, that was all too close to the bone. But what's left, he had thought, if these kinds of things were always ruled out?

Zhang was not a born liar. He knew that for sure. It was, as Mason had told him, something you had to be able to handle with ease. A spy's life was divided into boxes: big ones for this, small ones for that. It was a maze of separate compartments, and an operative had to straddle the lot. Bits of the real person might spill into this, or seep into that, but it was always contrived and under control. A spy's personality had to be tailored to suit each occasion. As Gao put it, 'an intelligence officer is a man for all seasons, but rarely one for his own'.

Instead, Zhang had mentioned an incident that occurred in his trade job, which elicited an analytical response from the Cicada about the impact on the Australian economy of the Whitlam Government's across-the-board tariff reductions. Zhang was glad he had no need to remember any of that.

Now, with a rare lull in the conversation, the Chinese was about to fill it by changing the subject and asking whether anything had yet been passed on to the *Courier*, when the Cicada pre-empted him by announcing that the boatshed was just down the road. Talk was suddenly overtaken by the observation of how perfect the weather was for a day on the water.

Shit, you've got to be fast, Zhang thought. Maybe spies are more assertive and that's where I'm going wrong. Still, there'll be lots of time on the boat.

He quickly reviewed his mental list of Gao's priority tasks, repeating them in his mind like a mantra, determined to show his colleagues what the intelligent layman could do. He relished the prospect of being able to say to Gao: 'Yes,

Comrade, as you told me, it's all about human relations.'

And the case was clearly worth the effort. Gao had told Zhang that the Cicada's product was of high quality, that his tradecraft was good and that he was generally focused as an agent. Beijing was ecstatic over his product and had stressed a number of times that there was no reason to doubt its veracity. The big questions were why he was doing it and how soon might he feel he had accomplished his goal.

At Newport they found a parking spot without any trouble. The Cicada jumped out and opened the boot. He took out the three kung fu videos that Zhang had given him at Kirribilli that morning. Examining them closely, he was very pleased with one in particular.

'Hey, I hadn't expected this Jackie Chan movie before the end of the year, and here it is now.' He was beaming.

'I've heard that the studio gave it precedence,' Zhang said. 'They wanted to clear the decks for something bigger that he's starring in, so they wound it up early.'

'I can't thank you enough,' the Cicada replied.

'Don't mention it, it's a pleasure. Oh, and by the way, there's something else.' Zhang pulled out a loosely wrapped package and opened it, revealing a small bamboo-framed cage, half the size of a shoebox.

'For cicadas!' the Australian said, immediately recognising its purpose. 'Now where did you get that?'

'In Chinatown. A friend of mine there brings them in from Hong Kong. I thought it might come in useful.'

'Jesus, mate, you can't imagine what this means to me.'

'Well, let's just say I'm happy if you are.'

They unpacked their gear from the boot, taking out two colourful towelling hats, Zhang's old-style cane hamper, and a small plastic coolerbox with a bright yellow lid. This the Cicada regarded as vital and carried himself.

They strolled across to the office, which was not much more than a shed, and were greeted there by a dark-haired young woman in a pale blue shirt. She had the collar turned up and a few buttons undone, displaying her cleavage. Her husband, she explained, had gone to pick up some clients. In the meantime, she would show them to their boat.

'Hey, wait a minute,' Zhang said excitedly. 'Can we go fishing as well?'

'Of course you can,' she replied. 'Not for marlin or anything like that – but, yes, we have runabouts that take you further out than you'll ever get in a dinghy.'

'Oh, look,' Zhang said, turning to the Cicada, 'we can't miss a chance like this. It's the type of thing I dream about when I'm bored with my job.'

Spending a few hours in a faster boat was strictly *not* what the Cicada wanted to do, for reasons he had no desire to share with anyone else.

'Come on!' Zhang said, noticing the look of doubt on the Australian's face. 'What are you worried about?'

The Cicada was in two minds, but feared looking weak and indecisive. 'Are you sure it won't mess up your bookings?' he asked the woman.

'Oh, hell no,' she replied. 'I've got something ready to go straight away, and there's a bit of bait here you can use.'

The boat was a red-hulled affair, wallowing languidly in the water, along with a dozen others of similar colour and size. They were tied to a low-slung wooden jetty that stretched out into the bay, as though floating on the high morning tide. A white metal railing ran the full length of one side, with a cluster of seagulls perched at the end. Zhang felt a pleasant air of expectancy. For him this was Australia at its best.

As they walked along the wooden planking, the Cicada suddenly handed the woman a number of banknotes, which caught Zhang off guard. Gao had insisted that Zhang pay, not for reasons of politeness, but because it was obvious that money was crucial to this walk-in and hence the Chinese should cover all costs.

Don't fight over it now, Zhang thought, but don't forget to raise it later. He stepped down into the boat and the Cicada passed him the hamper and the hats. Next came the cooler-box, packed with one of the Australian's favourite beers, Coopers Ale.

The young woman seated herself in the stern, to one side of the Evinrude outboard. She put the bait away, took up some rods, which were already on the boat, and set about rigging their lines.

'Where do you fellas reckon you'll head off to?' she said, turning to the Cicada, who'd followed her aboard.

'I suppose I'll take my friend out around Lion Island. That's a spot where I once had some pretty good catches.'

She smiled at Zhang. 'You'll love the scenery outside the bay.' It appeared she thought he was a visitor to Sydney with not long to stay. 'That whole foreshore over there,' she said, 'is a National Park – lots of cliffs and huge trees. It's pretty grand stuff, and unspoiled. You'll enjoy it.'

Zhang found the warmth of her voice alluring. 'I'm sure I will,' he said, with a glint in his eye. He was, at heart, a flirt who enjoyed this kind of encounter with women.

'Hey, do you want a beer?' the Cicada said, interrupting to offer her a Coopers.

She declined and he passed it to Zhang, ignoring the fact that the Chinese had said he never drank in the daytime. Zhang accepted it anyway. He had heard from Gao that alcohol and tobacco were tools of the trade, whether a spy liked them or not. With agent-handling, no matter how normal a traitor might be, the act of betrayal brought with it tension, and drinking and smoking seemed to provide some relief.

The Cicada opened another bottle and he and Zhang toasted the prospect of a good catch. When the rods were set up, the young woman climbed out of the boat.

'If you can wait a few minutes,' she said, 'my husband will be back and he'll start up the outboard for you.'

'I think we'll be all right,' the Cicada replied, seemingly eager to take charge.

They waved as she strolled up to the boatshed, looking back briefly at Zhang.

Moments passed as the two men enjoyed the sun sparkling on the water as the wash from a passing cruiser rolled in gently. Zhang was relaxed and the Cicada appeared to be, too. He opened another bottle of beer, his first already gone.

Zhang hoped he wouldn't go through them at this rate, but realised it was a warm day and that his companion did like his drink.

The Australian flicked the bottle-top into the water and moved away from the stern, where he had been sitting next to the outboard. Something had disturbed him, though Zhang had no notion of what it might be. Suddenly, the Cicada shuffled away from the fuel tank as if it were likely to bite him and joined the Chinese on the cross-seat in the middle.

I hope he doesn't expect *me* to start the engine, Zhang thought. 'Oh, by the way,' he said, 'I insist on giving you the money for the boat.'

'No, please don't worry about it. After all, I'm pretty flush with funds these days.'

'But that's cash for *you*,' Zhang said, remembering Gao's edict. 'It's for you to spend on yourself.'

'No, I meant that hefty sum in the Hong Kong trust account. That's set me up for life, in effect.

So you can't deny me a little generosity once in a while.'

'Yes, but they're not funds you can access at the drop of a hat.'

The Cicada's head jerked back. 'And what's that meant to mean?'

'Well, in the sense that the Hong Kong money's probably locked away for a while. Surely?'

The Australian stared at him, bewildered. His face had gone pale.

Zhang suddenly wished he had never raised the subject. Instinct, though, warned him to say nothing more, otherwise he might dig a deeper hole for himself. He smiled, but the Cicada seemed not to notice. He merely shrugged. Then he glanced back at the outboard, then looked at the fuel tank.

'God, a bloody petrol engine!' he said, punching his fist into the seat. 'Just what I need – like a hole in the head!'

Zhang had no idea why this should be so important but knew it would be unwise to ask. The Cicada offered no explanation and in a moment his storm seemed to have passed. But it worried Zhang and put him on full alert.

'Here, have another one,' the Australian said, handing a fresh bottle to Zhang, which he accepted.

The boat rolled lethargically as more wash came in from the bay, with the two of them lulled into silence by the rhythmical movement.

Why, Zhang thought, did his mood change so quickly? Why does he keep eyeing the tank as though it's a leopard about to pounce? Maybe he's allergic to fumes. No, there'll be more to it than that. Perhaps it's a phobia – something from his childhood. Or was it the mention of money? Yes, it must have been that.

The Cicada's face had grown even paler. 'Look, can I help you?' Zhang said, reaching across and patting him on the shoulder.

'No, don't worry,' the Cicada replied. 'It's just that I feel a little queasy.' He seemed appreciative of Zhang's gesture and tried to add something. But before he could, he suddenly lurched to the side of the boat and spewed overboard. It was no short affair, as he brought up everything he'd eaten for a day or more.

Zhang slapped him hard on the back, trying to be helpful.

'I think I might go back to the car for a while,' the Cicada mumbled, when he regained his composure. 'I feel so embarrassed.'

'Oh, come now,' Zhang said. 'You don't have to worry about me.'

'Thanks.'

'Look, why don't we skip the fishing,' Zhang suggested, 'and drive back slowly to the city instead. I'll take the gear up to the car – you go on ahead.'

'Yes, OK. That's a good idea.' The Australian climbed on to the jetty and staggered away, holding the railing.

Before Zhang had lifted anything out of the boat, the young woman came down from the office to help him. She had obviously encountered the Cicada on his way to the car.

Once the gear was packed into the boot, she refunded the money, which Zhang quickly tucked into his pocket. It was something he had no time to think about now. And it was he who drove the car back, while the Cicada, who was nothing but apologetic whenever he stirred, slept most of the way. For that Zhang was grateful, as it gave him plenty of time to replay the day's events over and over in his mind.

'Put simply, Adrian, the Government *doesn't* do things like that,' the deputy secretary from the Attorney-General's Department said.

He was calm and collected but realised instantly that McKinnon had been tipped off. The few details he had just provided vouched for that.

The *Courier* journalist stared him out, allowing only the most sardonic of smiles to show on his face. '*Doesn't?*' he queried, watching the bureaucrat like a hawk

The silence was icy and McKinnon had no intention of breaking it.

The deputy secretary found himself devoid of a line of retreat and opted therefore for a change of subject. But McKinnon jumped in fast. He was not letting go.

Unbeknown to the journalist, the targeting of him and the *Sydney Daily Courier* had been taken to farcical lengths. The Government had ordered ASIO to step up its monitoring of the newspaper's – especially McKinnon's – communications, despite Joe Pellegrini's advice to the contrary. Further, the Attorney-General had issued the *Courier* with a D Notice, warning that if material on the bugging were to be published, national security would be endangered. In all of this, a leaker in Canberra – the same one as before, McKinnon and Hull assumed – had been moved to supply more information. The pair had then readily agreed that McKinnon should fly to Canberra and attempt to interview the deputy secretary, who most investigative reporters were aware handled intelligence matters of this nature.

The request for a meeting had thrown the hierarchy of the Department into confusion, with most of the deputy's colleagues coming down against any direct contact with a journalist who was, effectively, the subject of the D Notice on his newspaper. It would be decidedly improper, they argued. But the Attorney-General himself had endorsed the deputy's view that it would be unwise to refuse dialogue with the *Courier* on the designated topic of 'Government–media consultation on protecting national security'. Stunt or no stunt, it was better to go through the motions. 'See him, and snow him,' the minister said.

But the deputy had never imagined that McKinnon might throw up what he did, as soon as their one-on-one meeting began: the assertion that he was being monitored by ASIO. The cat was clearly out of the bag, though the last thing this mandarin could do was corroborate the fact.

McKinnon's steely gaze cut through him now, like a laser. The deputy was about to speak, when McKinnon broke in abruptly.

'You see, with respect, all your D Notice has achieved is to confirm to us the veracity of the story we're working on. That's why I've been authorised to hand you this letter from the *Courier*, which — perhaps rather irreverently — suggests it's about time the Government got its house in order. If a newspaper, which has none of the resources that Canberra has at its disposal, can get wind of a story like this, how much more might already be known in the broader community?'

The deputy secretary grimaced. That was indeed one of his greatest concerns.

'So, you see,' McKinnon went on after a pause, and with a look that told the other man this was not going to be easy to take, 'it might have been more appropriate for the *Courier* to have served a D Notice on the Government, on behalf of the public, to stop the leaking!'

They knew it was going to be a very long night.

The sky was dark and the moon unlikely to appear. A skittish breeze came in from the south, adding to the chop on the sea below.

This must be the crankiest thing of all time, Lambert thought. *Us* training Chinese spies! Throwing sops to Beijing is meaningless. Now that they know their embassy's bugged, they'll be out to screw us for all they can get. Lambert, and others too, had openly criticised the idea of training the

Chinese, but Foreign Minister O'Sullivan had asked that the proposal be formally assessed.

Lambert checked his watch with a pencil torch. His fair hair was covered with a brown woollen beanie, which he wore down over the ears. The collar of his Army jacket was pulled up high.

'It's two past midnight, Joe,' he said in a low, husky voice.

Pellegrini, his ASIO colleague, sat on an army groundsheet beside him. A nuggety man, he was clad in the same sort of jacket but sported a camouflage hat and had a khaki sweat-rag around his neck.

'Fifteen minutes and they should be hitting the beach,' Lambert added.

'*If* they're on schedule,' Pellegrini said. Never one for patience on training exercises, he had a habit of getting tetchy unless things went like clockwork.

What they were waiting for was a landing by a dozen new ASIS and ASIO recruits who, in a carefully crafted exercise, would come ashore from a submarine and head for a nearby farmhouse where hostages were being held. In reality, the trainees were not going to rescue anyone. Instead, they would be apprehended along the way and subjected to a lengthy and gruelling interrogation at a 'deserted' sawmill, specially rigged with closed circuit TV. This was a common feature of intelligence training courses and much trouble was taken to guarantee authenticity. Trainees were assessed on their capacity to maintain their cover. But could such a course be offered to the Chinese?

(It had worked for others in the past.) That was what Lambert and Pellegrini had been asked to report on.

Positioned atop a high bluff, behind the gnarled stump of a tree, the pair checked out a rocky point below them through their night-vision goggles. The point dipped into the sea like a giant finger running beneath them. When the first inflatable Zodiac dinghy, with four trainees aboard, rounded its tip the action would start.

In his forties, and dark-bearded and balding, Pellegrini had risen fast in the system. Australian-born, of Italian parentage, he had a good intellect, a solid background in electronics and was the opposite of the Constable Plod image that still blighted his organisation. He was of a new generation, as was the perky Lambert in ASIS. The two had met during Lambert's SAS days, when Pellegrini was the sole ASIO participant in a risky Cambodian mission requiring technical knowhow. It was in the course of that venture that the idea had first come to Lambert to move from the military across to intelligence.

'What I'd like to know,' Pellegrini said, 'is who put this harebrained idea into O'Sullivan's mind in the first place. Foreign Affairs says our embassy in Beijing claims the Chinese Ministry of State Security wouldn't consider anything less than fifty on a course like this, if we make an offer. But even Blind Freddie can see they wouldn't be sending their best. They'd hold their smartest back. You don't parade your top talent so everyone knows who they are. OK, nobody's saying you can't make a gesture, but there are certain realities you just can't ignore.'

An owl hooted somewhere back in the scrub, providing a momentary distraction.

'All we'll do,' he went on, 'is let the Chinese check out our strengths and weaknesses – and at a time when on the espionage front they're leaving the rest of us behind in a cloud of dust. They'll be asking themselves: "What the fuck do the Aussies think they'll get out of this?"'

'I agree,' Lambert said, 'but I doubt this was a Foreign Affairs scheme. From what I've heard, the PM asked O'Sullivan to look into what we could offer Beijing if this bugging story blows wide open – even something we could throw their way before it happens. Something that might make us look less like a lackey of the Yanks, which in turn might suggest we were steamrolled into the embassy bugging op by them and that it's basically their show anyway.'

'Sounds like wishful thinking to me,' Pellegrini said, 'and anyhow, this surely can't be the best way of going about it.'

'True, but if you were O'Sullivan and Farnsworth asked you for ideas on China, who would you go to?'

'You mean Bass?'

'Too right I do. I can see his fingerprints all over this. See, in the last few weeks he's started talking a lot about the need for Australian intelligence to "open up new vistas in Asia". Mind you, for a while now he's given the training dimension a wide berth . . .'

Even in the dark, Pellegrini could see Lambert grinning, and he understood why.

'... but, for whatever reason, he's suddenly back on it again. He says the Brits and the French, for example, have made it into a lucrative industry, and we should be doing the same. We certainly shouldn't be letting European int services take our share of the training pie in this part of the world.'

'Well, there's merit in that argument,' Pellegrini said, chuckling, 'but as you and I know, Bass won't be putting this forward simply because it's a good idea. There'll be something more behind it.'

'That's what's worrying me,' Lambert said, though he refrained from mentioning what Mason had raised with him in Canberra a few days before about treachery. He had promised to keep that to himself.

If Bass *is* the one who's sold us out to Beijing, he thought, this is definitely the sort of thing he'd be steering their way.

What Lambert and Pellegrini had been chuckling about was an incident involving Morgandale a few years before, which both had witnessed up close.

A similar, one-off course had been jointly run by ASIS and ASIO for a unit from Kopassus, the Indonesian Army's elite special force. The men had been told that a business tycoon from their home country, who was a friend of their President, had been kidnapped while he and his wife were visiting Melbourne, where their student son lived. And that a rebel group from Aceh was holding them hostage at a farmhouse on the Victorian coast and Jakarta had recommended that the Australian Government use the Kopassus squad in the rescue.

Tougher than most trainees on such courses, the Indonesians had required special treatment. A vigilante group of look-alike Bandido bikies had been put together to test their resistance to interrogation, with Lambert included because of his background in SAS. Waylayed by the 'bikies' on the trek to the farm, the Indonesians were subjected to a wild tirade about Asian migration 'ruining Australia' and then carted off to a sawmill. They had been warned that if they could not explain who they were and why they were carrying weapons, they would be shot. Claiming they were spies on a training course would, clearly, only infuriate their captors.

Morgandale had elected to play a minor role himself, it was said, because he wanted to show that senior management could still contribute in practical ways. What happened was still a taboo subject in the Service, though Martin Clarke, when he got wind of the story, broadcast it widely. While a videotape of the incident was kept under lock and key, pirate copies were in circulation.

For Lambert and Pellegrini, the event was still fresh in their minds.

'You're a fucking liar!' the brawny bikie screamed.

The young Indonesian hardly flinched. Strong and muscular, he sat barechested on a stool in the middle of the room. Half a dozen hostile men – making no secret of their wish to beat him to a pulp – stood around ridiculing him. An electric bulb dangled on a cord from a rafter above, only centimetres away from his forehead. The light was blinding.

'Before, you said it was a three month university course. Now it's only eight weeks. Well, eight weeks, mate, don't add up to three bloody months!'

The room was the toolshed for the sawmill and stank of old grease, rust and stale sawdust. A pungent smell of urine laced the air. It was from other trainees who had had to relieve themselves. The group had been deprived of food, water and sleep for their first 24 hours in custody. All had been interrogated more than once. Requests to use a toilet had seen them shitting outside, guarded by abusive bikies with torches and snarling Alsatians. No paper or water was to hand, which made the degradation that much worse.

'What do you say, liar? Is it three months or not?'

'I've only ever said it was two,' the Indonesian replied, his English clear and his voice confident.

His answer was right, but the interrogator's purpose was to confuse him. He was the toughest trainee in the group, though none of the others lacked grit.

'If you don't tell me the truth, pissant, you won't be leaving here alive!' the bikie roared, close to the man's face.

He was ASIO's top interrogator and played the part to the hilt. His colleagues studied him closely as he tried to break down the Indonesian's resistance, egging him on for effect. One of those watching was Morgandale, who wore a silver-studded, black leather jacket. Lambert stood alongside him, dressed in similar garb.

Suddenly Morgandale interrupted, commandeering the script. 'Leave the bastard to me!' he shouted, stepping forward. 'I'll show 'im not to waste time.'

The interrogator was unamused, but desisted.

No one had any idea what had possessed Morgandale, beyond his well-known propensity for injecting himself into other people's affairs.

Although this unwelcome interference destroyed the momentum that the interrogator had cleverly built up, he refrained from debating the issue. After all, the whole process was being recorded on closed circuit TV, to be played back to the trainees in a wash-up. So what better evidence, he thought, of Morgandale's disruptive behaviour? For ASIO this would be like manna from heaven. Recognised as experts in interrogation, they never took kindly to interference from other parts of the system.

'Come on, all youse out,' Morgandale demanded, hamming it up as he dismissed the others from the room. 'Leave us alone and I'll show ya how to make brown scum like this talk.'

The interrogator said nothing. Instead he signalled to his colleagues to follow him.

Lambert, who was the last through the door, left it ajar. The rest of the bikies headed for the control room to pick up the action on screen, but Lambert chose to stay close. He was concerned about where this might lead.

Morgandale glanced around to check that they'd gone.

'OK, matey,' he said, swaggering in front of the Indonesian before going in for the kill, 'I'll take care of you.'

He pulled up an old wooden chair, reversed it, and sat down in front of the trainee with his stomach to the back of the seat.

'Look, I'll tell you straight out,' he said, in a low, conciliatory voice. 'My pals here are a pretty unsophisticated bunch. They're out for a bit of fun – that's all – and they love to draw blood. But if you give *me* the truth – just a hint of it – we could work up a story to tell 'em. See, there's a hell of a lot of face at stake here, boy, and unless you help save it, they're going to rough you up something terrible. They'll kill you just for the fun of it – all of you – do you understand?'

'Yes.'

'Well?'

'Well what?' the Indonesian said defiantly.

'Well, tell me the truth.'

'I've told you the truth.'

'Don't give me that crap!' Morgandale exploded.

'If that's what you think,' the Indonesian said, 'I can't help you. I'm sorry.'

Morgandale was dumbfounded. He seemed not to have allowed for any response other than what he desired. It threw him off balance.

He quickly realised the tables had turned. The interrogator was himself now under pressure – at least to come up with a new line of attack. In his younger days Morgandale's wits had been sharper. But now, years removed from hands-on experience, he was nowhere near as alert. He had misjudged things badly. Flashing through his mind was his own image on closed circuit TV. He knew that some of those watching understood Indonesians better than he did and had a healthy respect for their pluck and tenacity.

He panicked. 'Listen, you monkey-faced bastard. Don't stonewall me!'

The Indonesian sat tight, but Morgandale noticed him flinch at the mention of monkeys. Most Asians reacted this way. It put an idea into Morgandale's head.

'One of my bikie mates,' he yelled, 'would love to screw the arse off a brown kid like you. How d'ya think that'd sit with your Islamic beliefs?'

He raised his hand to strike the trainee, but before he made contact the Indonesian blocked the move and set upon him. In an instant he had Morgandale in a headlock, with the Australian's arm pinned agonisingly behind his back. It was no mere matter of point-scoring. The Indonesian planned to kill him. He had nothing to lose. Morgandale had pushed him too far. He had made the fatal mistake of leaving himself alone and unarmed with a strong and irate prisoner from whom he had removed all hope of survival.

In a flash, Lambert was into the room. He grabbed the trainee round the neck and pulled him back. It was a furious scuffle, but after a second or two it was clear that Morgandale's life was no longer at risk.

Clarke's deputy had saved the senior man.

'My Government and I would be humbly grateful if you could help in bringing our project to fruition.'

Sherrington smiled as he read the words aloud.

'Holy Jesus, a direct translation from the Japanese!' someone said.

Looking dapper in a white shirt and magenta tie, the Director had his jacket off and sleeves rolled up. He held the letter aloft for his three colleagues to see. Among the best minds in the CIA, they were seated with him in his long, wood-panelled office. One was a woman, the other two were men. He had called them in at ten that morning for a quick review of this intriguing development. The letter they were eager to read had been received by the White House only hours before, then been relayed by the President's chief of staff across to Langley.

Sherrington handed a copy to each of them now.

While they were reading he sat back in his chair, drawing gently on a small Dutch cigar. A packet of Henri Wintermans Short Panatella was never far from his side. None of his colleagues on this occasion were smokers, though they were in no way averse to the sweet smell of his tobacco.

The missive, on the Japanese Prime Minister's letterhead, covered one page.

> Dear Mr President,
>
> Urgency dictates that I write to you on a sensitive matter. My ambassador will elaborate when delivering this letter.
>
> Japanese gas exploration vessels under contract to the Russian Government are working in waters near the island of Sakhalin. A discovery of massive proportions has been made. The Russians have yet to be informed of the find. We believe that a workable development package must be offered at the same time as the discovery is declared.
>
> Crucial to the project's economic viability is the long-term contractual involvement of the Chinese. Regrettably, Beijing has not yet seen fit to convey to us a clear answer on its involvement. We believe this may be due to talks that they and the Australians are apparently engaged in on a possible energy agreement.
>
> My Government and I would be humbly grateful if you could help in bringing our project to fruition. Ambassador Nishimura will acquaint you with our deeper thinking on the strategic

importance of this matter and its positive impact on US interests. We see a vital role for American firms

Yours respectfully,
Masahiro Sakamoto
Tokyo, 19 May

'So, what do you think?' Sherrington said, when his colleagues had finished. He was grinning.

'Utterly Japanese,' his bony-faced deputy replied. 'It tells you everything and nothing. But why come to us so late in the piece?'

'Well, from what the President's told me,' Sherrington said, 'the ambassador was worried about Russian engineers. It seems they're joining the Japanese crews in a week or two, when they'll learn all about the big find. Of course, Tokyo's fears aren't that unreasonable. They have to give the Russians a deal they can't refuse, and they've got to place it on the table at the same time they come clean. Otherwise, Moscow will throw the whole goddamn thing open to the highest bidder and there'll be an unseemly scramble. All the oil and gas majors, including ours, will be in there bribing the Russians to oblivion. The upshot will be a dog's breakfast. Certainly not what we'd want. Hell, it's going to be difficult enough as it is balancing all the different dimensions of this – the economic, the political, the security angle, and a lot more as well.'

'True,' his deputy said, scratching his cheek, 'but one thing sticks out. Tokyo wants to control the *whole* project. That's it. Of course, we all know that without our expertise they won't get it off the ground. And naturally, they want to hog as much as they can, but they're hardly offering us a slice of the action just to be friendly. Why they're buttering us up at this stage is because they need our help to clear a few obstacles.'

'Well, rather than just *needing* our help,' Sherrington's top strategic analyst added, 'I think they're actually *desperate* for it. Frankly, the letter's obsequious. They want something really badly, but haven't got the guts to ask for it directly. Fancy the ambassador meeting with the President on something like this. Aren't we meant to know what they're up to?'

Sherrington grunted, which usually meant 'tell me more'.

'They're shit-scared,' the analyst went on, 'that the Chinese are going to get into bed with the Aussies, and if they do they won't bother with this Sakhalin thing. Or on the other hand Beijing will screw the Japs to the wall on price . . . '

Sherrington nodded, as did the others.

'You can almost hear what they're thinking. They know we'll come down in favour of a project like this. They know we'll see how it'll add stability to Russia, to the two Koreas and even to China. They know we'll warm to the prospect of cheap energy weaning Pyongyang off nuclear power. Let's face it, they're *sure* which horse we'll back. Not that we're against what the Aussies are after. Good luck to them. But they're rich enough as it is, and they're always on our side anyway. They've got nowhere else to go. But if their China deal does come off – further down the track, of course – we'll all be happy.'

Sherrington drew on his cigar then sat forward. He had something to reveal.

'Look, there's another matter that Nishimura raised with the President – something Tokyo wants kept off paper. You see, they have this plan to break Asian gas up into two main blocks – one in the north and one in the south. In the south, they want the Indonesians to link up with the Aussies in a way that gives the Japs, as well as us, backdoor entry into those huge Timor Sea deposits. Then there'll be this new Sakhalin thing in the north. And they want us involved alongside them in both.'

Sherrington's analyst was left with a wry look on his face. It was typical of the Director to allow someone to run in the way he had, before laying a new card on the table.

'Don't you love that bit about the Chinese and the Aussies,' the deputy said, '*apparently* engaging in talks? How tongue-in-cheek. We know the Nips have been busy Down Under screwing that lot senseless. They've spiked the Canberra–Beijing dialogue so that it doesn't produce a damn thing.'

'I gather that wouldn't be hard,' Sherrington said. He rose from his chair and moved back to his desk. Picking up a ruby-red folder, he studied it briefly before turning to his colleagues. 'Fresh in this morning from Sydney,' he said, holding it up.

All three confirmed they had briefly looked through copies of their own before attending the meeting.

The report was headed *Australia: Grounds for Betrayal*. Compiled by Ben Jameson, the CIA's Sydney station chief, it was a thinkpiece on the workings of the Australian intelligence community. It looked at the havoc that one or more strategically placed traitors could wreak. Jameson had assessed the nominal checks and balances and firewalls built into the system to prevent such a thing happening. What caught Sherrington's eye was the station chief's analysis of Australian cronyism – what he called 'mateship' – and the ways in which it negated mechanisms put in place to thwart improper behaviour. No CIA operative in Australia was unaware of the Director's attitude towards Canberra. He was a stern critic of its sloppiness in handling the human factor and the aberrations that that regularly produced. For this reason he had pushed hard and successfully for the National Security Agency to retain American control of the eavesdropping operation in Canberra, which was to be a window on the world of Chinese intrigue.

'Jameson's paper is right on the money,' he said. 'He believes the system in Australia has been subverted by forces that usually get weeded out in other societies – certainly in those where there's a stronger sense of survival. In Australia, it seems, it's the *most comfortable*, rather than the *most competent*, who generally get to the top. Now, it's in this area that Jameson focuses on our greatest concern – the question of how Aussie politicians come to be so dependent upon mediocre types in the intelligence world and other parts of the bureaucracy. He looks at why it is that that clique won't cleanse the system, and how it is that it harbours and protects traitors.

'He goes back into our own Agency holdings on that bunch of Aussie spies and diplomats we've heard about over the years, who are caught up with politicians and judges and the like. "Caught up" in the sense that they're too involved in servicing – what can we call it? – the "quirkier" needs of those types. So there's this network of dependency. You scratch my back, I'll scratch yours. That type of thing. And it's in there that Jameson suspects we'll find our traitor. That's the network that'll shelter whoever it is and give them succour. That's also why he's so much in favour of this guy, Mason. In effect, we've recruited our own "mate" – someone who can drive his mateship network to *our* advantage. Even though the guy's dropped out of the Aussie system, he's still in contact with honest mates inside – people who'll help him help us.'

Sherrington caught the eye of the CIA's tenacious counter-intelligence chief. She would translate all this into housekeeping terms. In her forties, she made no secret of her ambition to become the Agency's first female director.

'Well, I see a number of issues here,' she said, in her cultured Bostonian accent, 'and they're critical to what Beth Cantrell and her associates are grappling with in Sydney. What Jameson's done is to map out the web of rogue forces that

Mason is stalking his prey in. Whoever the traitor is – if indeed there's not more than one – they'll be part of that setup. And, as Jameson stresses, it will give them support and cover as well. So, as Mason closes in on his target, it'll take only one person to see that somebody's scouting around and the whole network will act as an early warning system to tip off the son of a bitch.'

Sherrington nodded, along with the others.

'Another thing,' she went on, 'is the Chinese. We know from the transcript our Japanese friends handed over that Beijing has struck it rich with its agent. That relationship's probably not only productive, but already quite settled. They'll be squeezing it for everything they can get. They'll also be on high alert for any threat to someone like that, and on the look-out for sleuths like Mason.'

'Which reminds me,' Sherrington said, 'has this guy made any headway?'

'He certainly has,' she replied. 'He's targeted key people inside ASIS. Both Jameson and Cantrell were in contact with us an hour ago and they're obviously pleased with his progress.'

'Well, let's make sure he gets all the help he needs,' Sherrington said, glancing at his counter-intelligence chief. 'This treachery's gone on for long enough.'

'The team's expanding fast,' she said. 'They've got another eight people on the ground now, including that gutsy FBI crime-buster, Linda Levi, who we've pulled in on secondment. So in terms of surveillance – physical and electronic –

we're laying a net right over the targets. It's saturation, John, like we don't often do.'

Nobody doubted her word. She usually got the results she wanted.

'Very good,' Sherrington said, turning to his deputy and the analyst alongside him. 'I'd like our stations in Nippon to zap this Sakhalin thing. You know, the better our intelligence, the harsher our demands on Tokyo in return for our help. I'd also like a thinkpiece on where this whole gas thing is heading. What happens if the Japanese get their north–south idea up and running? Where do US interests lie? Then there's the question of the embassy bugging and how the Chinese will make us and the Aussies pay for conniving against them. Canberra's all on its own on this one, with no leverage to speak of, and you can bet your bottom dollar the Chinese will exploit it ruthlessly. What can we do to assist? After all, none of our allies is perfect. And in the end, the Aussies are probably as good as we get, even if we *do* have to give them a hard time to clean up their act.'

This caused a ripple of mirth.

'All in all,' Zhang said, 'the only two things I think explain it are the possibility of petrol fumes and the mention of money. It certainly wasn't the alcohol.'

He had just described to his colleagues his experience with 'Chang Zhe Chan' – now commonly referred to as 'Chan' – at Pittwater a few days before.

'And it was the question of access to the Hong Kong trust account that seemed to worry him most.'

The group had gathered to review not only that development but something far more disturbing: the Cicada had missed a scheduled meeting with Gao in Sydney and had not called in on the designated number to reset the date. Moreover, the mobile he had been given was turned off.

Ambassador Li, like the other Chinese sitting around on the homestead's flag-stoned verandah, was silent. The consensus was that Zhang had gone straight to the nub of the issue, and it was one that was of vital importance to China in the strategic energy game it was currently playing.

It was just on eleven on 20 May and the sun was bright on this clear autumn day. One long wispy cloud, like a strand of scoured wool, hung over the mountains to the west.

Li and his deputy sat with Gao, Zhang, and Zhou – the psychologist – who had come down from Sydney. With them were the Canberra embassy's intelligence chief, Deng, and two of his offsiders.

The place they were meeting at was a secure retreat for the Chinese when sensitive matters had to be discussed. A few hours' drive from Canberra, it was a sprawling tract of land which had as its centrepiece an historic, two-storey Georgian mansion. Surrounded by a colonnaded verandah, the house stood on a rise among a profusion of mature English trees, yellow now in their autumn garb. The property was owned by a Malaysian–Chinese industrialist, Lee Kong Yam – otherwise known as Winston Lee – who was from the same clan and town in China as Ambassador Li, and who also played a unique intelligence role for the embassy.

In Sydney, Gao and Zhang had already analysed the Cicada's behaviour, together with Zhou, who had tracked the case from the start, five weeks before. They had also considered the possibility that he had taken fright and that they might not see him again. And worse, that someone may have twigged to what he was doing and informed the authorities. But now the ambassador wanted his Canberra colleagues to hear what Zhou thought.

'What do you think has happened?' he asked.

'Well, as Zhang's explained,' she said, 'I also feel it's a mix of Chan's past and his present. There's no doubt that some phobia from his formative years could explain the man's reaction to any fumes present or to the water. Remember how Gao and Zhang told us about the trouble he had with the fish tank at the Golden Orchid in Sydney. But the main thing is the present, and what is obviously his dire need for money.'

Both Gao and Zhang were nodding. It was encouraging for them to hear Zhou, on their behalf, articulating their views in her own independent way.

'Again,' she continued, 'you'd recall how he urged Gao at the restaurant to increase the amount in the trust account. Now, what I think might have happened is he's tripped over his own expectations. Maybe he's forgotten that we agreed that the million and a half was only *his* after three months of continuous service. It's possible, too, that he misunderstood Zhang on the question of access and thought Zhang meant that red tape might somehow double the period. Whatever, we now know that, for him, getting his hands on that money is crucial. But why, I can't say.'

Li turned to Gao for a comment.

'No, I can't say, either. But it's certainly got me thinking.'

'So, will we get him back into harness?' Li said, addressing the group as a whole.

'Yes,' said Deng, who was Gao's nominal superior. 'I'd say the odds are in favour of that.'

Laconic at the best of times, Deng had had little to say all along, which gave his pronouncement even more weight. Nobody disagreed, least of all Zhou.

'I think that's right,' she said. 'Up in Sydney we've considered this carefully and we think that, above all, his need for that money – call it his holy grail, if you will – virtually guarantees he'll be back. Also, though to a lesser degree, there's the new sense of purpose he appears to have gained from helping China out in this way.'

'And why do you think he's failed to make contact?' Li said.

'Well,' Gao replied, 'we believe it might be his way of saying: "Look, understand my priorities and don't get in my way."'

Li glanced around the group, but nobody had anything to add.

'*Hao le!*' he said: I see. He went on: 'That's all very interesting. But of course we still don't know, do we, if he managed to plant the rest of the eavesdropping story?'

'Correct,' Gao responded, as images flashed through his mind of his lunch with his boss, Wang, in Beijing.

'What do we do about that?' Li asked.

Gao thought for a moment as the others watched quietly. Ultimately it was his case, they knew, and only he could decide on the best course of action. No one could recall an occasion when Gao's judgement had proved faulty.

'Look,' he said, 'why don't I give him another day to come through, then I'll leave a message pressing him to make contact fast?'

He turned to Zhang as he spoke, the only other Chinese to have met 'Chan'. He agreed, as did Zhou.

'Of course, while we're waiting,' Li said, 'we're stuck with the spectre of those Nipponese *guizi* and the dirty games they love to play.'

Never averse to matching wits with Tokyo, the ambassador had endless ploys in his arsenal with which to foil Japanese smugness. Alongside other senior officials in Beijing, he knew enough to checkmate Tokyo more or less whenever he wanted.

'Well, if we can't use the media to spur the Government here into action,' he reflected aloud, 'we'll have to take a different tack entirely

– one that'll stop the *guizi* interfering in what we're trying to achieve with Canberra.'

The others leaned forward instinctively. Something heady was in the air.

'You may not be aware,' Li said, 'but the Matsutomo Corporation – that mob leading the charge against us here – has a few choice skeletons in its cupboard.'

He paused to light a cigarette, then took his time settling back in his chair, cradling the ashtray in his lap.

'You see, Matsutomo's brokered some huge trade deals with China lately, and many of them have been paid for with Japanese aid money. Now, that wasn't really justified in any sense, but it's come about because senior cabinet ministers in Tokyo used their influence to swing contracts Matsutomo's way. In return for kickbacks, of course.'

A gentle breeze carried the old man's smoke slowly out over the garden, where shocks of rust-coloured chrysanthemums marked the border of a freshly cut lawn.

'Naturally, *we're* not complaining. All we want is the business, however it comes. But the point is, they don't know that we know what they're up to, and even if they did, they'd probably assume we wouldn't care anyway.'

No one was surprised. This was common practice with Japanese firms, often desperate for business. Nevertheless, they were intrigued to know what Li envisaged building on this base.

'So, if we were to feed a story like this to the Japanese media, it'd burst like a bombshell, especially in their Parliament. There'd be some sort of inquiry – the usual perfunctory affair, needless to say. Hardly one intended to do more than slap a few people on the wrist. But it would keep Matsutomo pinned down agonisingly for the rest of the year, and that'd stop them queering our pitch here in Australia. Let's face it, with that in the news, the locals they're paying off here would be far more circumspect about doing Japan's bidding.'

His sardonic smile made the rest of them chuckle.

'Unquestionably, I'd prefer to run with the eavesdropping story. I'm sure that's a much faster way of getting what we want from this amateur bunch.'

The message in this for Gao came through loud and clear.

'Martin, it can't go on like this. There's no way I can defend you unless something changes – and radically.'

Clarke stared at the floor as Hestercombe spoke.

Despite the ups and downs they had been through, he trusted the ASIS chief. They had survived much together, including things that evoked little pride in either. Nonetheless, he had a lurking suspicion that Morgandale was involved in this turn of events.

'I've had that sanctimonious prick from AG's – the one you've got offside on the bugging committee – on my back to bring you to heel. And now, after *yesterday's* performance, I've had the head of Foreign Affairs badgering me as well!'

Hestercombe's stern look said it all.

The same Foreign Affairs official who Clarke had harassed at the meeting in the Attorney-General's Department had been present at a discussion on diplomatic cover for ASIS spies at new stations in Asia. While obliged to provide such slots for the Secret Intelligence Service, Foreign Affairs nevertheless had the upper hand when it came to the allocation of cover ranks and duties. Knowing this, the official had asked Clarke – discreetly, and away from the others at the meeting – not to be disruptive. But Clarke had still managed to cause a disturbance. It was the Service's loss, for the meeting had adjourned without any firm decision, which now left Hestercombe in a tricky position.

'Look, I'll be frank, Martin,' he said, 'I've had a number of people say recently that they'd far prefer Todd – that whenever *he* stands in for you, things run smoothly. If you see what I mean?'

Clarke glanced up and caught Hestercombe's eye, as much as to say: 'Your emphasis only rubs salt into the wound.' Images of Morgandale haunted him now.

The Director-General was the same age as Clarke, and though originally a diplomat, he had managed to keep the spy service out of serious trouble for nearly ten years. Survival for him came through a network of past colleagues and friends in the bureaucracy, who helped out when things in ASIS went wrong. It was mateship at its best, although, perversely, sometimes also at its worst. But anything intangible, like what confronted him now, he found irksome. And that was what Clarke had become: inexact and unreliable. He had always been lively, but very controlled, which meant there was a consistency in his ways that made him predictable. His charm and wide-ranging contacts had helped the Service out on many occasions, especially when things went awry with Asian intelligence liaisons. Admittedly, his Midas touch of earlier years had worn off, but his track record was still talked about by some in the system. Yet now his behaviour posed a serious challenge.

'OK, Martin, I won't go on, but you know my position.'

Hestercombe waited, hoping that some explanation might be forthcoming, but Clarke had nothing to offer.

The chief stopped himself going through a list of possibilities in his mind. He had already done that too many times. Even close confidants who knew Clarke well had no idea why he had become so cantankerous. Perhaps, some said, the strain of past work in the field had caught up with him. 'The bastard's plain burnt out,' Morgandale conjectured. 'God knows what he's got himself mixed up in.'

'Look, what if I arrange for some counselling?' Hestercombe said.

He saw this as an indirect way of broaching the question of Clarke either relinquishing his position to Lambert – if not to somebody else – or of leaving the Service.

'You and I know, Martin, that counselling can be fixed up discreetly and securely. It doesn't have to be some shrink in Canberra with lots of clients in this incestuous place. I personally know of someone quite good up in Sydney.'

He assumed that if Clarke had already considered parting ways, he might have a few ideas of his own. But then, if he had, he would have mentioned them. Arrgh! It was all so frustrating.

Clarke looked to one side, then back down at his hands. 'Thanks for your concern, Bill, but it's not what I'm after.'

'But Martin, can't *I* know what's bugging you?'

Silence.

Hestercombe was determined that Clarke would not leave the room until they'd got somewhere. 'You know, my friend,' he said, softening his tone, 'others have quit the Service and done very well. Think of Stirling in Thailand, for example. He's made a neat business for himself up there and earns ten times what he did with us, *and* he's still in regular contact. You could virtually say he's still on our books.'

Clarke nodded in a way that suggested there might be mileage in this.

'And what about Poulson and Imlach?' Hestercombe persisted, naming the two long-serving ASIS officers who had recently left. 'They've got Indonesia sewn up, *and* they're throwing business our way as well.'

Clarke grimaced, which made Hestercombe

realise he could have chosen a less sensitive case. After all, Clarke had taken their resignation much harder than most. Nevertheless, it was a fact that Clarke had a soft spot for Jakarta and regarded it as one of his main arenas of success.

'Shit, Martin, with your contacts there, it wouldn't take long to get something off the ground. And I could throw things your way as well. All that welfaring stuff with their intelligence mob, bringing them down here on swans, marlin fishing off the Reef – it's endless. We could run all that through you. And I could put you on a retainer. Let's be frank, you wouldn't really be leaving.'

'Well,' Clarke said, 'give me time to think about it.'

Wouldn't really be leaving, eh? he mused to himself. Bill's more concerned about his own future than about mine. Well, we'll see. It's amazing that, while he knows me so well, he's still totally unknowing.

Hestercombe had long ago confided in Clarke his own ambitions for retirement. His plan was to establish an Asian business consultancy, which would allow him to exploit his high-level contacts with intelligence services across the region, in addition to his unquestioned access inside Australia. He would effectively be running a private espionage agency, handling everything from government policy assessments to strategic and security advice. And as Clarke knew only too well, little if any of this would be aimed at enhancing Australia's national interest. His own assistance, he had been told more than once, would be important in getting this venture up and running.

And now this, Clarke thought. It's nothing short of betrayal. He gave a faint smile, which offered Hestercombe a touch of hope, as it was intended to do.

'Martin, take a few weeks, but for Christ's sake cool it. Don't give me any more trouble, right?'

'I'll do my best.' As Clarke turned to go he hesitated, then looked back at Hestercombe. 'I'll admit, Bill, that I can sometimes be less than discreet, but what you need to watch out for is that you don't whip up another firestorm. You and I both know how clever Bass is at playing that game. God only knows what his secret agendas are a cover for.'

The comment made the intelligence chief think. Morgandale was notorious for using disinformation to surround someone with heat, dextrously turning it up until his target self-combusted. Either that or the system demanded that the source of danger be removed before the fire broke out. This same tactic had had a lot to do with the recent resignation of the two experienced ASIS officers.

Yes, Hestercombe thought, that was certainly something he needed to take into account. But it was odd. Here he had Martin casting aspersions on Bass's loyalty, while Bass himself had been doing the same to Martin just a few hours earlier. It was bizarre.

NINE

Tokyo: Sunday, 21 May

'*Kampai*,' Toshio Nakagawa said, responding to his boss's toast.

He had arrived in Tokyo not long before the dinner with his president was due to begin, summoned to the Corporation's headquarters at short notice.

Both took a sip of whisky, then put their glasses back down on the black-lacquered table. They had already dispensed with their jackets and were relishing the cool conditioned air that wafted over the tatami mats on the floor of the room. It was a welcome respite from the heavy humidity outside. Elegant and exquisitely Japanese, this was the inner sanctum of the exclusive Odakaya Inn – a meeting place for business leaders and conservative politicians.

'Let me tell you, the Government here is under real pressure,' the president said, adopting a more intimate tone. It spoke of a willingness to take the younger man into his confidence.

'*Ah, so desu ka?*' Nakagawa replied, deferentially: I see.

'I believe you're acquainted with Yoshida from the Cabinet Research Office,' the president said.

Nakagawa nodded. The name gave him his first inkling of why he had been called up from Sydney, though he knew it would have to be related to energy matters.

'Well, he invited me round yesterday for a friendly chat, which — of course — is why you're here now. You're no doubt unaware of what they're up to with this gas business, but here's the story. And it's Top Secret too — as hush-hush as all that funding Yoshida's had channelled through to us.'

The president was a dignified and gracious man, with a reputation for being as hard as steel. In his sixties, he was an ex-rugby champion who tackled business like the game. Seated opposite him on the floor on a gold-covered cushion, Nakagawa was the son-in-law of the Corporation's chairman, though this brought him no special favours — that is, beyond a close but unseen watch that management kept on him in case his outspoken behaviour were to embarrass the firm.

'You see,' the president continued, 'Japan has less than two weeks before Russian engineers board our drilling vessels off Sakhalin. Then they'll get to see the extent of what we've discovered.'

Nakagawa was silent.

'So the Government's desperate to stitch up a package that Moscow will readily accept, but it can't get the economics of all this locked into place until China signs on as the main customer. And the Chinese, of course, are playing hard to get.'

Ah, the picture unfolds, Nakagawa thought. That explains all this antipathy towards the Chinese and Australians linking up.

'*Yappari, Chugoku no senryaku ga miyasui daro,*' the president said, with a typically masculine Japanese drawl: let's face it, Beijing's strategy isn't hard to pick.

Nakagawa, who was thinking the same thing, grinned. He listened with great interest.

'Naturally, those Chinese crooks are out to screw us senseless.' The president's use of such an intimate term was itself a gesture.

'I'll tell you what they're after,' he went on. 'Those bastards want Tokyo to feel China's got bigger and better things going for them in Australia. Actually, Yoshida's off to Beijing with a negotiating team tomorrow and he needs to know from us how much we've been able to slow things down. That is, down there in your *nawabari.*'

This one word put the spotlight on Nakagawa, making him feel far less relaxed. It denoted the beat that a criminal gang had under its control and its connotations pointed directly to the younger man's responsibility, indeed obligation, to deliver the goods, no matter the price or method involved.

'So, my friend, the leading question is whether this China–Australia deal is dead in the water or not. Or at least, weighed down enough to stop it making any progress.'

Though Nakagawa felt pressured, he remained confident that what he had to report would satisfy the charter given to his company by the Japanese Government.

'Well, it's not actually *dead*,' he said, 'by which I mean it's still on the agenda and being talked about. But, yes, I think we can safely say it's come to a halt, certainly in terms of anything realistic happening in the foreseeable future.'

'So we've bought a little time then for Yoshida and his band?'

'Definitely. That's what the gentleman asked for and that's what we've provided. You might tell him that the Chinese have no real leverage any more. Either they cut themselves into our Sakhalin deal as fast as they can or they'll be left out in the cold. The Australians could dither for years, especially with the "guidance" they've been getting from us. The plain fact is, China won't get any long-term commercial gas development in Australia unless Canberra coughs up concessionary finance and lots of other sweeteners as well. But the Australians, with a little help from us, aren't going to give them what they want, no matter how much pressure Australian business puts on Canberra to make it economically viable.'

'Well, that's very encouraging,' the president said, smiling wryly. 'As you'd imagine, Yoshida's concerned that Matsutomo's activities might blow back on the Government, and of course *I'm* concerned they might blow back on the company.'

He left his words hanging, which meant it was up to Nakagawa to assure him that all was well and non-attributable.

'I don't wish to sound smug, Shacho San,' Nakagawa said, using the president's formal title, 'but it's a well-oiled machine we have down there. You see, we've filtered money through to key people right across the energy field and they've responded. In terms of security, we've been extremely careful. We never show a Japanese corporate face on these sorts of things. In fact, we have a classical operator in Sydney who does it all for us. He's an Australian who's been with Matsutomo for twenty-odd years – smooth, wily and utterly reliable. A few months back I – or rather *we* – moved him off Matsutomo's books and made him an independent operator. Nothing's actually changed in the relationship he has with us, nor with his contacts. It's just that he's one stage removed and spends much more time in Canberra.'

The president's gentle nod spoke of satisfaction.

'And you're the prime coordinator of all this "intelligence work"?' he said.

'*Hai*,' Nakagawa replied, a note of pride seeping in: yes. 'It's one of the more interesting roles I play in Australia.'

'*Ah, so desu ka?*' the president said.

Though he had had only one brief meeting with Yoshida on the previous day, he could see how this subordinate had got up the bureaucrat's nose during Yoshida's visit to Sydney.

'*Gomen kudasai*,' a soft, feminine voice called from outside, interrupting the president's thoughts: begging your pardon.

A sliding door opened gently and two maids appeared. They were dressed in kimonos, one in peppermint green and the other in pale pink. The pair sat on the backs of their feet and were apologetic in the extreme. Laid before them on the floor were trays of sweetmeats, which they sought permission to bring in.

'*Dozo, dozo*,' the president said: go ahead.

They shuffled across and proceeded to lay out upon the table a variety of dishes. Each was a taste treat, with qualities as aesthetic as culinary. Two fresh whiskies were also included. The smell of grilled fish, soy sauce and pickles mingled with the draughts of cool air coming into the room.

The men were silent as the ritual took place. This was not out of fear of talking in front of the staff. Rather it was a matter of savouring a few moments of quiet. In Japan, silence was in no way sinister, which was too often the case in the West.

Alone, they picked at the food with their chopsticks.

'I'm seeing Yoshida again in the morning,' the president said, 'so I'm pleased to be able to tell him we've successfully handled the task. Mind you, I did ask if I could bring you along too, to explain how we did it, but Yoshida was adamant I come by myself.'

Nakagawa shrugged, stung by an honour withheld. His boss seemed not to perceive the hurt.

'You never know,' the president said, 'he might want to raise something politically sensitive. It may be that Indonesian thing that's been brought back to life.'

It was apparent from Nakagawa's expression that he knew nothing of this.

'Look, keep it to yourself, but a few years back the Government asked us to "plant a few seeds" in Jakarta. They had an idea of creating a southern oil and gas bloc, with Indonesia and Australia joining forces to develop those Timor Sea deposits. Of course, Tokyo would have to cough up the capital and help set the price. It was clever thinking at the time, but never got off the ground. Now, with Yoshida and his strategists working on this Sakhalin thing in the north, I gather he'll want us to heavy the natives down south again. The brown ones in Indonesia and the white ones in Australia. If that's what he's up to, he may need to call on your intelligence skills as never before.'

Nakagawa smiled politely, but something inside him had snapped.

He had a background unlike most Japanese, which allowed him to see the games that Japan played in a much broader context, and hence the shortsightedness they entailed. He was growing tired of his role as just another automaton in this overall system, someone whose talents were there to be turned on and off like a light switch.

He wasn't sure how much longer he could take it. There had to be more to life than this.

'My God, what's that?' Elizabeth Cantrell exclaimed. Rounding a thicket of young eucalypts on the narrow bush track, she had spotted a grand Gymea lily off to one side. It stood five metres tall, its stem capped with blood red, bell-shaped flowers.

'That's one of our most unusual plants,' Mason said. 'It's a relic of prehistoric times. Only grows on the coastal strip near Sydney.'

The two were in natural parkland at Balgowlah Heights, a wealthy residential area facing the outer harbour and the Pacific. Luxury homes bordered a large tract of bush, which dropped away sharply to cliffs and the sea. The scenery was spectacular and attracted walkers and photographers.

Cantrell stood in awe of the size of the plant. It made her feel like a midget. Mason had been walking ahead to clear branches hanging over the path. He stepped behind her now and put his arm around her shoulder. It was an instinctive gesture and one that typified the close working relationship they had enjoyed in Indonesia.

Arriving at Balgowlah Lookout early in the morning, they had found a Saturday art group setting up easels. It was a fine, brisk day, with a shimmer across the sea that made the water look inviting, despite the chill in the air. They were only a third of the way down the track to Washaway Beach when Cantrell discovered the huge lily. It was her first time in Australia and in the ten days she had been in Sydney she had warmed to the place. Her delight in the outdoors reminded Mason of her interest, seven years back, in escaping Jakarta to explore remote parts of the archipelago.

On the previous day, Mason had returned from a visit to Canberra where he had begun questioning contacts. Todd Lambert in ASIS had readily confided what was going on inside the Service. He had had suspicions himself about the two key suspects, Morgandale and Clarke. Information that others in Canberra had produced also reinforced the picture emerging. ASIO and the Defence Signals Directorate had come up trumps. One solid contact in each – particularly Joe Pellegrini in the former – had opened up liberally. Mason's quest had quickly tapped a body of angst among contacts troubled by Canberra's incapacity to cope with high-level security threats.

Meanwhile, in Sydney, Cantrell had coordinated a surveillance operation involving over a dozen American officers, some of them FBI specialists. Working from information passed on by Mason the group had monitored phone lines and uncovered promising leads.

Cantrell had collected Mason from the airport and the two had gone straight to a CIA safe house near the city. There they linked up with Jameson, the local station chief, and some of his associates who had flown in from America. One was Linda Levi, the FBI crime-buster and forensic psychologist. Over a sushi takeaway, the group had correlated the intelligence now coming in. All of Mason's and Lambert's initial targets for treachery had been screened. Surveillance had unmasked illegal activity on the part of some — money laundering, smuggling via the diplomatic bag — that would require separate investigation.

Cantrell's team had confirmed the probability of either Clarke or Morgandale being the culprit, with Pellegrini agreeing. The team's energies would now be focused on these two men, as much to expose their networks as to verify the likely betrayal.

In Canberra, Mason had spoken frankly with Pellegrini about what was under way. As ASIO's technical chief, he could provide vital assistance.

'Look, Greg,' he said, 'my strong inclination is to play an active role, and I will in some form. But I need time to decide. Actively joining your Aussie–US team would be a quantum leap. It has all sorts of implications for a person in my position — professional as well as ethical. Please, leave it with me.'

He had agreed to come to Sydney over the weekend to explain his decision. Cantrell and Mason were to meet him at eleven at the Lookout. But now, sitting on a rock ledge with the sea below and plenty of time to spare, they were enjoying the view.

'Who'd have thought,' Cantrell said, 'that you and I would find ourselves with a challenge like this — possibly exposing Martin as a goddamn traitor?'

'You can say that again,' Mason replied, laughing. 'It's one hell of a surprise. But with all he did to me, it brings up a classic conflict of interest. Checking him out is one thing; staying impartial is another. I can't afford to jump to conclusions, nor have it said that I'm riddled with prejudice. But yes, the prospect of putting that bastard away for the rest of his life does get me excited.'

He realised this might be going too far, even with Cantrell. 'If only in private,' he quickly added.

She smiled, sympathising with the sentiment. Clarke had destroyed not only Mason's marriage but also his career. Inevitably there was a legacy of bitterness. What worried Cantrell was that it seemed to have turned into angst, manifested sometimes in flashes of temper – nothing serious, but it had not been there before. Personally, she was saddened to see Mason's spirit sapped in this way.

'You know, Greg, I'll be as happy as you if that's the way it pans out. In fact, I hope that's what he gets. But naturally, for both of us, that can't be a goal in itself. We have to display perspective in front of the team. Both of us have to bend over backwards to be seen to be fair.'

Mason was encouraged by this inclusion of herself in the dilemma. It was a long way for Beth to have come, in light of her earlier fascination with Clarke. Despite Mason's close friendship with her, he had still not reconciled in his mind the fact that she had been close to the man. Her appearance in Sydney only reopened old wounds, even if the warmth that she brought was so welcome.

The problem confronting the pair, however, was a delicate one. Simply informing the combined team of their earlier involvement with one of the suspects might not be enough. Levi had already stated that, while knowledge of this kind could be crucial in assessing a target, its value disappeared entirely when professionalism and detachment were overtaken by personal antipathy. And Levi, who had the eyes of an eagle, would be watching for slippage.

'Well, Greg, two minds are better than one. I'll keep a watch on you, if you keep an eye on me. We'll be the epitome of balance and Linda won't pick up a thing – if we're lucky. You realise, of course, that she excels at forensic pursuits. Apparently she was an academic at Yale when the FBI called her in to crack some difficult case. Then she was persuaded to stay full-time. She's agreed to spend a week or two in Sydney to help track down our traitor, and Sherrington's keen for this to happen quickly – not only to show that the Agency and the Bureau *can* work together, but before some new priority drags her back to the States.'

How fast is fast? Mason thought.

'While you were down in Canberra,' Cantrell said, 'Linda checked all the data we have on your suspects. She's impressed, you know, with what she calls the "clinical way" you go about things. The rest of the team, incidentally, feel the same.

The consensus, Greg, is that we've chosen the right person.'

Mason shrugged, but he was heartened by the compliment. This confirms I was right, he thought, to throw in my lot with the Yanks. They obviously see value in a past that I've had to close off on. At last wheels are turning and with a bit of luck what's happening now might lead to a clean-up of ASIS – something long overdue, something that could never take place from within.

The strength of his conviction shocked him. Hell, I'm in deeper than I thought. This is driving me . . .

Cantrell cut short his ruminations.

'Anyway,' she went on, 'Linda's homed in on Morgandale with a vengeance. She didn't raise it at yesterday's meeting, but others have picked up on comments she's made. She's probably waiting for more evidence before she lays her cards on the table. In brief, she's riveted by Bass. It seems there's a certain "smell" about him and she's right on to it. She may be mistaken, but let's face it, her reputation says she's rarely wrong. For the time being at least, we'll have to give her all the leeway she needs to check him out thoroughly. Any activity on Martin will have to play second fiddle until she's convinced he warrants further attention – beyond what I'll make sure we maintain as a matter of course.'

'That's fine with me,' Mason said. 'After all, they might both turn out to be traitors.'

'Actually, at the moment, Greg, Linda's looking for links between the two. She's wondering whether they mightn't have something going together, even if they are direct opposites.'

Mason nodded. He had no objection, though he thought the chance of Clarke and Morgandale collaborating was negligible.

Beth Cantrell gazed at the sea. A sleek white liner was moving out through the Heads, its wash glinting in the sun. 'Talking of opposites,' she said, 'how different the quietness of this place is to the frenzy that's brought you and me back together.'

Mason was pleased that this remark was about them rather than about the roles they were playing. Both of them had been tossed around by life, he reflected, which gave them a lot of things to share.

Beth had been married in her mid-twenties, and happily so, but after five years her husband – a US Air Force pilot – had been killed in an accident in the South China Sea. Mason was aware that, for her, no relationship had lasted after that.

They lapsed into silence. The magic of the place pushed everything aside, until the sudden cry of a currawong brought them back to the present.

Their swim at Washaway Beach was not planned. They climbed down the cliff to the sand, twenty metres below. It seemed precarious to Beth until Mason showed her the footholds cut in the sandstone by long forgotten locals. Regulars who ventured down there looked after the 300-metre stretch of beach that it boasted when southerly swells hadn't reduced it to a rocky ledge.

On this crisp, sunny morning it was at its best and the sea was enticing. No one was around, so the pair stripped off and dived in, their preoccupations discarded along with their clothes. The hour they spent there was refreshing and pure, free and content. Apart from weekend runabouts fishing offshore and green-and-yellow ferries plying the harbour, Sydney could be a thousand kilometres away.

Back at the Lookout, they waited for Joe Pellegrini. It was close to eleven and he would arrive at any moment by taxi. The three of them would then take a bush track to the seaside suburb of Manly, a walk that would give Beth and Mason's ASIO friend a chance to talk. Pellegrini had already provided informal assistance. The question was whether he would come on board as a fully fledged member of the team. Lambert had made his choice and was standing with Mason, but both were keen to have Pellegrini alongside.

Mason leant against the railing at the carpark as Beth wandered off to take in the view. She scanned the horizon, overawed by the breathtaking expanse of the ocean. Back we go into our professional moulds, she mused, savouring the time they had spent on the beach. For a while this morning, she thought, he was his old self again – as he had been in Indonesia – impish, freewheeling and full of wit. And he was even cajoling her into taking up scuba diving.

'Come on, Beth,' he'd said, 'snorkelling's for kids!' It was as though he'd finally closed off on the worst of the past. But now she'd stepped into his life and rekindled it all, not only his old addiction to the int game, but his obsession with how it had stuffed up his life . . .

'Off with the fairies?' Mason called out.

'No, just thinking. Places like this help me see things more clearly.'

'OK, we'll run with it,' Don Hull said.

For the first time in weeks, he spoke confidently inside his office. A short time before, the best electronic sweepers in town had given that part of the *Courier*'s premises a clean bill of health. Hull had ordered this done, following Adrian McKinnon's initial tip-off that he was under surveillance.

Despite the 'all clear' from the sweepers, Hull still turned away from the window as he addressed McKinnon and the paper's news editor. They were the only others in the room. Seated at his piled desk, he was conscious of the jamming device the team had installed, which he could activate whenever he was at work in the place. It would stop ASIO, ASIS or anyone else from playing infra-red beams on the window and picking up speech patterns from vibrations on the glass.

'Yes, this is good enough for me,' Hull said. He had just read another of McKinnon's latest haul of classified documents. 'See, I wanted to be sure about Canberra not having the degree of control it should have and about Australia being disadvantaged as a result. If that's not in the public interest for readers, what is? *Our* obligation is to disclose. The readers' is to judge what we've printed. And to hell with the D Notice.'

Both McKinnon and the news editor nodded.

The papers they were examining left no doubt that the public needed to know. The three had pored over them for the past hour, missing lunch in the process. McKinnon had collected the sizeable package at a rendezvous with a Canberra contact of Jeremy Torrens, his colleague in Beijing. Torrens had got a safe message through which vouched for McKinnon's credentials and for the story he was working on. The person concerned was an interceptor with the Defence Signals Directorate and he had driven to Sydney that morning to hand over the wad of 300-odd sheets. A meeting had been arranged with the greatest of care, avoiding contact by phone or any other means vulnerable to attack.

The source was impeccable, and was someone Torrens had known since university days when they studied Mandarin together. He was responsible for liaison between DSD and the two American technical officers based in Canberra to handle raw feed from the embassy bugging. All three got on well, in effect speaking the same professional language. Electronic eavesdropping was an art form that bound practitioners together like nothing else could – at least in the English-speaking world of espionage.

His job was to process the yield passed on to the Australian side by the Americans, following detailed analysis in Washington. It was his task to divide the material into specialised items. Over time, he had noticed marked discrepancies between his US colleagues' comments on what they had gleaned, and what eventually wended its way back to Canberra. This was especially so in the case of economic and trade matters, where competition between the two countries was keen. Bugged Chinese conversations on pricing and tonnages of wheat from Australia had never bounced back. And that was some of the hottest intelligence Australia could expect to reap from an operation carried out on its soil.

Other shortfalls had also attracted the Australian's attention: on coal, cotton, live cattle, energy resources and some types of hi-tech equipment. In contrast, political reporting garnered from the Chinese came back unedited. Torrens's contact had actually tumbled to what was going on, well before the Chinese changed their communication patterns. That in turn had restricted to a trickle the flow of intelligence derived from the joint operation. The contact had on a number of occasions raised with his superiors the discrepancy issue, but had been instructed to keep quiet on the matter.

'There'll be higher forces at work in this. Just forget it.'

That was what one of his bosses had told him. He had also raised his concerns in private with bureaucrats he trusted, all of whom were regular readers of the material involved. They, too, confirmed his suspicion that Washington was holding back on material that would give US exporters a commercial advantage. He had then put pen to paper, formally registering his doubts. The upshot was further advice to desist, plus the impression that persistence would impact negatively on his career.

'Hey, look at this,' Hull said. He pointed to one Canberra analyst's comments on a US-provided document. 'This says it all. "A comparison with secret intelligence from other sources makes obvious the fact that the Americans gather more on these topics than they are sharing with us." And he lists other reports he's checked to reach that conclusion. Now, you tell me, how the hell did Canberra get itself into a blasted muddle like this?'

The chief rarely displayed such anger.

'Because we don't think things through,' McKinnon said.

The news editor, who had once worked in government, agreed.

McKinnon was relieved that the Chinese story was about to break, though the copy had yet to be written, as well as adapted, in light of these revelations. And that would be no easy task. There were minefields to step through, some legal and some related to the protection of sources.

'We'll have to fudge these identities,' Hull said, shuffling through more of the documents. 'Something like "high government sources" is probably best for a story like this.'

With that settled, Hull and the news editor were interested to hear from McKinnon about a 'second dimension' to the Chinese story, the existence of which he had alluded to earlier in their meeting.

'Look, I haven't much to go on at this stage,' McKinnon said, 'but if it's true, and we can find another source to back it up, it could leave this first copy for dead.'

Hull's wizened face took on a quizzical look.

'You see, Torrens's contact hinted that the Chinese themselves might *already* know they're under attack.'

'You mean, they've found optical fibre hanging out of the wall?'

'Worse than that. It appears they might've been tipped off. And if so, possibly by someone on *our* side of the fence.'

'You're telling me an Aussie's let the cat out of the bag?'

'So it would seem.'

'Shit!' Hull said. 'Where does this end?'

The news editor was shaking his head.

'God knows,' McKinnon replied. 'It's just that the DSD bloke said he's got the impression that Washington is really worried about why the Chinese are suddenly sweeping and changing their comms. He assumes the Americans feel it's something technical that's given the game away. But recently, the two technicians in Canberra closed up like clamshells. Apparently, they won't even speculate on what might've gone wrong.'

'Hell!' Hull said, rubbing his chin. 'How complex can this story get? I've seen a few rippers in my time, but this one takes the prize.'

'Look, all he'd tell me,' McKinnon added, 'was that he senses something big and nasty looming. Frankly, I think it's his concern over this that's prompted him to leak the documents. But he's adamant we should leave this last bit out – for the time being at least. He's promised to fill me in on the rest if he can find out what's going on.'

'In the meantime,' Hull said, 'do we have other sources we can pump?' He knew that with this star journalist the answer would hardly be no.

'Yes, a few,' McKinnon replied. 'But I'd prefer to get stage one up and running first.'

'I agree. Once that's out on the street it might encourage others to come forward and talk.'

'Exactly,' McKinnon said. 'So let's see how we go.'

Hull's grin spoke of his nerve and resolve in handling matters like this. They were qualities that McKinnon and his colleagues at the *Courier* always found reassuring.

'OK, then. Let's ready the ship for action,' Hull said, clapping his hands, as much out of professional excitement as to emphasise the need to get on with the job. 'You knuckle down, Adrian, and churn out your copy by ten tomorrow morning, and we'll take care of the rest.'

McKinnon smiled. He would work through the night.

'Well then, I'll round up the legal advice,' Hull said. 'We'll run your copy past the lawyers as soon as it's ready. Now that we're defying a D Notice, we'll want to keep ourselves out of prison. Let's see, today's Tuesday. What say we run with it on Friday morning? That'd be May 26. How does that sound?'

'Fine with me,' McKinnon said, gathering up the papers strewn across his boss's desk.

'Oh, and I'll try my hand at an editorial,' Hull added. 'One that explains why the *Courier*'s defying a government warning on an issue like this. It'll give the legal boffins something to chew on before they get their teeth into what you've written.'

'How do you do it?' Zhang said. 'It's amazing!' He gave Mason a friendly punch in the chest as he spoke.

'Not in Intelligence, mate. Memory training's one of the first things you get.'

'Maybe, Greg, but to me it's extraordinary.'

The two men were sitting in a coffee shop in a city hotel. Shortly before, they'd had a brief meeting with an Australian businessman interested in doing a deal with China. An acquaintance of Mason's, he was a Tasmanian manufacturer whose firm's products were sold overseas. For weeks he had been trying to contact producers of metal extrusions in Shanghai, but to no avail. 'It's bloody impossible,' he had told Mason when they bumped into each other in the lobby. 'Nobody replies.' Mason had called Zhang immediately. Not only was this good for cover, but for Mason at this time it meant contact with a Chinese friend who was almost certainly briefed on Beijing's Australian traitor.

When the Tasmanian met Zhang he had quickly reeled off a list of technical requirements, adding that if a positive response were forthcoming he was prepared to fly to China straight away. For Zhang this was a welcome commercial opportunity. Later, however, when writing up his notes in the coffee shop, he'd found himself battling to remember all the detail. 'Let me help you out,' Mason said. 'First, there were seven different types of extrusion. Not five. Four were ten millimetres thick and three were fifteen.' And on it went: types of sheeting, welding technicalities, sizes of mouldings, and more. Zhang's head was left spinning.

'Brilliant!' he said, putting down his pen. 'I'll get this off to Shanghai as soon as I get back to the office.'

'Well, I'm pleased to have been of assistance,' Mason replied.

Zhang put his notepad in his bag and sat back relaxed. He was quiet for a while, pleased not to have to concentrate any more.

'You know,' Mason said, musing aloud, 'I still feel bad about missing that trip with the medical technology people, but I had no option.'

Mason had been keen to be part of an Australian manufacturers' delegation to China, one in which Zhang had included him because of his affinity with the Chinese and his outstanding fluency in their language.

'I've got so much work on my plate at the moment, there's no way I could risk being out of the country. It's a pity, though. It would've been our first time in China together.'

It certainly is a pity, Zhang thought. There'd be a lot of human contact on a trip like that, well away from big cities. He'd have enjoyed every minute of it. So would I. Still, if he's busy, he's busy. And that's no bad thing. He's been much happier lately, and far more focused, so he's clearly thriving on whatever it is. Not that he says much about all these commercial deals that have suddenly come his way. I'd love to know more about them – it's strange he hasn't been more forthcoming with detail. Must be awfully confidential stuff, though surely it couldn't be as sensitive as the Sakhalin discovery he told me all about. Then again, look what I'm involved in!

'Well, these things happen,' Zhang said, 'but don't worry. To be honest, right now I'm more interested in hearing how you memorise things. I'd love to learn the technique.'

'Look, it's dead easy,' Mason said. 'You'll pick it up fast.'

He glanced at his watch, suggesting concern for Zhang's need to get back, although the Chinese seemed in no hurry to rush away.

'I'll give you a quick lesson when we have more time on our hands. But is there something else you want to raise before we go?'

'Yes, there is, and you're the best person to ask.'

Mason wondered what it could be.

'Naturally, Greg, this has to be strictly between us, but you see, what's happened is that

Ambassador Li's asked me to draw up a list of reliable security firms in Australia. People we can call on, perhaps, if we need something done here. I'm not sure what's behind it, but I think there might be a plan to have all our private homes "swept", as you put it. Not the homes of our embassy staff in Canberra, but of people like me in our consulates. Are there any firms you know, that you'd recommend?'

What Zhang kept to himself was the fact that Li had asked Gao to handle the matter, but with Gao overloaded with a rush of case officer work, he had passed the task on to Zhang. Gao was not unduly concerned. Whichever firms made it on to Zhang's shortlist he would screen himself.

Mason smiled as he worked on an answer. Yes, he knew of a few and would scribble their names down. What an irony, he thought. Me advising the Chinese on something like this!

As Zhang waited, a frivolous notion came to his mind. Ask Greg about 'Chan', the Cicada. Does he know what his real identity might be? More importantly, does he think he'll come back?

'Too right,' he imagined Mason saying. 'I know who he is, and I can tell you, all he wants is money.'

No, stop it, Zhang thought. You're back to those two different worlds of the spy and they're brushing up close. You'd better be careful or you'll get lost between them. But then, a general question on the craft shouldn't do any harm. It never has in the past.

'Tell me, Greg, purely as a matter of interest, if someone *weren't* able to handle memory training, plus those other skills I've heard you mention, how would they go in your old line of work?'

'Well, they simply wouldn't get in. They wouldn't pass the psychological tests to begin with.'

A slight look of puzzlement on Zhang's face caught Mason's eye.

'Why do you ask?' he said.

'Oh, no special reason. Just wondering.'

This set Mason thinking, causing him to review his earlier answer. No system's perfect, he thought, and ASIS's certainly isn't.

'Of course, the wrong types do slip through,' he said, 'now and then. Come to think of it, I know of a number who should *never* have been accepted – and when they were, they shouldn't have lasted long. But they did. I can see one of them now. Shit, how could I ever forget *him*?'

The two men looked at each other in a way they sometimes did, knowing they were at a point beyond which it was best not to go.

'Come on round some time and I'll show you my toggles and chops.' Alexandra Templeton mimicked Morgandale as she spoke on the phone. 'That, Greg, is what he told my friend Sarah, from ONA. What a great line!'

Templeton's real voice had a soft lilt, which Mason enjoyed. Though she was in her late thirties she sounded ten years younger. Her image was with Mason now as he listened: tall, brown-eyed and with the sort of presence that turned heads when she entered a room.

Templeton had called Mason in Sydney soon after arriving at her office in the capital at 8.30 that morning. She obviously had something significant to report on Morgandale, and with Mason's awareness of Bass's varied interests he had some idea of what it might be. In Canberra the previous week Mason had had a long discussion with Templeton and Pellegrini, seeking their views on the two primary suspects. He was interested in the extent of their private networks and how they operated.

'See, Sarah bumped into Bass at a Defence chap's birthday bash we were both at last night. He eventually got her out on the terrace for a private chat. She said she had a feeling he might be up to something when he asked how her hobby of woodcarving was going. He's apparently never shown any interest in it before, so no amount of charm could cover up the fact that there had to be an ulterior motive. He said he'd heard she loved doing birds and animals and things like that, then launched into a spiel on his own collection of Chinese ink seals and those toggle things – *netsuke*, aren't they? – that the Japanese used to wear on their belts. He said that all of his have the same motif too – insects, animals and the like.'

Mason now had an inkling of where this was heading. Morgandale had a renowned capacity to charm both women and men, though for different reasons. But with someone like Sarah, who had top-level access, he would be after far more than intimacy. Bass was a schemer and never wasted time with people unless they served a purpose.

Yes, he thought, it'll definitely be something in the professional domain.

'Next, Greg, he tells her he's heard from the birthday boy that she's toying with the idea of taking leave to do a residential course on European timbers, in Florence, but was baulking at the cost.'

Mason was now rapidly narrowing the possibilities.

'Then suddenly – and glibly – he hits her with this weird story about how he might be able to help her out – *if* she were prepared to do the same for him occasionally. See, he claimed he was working on some super-sensitive job on the side "for our Yankee friends" and ...'

'What!' Mason said, chuckling to himself. Normally, nothing surprised him about Bass, but this was bizarre.

'He hadn't got stuck into the beer, Greg, like he usually does, so she took it seriously.'

Mason had stopped laughing, which meant he was taking it the same way. 'And who the hell's he meant to be doing this for?' he said.

'For one of those "lesser-known bodies in the States that keeps a low profile". Apparently that's all he'd say. All very clandestine. And anyway, it was being done with the minister's tacit approval. "You know, we have to keep those Americans happy somehow."'

'Bloody oath!'

'Well, Greg, that's how Sarah reacted, so she pushed hard to find out more. But he just said it was a high-level monitoring task. Keeping an eye on your old lot and that broader community here in Canberra. Its responsiveness, reading trends in the craft, the rise of terrorism, impact of globalisation etc. – that type of thing. And if she were interested in helping him, he could slip her some cash from the budget he had, which he insinuated wasn't that small.'

'Oh, Alex, look, this is just too hard to believe.'

'Well, I know what you're thinking. So I'm planning on briefing Joe and Todd straight away.'

'Yes, definitely. The sooner the better.'

As Mason put the phone down, he was still shaking his head.

How *do* they do it? he thought. If it's not Bass spreading his evil tentacles, it's Martin Clarke – always exuding the image of the devoted professional, ever defending the national interest and that of the Service. God, you've got to give 'em credit. They may be fakes, but they're bloody brilliant at pulling the wool over the eyes of most of the people most of the time.

'So you're a good mate of my Jiminy Cricket?' old Jack said.

Puzzlement showed on Gao's face, which caused the Cicada's father to explain.

'I'm sorry,' he said. 'That's what I've called him since he was a kid – or at least, Jimmy for short. I'd have thought he'd have told you.'

'But why Cricket?' Gao asked, intrigued. 'Is that who the game's named after?'

'God, no!' Jack said with a laugh. 'He was a cartoon character back in the fifties.'

His voice was deep and rich and similar to that of his son, though Jack's had more feeling. Alert for 86, he had the same sharpness in his eyes, but came across as a less calculating person.

He leant on his stick as he and his visitor stood alone in the kitchen. His shock of scraggly hair – clearly left uncut for a while – gave him an Einstein-like appearance, along with a tanned and leathery skin. He wore tired brown trousers, held up by braces, and the sleeves of his lumberjack's shirt were rolled up, revealing strong arms above his large, well-used hands.

'So, you know Jimmy well?'

'Oh, yes,' Gao replied, 'we're pretty close.'

He thought that would do for the moment, until he could gauge why he was being asked. There were also issues of identity to grapple with. Jack had not been introduced with a surname, but if the name the Cicada had used for himself from the beginning was indeed an alias, there seemed to be no concern on his part that Gao might now learn the truth. It was all rather odd, and uncharacteristic of the Cicada, who had so far kept his guard up at every turn.

Jack nodded, as though the visitor's answer required careful consideration.

Gao was still amazed at his luck. He had not imagined he would meet the Cicada's father, let alone have time to spend with him like this.

Intelligence officers always planned for the worst, rather than the best, and here was a rare opportunity – one to be exploited to the full.

The Cicada had left Gao with his father when he went in next door at the request of a neighbour, an accountant who looked after the old man's affairs. Now Jack wanted to know more about the relationship. His inflection on the word "mate" had made Gao wonder whether he too was suspected of being a spy, if indeed the father knew his son worked with ASIS. The Cicada had described Gao as a personal friend who he often met at diplomatic functions, but Jack's inquisitive mind remained unsatisfied.

Following the Cicada's strange turn at Pittwater the previous week, Gao had waited a few days before leaving a phone message: 'Call me when you can. Would welcome a meeting.' That was all he had said, giving no name – the Australian would know the voice. A return call came soon after. Again the message was simple: 'Anne's place at seven; number four.' This denoted Jack's home in Annandale, a Sydney suburb known for its Victorian charm. Gao had noted the street name when he and the Australian first met in Chinatown in company with Zhang and had settled on meeting arrangements. Code-names had been allocated to each place involved. It was the first time this venue had been used. 'Seven' following the name indicated early evening on the day after the message was left, and 'four' meant the street number.

Gao had taken a taxi to the area and first had it detour through streets near the consulate in case he was under surveillance. He gathered that ASIO would be routinely watching Chinese diplomats, especially those with suspected intelligence links. And the Cicada had told Gao that his name was indeed on the list, though further from the top than deserved.

It was a chilly late autumn evening: dark and with the roads wet from a shower. Gao had jumped out a block away. He intentionally walked past the father's single-storey brick home in order to note its salient features. It was on the high side of the street and the roadway in front was potholed where it ran round the side of a hill. Halfway along, Gao doubled back in time to arrive right on seven. He wore a raincoat and carried an umbrella, unfurled because of the threatening sky.

Coming in through the gate, he had spotted newly scraped paintwork on the verandah. Someone had been at work. The garden was neat and obviously tended with pride. Climbing the well-trodden steps, he had pressed the brass buzzer near the door. The entrance was an ornate, wooden affair, inset with panels of brightly coloured glass. Illuminated by the hall light inside, red tulips, green leaves and small clusters of blue flowers came alive. The Cicada himself had opened the door. Dressed in a suit with no tie, he was cheerful, even ebullient. It had been a pleasant surprise for Gao, who had not known what to expect.

'Hey, my old mate,' the Australian said. 'I'm so glad to see you.'

Gao had taken his effusiveness as genuine, at least for the moment.

'Come and meet my Dad. I'm sure you two will get on really well.'

Jack had been watching TV in the front of the house but had turned the set off when they entered the room. He was gracious in welcoming Gao. They had had no time to chat before the Cicada was called in next door. Jack offered to make Gao a cup of tea and it was in the kitchen, while they were boiling the kettle, that he asked about the friendship the Chinese shared with his son.

Maybe, Gao thought, there's something in the vibes between 'Chan' and me that's told him there's some extra dimension.

'And you're in the same line of work as Jimmy, are you?' Jack said, as they walked back to the front of the house.

What does that mean? Gao thought, knowing he had only an instant in which to come up with an answer.

'Well, yes,' he said, 'in the sense that we're both in government service.' He hoped that would be enough for the moment.

'You know,' Jack struck up again, 'I've always wondered how you fellas handle the demands of a job like that.'

That still doesn't show, Gao thought, whether he knows about the intelligence side. But it looks as though he might. He resolved to remain neutral until the picture was clearer. Even if Jack did declare his son's status, that would be no reason for Gao to confirm his.

'You mean, overseas postings and that kind of thing?' Gao asked.

'Yes – that and all those *other* bits and pieces.'

Jack's conspiratorial tone established that he was at least aware of his son's involvement in something secretive.

'Of course,' Gao said, treading warily, 'government affairs cover a – what do you call it in English? – a "multitude of sins". Some of us are in one neck of the woods and others are in another, but we're all ultimately in the same boat, I suppose.'

This appeared to strike the right note, and Jack nodded. He was silent until well after they had returned to the lounge room and seated themselves. Jack placed himself at one end of a sofa, facing Gao, who sat in a bulky old armchair. The air in the room was musty and smelt of tobacco and polish. A large 1940s clock ticked away on the mantelpiece, hemmed in on both sides by an array of Oriental knick-knacks.

'Well, you know, it's a line that's served Jimmy pretty well over the years,' the old man said, contemplatively. 'It's given him the footing he'd missed out on in his youth.'

Gao was intrigued. This was territory he was keen to explore and he showed his interest.

Jack smiled. 'You mean, he hasn't told you about the accidents?'

'No, nothing at all.'

'Well, you see, his mother was killed in a train

crash when he was fourteen. Some carriages jumped the line and smashed into a power pylon. Jimmy took her death really badly. And to make matters worse, I was away a lot at the time with my engineering job, so I wasn't able to give him all the support he needed.'

He shook his head.

'Don't go too hard on yourself,' Gao said, catching the old man's eye. 'Who else could have gone out to earn the money?'

Jack smiled again, then said: 'See, Jimmy retreated into himself and really had me worried there for a while. But then, out of the blue, a schoolmate of his kind of took over.'

'Oh?'

'You mean, he hasn't told you about Raju?'

'No, never.'

'Oh, look, Raju was his saviour. He was from a Ceylonese family that somehow slipped through our immigration barriers at the time. He was the only real friend Jimmy had – at least, the only person he trusted. But Raju didn't have it easy either, not back in the fifties. If you had a different face then, you stood out like dog's balls, which made him a bit of a loner. So Raju's energies went into study, plus helping Jimmy out with his problems. If Jimmy was depressed, Raju took him off to some place like the Zoo, or down to the beach. Raju's ambition was to be an entomologist, an expert on insects and bugs. Jimmy got hooked on it too. He had things in cages in his room and out on the verandah, especially those noisy ones. What do you call them?'

'Cicadas?'

'Yes, that's right. Anyhow, Raju's family was big and close and they took Jimmy into their hearts. They loved the outdoors life here and went fishing in the weekends in a wooden launch they had. Whatever they caught went to a restaurant they ran, near where we lived. It was on one of those trips that the petrol tank blew up. Raju's lot got off pretty lightly, but Jimmy was badly burnt and spent months in hospital. It left him with a phobia that still freaks him out today.'

That explained the strange turn at Pittwater. But there were other issues Gao hoped to coax the father into discussing in whatever time they had left.

'Of course,' Jack went on, 'what really screwed him up was losing Raju too, in a crash. A mate lent them a motorbike, which they slammed into a truck at a crossing. Raju was killed and while Jimmy wasn't badly hurt he was shattered psychologically. His solitary crutch had disappeared. He started university and dropped out of that, but I got him back and eventually he did fairly well: economic history, political science – that type of thing. The next task was to find him a job.'

Gao was delighted with the direction the conversation was taking.

'See, he'd wanted to join Foreign Affairs,' Jack said, 'but they knocked him back. Which was when I had to pull a few strings.'

Gao smiled in a way that suggested all good people needed a helping hand.

'A chum of mine from school days, a doctor, had told me about his diplomatic clients, so I had a word in his ear. He knew a few top people in the Department. Years ago, when he set up a clinic, I'd lent him a hefty sum at no interest and he'd always been looking for a way to say thanks. Anyhow, someone from Melbourne contacted Jimmy and said they'd look him over again. But first he needed to go off to South East Asia for six months and travel around, especially in Indonesia. Apparently there was a dire shortage of people in the system who knew anything about the place. Well, he did that and they accepted him.'

'And he's never looked back?' Gao said.

He had no time to reflect on Jack's mention of Melbourne, which he realised would have been the site of the ASIS headquarters at the time.

'No, not really,' Jack said, 'though it hasn't all been plain sailing. I mean, he's enjoyed his postings away and that exciting part of the life, but I don't think he'd be an easy man to work with.'

Gao was all ears.

'What I'd like to see him do,' Jack went on, 'is retire and go into some business of his own – be independent. Actually, I probed a bit a few weeks back when he stayed here overnight – asked him if he'd thought much about what he'll do when he leaves. As a matter of fact, he said that was very much on his mind at the moment. I said it seemed a bit early yet, but he said it wasn't if you'd been dudded like he had. And that's all he'd say.'

Jack was clearly baffled.

Gao had ideas of his own, but chose to keep them to himself. 'It's not much to go on, is it,' he said.

Jack agreed. He had no way of knowing he had just given Gao a nugget of gold. He reached across and patted his guest on the shoulder. 'At least, with you,' he whispered, 'I know he's in good hands. I can trust you to give him the right advice.'

Even to Gao this was poignant. But moved or not, he had a job to do and that overrode everything else.

Their conversation drifted, ending up on gardening. Soon Gao was taken to see the old man's vegetable patch, which was bathed in light from the kitchen window. Gao's youth on the land came to the fore as they chatted, and it was then that he asked about Jack's family heritage. Had his forebears from England come out as settlers? Yes, they were farming stock from Kent and their name went back centuries in the district they hailed from.

'I see,' Gao said. 'That's very interesting.'

It certainly is, he mused to himself. It's nothing like the alias that Zhang and I have been given. But why have I been allowed to discover all this? Surely it can't be by accident.

When the Cicada returned he wanted to haul Gao off to eat somewhere nearby. As they left, the old man glanced at the Chinese. Their eyes met for a moment. His message was clear: you keep him under your wing.

Gao smiled, though his mind was elsewhere. 'Chan' is in big trouble, he thought, and it's his past that's catching up with him.

The Cicada chose a largely empty restaurant a couple of blocks away. As the two men sat down he said suddenly: 'Look, I'm still very embarrassed by that Pittwater business. It's just that . . . '

'Hey, don't worry,' Gao replied, seeing no need to harp on the past. 'Let's talk about more positive things.'

I want focus now and product tomorrow, he thought. And that's what I'll get. I'll show him who's got hold of the purse strings.

The Cicada ordered their food and drink, then settled back.

'So, how did you go with the newspaper?' Gao asked, wasting no time. 'Did you leak the rest of the story as promised?'

Oddly, the Cicada appeared relieved by the question, as though pleased to be back in harness. 'Oh, I'm sorry about that,' he said. 'You see, actually, I haven't been able to do anything at all.'

Gao let his bewilderment show. Was this flippancy, his boxer-like face said, or simply a statement of fact?

The Cicada reacted quickly. 'It's not that I've broken my word. It's just that I've been out of the office and haven't had a chance to get round to it. But I will.'

This type of thing Gao managed well. For him, relations with the Cicada were strictly professional.

It was business from beginning to end. The Australian had made a commitment and had failed to keep it. Gao wanted answers and was ill disposed to waiting. His own workday had been trying and his tolerance was lower than usual. He gave the Cicada a long, steely look and held it until he had a response.

'You see, I went down with an ailment,' the Australian said, a defensive note in his voice. 'Something I get fairly often.'

Gao's stare was harsh.

'I have this old gastric complaint that strikes without warning,' the Cicada said, feeling the heat. Beads of sweat formed on his brow.

The Chinese was silent.

'It knocked me flat for most of the week. I was spewing up all the time, so I came back to Sydney to have a few tests.'

Gao shrugged. This was of no interest to him.

The Cicada's sweating worsened.

Arrgh, Gao thought. He's no spy displaying good form. If he really is sick he'll have brought it on himself. All he's worried about is getting his hands on the money, yet he hasn't bothered performing on something as basic as this.

For Gao, things now fell into place. Zhang's pen-sketch of the mind of this traitor was one element. The analysis of the consulate's psychologist was another. Then there was the background provided by the old man.

As a picture it's unimpressive, he thought. Maybe I should push him even more and tell him I know his real name. Fancy leaving me alone with his father and thinking I wouldn't find out. What's got into the man? Maybe he jumped at the chance of joining the neighbour, knowing I'd question his Dad and pick up something warm and fuzzy.

The Cicada was squirming. He had inextricably knotted his personal failings with a dire professional act – a treacherous one from which there was no escape. His face had gone red. For him, much hung in the balance.

He knows, Gao mused, that if *I'm* caught running him – an ASIS man – I'll be drummed out of the country but only with a dressing-down. Back home I'll be a hero. But for him life won't be kind. As a traitor he'll be judged in the harshest of terms. No, he's thrown his lot in with China and only we can save him. He's sealed his fate and he knows it.

'So, what's the gossip in Canberra?' Gao said, reverting to normal. 'No doubt things are moving fast.'

'They certainly are,' the Cicada replied, again relieved. 'You see, there's been a major development. It's led to more meetings of that Attorney-General's committee. You know, the one trying to keep the lid on your embassy bugging. Now they're in a blind panic over news that's just come in. Apparently, the *Courier* reporter who's on to your story has worked up a draft and the paper's likely to run with it soon.'

'Why can't *you* get yourself to meetings like that?' Gao said, bluntly.

'Oh, we have a young bloke – Lambert – who looks after that for us.'

This was a name Gao had not heard before. He felt a fleeting sympathy for the Cicada's fellow officer, who would be furious if he knew what was happening. It reminded him of a comment his own boss, Wang, had made in Beijing, that if traitors could not be loyal to themselves and the people around them, why should they be loyal to their country?

'I see,' Gao said, 'but I'd like *you* to follow those things as closely as possible.'

Only the waiter's appearance on the scene broke the silence that followed. He was bringing their food and soft drinks. The Cicada had said he was off alcohol for the rest of the month. It was at his doctor's behest. Gao suspected that was not quite the case. The reality of what the Australian had got himself mixed up in, plus heavy pressure from inside the Service, must have rattled him and he was on some form of suppressant. He was abstaining because he had no other choice.

Wo bu dong: I can't understand it, Gao thought, as the waiter served them some fishcakes. Surely his peers in ASIS know he's got problems. How could they ignore all the signs? Shit, they're looking for trouble.

'So, where did this journalist get the key bits that were missing?'

'That's why the Government's panicking,' the Cicada said, rather more animated now. 'They don't know. Wherever it's come from, it has to be a high level source. The *Courier* wouldn't run with a story like that unless they had the very best stuff.'

'And *you'll* hear the details when you get back tomorrow?'

'Yes, and I'll let you know as soon as I can.'

Gao scribbled a number on a small piece of paper he took from his pocket and handed it over.

'Call me on this as soon as you can. If necessary, I'll come down to see you in Canberra, although I'd prefer to stay away from the place.'

'Oh, and there's something else,' the Cicada said, still trying to recover lost ground. 'It's something that that committee knows nothing about. See, I've heard on the grapevine that someone from national TV is also sniffing around.'

'Really? Do you think they know very much?'

'No, it seems they've only just got on to the story.'

'And no one in the system officially knows about this?'

'Correct. If they did, the panic would be double what it is.'

'Well, for the time being let's leave it that way. Meanwhile, see if you can get the name of the TV reporter.'

The Cicada nodded. His sweating had stopped. Now he was spooning curry on to Gao's rice. 'This dish is going to disappear,' he said with a smile, 'if you don't tuck in fast.'

Gao remained silent. He's not doing too badly, he thought, for someone recovering from a gastric complaint.

'I owe you a lot,' the Cicada said, acting humble, 'and I want you to know it.'

'Oh, I know it, my friend, only too well. Trouble is, I can't go on paying you unless I have something to show for it, if you see what I mean.'

'Believe me,' the Cicada said, momentarily distracted, 'I'm aware of the pressure for product. I'm doing my best.'

'Well, that's good. Just keep it that way. You give me what I want, and you'll get what you want, OK?'

The Cicada looked away, sighing.

'Look,' the Chinese said, 'if you and I get things back on track fast, there might be a way I can help you earn extra money, if that's what you want. You see, there's someone on my side who I know will pay big dollars for certain high quality economic information.'

The Cicada was listening intently.

'So, if you're interested . . . '

'Oh, yes, I definitely am.'

'Well, let me see what I can do,' Gao responded.

If it takes an incentive, he thought, to spur him on, so be it. What's important is to keep Rottweiler Wang happy, up in Beijing.

TEN

Canberra: Thursday, 25 May, 10.20 a.m.

'Do have one,' Samuel S. Greensborough said. 'I never touch them myself, but some people like a quality cigar.'

How did this fool, with his bow tie, get to be where he is? he thought, as he smiled at his guest. I can't stand men with bow ties.

The US Ambassador to Australia was a big muscular man of 70. A former property dealer from Oregon and contributor to party funds, he had been rewarded with the Canberra post in return for dogged support of the President. A self-made man with no time for pretension, he got on best with Australian entrepreneurs who had clever ideas, and had helped many prosper by introducing them to key players in the American market. This Australian in front of him, however, sorely tested his patience, though he felt it wise to contain himself a while longer.

Michael O'Sullivan, Australia's distinctive Foreign Minister, had picked up the silver box to study a bear-hunting scene embossed on its lid. Opening it, he had perfunctorily sniffed the cigars inside, then declined the ambassador's offer.

The two sat alone in the room in ornate Chippendale armchairs.

'It's a superb piece of craftsmanship,' O'Sullivan said, closing the box and putting it back on the table between them.

Except for the drone of a lawnmower outside, the plush upstairs office was quiet. The American watched as O'Sullivan cast an eye over the other things on the table. A celadon ashtray caught his attention, then a small Inca figurine.

Greensborough felt no urge to recount the story that lay behind each item – he had more serious matters to discuss. Whether the minister's curiosity was driven by courtesy or was a display of genuine inquisitiveness was of no consequence to him. He had a task to perform for Washington and preferred not to beat about the bush. While an admirer of Australian pragmatism and directness, Greensborough was disenchanted with the foppery of much of Canberra's elite, and here was a noted exponent.

The ambassador had telephoned O'Sullivan earlier in the morning to suggest the pair meet without delay. He said he wished to avoid formality and would sooner not come to the ministry. Where else, he pondered aloud, might they usefully meet? 'Oh, I'll come to you,' O'Sullivan replied. 'It'd be my privilege. I'll be over straight away.' It was an unusual gesture in protocol terms, but Greensborough was pleased that the response had been fast.

The sprawling brick embassy was classical Williamsburg and straddled a hill overlooking Parliament House.

Now the minister sat forward, eager to learn what was afoot. He brushed back his wavy grey hair as the ambassador contemplated this sticklike specimen of manhood. In his late forties, O'Sullivan looked as though he had led a protected life. An image flashed through Greensborough's mind of him struggling through army boot camp in the days of the Vietnam War. That would have toughened him up and sharpened his wits.

'I have a message for your Government, Michael, and to deliver it I'd like to dispense with the usual formalities. With your agreement, of course.'

'By all means,' O'Sullivan said, sensing something grave.

'You see, Washington wants this to be completely off the record, but I'm sure you'll know who else to share it with.'

The minister seemed to expect a confidence of no small proportion.

'To put it bluntly, our people are worried that your system's leaking badly, that it isn't – how can I put it? – hermetically sealed.'

He paused to let the message sink in, which it did. O'Sullivan's body language betrayed the extent of his fear. Grimfaced now, he instinctively changed his sitting position.

'It's the Chinese Embassy thing, Michael. Washington's concerned that the operation might have been blown.'

Oh, shit, O'Sullivan thought. Not that!

An astute reader of men, Greensborough studied his visitor closely. O'Sullivan was acutely embarrassed. He was an intelligent man, if rash, and his instincts warned him to watch his external reactions. But the American had him trapped and he knew it. For O'Sullivan, this was the sort of situation he dreaded. His defences commonly deserted him when he needed them most. His town planning friends had warned him about it when he went into politics. In the ebb and flow of ministerial work his affability generally carried him through, but pressure of this kind left him disarmed. He tended to channel his energy in ways that only exacerbated the problem. Whatever composure he gained with his eyes would be lost through pursing his lips.

'What – I – er,' he mumbled, his mouth forming words before his mind was in gear.

Greensborough had no wish to prolong O'Sullivan's agony. He had already learnt what he wanted to know: the minister had something to hide.

'You see, Michael, Washington's picked up changes in the embassy's cable traffic. I'm told their communications patterns reflect an attempt to get round something they suspect – or *know* – has been planted inside.'

O'Sullivan grew increasingly edgy as the ambassador homed in on reality. What the minister didn't know was that the Americans had been eavesdropping on more than the embassy. Two of the FBI officers who had come to Australia to provide technical support for Mason and Cantrell had secretly handled the task, working on it whenever time permitted. They were occasionally monitoring communications in and out of O'Sullivan's office, and it was this that had tipped the Americans off to a leak of 'gigantic proportions'. But they were still unaware that the *Sydney Daily Courier* had the story and was preparing its copy for print.

Washington had decided it was time for the Australians to be given a prod. First, the ambassador would rattle O'Sullivan and assess his reaction. Depending on what this produced, the President himself would call the Prime Minister and drive home the message that Canberra's house had to be put in order – quick smart. The CIA had strongly supported this action. Sherrington, its Director, was adamant that only concerted pressure on the Government would see anything done. Observers in Canberra, he said, who harboured suspicions of their own would be more likely to help if they felt change in the air.

'Something else you should know, Michael, is that a highly classified report has recently come in from our people in China. It alludes to a "bombshell" coming in this part of the world. Washington's not yet sure what that means, but I have to say, what it *wouldn't* want to be – and I'm sure you'd agree – is our Chinese Embassy operation. Now, I've been instructed to tell you that if that's what it *is*, the United States Government would have no choice but to review our intelligence exchange. And that means everything – all sensitive material, electronic and signals intelligence, all reporting from human sources, all defence material – the lot. You might recall, Michael, what we did to the New Zealanders when they tried to screw us some years back by stopping nuclear-armed vessels calling in. Let's face it, it can be icy out there in the cold.'

O'Sullivan grimaced. He knew precisely what this meant.

'Washington is utterly determined this time,' Greensborough said, looking O'Sullivan in the eye. 'They want your system cleaned up.'

The minister flinched. His hands were clenched on his lap as if praying. 'All I can – er – say is that I'll get back to you as soon as possible.'

'I'd be grateful, Michael, if that's what you'd do. Let's say, by this time tomorrow?'

'Yes, yes, of course,' the minister said, like a schoolboy chided for a minor transgression. 'By this time tomorrow.'

Greensborough sat back, his expression far from benevolent.

There had, in fact, been no report in from China and the ambassador was aware that that was the case. But Washington was indeed prepared to cut off the flow of intelligence.

Such disciplinary action would hurt the Australians. The absence of these extra, and often vital, perspectives would be felt very quickly. But worse, a deliberate American leak of the fact that the exchange had been stopped would, domino-like, lead to other intelligence allies reviewing their relations with Canberra. America was the biggest producer of this valued material and smaller recipients could not afford to be seen to be out of the loop. Even more dangerous, it would be devastating politically for O'Sullivan and his party. 'All the way with the USA' was still an article of faith with a large part of the Australian electorate. The Government's prospects at the next election would be dismal.

These alarm bells were ringing in O'Sullivan's mind when he suddenly realised that Greensborough was asking him if he wished to take coffee.

'No, no thanks,' he said, struggling to gather his thoughts. 'I think I'd better be going.'

'A wise choice,' Greensborough responded, smiling politely as both rose from their chairs. His sarcasm was undisguised.

For O'Sullivan it was a demeaning encounter and one that he sensed would not be his last. Not unless something happened quickly to arrest events already in train. What he wanted right now was to get out of the ambassador's office. Once back in his car he could get on his mobile and stir up some action. There was not a minute to lose.

The PM? Yes, he thought, glancing at the date on his watch. The boss was in town. Maybe the problem could be flicked to him and *he* could damn well worry about it. It wasn't his, O'Sullivan's, idea to bug the bloody Chinese.

'What do you reckon, Martin?' Hestercombe said. 'Within reason, you can have whatever you want.'

The moment the ASIS chief invited him to lunch at the Commonwealth Club, Clarke knew it would be something like this. Now he hated it even more.

'We could have you settled in London in a matter of weeks, if you want to move fast.'

Clarke felt insulted by the offer. There was no way he could accept. The Washington liaison post might once have constituted a gesture of sorts, but London was out of the question. He had never trusted the Brits anyway. He gave Hestercombe the type of look that said: 'You know what you're doing to me. Don't rub it in.'

Hestercombe had racked his brains over how to move Clarke out quickly, especially after the Secretary of Foreign Affairs started making noises about the crucial issue of cover. 'How do you expect my people to support yours in the field,' he quipped, 'if you can't control Martin back here at home base?' He had considered putting him on extended leave until he could find out what was driving Clarke's behaviour, but that was easier said than done. He had to be handled with care – if visible urgency – and would only be safe on the outside if he was happy with the way he had left. Clarke knew far too much, not only about skeletons in the Service's cupboard, but also about certain government activities that were not strictly legal. He had supporters, too, in various places, and even the minister enjoyed his company, though Bass Morgandale ensured that such encounters were kept to a minimum. The minister was *his* mate.

But the heat was increasing on Hestercombe – coming not only from Foreign Affairs – and if he failed to act soon he feared someone might go over his head. Morgandale himself was a running sore with a lot of people, both inside the Service and beyond. And the last thing the chief wanted was fires on two different fronts at the same time. Better to deal with the most threatening first.

At least, with the way Martin was reacting, he thought, he was acknowledging a problem that had to be addressed. That was an achievement of sorts. Now it was a matter of 'what' and 'when'.

The thing that most annoyed and worried Hestercombe was that Clarke had always confided in him on personal and professional dilemmas, but not this time.

Clarke took another sip of his wine, then looked out of the window. 'I trust you're not discussing this with anyone else,' he said, turning back.

'Of course not. It's just between us.'

Clarke nodded, though doubt lingered on his face. It was difficult for Hestercombe to gauge what might be going on in his mind. He found that whenever he assumed Clarke was mulling over a particular issue, it too often turned out he was grappling with something completely different. He knew that one thing Clarke feared was any involvement on Morgandale's part, which was precisely why he had mentioned the London job. The negotiation of any such posting would inevitably see Bass play a pivotal role. After all, he was the one with close links to MI6. In reality, what Hestercombe was hoping for was that Clarke would take the Jakarta option. Throwing up London was only a ruse, aimed at highlighting the fact that no posting arranged *within* ASIS would make Clarke happy. Leaving, and handling 'outsourced services', was the preferable – indeed only – alternative.

'Look, Bill, give me a while to think about it, will you?' he said. 'I'm still considering some of the other avenues we discussed before.'

Ah, perhaps progress at last, Hestercombe thought.

'Look, I don't know how to put this, Ewen, but I want to ask you a favour.'

The DSD Director wondered what Hestercombe was going to say. The two went back a long way and he could tell from his colleague's tone that, whatever it was, it had to be pressing and confidential. But to be broaching it on the phone suggested it could possibly be personal.

'Look, it's Martin,' Hestercombe said.
'Oh? What's he done now?'

'Well, that's the problem. I don't know. He's up to something, but I can't get anything out of him. He won't talk, which is quite out of character. We've been completely open in the past about all sorts of things – as you well know, Ewen – but not now. Not on this, whatever it is. See, my problem is I have a host of people breathing heavily down my neck, and if something doesn't happen soon, heads may well roll.'

The DSD chief was silent. He had heard about Clarke's recent behaviour – and Morgandale's as well – and hence had some inkling of what Hestercombe might wish to ask. It was the kind of thing he found perplexing, but a line had to be drawn. 'Informal intercepts' were risky at the best of times, especially at the moment.

'So, I wonder if, somehow – unofficially, of course – you could keep an eye on him? You see, I need facts to go on, Ewen, before I can take this any further. It might turn out to be some personal trauma – something of no great consequence – then again, it could be serious and . . . '

'Bill,' the Director cut across him, 'rest assured, mate, I'd love to help you, but you know as well as I do that I can't actually tackle jobs like this myself. I have to get *someone else* to do it.'

Hestercombe took the Director's point. Recent Government demands on DSD had caused considerable disquiet in the organisation. Some were openly questioning the ethics and legality of acceding to such requests. One more case might tip the scales and prompt a leak to the media.

'Bill, why don't you take it up informally with ASIO? It's probably more in their bailiwick than mine. Anyhow, let me know how you go. In the meantime, I've forgotten everything you've said, right?'

'OK, thanks.'

Bugger! Hestercombe thought. The last thing I want is to have to drag ASIO into this. I'd lose control of it straight away.

Canberra: Thursday, 25 May, 12.40 p.m.

> Disclosure of this information will seriously prejudice Australia's diplomatic and trade relations with countries directly involved in the operation. It will also impact on relations with other governments.

'No!' O'Sullivan snapped. 'This bloody affidavit has to point to a clear and present danger to national life. It can't be filled with codswallop.'

Australia's Attorney-General, Lou Cavanagh, who was his cabinet colleague, sat next to him in the minister's suite. Youthful for 50, and renowned for his good legal mind, he was unimpressed with O'Sullivan's intemperate language, even if he understood what his colleague was getting at. True, if the affidavit were to have the desired effect, it would need to be weighted. No judge of the NSW Supreme Court would grant an injunction against the *Sydney Daily Courier* to stop publication merely on the grounds of the Federal Government's preference for material like this not to go into print. But the minister's hectoring of Cavanagh's three most senior officers was not going to help produce the document the group was drafting in haste.

Alongside O'Sullivan sat the Department of Foreign Affairs' chief legal officer and the head of its China desk. At opposite ends of the table, by no coincidence, were the Director-General of ASIO and Bass Morgandale from ASIS, the presence of the latter requested by the minister himself. In all, it was too unwieldy a group for the task. Cavanagh had wanted his own officers to draft a working version of the affidavit, with a full meeting to consider it later. But no, O'Sullivan reacted vehemently. There was no time to waste. *All* should assemble in one room and, in that session alone, hammer out the final document as quickly as possible.

Cavanagh could live with that, but the personality change that O'Sullivan underwent whenever this sort of pressure came on militated against the views of others being heard. And that was a worrying thing. To be sure, the PM had told them: 'Just get the job done and don't muck around.' Still, there were proper procedures for handling such things, even when under great stress. And this was where the weight of experience embodied in permanent staff was meant to temper the rashness common among those elected to office.

'Hey, Michael,' Cavanagh said jokingly, 'do you think I might get a word in myself, if . . . '

O'Sullivan took offence and cut his colleague off tersely. It had only been a friendly attempt to remind him that others might have something to offer.

'For fuck's sake, Lou, let's move on. There's no time to squander on ritual. We have to make sure that the judge, whoever the bastard is, grants an injunction. We have to hit him with everything we've got that'll further the cause. That's all there is to it. Do I make myself clear?'

This was galling for Cavanagh, who was a trained lawyer. O'Sullivan had no legal experience, though he pretended that his time in diplomacy carried great weight.

The simmering glare he gave the group put the others on notice. Haughtiness was only part of it; it was driven more by panic. When he was in this mood few would risk open defiance. With Cavanagh the only cabinet colleague present, and a junior one at that, O'Sullivan was likely to get what he wanted.

David Goldman, one of the Attorney-General's officials, with the rank of first assistant secretary, had been keying a new paragraph into the draft on his laptop.

'How about this, then?' he said.

> The matter is of utmost sensitivity and goes to the core of national security. It poses a clear and present danger to the life of the nation. The Government must

> not, and will not, shirk its responsibility to protect Australia's well-being. A newspaper cannot be allowed to dictate foreign policy and impinge upon this most basic of obligations.

'Yes,' O'Sullivan said, 'that's much better. But we're going to need more on the "dire consequences" the country will suffer if this stuff gets into the public arena. It has to be so clear-cut in its argument, so compelling, that the granting of an injunction will be automatic.'

'One of the most powerful points we can make,' the Director-General of ASIO said in the brief lull that followed, 'has to be the American threat to cut off sigint and all other secret intelligence. Let alone the flow-on effect to our allies. That's something that comes through clearly in the record of your meeting with Ambassador Greensborough this morning.'

O'Sullivan smiled, pleased with what he saw as a note of support. He got on well with the ASIO chief and listened carefully when he expressed an opinion. The transcript he referred to was a hurriedly dictated rendition of what the American had said. It had been read by all at the table before proceedings commenced.

'You might wish to consider,' the chief said, 'attaching a copy to the affidavit when it's delivered to the court registrar in Sydney this evening.'

'Yes, that's good thinking,' O'Sullivan replied, casting a disparaging look in Cavanagh's direction.

'How about the *US–Australian Agreement on Intelligence Exchanges*?' somone else suggested. 'That might be useful.'

The others agreed, including the minister.

'So, what do we throw at the judge on China?' O'Sullivan said, gazing at a picture on the wall.

The Foreign Affairs desk officer, who should have been ready to answer, was lost in thoughts of his own. O'Sullivan noticed this and moved on quickly.

'What do *you* recommend?' he said, turning to Morgandale, who had had little to say. 'You know China quite well.'

Morgandale had won the minister's confidence some years before in a series of intelligence briefings. O'Sullivan was taken by his capacity to get to the point. Granted, he was outspoken – even a tad quirky – but he delivered the goods. And in a bureaucracy where mealy-mouthed diplomats and other functionaries were constantly at the minister's side, this was a quality much to be valued. Personality-wise, the two were remarkably similar and O'Sullivan found this reassuring, a fact that Morgandale was keenly aware of and exploited to the full.

'What I'd recommend is this,' he said. 'We have to come on strong – or, should I say, *emphasise* – the absolute certainty of losing the long-term energy agreement with Beijing if this story gets out.'

O'Sullivan was nodding. Of course, the energy deal, he thought – he'd completely overlooked that when he considered the extent of collateral damage.

'Excellent. Here's a paragraph, then, that we can add on that topic,' he said, indicating to Goldman – the man with the laptop – that it should be keyed straight into the draft.

> Of absolute certainty is the fact that after more than a year of difficult negotiations, and with a deal on the verge of conclusion, an Australia–China Long-Term Energy Agreement will be lost to the nation. This will impact heavily upon our balance of payments, to the extent of many billions of dollars over a thirty-year period, commencing with $2 billion next year.

'OK?' O'Sullivan asked, addressing the group as a whole.

Nobody dissented. Most were embarrassed at not having raised the matter themselves.

'I still feel we need something more,' he mused aloud, scratching at a wart on the back of his hand. 'Something on the danger of China being in a state of high dudgeon. How the leaking of this story might stir the dragon like never before. It might breath fire all over us in ways nobody can predict.'

After a moment of silence he readied himself for another burst of dictation. Those who knew him best had a sense of foreboding. The minister's forte was not by any means the Central Kingdom and its political affairs.

> An insular nation for all of its history, China will undoubtedly prove to be Ronald Reagan's Evil Empire of the twenty-first century. Rampant, indeed rabid, in its offshore espionage activities, its appetite for the fruits of the labours of others already outstrips the perfidy and deceit of the Japanese. The Chinese can never be trusted, and in coming battles on the new global stage their venal standards will be projected through an unscrupulous application of force. It was for this reason . . .

Some around the table were unsettled. Brash statements of this kind were risky and in the eyes of the judge might debase the currency of the more practical issues that the affidavit was addressing.

Cavanagh was on the verge of expressing precisely that view, which he could sense the others were thinking.

'Arrgh,' he said, displaying distaste. 'I really don't . . . '

'Bloody oath, Lou,' O'Sullivan growled, his manner bordering on rudeness. 'This is no time to cower to politeness and protocol. We have to have focus and punch if we're to get what we want. You won't find me going to jelly just because the going gets tough.'

This silenced the room. It was O'Sullivan at his most querulous. Turning back to Goldman, he cleared his throat before speaking.

> It was for this reason that the Australian and American Governments jointly determined to undertake the technical operation against the Chinese, which is now so seriously threatened. Unless Western allies like us, similarly endowed with standards of justice and decency, cooperate to tame this beast, it will be out of the cage and upon us before we can put up a defence.

He paused.

> In ours, a most inventive of countries, we find Chinese espionage activity on Australian soil a menace of relentless proportions. The yield from our technical operation on the Chinese Embassy in Canberra has provided us and the Americans, and our allies as well, with a vital means of protection. In addition, it has significantly enhanced our ability to negotiate wheat sales to feed the Chinese.

The ASIO chief was left scratching his cheek.

'Troubled by something?' O'Sullivan said, looking at him benignly.

'I must confess, Michael, I am. I'm worried that emotiveness in a document like this might defeat the purpose ... '

'I hear what you say,' O'Sullivan cut in, 'but we'll only get one bite at this cherry, so we have to get it right.'

'I must say, Minister,' Morgandale chimed in, as silence took hold, 'I'm with *you* all the way.'

The statement shocked everyone, intent as they were on dragging O'Sullivan back to reality.

'You've described China for what it is,' Morgandale said, as the minister's expression softened. 'I can't see what's wrong with telling the judge how you see it. It's no use pretending that all we'll end up with, if the story blows in the press, is a diplomatic tiff – something that'll pass like a bad case of wind.'

No one laughed.

Morgandale was way out of line, but his support was all the minister needed.

'How soon can you give me a printout?' O'Sullivan asked Goldman.

'Another five minutes, I reckon.'

'Right. Once that's ready to go, we're cooking with gas.'

O'Sullivan was pleased with himself and it showed. His colleagues were resigned to the course he had outlined. Sixteen attachments, few of them small, would accompany the affidavit to be delivered by Goldman, who was compiling it now. He had already liaised with the Registrar of the Supreme Court in Sydney. A meeting had been set for six that evening.

'Oh, and make sure you give him a copy of the article the *Courier*'s planning to run.'

Most in the room were appalled. It was one thing to explain in the affidavit how the Government had learnt that the *Courier* was on to the story. That was touchy enough. It might even cause a judge to conclude that rights had been infringed from the start. But this was ridiculous and would serve only to highlight the point.

The Government, in panic, had ordered the Defence Signals Directorate to monitor communications between the newspaper and its legal advisers. DSD had been averse to acting this way, but threats were made and the deed had been done.

The instincts of the editor-in-chief of the *Courier* had been deadly accurate. Security within the paper was crucial. A lawyer from Buckridges, the law firm that customarily screened sensitive copy on which the *Courier* sought legal advice, had come to the paper's premises. There, at ten that morning, he had gone over the story that was now ready to run. He had asked to take a copy on disc back to his office where he would consult with other specialist partners. Permission was granted on the condition that nothing was emailed or faxed back to the *Courier*. Nor would the matter be discussed on the phone. But the lawyer, without thinking, had emailed a copy to a partner who was working at home.

DSD, in breach of the law, had been waiting to pounce. The story was intercepted at the time of transmission and delivered straight away to the Government. O'Sullivan and Greensborough had just sat down in the ambassador's office when DSD sounded the alarm.

But now, for the Government to include the article as an attachment to an affidavit that sought to block publication was looking for trouble. It was a Pandora's box which, once opened, could never be closed. Questions would arise that the judge could not ignore. He might even consider the nature of the intercept worse than the story whose publication he was being asked to prohibit.

'Frankly, Michael, attaching the article worries me too,' Cavanagh remarked. 'Surely the other stuff is enough. There's also the question of warrants. Were they issued at all? Were they adequate and appropriate?'

'OK,' O'Sullivan said. 'While I don't doubt that your counsel is wise . . . '

The words likely to follow were in everyone's mind.

'. . . I want the article included.'

A wave of dismay swept round the room, even unnerving the minister slightly. He coughed. 'That's all there is to it.'

Cavanagh made no further protest, nor was anyone else willing to try. An uncomfortable quiet fell over the group.

'So, David, you're ready to go?' O'Sullivan said, turning to Goldman. The question was perfunctory, but filled in the gap.

Goldman nodded.

'Anybody else want to join him?' O'Sullivan asked, for want of something to say.

No one responded, but Morgandale straightened his tie; an insignificant act in itself, yet enough to catch the minister's roving eye.

'Oh, would you like to go?'

It was beyond dispute that Morgandale should not be part of the process. And anyway it had been agreed from the beginning that only one person would deliver the papers.

Nonetheless, before Morgandale had answered, O'Sullivan was ruminating aloud. 'Yes, it'd certainly be useful to have an ASIS man there. Someone who could speak up on China in case the judge needed convincing. Yes, I like the idea.'

'Fuck!' the China desk officer mouthed to himself. Bass is always ready to pull some stupid stunt like this, he thought.

He glanced across at the minister and recalled something vacuous he had once been told by O'Sullivan about Morgandale: 'Anyone who understands Chinese art like he does, has to know how their minds work.'

'Let's face it, Martin,' Hestercombe said, 'it'll get you out of this place for a while, even if it's just a short trip.'

It was actually Morgandale who had suggested to the ASIS chief that Clarke fly up to Sydney, though not alongside him and Goldman. It was only a temporary expedient, but one that would give the chief yet another opportunity to project Lambert as Clarke's logical successor. There were important meetings on now, one after the other, and the few that Lambert had attended by himself had elicited comments like 'What a breath of fresh air!' And anyway Clarke would have no duties to perform in Sydney, other than 'being a general dog's body, helping with paperwork and whatever else', as Morgandale had sarcastically put it.

'Well,' Clarke responded, still in two minds. 'I suppose ... '

'Oh, come on, Martin. Look, the rest of management will simply see it as two senior officers going off on a sensitive mission. And I can promise you, Bass will stay out of your hair.'

'OK, then.'

'I want to ask you something,' Mason said, adopting a serious tone.

'Oh?' Beth Cantrell rolled her eyes mock-seductively.

They were walking to a late afternoon meeting and Mason had anything but hanky-panky on his mind.

'It's that energy deal with China,' he said, knowing that Cantrell was aware of Australia's negotiations with Beijing. 'My friend Zhang has come up with an interesting twist that his ambassador's picked up from an Indonesian contact.'

'Really?'

'Apparently some Tokyo mandarin by the name of Yoshida has been visiting Beijing. The Japanese are desperate to rope the Chinese into their Sakhalin gas project and it seems he was there to prod them along. The trip was all very secretive, as was his other port of call before heading home. As the story goes, he spent two hours in Jakarta with the President and offered all sorts of sweeteners if the Indons would pressure us Australians into some sort of regional gas tie-up. Tokyo's pretty keen that we drop any long-term deal with China.'

'Nothing the Japs do would surprise me,' Cantrell said.

She was an old energy hand and, as such, well acquainted with Tokyo's understandable quest to guarantee supplies of oil and gas.

'Mind you, this regional concept isn't without merit,' she said. 'But of course, they're only pushing it because they want the best of both worlds – *no* Australia–China deal and them controlling Sakhalin gas as well as the Timor Sea deposits.'

'Exactly, but from what I've heard in Canberra, Beth, we're not too receptive towards Jakarta. It's Beijing we want to jump into bed with. To be honest, what's set me thinking is a comment a Japanese mate made in a letter the other day. He's Fujisawa, the bloke I first heard about Sakhalin from when I was in Tokyo. I'd asked him if he could give me an update on how the project was going. All I got back was a few pages on his family, which was like saying: "Look, I can't tell you any more than I already have." But he added a cryptic PS about how the grass always gets trampled when elephants fight. Now that can only mean Japan and China, with Australia underfoot.'

Cantrell had no comment to make.

'I'm wondering,' Mason said, 'what your lot might know about this.'

He was eager to read her reaction. As one of the CIA's top energy specialists, she should be *au fait* with what was happening, even if she had been away from Langley for the past few weeks.

'Look, let me check it out,' she said. 'We should have a good flow of humint from Jakarta on something like this.'

Mason knew what she meant. He was also aware of the identities of some of the CIA's key local agents there, not that all of their product would be shared with Canberra. His reason for asking was not so much to find out what the Agency knew; rather it was an indirect way of saying: 'Where does the US stand in all this?' American oil giants were heavily involved across Asia. What were they telling Washington about where US interests lay? Who would have Australia's economic good at heart?

Cantrell knew what he was doing as soon as he asked. For Christ's sake, she thought, don't say he's getting cold feet! That was the last thing she wanted.

Sydney: Thursday, 25 May, 6.10 p.m.

'Uh, ha,' the judge said a number of times. His elongated vowels implied that he was aware of the Government's ploy and was unamused. The air in the room was like ice.

Mr Justice Garran went on studying the affidavit with meticulous care.

Ten minutes had already passed as he moved methodically through its 22 pages. Like most top lawyers he was deft at extracting the essence from swathes of printed material. In his mid-sixties, he was a dignified man who valued good health as much as knowledge and reason. Studious and careful, he was also laconic. In his conservative charcoal grey suit, he could pass for a university chancellor or the chairman of a British bank.

Three men and one woman sat in front of his desk in his book-lined chambers. The woman — his legal associate — was off to one side, perusing a file on her knee. The court registrar was at the opposite side, also engrossed in his papers. In the middle sat David Goldman from Attorney-General's and Bass Morgandale.

The ASIS man was ill at ease, frequently changing position. His chair's tight leather covering scrunched each time he moved, apparently disturbing the registrar.

Not quite 40, Goldman was a high flier. He had risen fast in the ranks of his department where he was renowned for his brilliance and intellectual bounce. He sported a bright red pocket-handkerchief with the corners hanging out, though not enough to look raffish.

The meeting with Garran had started right on six. After polite introductions, he got straight down to business. First, he scrutinised each of the attachments, then read the covering letter from the minister. It was co-signed by the Attorney-General. He then homed in on the affidavit. As the primary document, this commanded his fullest attention. Silence had ruled from the start.

Goldman, tense himself, spent his time studying Garran's facial expression as well as his body language. Having compiled the affidavit himself, he knew its every clause and inflection and felt he could pinpoint exactly where the judge was in his reading. Here and there an eyebrow rose ever so slightly, indicating surprise at O'Sullivan's intemperate language. The minister's wilder assertions even caused the judge to look away for a moment and think.

'I have a technical question,' he said, peering over his glasses. His eye fell upon Morgandale, then shifted to Goldman. 'Presumably warrants were issued for these intercepted calls – the ones between the *Courier* chap here in Sydney and their correspondent in Beijing.'

'Yes,' Morgandale said, jumping in.

Damn, Goldman thought. It's not for him to respond. God knows what he'll do next.

'I see,' the judge said, nodding as he returned to his reading.

Progressing at a uniform pace he arrived at the spot where O'Sullivan had commented on threats made by the US Ambassador earlier in the day. He skimmed it quickly, then turned to the transcript of the conversation itself. This brought a distinct frown, though he kept his view to himself. Goldman was certain that a hitch would arise over China, which was coming up soon.

'So, how many people get to see this signals intelligence from Washington?' Garran said, totally out of sync with what he was reading. 'And I'm not referring to whatever the Americans glean from the Chinese Embassy exercise. I'm talking about signals intelligence in general. How far does it spread inside the system?'

Goldman had no idea, but in his head he was making a quick calculation. 'Oh, I'd imagine no more than fifty for the unedited version,' he said, trying not to look flustered. 'But if you were to include those who get summaries, it might go up to three or four hundred, or perhaps . . . '

'But do you *actually* know?' Garran interrupted, his manner in no way offensive.

'Well, no, I don't,' Goldman said, trusting honesty to be a virtue this man would respect.

The judge nodded, then focused on Morgandale. 'And do you know the answer?'

Garran's new target had feared this might happen, but it all came so fast. He had imagined – foolishly, he now realised – that in such an event he could seek leave to quickly call a colleague. That was Clarke, who was back at the hotel where they were spending the night. He was equipped with a laptop with a direct and secure link to their headquarters in Canberra, whence he would be able to speedily retrieve sensitive information on request. But the judge's demeanour left Morgandale in no doubt about how he would react if recourse were sought to any such backup.

'Oh, no more than a hundred, Your Honour.'

Morgandale's answer only served to muddy the waters.

The judge's eye moved on to the registrar, and via some psychic consensus they seemed to agree that the matter was best left where it was.

'It's interesting there's no precise figure on that,' Garran observed to no one in particular.

He turned another page and read the top paragraph before looking at Morgandale again. 'And how many people in your organisation know that the Chinese Embassy's been bugged?'

Garran's stern visage left no doubt that this time he expected an accurate reply.

'Twelve,' Morgandale replied, without a moment's hesitation.

The judge looked surprised. It was hard to say if he accepted the figure as true, especially in light of the haste with which Morgandale had responded. He shrugged, almost imperceptibly, then returned to the affidavit, reading to the bottom of the page. It was there, Goldman knew, that another ministerial excess lurked.

The judge perused O'Sullivan's utterances on Chinese espionage and his awkward reference to Reagan's Evil Empire. These were digested without remark, though his right eyebrow lifted a number of times.

'Do you really think we might lose this energy deal?' he asked Morgandale.

This had Goldman seriously worried. He regretted having introduced his companion as 'ASIS's deputy chief – someone well versed in things Chinese', but there was nothing else he could say.

'Most definitely,' Morgandale replied, 'and if the deal's lost, it's gone for good.'

This time his speed of reply confirmed that his only task was to bolster the case of the Government. It also implied that he might be someone with no mind of his own on issues of professional importance.

'And what, precisely, might your opinion be based upon?' Garran said, his manner procedural.

He was himself well acquainted with China. But Morgandale, unlike his colleague from Canberra, had done no research on the judge's private interests and travels. In fact, as Goldman knew, Garran was a regular visitor to China. He had extended to that country judicial assistance in a variety of ways. There were longstanding friendships with Chinese counterparts, which bridged the great gaps in practice and custom. He was also an avid reader on Chinese history, especially on the lesser-known contributions made to the West. In short, Justice Richard Garran was seen on the Bench as a China buff of no mean repute. Goldman, however, had volunteered nothing to Morgandale, who he feared might exploit with the judge any shared interest in China. Much better, he thought, to keep this ASIS maverick in the dark.

'Why I think the deal could slip through our hands,' Morgandale said, 'is because of the *face* that will be lost if this bugging story comes out.

You see, the Chinese would get such a kick in the guts — if I might put it so crudely — that they wouldn't be seen dead cooperating with Australia after all the publicity the story would get.'

Morgandale was fired up and ready to go, but Garran merely nodded and left him up in the air. Again silence engulfed the room and a few minutes passed before he finished the affidavit.

He sat back in his chair, contemplating the papers neatly laid out on his desk. Removing his glasses, he swung them gently, this way and that. All except Morgandale, who had no feel for the law, realised that the judge had made his decision.

Goldman readied himself.

Garran peered out of the window, pondering the city lights. Then, replacing his glasses, he studied the *Courier*'s draft article once again. Finishing, he was quiet for a while before electing to speak.

'I must say, I'm *greatly* disturbed to discover this piece and to see it slipped in here as if it were some incidental appendage.'

This was not what Goldman wanted to hear.

'I won't ask *how* it was obtained, but I *will* ask again whether the appropriate warrants were issued. And I'd like a straight answer.'

Goldman had no idea what it was. He had raised this very point when O'Sullivan insisted the article be attached, but in the heat of the moment it had gone unaddressed. Inside, Goldman was furious. He should have thought of the warrants, he realised, on the flight up from Canberra. He'd reviewed each of the case's other dimensions. And there would have been time, too, to call from the airport. But bloody Bass was a constant distraction.

Now the judge was looking Goldman in the eye, expecting an answer.

'Well, I believe warrants would've been issued.' He put the best possible spin on his words, but they were devoid of conviction and his embarrassment showed.

Justice Garran was disgusted with Canberra and that was apparent as well. He let his glasses drop to the desk.

'You "believe they would have been issued", Mr Goldman? Come now, you and I know that's not good enough. What you mean is, the Government cut corners. That expediency pushed propriety out of the window.'

To Garran, there was a cavalier side to this whole sorry affair, and Michael O'Sullivan's fingerprints were all over it.

'In these sorts of matters, Mr Goldman, *knowledge* marks the man. *Belief* is simply blind faith. And I doubt that anyone's faith would be well placed in a Government that does things like that.'

Goldman bowed his head. He felt that humility was the best way to display contrition.

Morgandale, to the relief of both, had nothing to say.

Twenty-five minutes had elapsed since the meeting began.

Garran put on his glasses and glanced at his watch. 'You've prepared a draft court order?' he said, looking at Goldman.

'Yes, Your Honour. I have it here.'

The judge read it quickly, shaking his head at almost every point. Goldman's hopes retreated like an ebb tide.

Garran took up his pen, holding it over the print as he reflected, much like an eagle searching the ground for its prey. Then it dived on the paper. He ruled a line through Clause One and another through Two.

'I won't grant the Government an injunction "in perpetuity". That's out of the question, though I will place a suppression order on the affidavit itself, for as long as you want. That sort of thing should *never* find its way into the public domain.'

Telepathically he knew what Goldman was thinking: thank God for that!

'What I *will* grant is an injunction from this evening, Thursday – *pro tem* and *ex parte* – and I'll mark a return date of Saturday, 27 May, at ten o'clock in the morning.'

During that time the *Sydney Daily Courier* would be forbidden to publish. Instead, it would have its lawyers prepare to argue a case, as would the Government, for or against an extension of the injunction.

Garran added: 'We'll meet here and *in camera*. And I suggest that the time in between be used to find answers to the questions I've posed.'

Sydney: Thursday, 25 May, 8.15 p.m.

'*Bu xiangxin!*' Zhang exploded: I can't believe it! As he spoke he was both excited and worried.

'I'm dumbfounded, too,' Gao said, shaking his head. 'Seriously, though, the question is, will they get a long-term extension?'

The pair sat in Gao's office in the Sydney Consulate discussing the coup. They had pulled two swivel chairs up to his desk. Gao was keen to run the Cicada's documents past his colleague because of Zhang's superior knowledge of English, but Zhang's mind had already wandered far beyond language. He found the whole thing unreal, even disturbing. True, it was a great win for China, but for Zhang as an individual, it threw his value system into confusion.

If, behind the scenes, he thought, the whole world functioned like this – with traitors constantly plying their trade – who the hell was *he* working for? How immune was China to these ugly practices?

Less than an hour before, Gao had met the Cicada in Sydney at the Australian's request. It transpired that in Canberra, the Cicada had managed to copy the newspaper article that the *Courier* was planning to run. He had also made copies of the smaller attachments that were passed to the judge, including the transcript of O'Sullivan's conversation with the US Ambassador. But taking pride of place in the dossier was O'Sullivan's affidavit.

The Cicada had insisted that Gao wait until later to examine the documents. He preferred instead to brief the Chinese verbally, and quickly, on what had occurred. In the Cicada's view, which he stressed was also that of the Attorney-General's official from Canberra, Justice Garran might extend the injunction for a week, but probably no longer. Key parts of the *Courier* story, such as US involvement in the bugging operation, could well be excised and suppressed for an indefinite period. But in a greatly reduced form, the article might soon get a run. As for the affidavit, that bizarre piece of work would presumably never resurface, so damaging had the judge assessed its contents to be.

'Tell me, how does "Chan" do all this?' Zhang said. 'How can he betray his country so casually, without any compunction? OK, this is nothing new to you, but it is to me.'

'Look,' Gao said, 'I'm not into solving riddles. I just focus on what I can screw out of him at any point. All I know is he wants money, whether we pay him in cash or stick it in his Hong Kong account, and he's willing to produce useful material to get it. His interests and ours happen to coincide at the moment, for however long that turns out to be. Granted, we've learnt a lot now about him as a person and about his background, but none of that answers the question why he's doing this. I've tried to get it out of him; I've hit a brick wall every time. The only thing that's beyond doubt is that money's crucial to his future – and in the short term, I'm sure. There's nothing long term about this. He's working to a plan, and money's the key to it. To me, it's as simple as that.'

'Maybe, but I still can't understand how he hides doing things like this from his colleagues.'

'Well, from my experience, these types are exceptionally clever at covering up extra dimensions in their lives. They're somehow able to spend great amounts of energy on maintaining . . . oh, you know, a totally normal front. And it works. No one suspects what they're up to. Anyhow, enough of that. Let's see what he's given us.'

Zhang was left scratching his head as they pulled their chairs in closer.

The first thing Gao chose for scrutiny was the article that the *Courier* was eager to print. They carefully read through it together. Double-spaced, it ran to 33 pages, and it soon became apparent that hardly an operational detail was missing. There was much more information than they'd imagined the newspaper possessing. There were elaborate descriptions of how far the original optical fibre network had reached into the embassy, and enlightening accounts of how much of the yield the Americans had held back from their partner. On and on it went, with aspects and angles that even the Cicada had failed to disclose.

Next came O'Sullivan's notes on his conversation with Greensborough.

'Unbelievable,' Gao said. 'It's like a father browbeating his son.'

Though O'Sullivan had compiled the notes himself, the atmospherics of the tension-packed meeting had come through undiminished. As they read on, the two Chinese glanced at each other, grimacing in feigned agony over what the minister had had to endure.

They only cursorily examined the *US–Australian Agreement on Intelligence Exchanges*. Gao was already conversant with that. A copy had come his way two years before, when a recruited agent in the Department of Foreign Affairs had needed cash to renovate his house in Canberra.

'*Hao le! Xianzai zhege,*' Gao said, choosing a fresh document: right! Let's move on to this. Playfully, he waved the affidavit in front of Zhang.

'According to "Chan",' he said, his tough face aglow with excitement, 'this is "one fucking hell of a read", whatever that means.'

The opening pages were nothing out of the ordinary, merely outlining the technical parameters of the bugging operation. The construction of a new Chinese Embassy in Canberra had, it was claimed, been 'an opportunity, too good to miss'. The 'intimate and fraternal relationship with the Americans could only be enhanced by this cooperative venture'. When they progressed to where O'Sullivan had a full head of steam, Zhang and Gao started smiling. Soon they were laughing.

'Hey, see this,' Gao said, reading aloud in his accented English:

> ... China will undoubtedly prove to be Ronald Reagan's Evil Empire of the twenty-first century. Rampant, indeed rabid, in its offshore espionage activities, its appetite for the fruits of the labours of others already outstrips the perfidy and deceit of the Japanese.

'Wow!'

Gao had the full sense of the meaning, though he checked with Zhang on the significance of less colloquial words that O'Sullivan had used.

'Evil Empire, hmmm?' he said, tut-tutting. 'That's pretty strong stuff.'

'You realise it puts us in the same league as Saddam Hussein,' Zhang replied, infected by his colleague's enthusiasm.

'Imagine quoting this back to the Australian Government,' Gao said, grinning. 'It'd be pretty painful, eh?'

'The thought had passed through my mind.'

'And to top it off,' Gao said, 'we Chinese outstrip the perfidy and deceit of those bastard *guizi*. Now there's an accolade we'll never live down. What a pity we can't share it with the Nips.'

Zhang laughed at the prospect.

Reading on, Gao soon found himself snagged once again:

> Unless Western allies like us, similarly endowed with standards of justice and decency, cooperate to tame this beast, it

will be out of the cage and upon us before we can put up a defence.

'Oh, how rich can you get?' he said, laughing so much he had trouble talking.

'For a Communist Party edict back home,' Zhang said, 'you'd get an award for language like that. But not here. Not in a place like Australia.'

Zhang, who was reading ahead of Gao, spotted something else that was worthy of comment. He was intrigued by its raw exposition of Canberra's thinking. The intelligence game might be dirty, he mused, but at least it gets you close to the truth. He read aloud:

> . . . we find Chinese espionage activity on Australian soil a menace of relentless proportions.

'*Gao Tongzhi*,' he said, slapping his colleague on the back: Comrade, this has to be the finest tribute you'll ever get.

'Well, it's no matter of shame,' Gao replied. 'You know, I could crack a promotion on this alone. After all, this stuff's from the inner sanctum of Canberra, and you can't go much higher than that for a reference in my line of work. But I see a gong in all this for you, too. The Australians clearly want your energy deal like you've never imagined. Billions of dollars coming into the coffers over the next thirty-odd years, they say. And they believe it's of national importance.'

Zhang nodded. Indeed, it was there in writing, if exaggerated for the occasion.

'And that, my old mate,' Gao said, lowering his voice for effect, 'is where Beijing will nail them to the wall.'

ELEVEN

Sydney: Thursday, 25 May, 9.20 p.m.

'Do you read us? Over.'

'Sure do, Ma'am,' Jason, the FBI man in the surveillance squad, replied. Wired for the occasion, at the InterContinental, he was posing as a businessman waiting for somebody.

'He should be there any minute,' Cantrell explained. 'He said around twenty past and it's right on that now.'

Before she had finished speaking, Sebastian Morgandale appeared. He walked straight past Jason and headed across to the reception desk. But before he had a chance to talk to the young lady on duty, someone called to him from nearby. It was a short, chubby Chinese man in his sixties, with glasses and oiled black hair, who Jason had already spotted sitting there with a briefcase on his lap.

'Hey, Bass!' he said, extending his hand as Morgandale swung around quickly. 'I'm so pleased to see you.'

The pair greeted each other warmly.

'Look,' the Chinese said, 'I suggest we head off immediately. I've told the restaurant we'll be late, but still, we don't want to waste time, do we?'

'No, that's fine with me,' Morgandale replied.

As they strode outside to a waiting hire car – the Australian with a satchel under his arm – Cantrell's operative sauntered past them to flag his own vehicle. It belonged to a squad that was ready to follow the pair to Doyles. Out at the ocean end of Sydney Harbour and renowned for its seafood, it was one of this foreign visitor's favourite eateries.

Only the day before, Cantrell and her team had discovered that Morgandale had another mobile phone, in addition to the one he customarily used for work. By monitoring this full time she had learnt of his pending assignment with this wealthy Malaysian industrialist, Winston Lee. Lee was as close to Beijing as he was to his confidant and comrade, Ambassador Li. An elaborate surveillance operation had been launched to find out what the link was between Morgandale and Lee. It was coordinated from the CIA's safe house near the city and Cantrell, Linda Levi and others were there now, listening in.

'We have lift off!' Levi said, clapping her hands. Middle-aged and solid, she was intimidating without even opening her mouth. 'Think of it. This may well be our traitor.'

Cantrell found this puny attempt at being deferential to them almost insulting. She and the others knew what Levi meant: this *is* our man.

'What did I tell you?' the woman persisted. 'It so often turns out to be the ones closest to their political masters. Thank God we've put our resources into this guy and not into Clarke.'

Cantrell bit her lip. Say nothing, she thought, until we've seen what transpires.

Levi already had her offside with her constant urge to take charge. There had been an argument that afternoon over whether a listening device should be planted in Lee's hire car. Cantrell had put her foot down and refused. It was unlikely, she said, that much would be discussed within earshot of the driver. The team's resources could be better applied elsewhere.

Lee had flown into Sydney the previous day from Hong Kong. His plan was to meet up with family members now gathering at his property near Canberra. On landing, he had contacted Morgandale in the capital on the latter's special number and in the course of that conversation Morgandale had made a guarded allusion to material he was putting together for him. It was plain the two had something going, which was a revelation that caused Levi's face to light up. 'I've booked two rooms at the hotel,' the Malaysian said, 'and naturally, I'm covering your costs as well.' That was before Morgandale had known he would be coming to Sydney anyway, and staying in other accommodation.

Cantrell already had a two-man squad on site at Doyles. One operative, Jay, had been into the restaurant, posing as a hotel assistant. He said he had come to check the table: no airconditioning ducts overhead, no open windows close by and a reasonably quiet spot. The manager had shown him the table and left him alone. With a device in hand, he had seated himself and managed to slip it underneath without being seen. The bug was later fine-tuned from outside. Reception was good: sharp, and with little ambient noise from round about.

At the safe house, where Cantrell was keen to avoid chatting with Levi, she quickly struck up radio contact with her squad at the site.

'Do you read me?' she said, speaking into a mike.

'Loud and clear,' Jay replied.

'Our friends are heading your way. Might be twenty minutes, with luck.'

'OK, Ollie's set to go in right away.'

This other operative would position himself at a table already booked within sight of the targets, and would enjoy a quiet meal over a folio of corporate plans.

'All going smoothly with us,' those who were tailing the hire car cut in. They were locked into the same radio grid.

On arrival, Lee and Morgandale strode into the restaurant and went straight to their table, accompanied by the manager, from whom they ordered Scotches and a large seafood platter.

Lee pulled from his briefcase some photos, which he seemed pleased to show Morgandale. They were shots of major manufacturing plants he had developed in China, he explained, and were taken on his most recent trip a fortnight ago. Ollie, who had a good line of sight from where he was sitting, listened in to what they were saying. Occasionally, by resting his chin in his hand to hide his mouth, he was able to describe what was going on at the other table.

Back at the safe house Levi was finding it difficult to contain her excitement. Thankfully, though, she was silent. It had been agreed that, with everything from the bugged dialogue being recorded, nobody would talk while the operation was under way. Tapes could be replayed later if required.

Morgandale took from his satchel a large brown envelope and passed it across.

'Here,' he said, 'this is for you.'

'Oh, thanks,' Lee replied, routinely.

And that was all.

Leaving it unopened, he simply slipped it into his briefcase, along with his photos. Next, he produced an envelope of his own – a smaller, white one – that he laid on the table.

'Here are a few more "shots" you might like to see,' Lee said.

Morgandale clearly understood what that meant. 'Oh, your generosity, my friend, is excessive.'

'There's no sign of bashfulness over what they're doing,' Ollie whispered.

Levi, with a look of smug satisfaction, turned to Cantrell, as much as to say: 'What would you expect from a pair of experienced spies?' She had no need to explain what she was thinking:

Morgandale's our man. Other Americans in the room appeared to agree. Cantrell, though, still had faith in Mason's belief that Clarke was the one they were after – even if *this* was another case of treachery.

Morgandale now launched into a rundown on what he had just handed over. It was apparent that the matter had been previously discussed. A check carried out earlier that day had revealed that Lee had been in Australia some six weeks before. Levi had already worked out that this coincided with the first hint the NSA technicians in Canberra had had of changes in the Chinese Embassy's communications. To her that was simply more evidence of Morgandale's guilt.

'The stuff you wanted on China's all there,' Morgandale said, his voice confident. 'Beijing, Shanghai, Xiamen, Wuhan and three other places too. You'll find the field comments useful – they're at the foot of each report. Let me know if you need more. I should have updates fairly soon.'

Levi was ecstatic.

Sydney: Thursday, 25 May, 10.45 p.m.

'If you could pass this on,' Gao said, handing the large envelope across, 'we'd be eternally grateful.'

The Australian politician smiled. After all, he was merely playing the role of a go-between. And what the Chinese had told him about the TV journalist in question sounded quite reasonable. It was a straightforward task.

'And *no* attribution,' he said, checking his instructions.

'No, none at all,' Gao replied. 'It just fell off the back of a truck, as you say in English.'

The politician grinned.

During their brief meeting in Sydney the Cicada had remembered to pass on to Gao the name of the National TV reporter who was looking into the embassy story. Averse to contacting the journalist directly, Gao had telephoned the NSW State parliamentarian, who he knew to be someone who could handle the job.

Onside with the Chinese for more than a decade, he had been brought into their stable of contacts by one of Gao's predecessors in Sydney. The Australian involved, together with his wife, had been running a travel business which, through careless management, hit the wall. But before it went down, the consulate, already known to the couple, stepped in to provide much-needed succour. Long years of good service and countless bookings to China were rewarded in kind. The husband later entered parliament, while his wife continued to run the business. It was in this way that agents of influence were often created.

Now, with delivery of the envelope ensured, Gao felt pleased with himself.

But what neither he nor his messenger knew was that the journalist already had most of the story, having acquired it through his own skill and persistence. All he lacked was an awareness of the injunction process and the fact that the *Sydney Daily Courier*, too, was ready to run.

The documents were handed over within an hour.

On reading the material the Cicada had provided, and finding that Adrian McKinnon, an acquaintance, was the writer of the *Courier* article, the TV journalist decided to drive round to McKinnon's apartment.

McKinnon grinned when he finished scanning the documents. 'Yes,' he said, 'this is certainly a story that should go out as soon as possible — except for this bloody affidavit, which is right over the top.'

His friend agreed. 'National TV's likely to run with its main points, Adrian, as early as tomorrow evening's news.'

'Which will presumably bust the injunction,' McKinnon responded.

'Oh, without a doubt. That sort of exposure would blow it away.'

'And if all goes to plan,' McKinnon said, 'you'll see the *Courier* follow up with all the detail in Saturday morning's edition.'

'Hopefully,' the TV journalist replied. 'But as you and I know very well, a plan like this is only half the game. The other is to keep it away from the Government. They'll fight hard and dirty to make sure this story stays under wraps.'

'True, so let's run over that aspect of things carefully,' McKinnon said.

Canberra: Friday, 26 May, 6.45 a.m.

'You know,' Mason said, 'after sleeping on it, I see a few things coming together.'

'Well, I'm glad it's been of use,' Lambert replied. He was referring to a thinkpiece he had compiled and handed over the previous day.

The two men were on the return leg after jogging to Black Mountain, which, together with its communications tower, formed a backdrop to Canberra. On Mason's earlier visit to the capital he had asked Lambert to record anything of interest in the behaviour of Clarke, Morgandale and the other suspects on the list.

'I'm intrigued, Todd, by what you say about Martin's antics. OK, he's always been a stirrer, but this business of harassing the Foreign Affairs bloke and those other people is weird, especially when you think the main person it impacts on is him.'

'Well, that's how it struck me. But the question is, what's driving it? He's trying to make a point, but to whom and for what purpose? That's the puzzle.'

'And only one, at that,' Mason said. 'Another is what you've said about Poulson and Imlach. Instinct tells me also that what they did is somehow the key to all this. It might be what triggered it off. But where China comes into the picture, God only knows. Not that the two have to be mutually exclusive.'

'Greg, I really don't think anyone else in the Service understands the impact that that "desertion" had on Martin. With those two suddenly taking off like that and setting up shop in Jakarta, he was thrown completely. Yet he covered his feelings up well. Granted, he's normally pretty controlled, but that could've had him raving about how there'd been no forewarning, no security review of their plans – all that sort of thing. "You're defectors. Good riddance to you!" That's the outburst I'd have expected. But instead, what did we get? He just dismissed the whole thing with a wave of the hand. It doesn't fit in.'

Mason nodded. Lambert was taking him back into Clarke's mind: that sinkhole he had spent endless hours trying to fathom. He recalled a quip that one wag in the Service had made about Clarke: 'Mate, don't seek logic where it doesn't exist.'

'No, I tell you, Greg, with them pissing off like that, back into his old stamping ground, he was devastated. They didn't even discuss it with him, nor did they seek his endorsement. That's what really shocked him.'

'Yes, that's interesting,' Mason said, 'particularly if you link it up with old Alfie's suspicions about what Martin was up to in Jakarta. See, what we've got here are key pieces of a jigsaw, with China sitting right in the middle; but how they all fit together, who can say? I just can't imagine Martin getting mixed up with the Chinese unless it's for money, and in large sums that he'd want fast.'

'You know,' Lambert responded, 'I've long seen him getting himself caught up in a mess like this, one in which none of the checks and balances come into play until it's all over and done with.'

These were Mason's sentiments exactly.

The pair ran on in silence for a while, pausing on a bend to admire the view over Lake Burley Griffin.

'Say,' Mason struck up again, 'what do you think about O'Sullivan sending Bass up to Sydney? I can't see how he'd ever pull the wool over a judge's eyes.'

'Exactly. I gather the AG's bloke was spitting chips when he found he'd have him as a travelling companion.'

'And Martin got to go too, eh?' Mason observed.

'Yeah, well that was just to get him out of the office. There's a key meeting today with Foreign Affairs, where we're trying to settle that cover problem once and for all. We had virtually all the slots around Asia we wanted until Martin buggered it up last time round. So I'm fronting in his place.'

'Well, don't let it go to your head, will you.'

'I'll try.'

Sydney: Friday, 26 May, 10.20 a.m.

'Dammit!' Ben Jameson snapped. 'What are they doing down there?'

His display of petulance was aimed at pre-empting a walkout by Levi. Tetchy at the best of times, she believed that video linkups – whether secure or not – were a waste of time, time that could be spent doing the job.

Jameson sat alongside her and other members of the team in the CIA safe house. They were waiting to discuss with colleagues in Canberra what had occurred during Morgandale's dinner with Lee on the previous evening. It was an all-American dialogue at both ends. Mason was busy elsewhere.

'Look, I'll call someone and . . .'

Suddenly, Greensborough's booming voice crackled on the line, followed by the image of him and a stiff Norb Schneider, the Agency's top representative in Australia, sitting alongside. The NSA technicians sat behind, looking uncomfortable about being on camera.

'Listen, Ben,' the ambassador said, 'we're getting no damn sense from this Government down here. None at all. But don't worry, we've been doing a bit of nifty interception work at this end and that's given us some idea of what's going on. You see, we now know what the *Sydney Daily Courier*'s up to, and to top it off, we also have a copy of an affidavit the Government's presented to a judge in Sydney – some guy called Garran. It seems he's already granted them a short injunction on the newspaper story, though the prospect of that being extended for long doesn't look too good. So, Ben, we think it might be time to touch things along.'

Those watching in Sydney sensed Greensborough's determination.

He was like a terrier when he sank his teeth into something he believed in. He was not always easy to handle, but he was levelheaded and *not* a loose cannon. And, with any ambassador overseas, that meant a lot to the CIA, especially to Jameson for whom Greensborough had a great liking. He had not yet met Beth Cantrell.

'The consensus is, Ben, that I get on to President Dunbar direct and ask him to put the fear of God into this pipsqueak Prime Minister here.'

Off camera in Sydney, Levi punched the air. 'Now *that's* what I call good thinking,' she said, loud enough to be heard.

She felt this might appeal to Greensborough, which it did. He liked openness, and hence his arm's length relationship with Schneider, who he had privately described to Jameson as 'that anal-retentive prude'. Jameson was an experienced field officer, while Schneider – one of the Agency's new breed of managerial diplomatists – was not.

'We'd be grateful for that, sir,' the Sydney station chief said, scanning his colleagues alongside as he spoke.

It was just what the team wanted. Better, though, for the ambassador to have suggested it and for the Agency to agree, otherwise someone back home might claim they were unable to handle the task.

Greensborough sat back in his chair. He had noticed Cantrell glancing at her watch and was aware that Schneider also had urgent issues to raise.

'Ben,' Schneider came in, 'before we hand over to Linda and Beth, I should tell you that Greg Mason dropped in last night and laid his cards on the table. We decided to come clean and tell him about the other bugging we've been doing down here. He's a straightforward sort of guy, so it went fairly smoothly. He wanted to know what we knew about what Canberra's been hiding, which led to the question of what he thought he should or shouldn't be passing on to us. It's that old issue of where the line should be drawn – the same thing that came up in Beth's chat with Joe Pellegrini. Whatever, it's a relief that we've cleared the air. Now, with ASIO's technical chief on board, and Lambert as well, it's a potent force we have here in Canberra – particularly with Todd being deputy to the number two suspect!'

Schneider spoke with a large grin on his face.

This greatly annoyed Cantrell, though she tried not to let it show. There had been no agreement yet on which of the prime targets was the likely traitor, but clearly Levi had been in contact with Schneider and left him in no doubt about who she thought it was. She had also rejoiced in news of Morgandale's attempt to recruit Alexandra Templeton's friend and colleague at ONA, Sarah, to gather intelligence on his behalf, though Washington had confirmed that no American agency had employed him. 'It's still very worrying,' Schneider had said in an earlier video link, with Levi tripping over herself to agree.

'We clearly have quality people,' the ambassador interrupted, while Cantrell was deciding whether or not to object. 'I've liked the cut of Mason ever since I heard how he helped us out with that Omega Blue operation. He's a man whose instincts we should follow carefully. I met him this morning, you know, and I asked him how he thought the Chinese might react to the bugging. It was interesting hearing what he had to say about the high price they'll exact from us, and on *how* they'll go about it. That's where his understanding of the Asian mind comes to the fore. Actually, I've asked Norb here to do some notes to send back to Washington.'

Cantrell wondered whether this was Greensborough's way of saying that, if Mason had put his money on Clarke, then that too was the horse he would back.

The same thought had obviously struck Norb Schneider, who was monitoring Levi's body language closely. That was why he quickly reverted to his earlier and more general theme.

'These Aussies,' he said, 'are sick to the teeth with what's going on in Canberra. But let's be sure of one thing. They're in this to clean up *their* system. Not just to be helpful to us. OK, our interests coincide, and in a way *we're* as recruited to their cause as they are to ours, but if they see any divergence from that one central aim, they'll pull back without hesitation.'

Silence at both ends of the linkup confirmed that the point was well taken.

'We had all three in here earlier this morning,' Schneider went on, 'and worked out where everyone fits in on a delicate mission like this. Pellegrini said he couldn't risk diverting ASIO resources unless, ironically, there's leverage from outside – like Washington putting pressure on Canberra. At the moment, it seems much of the Government's effort to weed out the traitor is bogged down in a study of who's had access to what. They've identified everyone officially in the know, but seem to have no idea how far word might've spread beyond that. Mason and his mates feel there's a handful of people at the top who are actually desperate for the traitor never to be found, yet equally keen to appear to be vigorously searching.'

Levi was nodding, which Cantrell found positive.

Indeed, this was the area that Cantrell herself wanted to explore when she had sufficient resources to devote to Clarke: what sort of network was supporting him? Ultimately, she believed, the fight they were engaged in would be as much about disarming that, as about surgically removing Clarke from its protective embrace. She was aware from experience that no one in a network like this could risk breaking ranks: the worse the crime, the closer the pack rallied around the offender.

'Apparently, the rest of their energy's focused on the *Courier* in the hope of finding out who's been feeding them copy and . . . '

'Oh, by the way, Ben,' Greensborough jumped in, politely patting Schneider on the arm in the process, 'Pellegrini says Clarke's been spreading a story around that it was the *Courier* itself that tipped off the Chinese and that they did it through asking amateurish questions about rumours the embassy was bugged. Joe doesn't believe that's what happened at all, nor do we, but it's a line that Clarke seems intent on pushing. Joe told us he put Clarke on the spot by asking what evidence he had, but he just rambled on about how he'd heard it around the traps.'

Mention of Clarke, yet again, proved too much for Levi. 'Look, with respect,' she said, breaking in tersely, 'if you want to hear what happened last night in Sydney, we're going to have to move on.'

Greensborough was taken aback. He had not finished what he wanted to say. 'All in good time, blossom,' he shot back, scowling to show his dissatisfaction. 'Don't wet your knickers, now.'

It was a grand putdown, but no one dared laugh, even if most wanted to.

Levi was nonplussed. Would she react, the others thought, or would tact dictate a better response? She sat tight, although her frown did nothing to disguise her fury.

Schneider, thinking quickly, gave the ambassador an out. He pointed to the time, suggesting Greensborough had another appointment to keep. Greensborough responded smoothly to the reminder and readied himself to leave. He had resolved to bow out – for the time being anyway. He had, after all, made his case, which was why he had 'offered' to sit in in the first place. Before the linkup started he had told those in Canberra that, while he believed Levi had some attractive professional attributes, he was still not sure how effective she would be overall.

'True,' he'd said, 'she might have an impressive reputation, but as Pellegrini's warned us, her US expertise is going to have to adapt to a culture she wrongly assumes to be identical to her own.'

But once the ambassador had gone, Schneider looked content again.

If Linda's on the right track, he thought, with this Morgandale guy, we might wrap up this whole sordid affair before it goes any further.

Canberra/Sydney: Friday, 26 May, 11.50 a.m.

'Hello, it's me.' Cantrell recognised Mason's voice immediately, and his serious tone. It said: 'Let's avoid names. This is not a personal call.' His failure to name himself told her as much.

The video linkup had not long finished.

'What's new?' she said.

'I'm still in Canberra. We can talk more tonight. "T" and I are driving up and should be in Sydney about ten,' Mason said, alluding to Todd Lambert. 'In short, we're on to something. We're pretty sure "Miss L" is barking up the wrong tree. She's correct in the sense that the bloke she's targeting *is* mixed up in something, but "T" agrees with me that it's almost certainly a private trade he's doing in economic material. It's probably been going on for years and with more than one party. But he's not the one we're looking for. "T" and I still think it's the other chap, and we'll tell you why.'

Though convoluted, Cantrell understood easily.

'More on that later,' Mason said. 'But before I go, something else to keep under your hat. I've just heard that "Miss L" called your prudish boss down here, soon after the end of the linkup you had. She doesn't think it's wise to move resources across on to "C". It seems her line is that, first, "Bass Strait" has now been conclusively identified, and second, you and I share a known relationship with "C", which colours our judgement. And third, and I hope you're ready for this . . . '

'Try me.'

'That you and I are *emotionally involved.*' His enunciation spoke of sarcasm and ridicule.

Cantrell was silent.

'I gather someone will raise this with you fairly soon. Anyhow, I must go. We can talk later.'

'I look forward to it, but be careful your feelings don't show!'

He laughed in his familiar way.

Cantrell admired Mason for staying on top in adversity. She had seen it before. He was that sort of person. He had a strength of his own and she liked it, especially now that he was back in full operational mode. Her mind was already at work on how to foil the FBI guru.

Canberra: Friday, 26 May, 5.00 p.m.

> In news just to hand, it has been revealed that Australian Intelligence, in conjunction with an American spy agency, has for more than five years been engaged in an extensive eavesdropping operation against the Chinese Embassy in Canberra. A wide-reaching network of listening devices was installed in the new embassy building while it was under construction.

Ambassador Li flashed a grin at the others, all listening intently. He kept rubbing his hand over his bald head, a habit he had when something tickled his fancy.

Five of his senior staff sat with him in his office, with their chairs arranged in front of the television set. The sense of relief in the room was palpable. At last the story was out. And right on schedule on the five o'clock National TV News.

Li gestured to them to keep quiet. This was a moment to be savoured — not one to be disrupted by undue elation. He had earlier asked that his colleagues, three men and two women, hear the report to the end.

> Sophisticated optical-fibre devices were originally put in place by ASIO, the Australian Security Intelligence Organisation, though the operation has since been controlled by the US National

> Security Agency, which specialises in electronic intelligence-gathering. Top Secret information gleaned from the venture and picked up by a relay station near the embassy is transmitted direct to Washington. Australian intelligence sources have revealed their concern that vital information, especially on economic matters, has not been filtered back to this country.

Not a murmur could be heard as the bulletin went deeper. A clenched fist was occasionally raised or a guffaw restrained.

Four minutes later the report drew to a close and the newsreader moved on to a multiple pile-up on a highway near Brisbane. Li used the remote control to turn down the sound, then they all erupted with joy.

Deng, the Canberra-based intelligence chief, uncorked a bottle of champagne. He had been quietly readying it in the bulletin's final stages. Thin and gaunt, he was on top of the world. Holding the bottle aloft, he glanced at Li for permission to pour. The embassy's counsellor, a senior woman of sixty, passed the glasses around, handing the first to her beaming ambassador.

Li religiously shunned alcohol, except for a perfunctory sip on formal occasions. But when news had come down the line mid-afternoon from Gao in Sydney, that five-o'clock might be the moment they were waiting for, Li suggested celebrating with a top local brand.

Their glasses charged, he proposed a toast. 'To devious plots foiled – *Gongxi, gongxi.*' Congratulations. He spoke with theatrical flair.

The others repeated his words.

'And to turning the tables,' he said. *'Gongxi, gongxi.'*

They all drank to that.

'And,' he said, just when they thought he had finished, 'to Master Spy Gao.'

'To Master Spy Gao,' they echoed, with a gusto that spoke of genuine esteem. *'Gongxi, gongxi.'*

Gao had done a professional job. Li and the haughty Deng understood this only too well. Without his speedy action on the previous evening, and the help of the consulate's parliamentary friend, none of this might have happened.

But when another round of champagne was poured out, Deng refrained. Instead, he removed from the ambassador's video set the tape he had earlier inserted.

'It won't take long to transcribe,' he said to Li. 'Our on-the-spot version might be helpful to the boffins back home.'

Gao's tip-off to the embassy in Canberra had been quickly relayed to Beijing. His summary of the documents handed over by the Cicada was passed on as well. The Ministry of State Security – so its desk officer for Australia said – would monitor the broadcast directly. But the embassy's own interpretation would be useful. Local atmospherics, they knew, were often lost on transcribers remote in the motherland's bosom.

'Tell them about the affidavit,' Li said, as Deng was about to leave the room.

It was a point Gao himself had made, just before five. If that document were to fail to rate a mention in the bulletin, it might possibly be banned from the public arena for good. After all, it had been acknowledged as political dynamite. And for that very reason, for the Chinese it had a value all of its own, which now reminded Li of a duty he had to perform.

'*Hao le, hao le,*' he said, clapping his hands in a sign that the party was over: OK, OK. He went on: 'I need to put pen to paper myself. They'll want ideas on the mileage to be gained from a stunning event like this. Let's face it, it's virtually a Mandate of Heaven – a licence to print money, which the Australians will have to honour in return for our silence.'

Deng laughed from the doorway. 'Exactly my thoughts,' he said, 'and if anyone knows how to milk it, it's you.'

The others understood that this was not flattery. Rather it was simple fact. Li loved a good fight and the more strategic and cerebral it was, the better. He made a courteous bow of the head.

'I'll get a quick note off to Beijing,' he said, 'before we're attacked by the media.'

He turned to the embassy's press officer, who was also part of the group.

'Please tell all staff, wherever they are in Australia, that the message is "No comment". We have *absolutely* nothing to say.'

'Ambassador,' Li's secretary called from her room alongside. 'Miss Wei says the switchboard's jammed with inquiries.'

Canberra: Friday, 26 May, 5.35 p.m.

'Well, it's not the sort of thing any of us enjoy having to deal with, is it?' Li said, smiling warmly. From his point of view, commiseration with Prime Minister Farnsworth over his unenviable position could only oil the path nicely.

'No, it's not,' the PM replied.

His call to Li on the ambassador's direct number had been made without consulting the Foreign Minister, Michael O'Sullivan. 'Yes,' Li had said, 'let's meet in your office.'

Now, having only just sat down for a one-on-one chat, Li chose to set the pace. 'Knowing we both have a lot to do,' he said with unusual directness, 'why don't we get straight down to business?'

'Yes, yes, of course.'

'Naturally, you'll understand I'm still awaiting instructions, but I do think it's safe to say – strictly off the record, that is – that if you can offer up some sort of "political accommodation", then I'm pretty confident Beijing will refrain from public comment on this unfortunate thing. At least, until you're able to sit down and parley.'

Oh, what a relief! Farnsworth thought. That's just what I want.

Li knew that it was.

In reality, the ambassador was authorised to handle the matter in whatever way he saw fit. He had already suggested that a small delegation fly down in secret to see what could be done. The group would leave for Sydney the following night. He had also agreed with Beijing as to who should head it. In fact, it was a mission for which that hardnosed negotiator had a particular bent. Indeed, that was why they had asked China's leadership to throw it their way.

'Can I get you a drink, perhaps?' Farnsworth said, exuding politeness.

Li had allowed a silence to settle upon them, and the PM had been unsure how to fill it.

'Yes, a tea would be nice, but please excuse me if I don't stay very long.'

Sydney: Friday, 26 May, 6.30 p.m.

Justice Garran sat quietly at his desk peering over his spectacles. His visitors were still taking their seats. Extra chairs had been brought in to his chambers. The atmosphere was a mixture of relief, trepidation and downright dismay. Michael O'Sullivan sat alongside David Goldman from Attorney-General's and another man, who was the Federal Government's barrister. The original delegation from Canberra was supposed to be bigger but had been drastically reduced in light of what had occurred a short time before. The National TV news had injected into the equation a new and unexpected dynamic. Hull, the editor-in-chief of the *Courier*, was also attending. With him were two partners from Buckridges, the paper's legal advisers, and their Queen's Counsel. The court registrar and the judge's associate sat quietly off to one side.

O'Sullivan was embarrassed as well as despondent. He felt intimidated by the ticklish position in which he now found himself. Things had spun out of control and his colleagues were demanding he shoulder responsibility for the whole damned affair. As a politician, he could usually talk his way out of anything threatening, with a largely compliant Opposition rarely testing him on the floor of the House. The media, he also believed, he could handle, as he could the occasional choleric constituent with too much to say. But this sharpwitted jurist, Garran, was a different matter entirely. O'Sullivan found himself back in a schoolroom in front of a master about to cane him for acting the goat. Neither mealy-mouthed words nor the twisting of logic could help him talk his way out of this.

The judge appreciated the minister's discomfort and his urgent need to focus both political and diplomatic talent on repairing the damage. But after what Garran had seen in the earlier affidavit, his sympathy stopped at that point.

Silence pervaded the room, folding into suspense, as procedures got under way.

O'Sullivan drew from his bag a new affidavit, though one much thinner this time. Attached to it was a letter from the Prime Minister. He passed these to Goldman, who in turn handed them to Garran. Copies were also given to the Buckridges team.

The judge read the two-page letter with precision and care, nodding ever so slightly as he moved on from one paragraph to the next. Thank God, he thought, this is more balanced and measured. It's even convincing, compared to what they dished up last night. Finishing, he moved on to the affidavit, which he read quickly. Excellent, he thought. No more of that nonsense. This is Goldman's drafting for sure, and with no interference.

He laid the affidavit down on his desk then slowly removed his glasses. 'Thank you,' he said, looking at O'Sullivan. Next he turned to the Government's barrister. 'Is there anything you wish to add?'

The barrister shook his head politely. The deference the two afforded each other suggested they had been through this ritual before.

Garran then turned to the QC from Buckridges. He was another friend from the tight-knit world of the law and displayed the same serious demeanour as Garran. Both approached their profession with the gravitas that marked a top surgeon out from the pack.

'Perhaps we should hear what you have to say.'

'Thank you, Your Honour. My client would respectfully submit that, because of the nature of the television broadcast, of which we're no doubt all aware – a video of which is appended to my client's affidavit, if Your Honour wishes to see it – that the injunction placed upon the *Sydney Daily Courier* should be dissolved. More than enough detail of this eavesdropping operation is now freely available in the public domain.'

It was a case plainly stated for a lawyer.

'It so happens,' Garran said, 'I am aware of the bulletin and I have no reason to disagree with what your client asserts.'

The hare was off and running.

Without further comment he turned to O'Sullivan. The minister squirmed. The moment of decision hovered over him like an executioner's sword.

Garran's face gave nothing away. O'Sullivan was speechless, not knowing whether he was expected to comment or what he should say.

Moments passed with an interminable grind. Then Garran gave up and moved on.

'Well, Mr Goldman,' he said, addressing a man who, he knew, understood what was coming. 'Is there anything *you* wish to add?'

Goldman shook his head.

Catching the minister's eye again, the judge paused as O'Sullivan nervously ran a finger round the inside of his collar.

'For reasons already outlined,' Garran went on, 'as well as for others, I will lift the injunction completely.'

O'Sullivan's jaw dropped, as though nothing could have prepared him for this.

'I see no clear and present danger to the nation,' Garran went on, his tone procedural, rather than didactic, 'nor do I believe that the content of the television bulletin – nor, indeed, of the *Courier* article – in any way poses a threat to the nation's security. In this matter, therefore, I come down in favour of the public interest and the right of the public to know.'

Hull turned to his lawyers and smiled. He was careful not to aggravate the position in which others in the room found themselves. Goldman was unfazed. He just wanted it over. His eyes were lowered. O'Sullivan, though, was badly tested by this turn of events.

'But Your Honour,' he said, stumbling and with none of the swagger he customarily displayed when things were going his way.

'Yes, Minister?' the judge replied, his tone bordering on exasperation.

'The Government's first affidavit,' O'Sullivan said. 'We can't let *that* out!'

Garran's view was no different. In fact, it was the next thing he'd planned to broach, but the minister's impatience now caused him to question how benign he should be in responding.

I'll say nothing, he thought, and see what he does. His raised eyebrows egged the minister on.

'Good grief, that sort of thing could be fatal if published,' O'Sullivan said. He glanced at Goldman for moral support, but the younger man was engrossed in the weave of the carpet.

'You and I know, Minister,' Garran said, 'that *moderation* is a virtue in public affairs. And therefore I have little option but to accede to your request. In effect, to protect you from your very own hand.'

This was scathing. It was rare for a judge to make such a comment, even *in camera*.

'As a consequence,' Garran said, 'the injunction on the affidavit will remain – in perpetuity.'

O'Sullivan's relief was manifest.

An odd quietness fell over the room, broken only by the registrar rising from his chair. The judge had earlier glanced his way. There was paperwork to attend to but, all up, the meeting was over.

'I thank you for your assistance in this difficult matter,' Garran said, smiling graciously at his visitors, who were still sitting tight in their chairs.

Sydney: Sunday, 28 May, 10.30 a.m.

Wang Meijian, China's intelligence supremo, settled back in her fine cedar chair, waiting for the meeting to start. The sound of her fingernails tapping on the polished table evoked an image of galloping horses.

'*Bu xiangxin?*' she said to her colleagues: you don't believe me?

Zhang laughed in response, which was just what she wanted. She had earlier told her team that if these *xiangbalao* – country hicks – proved incapable of facing reality, she planned to walk out. 'Up and over the table and out through the door,' she said.

The Australian side had no way of knowing what had transpired. That was why she had said it. At a time like this, she thought, humour's the least of *their* weapons.

The group sat in the dining room of Admiralty House, once the home of the commander of the British Squadron in colonial Australia. It was one of Sydney's stateliest rooms, high ceilinged and elegantly furnished. The Chinese delegation of six sat in the middle on one side of the long table. A low-slung floral arrangement of yellow and white roses decorated its centre.

It's appropriate, Wang thought, that they chose to talk here, torn between their past and their present.

On this bright sunny morning, two large windows in the room were wide open to keep the air fresh. Wang had asked Zhang to request that this be done. It was something rarely feasible in dusty Beijing. She had slept well on the overnight flight from China. The rigours of tough times in her youth had taught her to grab every moment of slumber. At the airport she'd got Zhang to take her to the sea for a swim, and to join her as well. On the way, they changed at the consul-general's residence, where Wang and her three male colleagues were to stay overnight. She had relished her hour at Bondi, enjoying the surf like a child, despite a chilly May bite in the air. It was nothing compared to the task that had brought her to Australia. It would undoubtedly be a day neither side would forget.

Wang was dressed in her trademark pale grey slack-suit, with which she always wore a plain ivory blouse. Pinned to her lapel was a small red flower picked from the consul's garden.

David Farnsworth, the Prime Minister, was embarrassed by the delay, which Wang's table tapping had only made worse. 'We'll be under way in a moment,' he said, frowning at O'Sullivan and Carl Maynard, his Trade Minister, both of whom were still organising their papers.

Maynard posed no risk in tense situations like this, but O'Sullivan did, for which reason Farnsworth had told him to keep quiet unless invited to speak.

'Take your time,' Wang replied, using Zhang to interpret, despite her own impeccable English. Zhang sat on her left, with Ambassador Li to her right.

The three-man Australian team found this formidable woman daunting.

Stories were legion of her Rottweiler habits when fools were around.

As she waited, she flicked through her briefing notes in Chinese, reading again the entry on Farnsworth. 'A portly and balding man of 57,' the entry ran. 'He is known for his shrewdness, quick wit and political cunning, but you can expect that O'Sullivan's tendency to pour petrol on the fire, trying to extinguish it, will test him sorely.'

She had agreed with Li's suggestion that she speak only through Zhang, though Li had told Farnsworth he assumed it would all be in English.

Silence would also be used, and with exquisite finesse. For the Chinese it was like a diamond: it had more than one facet.

Farnsworth coughed to warn his ministers he was going ahead. 'My colleagues and I welcome you in these most trying of times,' he said. His voice was clear and authoritative.

Zhang whispered his interpretation to Wang. The other Chinese were impassive and stern, though in no way uptight, which Farnsworth found mildly disarming. Perhaps, he thought, I could've put it better than that. Times are anything but trying for them.

'To begin with,' he said, 'I must apologise for what we've done to your embassy. There are no two ways about it. I appreciate that even those words mightn't hold much value in light of the act we've committed.'

The Chinese sat stonefaced.

Wang looked Farnsworth in the eye, nodding politely to acknowledge his words. The fact that she bothered meant something. He knew she would understand his dilemma only too well: how to broach compensation for the bugging, while in return asking China to keep quiet at all costs.

Something that Wang did not know was that her American counterpart – the CIA Director, John Sherrington – was also flying in with a team. He was due to arrive later in the day. Secret talks between the Americans and Australians would begin in Sydney early the next day, Monday. The PM, therefore, was under great pressure to reach agreement with China within 24 hours. The prospect of meeting with an irascible Sherrington, *without* a Chinese settlement under his belt, was enough to make the normally unflappable Farnsworth shudder.

'Right, let's get down to business,' he said, seeing no other way but directness. 'I thank you for holding back on public comment until we could talk.'

Wang's eyes were narrow and crafty. Their message was clear: just get to the point.

'No doubt the main thing to deal with,' Farnsworth said, 'is the question of refurbishing your embassy. That is, making it secure in whatever way you want.'

Wang listened until Zhang's rendition had ended, as if she had not understood a word. She pondered a moment, then looked back at Farnsworth.

'*Women yao* xin *de dashiguan*,' she said forcefully: we want a *new* embassy.

What Zhang said in English replicated her robust delivery.

The PM's advisers had considered the likelihood of the Chinese pushing for this. Nevertheless, it came as a shock to hear it stated so bluntly.

'Of course, we'll do all we can,' Farnsworth said, 'to fulfil your needs.'

He showed no sign of nervousness, but inside he was far from serene.

'Actually, we see a number of options,' Wang said, via Zhang, 'including rebuilding on the site.'

Farnsworth was unconcerned about cost. It was profile that preoccupied him, as well as the time it would take to put the matter to rest. It would be agony if the Government had to demolish the existing building and replace it with a new one.

Shit, if they stick to this line, he thought, we'll get nowhere. There'll be no chance of a political accommodation today.

He recalled scenarios that his minders had outlined before the Chinese arrived, and it was the energy deal, which Beijing had been promoting for more than a year, that came out on top. Yes, that's it, he thought. That's what they'll be aiming to clinch. Now the sooner that card's on the table, the better.

'I note what you say,' he said, 'but perhaps there are other areas we could usefully explore – to mutual advantage, of course.'

Maynard and O'Sullivan, who were looking quite glum, perked up visibly at mention of this.

'Other areas?' Wang replied.

'Yes, where we may find room for agreement.'

Wang sensed that her tactic had worked. She wanted nothing more than to range over options.

'It might be useful to name them,' she said.

'Well, to start with, there's the long-term energy pact we've been talking about. If we could work out something on that, there'd no doubt be benefits for both sides. And on a huge scale as well.'

Inside, Wang was riled by this resort to mutuality as a way of easing the pain.

'But that's been blocked for so long,' she said. 'Surely, it's hardly worth raising. And anyway, *we're* already working on alternative sources.' Her short laugh was one of derision, as well as impatience.

Farnsworth was careful not to overreact. His pause, however, after Zhang had finished interpreting, had the opposite effect.

So, nothing to say? Wang thought. Well, let's see how much homework you've done.

'Somehow, Prime Minister, you seem unaware of a major gas-field the Japanese have discovered near Sakhalin. It's mammoth in size. Your American friends, as well as the Koreans, the Russians and others, are all working hard to develop it – and, of course, also working on a long-term contract for gas sales to China.'

This came like a clap of thunder to the Australians. No mention of it had been made in their briefings. How could Canberra not know? Was it true? It had to be.

'I'm surprised,' Wang said, 'that you haven't been told.'

The silence that followed was plaintive.

Farnsworth and Maynard were in control, but O'Sullivan was like a piano wire ready to snap. ASIS had failed to pick up this crucial intelligence and he was the minister in charge of the Service.

The Chinese sat quietly, tirelessly studying the décor of the room. Ambassador Li pulled out his Hongta cigarettes, checked how many were left, then casually put them back in his pocket.

'Perhaps you'd like a break?' Wang said. 'It might help you to gather your thoughts?'

'No, thanks,' Farnsworth replied, trying not to look rattled. 'I'd rather carry on as we are.'

Zhang's interpretation in Mandarin was wicked. It came across as: no, my colleagues and I prefer to keep floundering around. All the Chinese heard the joke, but nobody laughed or even smirked. Wang merely nodded in consent.

'With the energy pact,' Farnsworth went on, 'I'm sure we'd be able to speed up the process at our end.'

'Just like that?' Wang responded, quick as a flash.

'Well, yes, more or less. So that China ends up with what it wants and both sides are happy. It'd probably be more productive than negotiating new embassy sites and that sort of thing . . . '

He let his words hang. He had no wish to appear presumptuous, though Wang already had that impression. What the Australian Prime Minister wanted was no longer a secret. Wang saw a strategic opening and went in for the kill.

'So, what you're saying then, Prime Minister, is this. If we can strike a deal on the energy front, we can put all these other issues to rest?'

'Yes, I suppose that's it in a nutshell.'

'In which case, it's simply a matter of *this* or *that*?'

'Well, yes,' Farnsworth said, 'if you choose to put it that way.'

'You know,' she mused aloud, 'you Westerners puzzle me. You have such strange ways of thinking.

Everything's either this or that, black or white. In *our* world — and who's to say which is best? — we tend to see things differently. True, there are times, anywhere, when it *is* a matter of this or that. But mostly life's more about complex questions that entail *both* this *and* that, if you see what I mean. It's rarely a simple choice between the two.'

Zhang's rendering into English was skilful. Nothing was lost. It was a subject in which he too had a great interest.

The diversion intrigued the Australians.

'I gather,' Wang said, 'that that's where our idea of *holism* comes from. That's what our concept of *yin* and *yang* is all about.'

Farnsworth sensed he was trapped. Maynard felt the same way. O'Sullivan's mind was still locked into ASIS's failure and the implications for him.

'Let me be frank,' Wang said. 'China can have *both* the energy deal *and* a new embassy, if that's what it wants, though your energy deal's currently off the agenda for the reason I've told you.'

Farnsworth realised what Wang was about. She planned to take everything. In reality, for the Chinese, there was little if anything up for negotiation.

'Of course,' she said, 'we do have other requirements, unrelated to energy. Things like human rights. Things that might — how can I put it? — fill in the gap.'

Human rights, Farnsworth thought. Holy shit! That's the last thing we want. It must be a tactic

– what she's really after is good terms on the energy pact.

'Before we give up on energy altogether,' he said, 'I might just run past you, if I may, what we could do on that front.'

Before Zhang's interpretation was over, Wang had turned to one of her colleagues. An astute-looking man, he had come with her from Beijing. Without a word, he drew from his bag a document of twenty-odd pages and placed it on the table in front of his boss. Wang swung it around and pushed it politely across to the Prime Minister.

'If you insist on discussing the matter,' she said, 'here's an outline of what we'd accept. It's in English, which might save you time.'

Farnsworth digested the title in a glance: *Basic Conditions for a Sino–Australian Long-Term Energy Agreement*. Opening it, he ran his eye over the table of contents.

1. Enhanced Terms for Concessional Finance.
2. Outline of Australian Assistance with R&D.
3. Technology Transfers.
4. Australian Provision of Port Facilities in China.
5. Australian Construction of LNG Processing Plants in China.
6. Australian Assistance with Oil Shale Technology.
7. Australian Funding for Purchase of LNG Tankers.

8. Australian Assistance with Coal-Fired Power Plants.
9. Australian Assistance with Electricity Transmission.
10. Provision of Training in Australia in Energy Fields.

Farnsworth skimmed the document. At the back he noticed his name and Wang's below a heading, *Declaration of Intent*. All it needed was signatures. He passed it to Maynard, who checked it quickly. O'Sullivan was left out of the game.

Nobody uttered a word.

Farnsworth flicked through it once more. 'You realise, we'll need time to go over something like this,' he said, feeling the pressure. 'I mean, we'd have to coordinate things inside our system before we could agree to this sort of package. Then there's . . . '

'*Name shijian, meiyou!*' Wang interrupted, slapping her hand on the table.

'I don't have that sort of time!' Zhang said in English.

Farnsworth was shocked. 'But there's no way we could . . . '

Wang cut across him again. 'Take thirty minutes if you want, but I won't wait any longer.'

She glanced at her watch for effect.

'Please remember, Prime Minister, I haven't come all the way down here just to lodge a complaint. I've come to reach an agreement. We know only too well how long it takes you

Australians to "coordinate things in your system". We've been subjected to that for more than a year. But things have changed, and now *you're* the ones wanting the energy deal. Anyhow, now that you know what we'll accept, you can take it or leave it. If you can't make a choice, then I'm wasting my time.'

She took another look at her watch. 'Why don't we say an hour? That should be enough for you and your colleagues to sort yourselves out.'

Farnsworth realised that if Wang walked away, any prospect of Chinese silence would be lost. He had no doubt she was authorised to decide for herself which path to take. Either way, he thought, Beijing will get what it wants. Which path is the cleanest for us is what I have to decide.

'OK,' he said.

The Chinese peered down from the sea wall, intrigued by a school of fish teeming in the clear harbour water.

The Admiralty House butler had politely excused himself when Ambassador Li indicated they would need no refreshments. They were happy just to take in the view, and happier still when he left. All they wanted was to relax and speak freely.

A large red container vessel with the shipping line's name in bold letters along the side glided past a few hundred metres away. Wang followed its progress as it passed the soaring shells of the Opera House opposite. The sky was clear, with a faint pastel blue haze hanging over the scene.

Turning to Li and the others, she smiled. '*Zenmeyang?*' she said, addressing the ambassador: what do you think? Li was a man she had known for three decades.

'Well, Farnsworth's certainly got the message,' he said. 'There's no doubt about that. And if he's anything, believe me, he's the consummate politician. Which means he'll go to extraordinary lengths to keep the lid on this mess. If it boils down to money, training, facilities – things of that nature – then we'll get what we want. They can hide that expenditure away in their system. But anything with a public profile terrifies them. The prospect of having to build a new embassy, or pull down the old one, worries them sick.'

'Yes, you do have a point,' Wang said. 'One must admit, it could drag on for years, and in full view of the public.'

Her wry smile told her colleagues how much she was enjoying the game.

'You know, while we were sitting there,' she went on, 'I was wondering how Farnsworth would react if I were to casually mention that Beijing found O'Sullivan's habit of calling China the Evil Empire highly entertaining.'

The group burst into laughter at the thought of such a cruel act. They knew that the minister's affidavit was worth its weight in gold. It was a trump card for Beijing to keep up its sleeve.

'Seriously, though,' Wang said, addressing Li, 'what do you think our next move should be?'

'Well, that we keep playing it tough. But I think you should throw in something specific that shows how we might let them off the hook if they do as they're told. Perhaps we should tell them precisely what it is they have to do.'

Wang was curious to hear what this master tactician was planning.

'Look, what I propose is this,' Li said. 'When we go back to the house we'll make sure we're early. You can wander around in the garden, and I'll go inside to let Farnsworth know we're ready. I can't swear to this, but he'll almost certainly pull me aside. He'll be desperate for a tip-off on what's likely to happen. I'll tell him you intend to fly back to China tonight, unless he comes to the party. Otherwise, Beijing's not going to hold off on a public response to the bugging. After all, China's lost enough face as it is. But to reach the kind of "accommodation" that'd guarantee silence for good, we'd have to see four firm commitments made before proceedings wind up today.

'One's Farnsworth's signature on the Declaration of Intent, as per our draft. On that, I'll tell him that when the energy agreement itself is finally signed and announced, we'll turn a blind eye to any fudging of terms and conditions. Let's face it, he'll have to do that to keep the truth away from the public. The second is a figure of, say, thirty million to "refurbish" our defiled embassy in Canberra. And again, as far as his constituency's concerned, it'll be all on the quiet. Third, a secret agreement on human rights.'

Li grinned as he spoke. The others had earlier noted the look of horror on the Australians' faces when Wang briefly touched upon the matter.

'That'll ensure they stop their critical line,' Li continued, 'as well as work with us to help keep that whole confounded question off the international agenda. As a result, there'll be no more Australian support for those cursed US-sponsored UN resolutions attacking us. Instead, we'll let them send parliamentary delegations to China every couple of years to check on our "improved performance". Of course, we'd only show them what we wanted them to see.'

This drew another chuckle.

'And last but by no means least, we'll want a reaffirmation of their support for the One China Policy. So whenever we hear rumblings of independence in Taiwan, we'll soon afterwards hear Australia unequivocally supporting *our* line that Taiwan is an integral part of the motherland. You know, I really think we should go in hard on Taiwan. It worries them silly. They have this massive trade with the place. In fact, we could tell them that if Taipei ever wanted to strike an energy deal of its own with Australia, particularly on gas, we'd want to know the details in advance.

'So there you are. I'd imagine an attack on those four fronts would keep the pressure on Farnsworth and convince him to do the right thing.'

'Well, that's good enough for me,' Wang said. There was a glint in her eye, and her hard, well-worn face was alive with excitement. She loved a good fight. 'What does everyone else think?' she said, more out of courtesy than because an objection was likely.

To a man, they agreed. No one lacked confidence in Li's thinking, nor in Wang's capacity to deliver the goods.

'It'll put the *guizi* back in their box,' she said. 'So, for the sake of our Nipponese brothers – and to make it as excruciating as possible – we must force these Australians to pay full price for their chronic ineptitude.'

It was a dig the others enjoyed. The prospect of giving Japan a run for its money over Sakhalin was tantalising. All were aware that in the past few weeks Tokyo had stepped up its campaign to block any energy deal between Australia and China. Japanese 'lobbying' in Canberra was intense and Beijing was on the verge of delivering to Tokyo a blow that would cripple its style. Now, though, the tables had turned and Japan's scheming might be brought to an end. As soon as China had Australia's signature on the Declaration, it would be used for leverage with Tokyo. With a good Sakhalin deal clinched, China would take its time over signing a long-term agreement with Australia. Indeed, the process might be strung out for months – even years.

'If we play our cards right,' Wang said, 'we'll end up with the best of both worlds.'

'An achievement to rank with that doll on your shelf,' Li added, beaming.

Wang laughed.

She explained to the others that only a few days before, Li had sidled up to the Japanese ambassador at a diplomatic function in Canberra and had apologised for passing on to someone else the kind gift recently presented to him. Knowing as he did that China's intelligence chief, a woman of outstanding repute, was a collector of art works, he had sent the intricately crafted Kabuki doll to her in Beijing.

'Always good to have one's spy service onside, huh?' Li had observed with a wink, though no nudge.

The Japanese abassador, stodgy and desperately formal, was lost for an answer.

Sydney: Monday, 29 May, 9.50 a.m.

Farnsworth was bruised by John Sherrington's hectoring tone and by the barbs in what he was saying. There was no alternative, though, but to sit tight and take it. Or most of it, at least.

The two were alone in the American consul-general's office.

The top CIA man punched his fist into the padded arm of his chair. 'It just won't do, David. You say you've got good people in security here. Of course you have, and over the years I've met some of them. But the problem is they can't get on with the job because of incompetence — even treachery — on the part of cronies at the top. They're the ones you have to weed out.'

God, Farnsworth thought, if only I'd kept an eye on that bloody fool, O'Sullivan, I might have avoided this whole galling process. OK, there were other things going on, but I was stupid to take that bastard's assurance that everything was under control. That was a slip of the first order.

'The President's asked me, David, to tell you that the intelligence exchange between the US and Australia is off, as from Friday night's TV bulletin. There'll be nothing coming from us. That's what Washington's decided. You mightn't like it, but you and I know it's been coming for years.'

Farnsworth was smarting from the severity of the message, dressed up as it was as a presidential decree. He knew only too well that Sherrington himself would have been the key proponent of action like this. He would have been the driving force behind it. And his contrived air of detachment only rubbed salt into the wound.

'Oh, come on, John, let's not go overboard,' the PM said. 'It's been a useful two-way street, this exchange. You'd never have bugged the bloody embassy in the first place, without our help. And from what we all now know, it's been of much greater benefit to your side than to us. So let's be realistic. We all have problems like this from time to time. Even in the US, you're regularly exposing traitors.'

'Yes, but *we* find them ourselves. Or if someone tips us off, we act straight away. You lot have to be dragged kicking and screaming to the point where you'll even acknowledge they exist. Then you never have any luck in tracking them down. You've never convicted anyone. You lot have your heads in the sand and your arses stuck up in the air. That's no way to run a country, David.'

Whenever Sherrington was on a roll, he found it difficult to desist.

'The fact is, David, *you've* landed yourselves in this shit and *you're* going to have to work your way out of it.'

He held up the front page of the *Courier*'s Saturday edition, which featured the full story on the eavesdropping operation, including finer details missing from the television coverage the evening before.

'Intelligence cooperation with allies,' he said, turning the knife, 'shouldn't end up like this. Judging by the score at the moment, the *Courier*'s investigative skills far outstrip those of your Government. Godammit, David, take your National TV. It's a government-funded organisation, and do you know where they're getting their material from?'

The PM was silent. Despite his briefing, he knew the answer was no.

Sherrington was shaking his head. He appeared satisfied that his point had been made.

The Director had been accompanied on his trip to Australia by a handful of officials from his Agency, as well as from other parts of the US intelligence community. He had pushed strongly to meet at the consulate, wanting Farnsworth to receive the President's message on what was technically American soil. The PM felt obliged to accept. Nothing would have been achieved by

359

resisting. Sherrington had made light of the so-called agreement that Farnsworth boasted of reaching with the Chinese. To be sure, Beijing's promise to keep mum on the bugging would dampen publicity, and that was a plus. But what Washington wanted and was determined to get was action here in Australia to clean things up once and for all. He had refused to meet with O'Sullivan, whom he openly mocked. His disdain implied that unless the Foreign Minister, too, was cleaned out, along with the rest of the 'trash', then the intelligence taps might stay dry for some time.

'You see, David, what we want,' he said, in a tone less harsh, 'is your Government's permission to put our own people on the ground here to work with your best. Together we have to cut out this cancer that's infected your system. We simply won't tolerate another Omega Blue situation.'

The PM had not heard mention of that operation for years, but recalled enough to know that it had caused considerable embarrassment.

Sherrington sat back, eyeing Farnsworth as the PM weighed up the cost of withholding consent. It was a choice between Canberra's capacity to handle its problems itself and the symbolism entailed in having outsiders involved.

Farnsworth's gaze fixed on the Stars and Stripes draped from a spearlike pole in the corner.

'You either have enough lead in your pencil, David, or you don't. That's what it boils down to. In matters like this it doesn't pay to be lacking, otherwise your country can find itself out in the cold – like New Zealand.'

Sherrington pulled out a packet of his favourite cigars and lit one. Sinking back in his chair, he drew heavily, then blew the smoke upwards with studied affectation.

The sky outside was leaden. A storm was coming in from the south.

The PM's greatest fear was that news of a US freeze on intelligence would leak. With a general election around the corner, the Opposition would have a field day with that. 'Incapable of defending the nation', would be the charge they'd make. The Government would be decimated at the polls and along with its loss of the Treasury benches would go Farnsworth's own place in history. He would suffer the ignominy of reducing the US–Australia relationship to its lowest level ever.

If that were to happen, it would be a cross he would bear for the rest of his life.

TWELVE

Sydney: Monday, 29 May, 10.42 a.m.

Zhang found the abject silence perplexing, but he was determined not to let it get at him. He would carry out the task to the best of his ability.

He and the Cicada had made contact ten minutes before, not far from the Town Hall, where they had jumped into a taxi. The Australian had not uttered a word since, except to direct the driver to Mrs Macquarie's Chair, a landmark down by the side of the harbour. Out on the coast the sky was black, and dark clouds hung over the city. Zhang wore a raincoat, though the Cicada seemed immune to the chill in the air. He was clad in a light summer suit.

He had been asked by the ASIS chief to spend the weekend in Sydney, and Monday as well. He might be needed, it was said, while the CIA Director was in town, though personally he thought it unlikely the two would actually meet.

Sitting alongside the Chinese in the back seat, he had lost much of the colour in his face. His customary animation was missing and he was obviously deeply troubled.

Just ride it out for the moment, Zhang quietly counselled himself. There'll have to be dialogue sooner or later, and when there is, I think he'll be pleased with what I have to tell him.

From today, it was Zhang's case to run and the best way to stay on top, he knew, was to follow Gao's advice: be guided by instinct. That was ironic, he thought, because his instincts had warned him to stay well clear of this business. But orders were orders, and on this occasion they had come from both Beijing and Ambassador Li. And, everybody stressed, it was for the good of the country. A hackneyed line that might be, but not one easily ignored.

Anyway, what can 'Chan' say at the moment? Zhang mused. He's hardly going to broach anything serious while we're in the back of a cab. But there's got to be more to it than that — much more. And whatever it is, it'll go to the heart of what he's got himself mixed up in, with us. At least we know much more about him now, and we've got in behind his alias, thanks to the clues we got from his father.

Not long after Friday's TV news, Beijing had instructed Gao to lie low until a decision had been made on his future. Contact between him and the Australian was to be suspended after their next scheduled meeting. It was decided that Zhang should take over, at least until the dust had settled. He had a well-established trade role and lacked intelligence links, both of which provided valuable cover at a time like this. Moreover, it was essential for 'Chan' to be minded by somebody he knew. Beijing well understood how heavily the Americans would crack down on Canberra after such a major intelligence blow. No effort would be spared to bring the recalcitrant Australians into line. A witch-hunt had probably started within hours of the news program going to air. And Gao's stable of high-calibre agents in Australia was too important an asset to risk over this. Chinese deep-cover operatives in other parts of the country could keep his main cases moving along until a replacement was found.

For that reason, at Gao's Saturday meeting with the Cicada, a method for handling contact with Zhang had been quickly devised. A new mobile phone was given to 'Chan' for the purpose and a detailed list of places to meet was also compiled, then reduced to code. The Australian appeared to take all this in his stride. He had raised no objection to Zhang taking over, with the change even bringing a smile to his face.

With the Australian Government having agreed to Wang's list of demands by her final Sunday deadline, Beijing had resolved to go further and pull Gao out fast. Now that the eavesdropping story was out and the hunt to find the traitor was on, the stress on the Cicada might make him a serious threat. The pressure might cause him to stumble, leaving a trail back to Gao. Better, therefore, to have Gao out of the country. He had left on a flight that evening for Singapore, whence he would slip back into China unnoticed.

The taxi rounded Hyde Park and headed into a tree-lined drive to the Art Gallery and Botanical Gardens. Branches of huge Moreton Bay figs closed in over the road, forming a tunnel. It was one of Zhang's favourite places, although he had rarely seen it in this gloomy light. He gave 'Chan' a nudge, pointing to the green lawns of the Domain on their left. *Fine sight, eh?* was what the gesture was meant to convey, but it drew only a grunt in response.

A minute or so later the driver pulled into the parking area at the end of the road. It was on a high grassy knoll, with more trees dotted around. The views over the harbour's gunmetal waters were striking. Despite the weather, tourist coaches laden with Japanese and Koreans were disgorging their loads at the site. It was a prime spot for group photographs, with the white shells of the Opera House and the Harbour Bridge as a backdrop.

'Wait for us here,' the Cicada said to the driver, as he and Zhang got out. 'Don't worry, we'll cover the cost, whatever it is.'

They strolled down the slope, leaving the tourists behind, with the Australian hanging back like a Japanese wife. Zhang said nothing as he headed for a park bench below. Finding it wet, he wiped the water away with his handkerchief, then sat down at one end. He stretched his arms high and flexed his muscles, as the Cicada joined him quietly.

'Look,' the Australian said after a time, 'I'm sorry I put on that turn up at Pittwater. It's just that I lost it – completely. You mightn't believe this, but I'm finding it hard to handle the strain. I thought I'd be able to juggle all this, but now it's getting at me. When I cracked on that trip, I really frightened myself. And you're the last person I wanted to do that in front of. I've always seen you as an anchor – more of a lifeline now, I suppose – which is why I came to you in the first place, six weeks back.'

'Come on, don't flatter me.'

'I'm not. I have something serious to raise.'

'So do I.'

'Well, you go first, then,' the Cicada said.

Zhang launched straight in with a list of priorities that Beijing had sent down the previous night. He had committed them all to memory, using the system that Mason had taught him. There was one main proposal that Beijing wanted the Australian to consider if things got too hot.

The Cicada listened carefully, then thought for a while, and when his answer came it was with a speed that took Zhang by surprise.

'So, what is it that you wish to raise?' the Chinese said after a moment.

'But that's it. You've just taken the words right out of my mouth.'

Ah, I see, I see, Zhang thought. So that's what

this was all about. He's been one step ahead of us, but didn't know how to broach it.

The Cicada's new minder was feeling the thrill of the craft and it left him unsettled.

Sydney: Monday, 29 May, 12.20 p.m.

'Greg, it's not just the *guizi* pushing Indonesia,' Zhang said. 'The Americans are in it, too.'

Mason shrugged, implying that he'd suspected as much. He had heard rumours about this strategy from business contacts in the energy world. Inside, he was seething.

'Ambassador Li,' Zhang went on, 'picked it up from a contact in Indonesia – somebody close to Subroto. As you know, that schemer Yoshida, from Tokyo, worked the President over when he stopped off in Jakarta. The Japs want Australia and Indonesia locked into some kind of regional gas grid and that means you Aussies have to be kept out of the China market altogether. Well, apparently the US Ambassador to Jakarta called on Subroto straight after Yoshida and explained how the American energy majors might help the plan along.'

'Oh, lovely!' Mason said.

There was a pause while Mason digested the implications of such a radical development. Zhang took a sip of his coffee, waiting.

'It's a dirty business, isn't it?' Mason finally said.

'Well, as far as I can see, no one doubts that the Americans have teamed up with Tokyo on this.'

'I agree, and I reckon the aim is to get hold of those Timor Sea deposits and keep other international majors out. I gather the Japanese will throw in the bulk of the capital and take half the output, with the rest going off to the States.'

'And the expertise you have in Australia,' Zhang said, 'plus all those North West Shelf facilities nearby, would slot in very nicely. Oh, and by the way, something else my boss told me that you might find interesting. He bumped into Ambassador Greensborough the other day at Canberra airport, and guess where he was heading – up to Darwin.'

'Darwin!' Mason realised immediately what the attraction would be. That was where a gas processing plant would almost certainly be built to handle the yield from the Timor fields.

'Li said Greensborough told him it was just a quick overnight trip to show the flag, but who'd believe that? Li thinks Washington's sent him up there to work on the chief minister to put pressure on Canberra. Imagine how excited the Northern Territory Government must be over the prospect of billions of dollars of investment flooding in. The processing plant alone would employ a thousand or more, then there's all the other spending that goes with it.'

'Yes, they'd be over the moon.'

Mason was annoyed that no one had briefed him on this. So much for getting close to the Yanks, he thought. First chance I get, I'll see if Beth knows what's going on. This is ridiculous –

you help them with one hand, while they're biting your other hand off!

Canberra: Monday, 29 May, 1.35 p.m.

'I'll take this any day,' Toshio Nakagawa, Matsutomo Corporation's Australia-based wheeler-dealer, said. He took a deep breath of the eucalyptus-laced air as he leant on his bike. 'It certainly beats the office in Sydney, which isn't much fun at the moment. Not with all the pressure we're under.'

Stephen Needham, who handled government affairs for Matsutomo, knew only too well what he meant. After all, the blowtorch was currently on him more than anybody else in the firm.

Paunchy and out of condition, Needham was not one who shared his boss's enthusiasm for cycling. In his forties, he found it hard to keep up, but with Nakagawa so athletic the effort had to be made. He had done well out of the Corporation and wanted to keep it that way — at least, until he was ready to run with options of his own.

A breeze wafted up from the lake over a thicket of willows already bare for the winter.

'*Jaaa, iko,*' Nakagawa said, though Needham spoke no Japanese: let's go.

He had flown to Canberra at midday, wanting to be alongside Needham while the Australian did the rounds of his contacts. Too many important questions remained unanswered. How was the Government reacting to the bombshell of the Chinese Embassy bugging? How were policy-makers and advisers grappling with the implications of Friday's TV news and the lurid detail that the *Courier* had gone on to provide? Would trade between Australia and China be affected? Would Beijing exploit its advantage to win an energy deal? Would trade be restricted if diplomatic relations were temporarily frozen? These were things that Matsutomo wanted to know, and quickly.

Needham had already spent the weekend probing, in the knowledge that Nakagawa was eager to get an accurate assessment off to Tokyo in the next 24 hours.

The firm maintained an apartment in the capital, not far from the lake. Needham used it on frequent trips and viewed it much as his own. Company visitors from Japan always stayed at the Hyatt, but Nakagawa bunked down in Needham's spare room. As a Japanese, he liked to feel he had his ear close to the ground.

On the cycling track that circled Lake Burley Griffin, Nakagawa had set a vigorous pace, leaving Needham far behind. Whenever the Australian pulled into the next rest stop, his ambitious colleague was always waiting to have a go at him again.

'It's extraordinary,' the Japanese said, 'that no one here knows what's going on. Surely somebody has their finger on the pulse.'

His tone suggested that Needham might not be as good as he thought. The issue had first come up on the drive in from the airport and Needham had found it offensive. Nobody worked Canberra like he did – and he said it – but he guessed it would crop up again.

'I wouldn't call it extraordinary,' he said. 'The place is buzzing with rumours, but when you get close to the top you slam into a brick wall – into a vacuum.'

Nakagawa shrugged, insinuating that this was not good enough.

'Look, by "vacuum",' Needham said tetchily, 'I don't mean that nothing's happening at all. It's just that the PM and the people around him are preoccupied with the embassy mess. They're not doing *nothing*. They're bloody panicking, but in private. And until it's resolved, and a decision's made, the system will just have to wait. As we have to, too.'

Nakagawa grunted, which Needham thought preferable to the sarcastic rejoinder he expected. He found it galling to have to admit he was not privy to the Prime Minister's thinking, for he often boasted that he had privileged access to Farnsworth's advisers.

'They're not only playing their cards close to the chest,' he said, 'but they're covering their tracks very carefully. I've heard that the PM's been up in Sydney since Saturday night. He's not due back until late today. Normally there'd be nothing special in that, but it's significant that this time his movements have been deliberately fudged. The official line that his aides dish out is that Monday's been taken up with medical checks. "Nothing serious, just routine." But if that's the case, why cancel high-profile appointments for it? I've heard from inside his office that the medical thing is just a cover. It's really to do with the bugging. There are rumours that Farnsworth's been up in Beijing and that the Chinese summoned him there to be lectured, but I know for sure that's not true. Anyhow, whatever they're up to, it's all happening in Sydney. And believe me, by this time tomorrow I'll know what it is.'

'Yes, well,' Nakagawa said, disgruntled, 'I had the impression you were more plugged in than that.'

It was a tactic he regularly used. Nothing spurred Needham on more than a suggestion that he was losing his grip.

Nakagawa understood the pressure that Beijing would be putting on Canberra. China's silence so far had virtually confirmed it. It would be a chance too good to miss and the Chinese would exploit it relentlessly until they got what they wanted. There was no way, he knew, that he could risk letting Needham in on the secret that Matsutomo's president had divulged in Tokyo. The Sakhalin story was still under wraps. Japan had only a week left to pull its gas deal together. Bad weather, the Russians had been told, had delayed the last of Japan's exploratory drilling.

Tokyo, therefore, was on borrowed time and desperate to know what the Chinese were trying to squeeze out of Canberra, let alone what the Australians were likely to concede.

'*Jaaa, iko,*' Nakagawa said, jumping back on his bike. 'I'll beat you to Scrivener Dam.'

A low barrage that held up the lake, this was the halfway point on their ride and a place where Needham was usually nearing collapse. He was still adjusting his pedals when Nakagawa took off. What's the fucking hurry? he thought. It's not a race. It was then that he realised he had forgotten to mention something. It was a bit of hot gossip he had picked up on that consultant whose services Matsutomo occasionally used. Greg Mason was his name and his judgement was highly valued, so Nakagawa would appreciate hearing the story.

God knows what that poor bloke's up to, Needham thought, but it's clearly not going to enhance his career.

Sydney: Monday, 29 May, 2.50 p.m.

Norb Schneider, the CIA station chief from Canberra, held aloft the letter from Prime Minister Farnsworth for his colleagues to see. It was addressed to John Sherrington, the Agency's Director.

His usual serious self, Schneider proceeded to read it aloud.

> My Government hereby grants unrestricted authority to a limited number of designated Australians to act on their country's behalf in cooperation with representatives of the

> United States Government. This relates to our joint quest to track down those responsible for informing the People's Republic of China of the combined intelligence operation carried out on its diplomatic mission in Canberra.
>
> At the express direction of the Australians so nominated, investigative activities may legitimately involve American counterparts operating on Australian soil.

'There we have it,' Schneider said. 'It might be political-speak, but it pretty well covers what we're engaged in.'

The group of fifteen were crowded into the safe house. All were Americans, except for Mason, Pellegrini, Lambert and Alexandra Templeton. Mason was brooding and testy, which was unlike him. Only Beth Cantrell understood why. The pair had had an altercation before the meeting began, over Timor Sea gas and American interests. She had pleaded with him not to raise the issue with the others, certainly not with his three compatriots who had managed to make it to Sydney. After all, there was now an ace card to play. 'Let's not pass up the chance,' she said, 'to exploit that to the full.'

Schneider too, had come up from Canberra, in company with Ambassador Greensborough, for talks with Sherrington. That had followed the Director's confrontation with the PM. The two

Americans spent some hours with Sherrington over lunch, before his jet whisked him away on another secret mission – this time to Indonesia.

Now, along with the others in the room, Schneider was sensitive to the position of the Australians and appreciated that, of the Americans, Cantrell and Ben Jameson were closer to the practicalities of it than anyone else. Linda Levi had her own views on how much they were contributing, which Schneider had asked her to keep to herself.

Templeton's sharp mind, coupled with her detailed knowledge of the 'plumbing' via which secret reporting circulated in Canberra, had already proved vital. Additionally, her understanding of the personalities involved and their interrelationships was unmatched. When Mason told her what had been uncovered on Morgandale she was not surprised, though she was disturbed by the reduced focus on Clarke. Like the other Australians, she believed that he warranted far more attention. And he had briefly had it, too – until Levi homed in on Morgandale. Her influence had flourished with the product of that target's meeting with Winston Lee.

Cantrell's views were now aligned with those of Mason and the others. She agreed that the exposure of Morgandale's activities was significant, but had her own reasons for believing that he was not the traitor who had blown the whistle on the Chinese Embassy operation.

Now, having read the letter, Schneider moved on.

'Farnsworth explained to the Director,' he said, 'what his Government's been doing. And let me tell you, the boss was far from impressed. He says it's just the same old script reworked. Searching from the bottom of the hierarchy up, but *never* all the way to the top. That supports what Joe Pellegrini's been saying. His view is that Canberra's done some useful work on access, but – as ever – things are going round in circles. Well, what we need to know is how cronyism drives that circular motion and who the key actors are in it. How, exactly, are they supporting Morgandale? Now, to answer that kind of question we're going to have to drill down into each of his top contacts to see who they're linked to. Naturally, that throws up another network – one that spreads out through the system like the roots of a tree.'

Schneider scanned the faces in front. Eye contact between the Australians and Cantrell reminded him not to push his luck, even if keeping Levi on side was a priority. Mason's glare said it all.

'Of course, we can't forget Clarke,' Schneider said. 'We made a good start on him before the breakthrough with Morgandale, so we'll need to look at revisiting that.'

Cantrell briskly flicked through the pages on her clipboard to display her frustration.

'But alas, enough from me,' Schneider said, beating a tactical retreat. 'It's time we heard from those at the business end of this thing.' He signalled to her to take the floor.

Cantrell's personable nature gave her an immediate presence. She smiled at the Australians, which was a simple act in itself, but one that took the group back to its point of departure. First and foremost, this was an exercise on Australian soil to catch Australians who had betrayed their country's national interest, and in the process, that of America.

'To begin with,' she said, with a deadpan look, 'there's been a development. One that could change things considerably.'

A buzz went round the room. Those who knew Cantrell sensed it would be good. Mason and his colleagues were aware of the details, but Schneider and Levi were not.

'It's come from something we've been keeping a close eye on, despite what the group's been preoccupied with recently. It relates to the movements of Chinese diplomats in Australia. You see, we've run a check on their travel and nothing suspicious cropped up on any of them – *except one.*'

Levi looked worried.

'The man involved goes by the name of Gao Chun, and he works out of the consulate here in Sydney with the cover of a science and technology consul. He's been on our watch-list for a while and when we raised his name with Langley they threw up a report that said he was 'hot enough to glow in the dark'. Well, the news is, Gao's flown the coop!'

Levi looked at Schneider, but all he did was shrug.

'He left for Singapore last night, at very short notice. Bookings were made only hours before, plus there were *no* onward reservations and *no* return ticket. Yet his family's still here. Now, earlier this afternoon, Alexandra did a bit of investigative work of her own.'

All eyes turned to Templeton. She smiled but said nothing, merely watching as Cantrell flicked the speaker switch on a panel nearby.

'Hello, Chinese Consulate-General. How can I help you?'

'I'd like to speak to Mr Gao, please.'

'Oh, I think he's . . . '

'Look, just put me through to his number, OK?'

'Well, I'll try . . . '

'Hello, I believe you want Gao.'

'Yes, is he there? See, I'm his girlfriend.'

'Oh – no, he's not – he's – he's just out at the moment – but – but maybe I could pass on a message.'

'A bloody message! Look, I cooked dinner for the bastard last night and he didn't turn up! Now where the hell is he?'

'Oh, he's – he's been called away – urgently – he's . . . '

'Called away? Where? When's he coming back?'

'I'm not too sure. I think he'll – I – look, maybe you should call back later.'

The line went dead.

The room filled with guffaws.

Cantrell noticed that Schneider and Levi were shocked. The realisation had struck them that Gao had been running someone else, and there was little doubt it was somebody other than Morgandale.

'Oh, Alex, baby,' Jameson said, laying on a thick Southern drawl, 'lil 'ol Mrs Gao ain't goin' to like this one bit!'

The mirth kept rolling on.

Jameson was a popular man and had taken the Australians to heart, which was something he made no effort to hide.

'It damn well won't endear her husband to her,' Cantrell said, 'though it'll warn her the girlfriend's got spunk. But joking aside, we need to know a lot more about this guy. Namely, who's he been running and is it the traitor we're after?'

Levi was dumbstruck.

'I'm sure we'd all agree,' Cantrell went on, 'that it's just too much of a coincidence he's departed like this, so soon after the TV news bulletin and what the *Courier*'s put out. Let's face it, Gao's almost certainly a spook and the Chinese have moved him out fast to protect his stable of agents. Yet they've achieved just the opposite. They've given us one hell of a lead. OK, Gao might've been Morgandale's case officer, with Winston Lee in a secondary role, but we've seen no evidence at all of them being linked.'

Cantrell avoided looking at Levi, knowing she would already have tumbled to where this was leading.

'Then again,' she said, 'if Martin Clarke *is* the one we're after, we could well find that Gao's been his case officer. That he's been running Clarke out of Sydney, rather than someone else handling it from the embassy in Canberra. And on top of that, Gao might've . . . '

Levi could hold back no longer.

'Look,' she said, 'we can go on for hours like this, but what's the point? We *must* stick to the things we know to be true, and the facts we have are all about Morgandale. It's as simple as that. OK, Gao's gone, but the question of who he might've been running is separate and secondary. It's something the Australians can deal with later.'

Mason was restless again, which Levi picked up. She had clearly overstepped the mark and she knew it.

'All I'm worried about,' she said, backtracking, 'is that we'll spread our resources too far. I'm not saying that's what's happening now, but I'm concerned it might.'

Schneider was uneasy and seemed on the verge of interceding when Mason cut across him. It was the moment the Australians had been waiting for, having earlier agreed that Mason should state their case.

He rose and stood next to Cantrell.

'With all due respect, Linda,' he said, 'there's a

whole extra dimension to this and it's one that has to be raised.'

He spoke forthrightly and with authority. His openness had served the group well and was an attribute that Levi, too, acknowledged.

'But first, let me mention one thing. I know I speak for all of us when I say that in the time we've been working together we've achieved a hell of a lot, and that's only because it's been possible to organise a group like this. If the task had been left to Canberra there'd be virtually nothing to show for its effort. As you know, that's why we Australians have teamed up with you.'

He looked straight at Levi.

No one made a sound.

'What's bound us together has been our mutual quest to find out who betrayed the embassy job. Well, *we* believe that only one person's responsible for that and it's Martin Clarke. But along the way Morgandale's antics have overshadowed him. Now, Linda, don't get me wrong. I'm not saying that that's all been useless. Quite the contrary. He's clearly a nut we wouldn't have cracked without your expertise. But I'm afraid that in the process there's been this perception on your part that Beth and I, and maybe Todd as well, have been too close to Martin. "Emotionally involved", if that's the way you want to put it.'

Levi accepted his comment. She liked Mason and found his intellect as sharp as his wit. But it was true that she felt his past contact with Clarke had coloured his judgement and that of the others.

'In different ways, Linda, we've all paid a price for knowing Martin. I'd be the first to admit that emotions can easily get in the way, even with people engaged in the detached and clinical art of spying . . . '

Levi grinned. She enjoyed Mason's sense of irony and minded little that he used it now to soften her up.

'. . . but that shouldn't obscure the fact that we Australians have unique insights into Martin's psyche, and we have them *because* of our involvement with him.'

Levi appreciated that Mason wanted resources diverted to Clarke and was determined to get them. For her the weight of his words was minor compared to the strength of his conviction. It was true, too, that his contribution to Operation Omega Blue, which she had studied in detail, could not be ignored.

Schneider and Cantrell let things run. Mason appeared to be on the brink of a coup, one that might leave everyone happy.

'Why then,' Levi said, 'don't we give the Morgandale case another four or five days, after which . . . '

'I'm sorry, Linda, that's out of the question. I'll settle for nothing more than twenty-four hours.' His expression left her in no doubt that he meant what he said.

Both knew that a meeting in Sydney the following day, which would involve Ambassador Li, might put the Morgandale issue to rest once and for all.

'OK, twenty-four hours, then we home in on Clarke,' she said.

Even Levi herself breathed a sigh of relief, though no more so than Cantrell, who had been afraid that Mason might explode. She had told him about the briefing she'd received from Langley, called for at his request. Yes, it was true that the Agency was helping US oil and gas majors and that it was aware of the game that Tokyo was playing.

Sydney: Tuesday, 30 May, midday

'I hear some Treasury blokes are on a secret mission to China,' Adrian McKinnon said. As the *Courier*'s top gun he was often way out in front. 'Not that I can put my finger on what they're up to. I thought you might know.'

Mason shook his head. It wasn't that he distrusted McKinnon. Far from it. But the Government's payoff for China's silence over the bugging fiasco was not a topic he wished to discuss with a journalist. He was indeed aware that officials were in Beijing to work on the detail of the financial package that the two sides had agreed upon.

Adrian would go well as an interrogator, Mason thought. He's certainly as good as any I've met in the game.

The pair shared a bench seat at Darling Harbour, with the *Courier*'s premises in view. A gaggle of European tourists went past, heading for the Maritime Museum.

'Now listen to me,' McKinnon said, jesting. 'I can hear what's rattling around in your head.'

Mason laughed, though his expression made it clear he was disinclined to open up. They had been acquainted for years, but had never had time to develop a friendship. McKinnon, who was aware of Mason's ASIS background, had called him late the previous night on a public phone. The call came as no surprise. Mason was toying with the idea of making contact himself. He wanted to check on Clarke's claim that it was the *Courier* that had tipped off the Chinese. McKinnon, in his mid-thirties, had a mind like radar which picked up stories that others missed. It was a quality that Mason found attractive.

'Look, Greg,' McKinnon said, sitting forward, 'I've been wondering if there isn't common ground between us on this embassy thing. See, what interests me and perhaps you even more is the question of who leaked what to whom, and when.'

'Why do you think I'd be interested in that? After all, I'm just a consultant. Not some government sleuth.'

'Oh, a gut feeling tells me you might.'

The wisp of a grin on McKinnon's face confirmed Mason's suspicion. He's on to something, he thought, and it's hot.

McKinnon waited for Mason to make the next move. It was a game that journalists and intelligence officers played, though rarely with each other.

'Look, Adrian, in the unusual event that we were to discuss something like this, you'd obviously appreciate we'd need to lay a few cards on the table.'

McKinnon nodded. His eyes lit up at the prospect of Mason being candid.

'First, it would have to be strictly off the record,' Mason continued, 'and no doubt as much from your standpoint as mine.'

'Of course.'

'Well, you lead the way, then,' Mason said.

'OK, let me start with how I first got on to the story. You see, way back I had a contact who worked on the embassy site when they put that new building up. He told me at the time that spooks – our spooks – were crawling all over the place posing as engineers. He said it was a bit stupid really. The professionals all knew they didn't belong. Anyhow, I learnt from him that the place was rigged with optical fibre. I haven't got much more out of him since, but I've followed it up with others here and there and pieced together a fair bit of the story. You know what it's like – a fragment here and another one there.'

Mason smiled. They were speaking the same language. Both crafts involved the slow process of building up a picture, rather than simply waiting for a scoop.

'Most of my leaks on this,' McKinnon said, 'have come from contacts in ONA and DSD. People who are crapped off with the way the Yanks have been giving us a raw deal on the "take", especially on trade issues like wheat.

They've had a gutful of Canberra failing to take a stand. I've come to know some of them fairly well and they've really opened up over the past year or two. One bloke's even briefed a few of the brighter types in the Opposition on what's going on and the impact on the national interest. But evidently the pollies concerned have been forbidden by their seniors to raise it in Parliament. You can imagine how this bloke felt about that.'

'Same old story,' Mason said, shaking his head.

It was a subject on which both knew they could easily digress.

'Too right, Greg, but that's only half of it. What finally pushed this fella over the line was when he heard from a technical mate in Canberra that the operation had been betrayed from inside. That's when he decided to give me a bundle of stuff – a great wad of documents – that, for me, filled in the gaps. And in turn that's what finally convinced my editor to run with the story.

'National TV had bits and pieces as well, though apparently not enough to do anything with. It seems their breakthrough came with a similar leak last Friday – an envelope full of sensitive papers from some reliable source. And of course they ran with it on the news. Now, this is where things get interesting, Greg, and maybe where you and I can compare notes. I've been told that that envelope contained a copy of *my* draft article, which the Government somehow managed to get hold of and tried to injunct. And that's not all. There was also a copy of the injunction itself and an affidavit that went with it. And what a read that was!'

Mason's astonishment showed.

'I'm not joking,' McKinnon said.

'But where did it come from?' Even as he spoke, Mason was thinking of people who would have had access to that type of thing.

'That's what I'm asking you,' McKinnon said. 'See, some of my contacts have recently sneaked up here from Canberra to talk. Naturally, they're worried about being seen with a journalist, so even in a big city like Sydney we've had to get together in pretty strange places. And in all of this, Greg, something's come up that involves you.'

Mason was jolted. His mind went straight to what he was doing with Cantrell and the rest of the team.

'One of these fellas told me — and, I stress, with no lack of goodwill — that he's heard that *you've* been sniffing around in Canberra.' McKinnon raised an eyebrow that asked: could this be true?

Mason smiled wryly, suggesting it might. He knew McKinnon had excellent sources. The remark, therefore, told him a lot.

Shit, he thought, my trips there have been deliberately short but it's such a small place and . . .

'On the positive side,' McKinnon said, cutting across his thoughts, 'some who've seen you have actually considered saying hello and having a chat, which is all very nice. But unfortunately it appears there's another dimension to this business of you being spotted.'

Images flashed through Mason's mind.

'Somebody else,' McKinnon went on, 'who's seen you around is apparently making more of it, and it's far from benign. Whoever it is, they're spreading a story about that you have a sinister interest in all this. One that's clearly unwanted. Now that, Greg, is nasty, as I'm sure you'd agree.'

The look on Mason's face confirmed that he did. 'OK, I'm grateful for the warning,' he said, 'but tell me, what do you think's going on, let alone why I'm meant to be mixed up in something dirty?'

McKinnon rubbed his cheek. 'Here's how I see it. To start with, someone's pumping out disinformation. There's a deliberate attempt at confusion. For example, the story doing the rounds is that it was *us* at the *Courier* who tipped off the Chinese. That we got wind of the bugging, then asked them for a comment. I mean, that's crazy! Nevertheless, it's a line that's gained traction.'

To Mason, this was the story that Pellegrini had heard Clarke was putting around. If this isn't proof, he thought, that Martin's the one we're after, I don't know what is. It's clearly a red herring to divert attention.

'You know,' Mason said, 'even *I'd* heard that the *Courier* was to blame.'

McKinnon shook his head, but chose to go on. If it were important to know how Mason had learnt this, he would say.

'What all this tells me, Greg, is that the Chinese really were tipped off. But if it wasn't us or National TV – and I'm sure it wasn't them – then who the hell was it?'

'Yes, that's the key question.'

'And I suspect that you, Greg, know the answer.'

'Well, a few suspects do come to mind, but pinning them down isn't easy. Do *you* have any ideas?'

'Look, it's hard to say, but whoever it was they'd have leaked it some time back. I think Beijing's been aware for a while and played the thing to advantage. And our Government's bearing the brunt of that now. Whoever spilt the beans to the Chinese must know that the whole system's after them. If they weren't paranoid before, they'd have to be now. They'd be feeling the pressure, I gather, since National TV and the *Courier* blew it wide open. No doubt they'd be working their crony supporters like hell to put the trackers off the scent. That, Greg, is what I think's going on down in Canberra. And for whatever reason, they see you as a threat. Somehow, you've been identified as the one who's closing in. You're the one who has to be stopped.'

Mason nodded. It was not unusual for McKinnon to be so near the truth.

A quiet settled on them. Each sensed what the other was thinking: we both have principal pieces of the jigsaw and it would be a pity not to fit them together.

'It's not a matter of pressuring you,' McKinnon said, breaking the silence. 'Let's face it, you and I know there's a second big story brewing in this. In effect, the cover-up is bigger than the embassy story itself. And I'd like to run with it. I have enough at the moment to cover the front page again. But as I see it, Greg, the challenge is how you and I avoid tripping over each other. Not only that, but possibly even joining forces to accomplish a goal, and enhance Australia's interests in the process.'

Mason thought for a while. McKinnon's sentiments were the same as his. Pre-emptive publicity would forewarn Clarke that the noose was tightening. That was not what was needed. To get the *Courier* to hold off for a while was vital. McKinnon's investigative efforts had consistently attacked the hold that certain elements had on the system, and it was for this reason that Mason had long been a defender of the *Courier*'s robust approach to its duties in the public arena.

'Look,' he said, 'you mentioned pressure, right?'

McKinnon nodded.

'Well, take your mind back, Adrian, to something we've talked about over the years, about forces that need to be rallied outside if we're ever to bring about change in this place.'

McKinnon grasped the point instantly. 'Ah, so that's it,' he said, smiling. 'You know, I twigged to some US involvement in all this when my main sources opened up. Then as soon as I heard you were buzzing around I thought, that's it for sure. So, you're right in the thick of it, eh?'

'Well, let's say I'm playing a part. But it's all much bigger than me, Adrian, as you wouldn't find hard to imagine.'

'So, how close are you to nabbing the culprit?'

'On the verge of it. Give us a few days and we might bag more than one, as well as much of the network that goes with them. And, believe it or not, we might also get to use polygraph testing to check how far their influence spreads. The Yanks have forced it on Farnsworth and offered to send out specialists to make sure it's done properly.'

'Well, I'll be stuffed! I should've known you'd be up to something like this.'

'Thanks for the compliment,' Mason said. 'But I tell you, it's not over yet. Not by a long shot. What we need, Adrian, is time. We're so close, mate, to bringing this off.'

'OK, I get the message. I'll hold off for as long as you want.'

'Thanks. And in return, I'll make sure you get the story before anyone else.'

THIRTEEN

Canberra: Tuesday, 30 May, 12.20 p.m.

'I tell you, Todd,' Clarke said, 'you've got to hang in there and make sure bastards like Bass don't fuck up ASIS for good.'

For Lambert, alarm bells were ringing. The comment had to be driven by more than the influence of alcohol. An image raced through his mind of what Clarke had done to Mason and to other Young Turks in the Service. Morgandale's influence would be nowhere near as great now if fewer officers of that calibre had been expunged.

And here's bloody Martin, of all people, Lambert thought, advocating generational change!

Clarke had turned up at ASIS headquarters at 8.20 that morning. Lambert was already in the office. The two chatted for a while about instructions given by the Prime Minister to the Attorney-General's investigating committee to 'find that bloody traitor quick smart'. At 9.30

Clarke had attended an internal ASIS meeting with the chief and others to discuss Farnsworth's request. It had lasted two hours, after which he returned to his office bleating about how 'that dickhead, Bass, always has too much to say'. 'It wasn't half obvious,' he said, 'that he was covering his tracks.' In a rather agitated state, Clarke had rummaged around searching for something. Then at noon he had cancelled an appointment and instead invited Lambert out to lunch. The two rarely had meals together.

They sat in an outdoor café in the trendy Canberra suburb of Manuka. Lambert had expected Clarke to drive his own car, but he insisted on taking a taxi. As soon as they were shown to their table, Clarke had ordered two double whiskies, then asked for a couple more.

'You see, the problem is,' he went on, 'that nobody listens to my lot any more. It's younger guys like you, the ones coming up fast, who have to speak out. Otherwise, people like Bass and his cronies will sit on the place for years – like a concrete lid – just smothering things. You already know they only ever promote people who share their own lack of scruples.'

What the hell's got into him, Lambert thought? He's been worked up before, but never like this. OK, the fact that Bass is screwing him over and trying to get him out of his job is one thing. But that can't be all that's driving this. There has to be some other motivation – something really powerful.

'But what about people like Wally?' Lambert said, naming a senior manager who was highly regarded, both inside the Service and out. 'And Max. Now he's certainly no fool.'

Both men maintained a good working relationship with Morgandale, though neither had any particular liking for him.

Lambert was intrigued to see how this might draw his boss out.

'Arrgh,' Clarke replied, 'they're the same as the rest. They've never spoken up. Certainly not like I have over the years.'

Lambert sensed it was useless debating the issue, so he just shrugged. He was close to both officers and later that day would probably hear more from them about what had transpired at the meeting that morning. Clarke's own cursory account had revealed little.

'Fancy,' Clarke said, 'a traitor in ASIS! And even if it were true, how could a toff like Bass help suss him out? *He* of all people! Shit, he regularly consorts with the Chinese behind our backs, and hasn't got the guts to come clean on it. If it's all hunky-dory, why keep it quiet?'

This is certainly a new line, Lambert thought. If he's known about this for so long, why hasn't he mentioned it before?

Clarke construed Lambert's shrug as a sign of agreement, failing to sense it might be deliberate.

'Of course, you know where he meets them?' Clarke clearly wanted Lambert to hear the full story.

'Well, patently *not* in the embassy.'

'No, no. He sees them out on that property that old Ambassador Li has the run of. You know, that one on the road out to Braidwood.'

'Really?' Lambert said, feigning surprise. 'But Martin, have you told the ASIO blokes about this? Surely they'd be pretty interested.'

'Frankly, I wouldn't bother,' Clarke said, scoffing. 'No one takes any notice of me. Whatever I say just gets dismissed as sour grapes, because of how I've stood up to that bloody crook and often come off second best.'

'But I'd still tell them,' Lambert said. 'It could be a vital piece of information.'

'Well, I'll think about it.'

That didn't go very far, Lambert mused to himself. He must feel he's made his point and it's time to roll on.

Suddenly, from inside his jacket, Clarke produced an antique gold cigarette case, which he displayed with great reverence. Its fine filigree work had worn smooth, but the name *Albert Grenville Clarke* was still legible on the lid. He handed the case across. Lambert opened it and found it filled with fresh cigarettes. Inside was another inscription: *Presented by Balmain Mechanics Institute, March 1897.*

'Albert was my granddad,' Clarke said. 'He died years ago, but he left this to me.'

Clarke was smiling. He seemed pleased that the thing had aroused Lambert's curiosity.

'It has character, eh?' he said, as Lambert snapped the case shut and handed it back.

'Yes, it really does.'

'Go on, have a cigarette,' Clarke insisted, though neither of them smoked.

'But I don't . . . '

'Neither do I, but it won't do us any harm. After all, you and I have had to put away thousands between us to keep agents company.'

Clarke had a point. Lambert took one and Clarke lit it for him with a modern lighter he also had with him. He lit another for himself, then sat back, apparently content with what he had done. Lambert was baffled. Why such a big deal?

'Reminds you of overseas postings, doesn't it?' Clarke said, blowing a stream of smoke into the air.

'Yes, in a way.'

Lambert sensed that the anchor that had kept Clarke's life fixed had broken away. He was floundering.

Images flashed through Lambert's mind of Mason and the rest of the team.

Earlier that morning, while Clarke was attending the meeting in ASIS, Lambert had gone down into the basement. There, in the carpark, he placed a fresh tracking device under the rear bumper of Clarke's ageing BMW. An earlier one had been positioned when the combined team had first had him under surveillance, but had worked itself loose. Now, with the focus swinging back to Clarke, Pellegrini suggested they try again. Later, when Lambert returned to his office, he had placed a similar device inside the base of Clarke's old-fashioned briefcase. Only Lambert had a spare key to his boss's office, which was locked whenever Clarke was away.

He had run an eye over files that were left open on the desk. One contained the latest reporting from ASIS's North Asian stations. Another dealt with an ASIS proposal to place additional deep-cover spies in China and Indonesia. Also open was a posting schedule for ASIS intelligence officers and support staff right across Asia. It not only listed cover ranks but also named those undertaking in-country language training and others attached to embassies for whatever purpose. It was a roadmap to ASIS on the operational front.

'Now listen,' Clarke said, pushing the cigarette case — which was still on the table — back across to Lambert. 'I want you to have this.'

'But Martin, why me? I mean, it's not that I'm ungrateful. It's just that there must be lots of people in your family who'd treasure it.'

'No, mate, I want you to have it. Let's face it, you're one of the brightest blokes I've ever worked with and I really admire your guts and conviction. Don't ever lose those qualities, Todd. They're all that counts in the end. So let this be my tribute to you.'

What the hell's he up to? Lambert wondered, knowing that Clarke was not one for soft talk. He's so full of mystery, but how's it significant? Is he joking, or sending a message? Something's brewing and it's big. That much I can tell. The sooner we pin the bastard down, the safer I'll feel.

Lambert's instincts were alive. He would act as soon as they parted company.

Sydney: Tuesday, 30 May, 12.35 p.m.

'*Ima, doko ni iru no?*' Toshio Nakagawa asked: where are you at the moment?

He spoke in the guttural vernacular of Japanese men who know each other well. It was the form by which Mason was customarily addressed, and for a foreigner it meant you were fully accepted.

'*Shinai no ho,*' Mason replied: I'm in the city.

He had just finished his meeting with Adrian McKinnon and was heading off to join up with Beth Cantrell and the team. Nakagawa had called him on his mobile after failing to reach him at home. There was urgency in his voice.

'*Kaisha kara, toi no?*' he said: are you far from my office?

'No. Close, actually.'

'*Hirumeshi wa, do?*' he went on: how about lunch?

'I'm afraid that's a bit tricky,' Mason replied, with an appropriate hint of regret. 'You see, I'm doing a boardroom briefing at one o'clock sharp.'

Mason's priority was the team. He had already handed over his energy report to the Matsutomo Corporation and felt no professional obligation to make himself available right now.

The team was coordinating a number of surveillance squads that were trailing Winston

Lee in Chinatown. The squads had already monitored a series of meetings which the Malaysian had had with wealthy local Chinese. Some, like him, were closely linked to Beijing. The event of the day was due to begin at 1.30 when Ambassador Li, having flown in from Canberra, would meet Winston at the Scented Lotus, a restaurant the businessman owned. The squads, backed by Pellegrini and ASIO colleagues, had wired the pair's private room in advance. Intercept posts had been established nearby to ensure that nothing was lost in transmission. Mason had been heading for one of the posts when Nakagawa rang.

'*Gofun dake, dekiru?*' he pressed Mason: can you spare me five minutes? 'It's nothing to do with work, though it might be important' – he hesitated – 'important to you, that is.'

His inflection in Japanese anticipated a positive response. Mason knew him well. Nakagawa was one Matsutomo operative who never wasted time, unlike most of his compatriots, who slackened off on their Australian 'sleepy hole' postings. Nor was he one to blow things out of proportion.

'I'll be there in a jiffy.'

Mason jumped in a taxi and rang Cantrell to let her know he would be slightly delayed. She had no problem with that. An intercept on Ambassador Li's car phone had indicated he would be at the Scented Lotus half an hour late.

'By the way, Beth, you might remember "Big Mac", the man I've just been with,' he said, alluding to McKinnon.

'I do.'

For the past week Mason had kept the combined team informed of his movements. People like McKinnon had been allocated codenames, which the whole group understood.

'Well, "Big Mac" told me that nobody was tipped off by his bunch. They sought no comment from anyone. Not only that, but until the very last moment only a handful of people inside his setup knew what was coming.'

'So it's "C" who's been spreading that story about,' Cantrell said, referring to Clarke. 'That clearly points the finger at him.'

'Correct, and I'll leave it to you to tell Linda that that's what we think.'

Cantrell was still laughing when he rang off.

When Mason emerged on the building's 28th floor, Nakagawa was waiting at Reception. The two shook hands, with the grip of the Japanese firmer than usual. He led his guest into a meeting room off the lobby and closed the door quietly.

Fawn leather armchairs surrounded a low wooden table. Some backed on to the wall and others the window. The views of the Opera House and Circular Quay were spectacular. Nakagawa invited Mason to take the seat that a visitor would normally occupy. He then sat alongside him, instead of opposite, which for a Japanese was a gesture he knew would not go unnoticed.

'*Jaa, chokusetsu ni,*' he said: I won't beat around the bush.

'Feel free.'

'I was down in Canberra yesterday,' Nakagawa said, 'and I spent a bit of time with our guy there – an Australian who handles our liaison with government.'

Mason nodded. There was no need to ask for a name. Nakagawa would assume he knew who it was, which he did.

'He'd been to see some contact of his in your Foreign Ministry. Someone called Roland Longfield. I think the two of them did a training course together way back. Anyhow, he tells me that *Nagabatake* works on the Indonesia desk.'

Mason was intrigued by this rendition of the diplomat's name into Japanese, something as unnecessary as it was unusual. It was, at the very least, mildly dismissive. It's as though it's a secret code, he thought, one that only we share.

He knew of Longfield and held him in no great regard. Self-serving and in his forties, the diplomat had the nickname of Rasputin. He was low in both profile and principle, with his time and energy largely devoted to feathering his own nest. And the position he occupied provided ample opportunity for that.

'I'm told, Greg, that Longfield had a real dig at you. Apparently he and Stephen Needham were talking about trade when he suddenly spat out something quite nasty. Needham wrote it down afterwards.'

Nakagawa drew from his shirt pocket a small piece of paper. Unfolding it, he read out the words that the Matsutomo employee had noted down.

> That prick Mason – one of your company's consultants – could ruin your whole business. He's bad news around Canberra. Take my advice and stay well away from him.

Mason sat tight. His expression gave nothing away. It was extraordinary for a Japanese to pass on information of this type, and in such a direct way. But he felt that Nakagawa was somehow onside.

'Needham was surprised, Greg, to hear you attacked like this. He says your name's never come up before, nor was there any need to raise it. But from the way he told me, Longfield said it with real venom.'

Mason remained silent, though he was careful not to look offended.

'I don't know what relevance this might have,' Nakagawa went on, 'but I'd ask you to keep the source to yourself. I promised not to pass it on, if you know what I mean.'

'*Yoku wakatta*,' Mason said: I understand fully. 'Rest assured, it's an invaluable tip-off and I'm most obliged.'

Nakagawa smiled warmly, and in a way that Mason had not previously seen. Then he glanced at his watch.

'I know you have to go, so I'll say only one thing. I'm sure you're asking yourself why I'm telling you this.'

Mason nodded. Words were uncalled for.

'You and I know, Greg, that life in business is

no easy thing. Wherever one goes, it's "dog eat dog", and my time in Australia's been no different to anywhere else. What I'm getting at is this. I respect what you do for your country. That's putting it plainly. I'm sure Australia could do with more people like you.'

Mason looked politely askance. This is unprecedented, he thought, coming from a company *apparatchik* like Toshio.

'For some time now,' Nakagawa continued, 'I've been watching quietly and, you know, I like the way you believe in this place and fight for it. I know you were born in Japan and came back here as a kid – I suppose, as an "outsider". And that, no doubt, gives you a clearer perspective than most on a wide range of things.'

Mason quickly rumbled to what Nakagawa was doing.

Once, after a day on the golf course together, he had told Mason – over more than one drink – the story of his own disjointed childhood. His father had been an engineer, also with the Corporation. An expert in textile machinery, he was stationed in America for the whole of the 1960s. His large family had remained in Japan, but one son – Toshio – had spent the last five years in the US with his father. The wish of the parents had been for their brightest boy to master English and the Western way of thinking. That goal was achieved, but when the young man returned to Japan he had been made to feel out of place. As he explained to Mason that day, it had taken him years to catch up.

Ultimately he felt he knew more about the Japanese than they knew of themselves, though this was something he was rarely able to share.

Mason remembered the conversation well. What he had not realised, however, was the extent to which Nakagawa identified with him over their similar backgrounds. Mason imagined there might be more to it than that. Nakagawa, after all, was a dab hand at another Japanese art: that of creating and calling in favours. But oddly, this seemed totally genuine.

Something – or someone – Mason thought, has got to him, and I suspect it might be a fellow Japanese.

'You see, Greg, that's why, when I heard this story in Canberra, I felt I had a duty to tell you.'

He rose, smiling, and extended his hand. The meeting had ended in less than ten minutes.

Longfield and I hardly know each other, Mason thought as he went down in the lift. So he's projecting somebody else's hostility, spreading shit around for someone. But who? Bloody Clarke – that's who it'll be!

Sydney: Tuesday, 30 May, 2.45 p.m.

'In the end, Zhang's efforts paid off,' Ambassador Li said. 'All that hard work on the energy deal stood Beijing in good stead when the story finally broke.'

'I see,' Winston replied, rubbing his chin. 'And of course, Wang the Rottweiler was ready to pounce with a list of demands. Oh, I can just imagine her screwing the Government here for everything she could get.'

The interception team listening in were surprised to hear the ambassador giving his friend such a detailed rundown on what had transpired at Admiralty House.

The two men sat alone in a private room at the Scented Lotus. They had known each other for 40 years and at one time had served together in London: Li with the Chinese Embassy, and Winston with a bank. Later their close relationship proved highly productive in the business arena, where Winston was one of the first foreign investors to help modernise Chinese industry. Li had facilitated this by using his influence in Beijing, and money changed hands to make it worthwhile. Never one for ostentation, Li had spent most of it on overseas education for the brightest young members of his family.

'I've always told you,' Winston said, 'that Zhang's one of the best officers you've got here.'

Li, who was not eating much, sat back and lit a cigarette.

'Plus you've had that unique insider's view as well,' the Malaysian added.

'*Lu gong liao chin gam,*' Li responded earthily: yes, we certainly have. He'd reverted to the hushed tone he used when discussing sensitive matters.

'Look,' Winston said, 'you don't have to whisper. I'm assured the place is regularly checked. And after all, I own it.'

In their hideaway Damien Khoo, an ASIO interceptor, and Mason smiled at each other. Khoo always had a cigarette hanging out of the corner of his mouth. The ashtray on the narrow desk they were sharing was filled with butts from the packet he had already gone through. 'Helps the concentration,' he had said, when Mason first noticed the habit.

The pair were manning one of the listening posts set up in a small upstairs room in Chinatown to cover Li's lunch. Though Mason had only a patchy knowledge of Hokkien Chinese, he was able to follow the general flow of the conversation, aided by notes which Khoo occasionally scribbled.

'*Ho la, ho la!*' Li replied: OK, OK, I take your point. 'So you see,' he went on, 'for six or seven weeks now, we've been on top of everything that's happened. We've been as prepared as anyone could be. It's been a dream run really, whichever way you see it. And it's left those cretin Nips right out in the cold, which is just where we want them.'

Again Winston appeared conversant with the fact that the Chinese had known for some time that their embassy was under attack. It was clear that Li felt no need to fill him in on the detail, nor on the existence of the well-placed Australian informer who was such a prolific producer.

'What we aim to do,' Li said, 'is to use leverage from this Australian energy deal to squeeze better terms out of the Nips. If they want us to buy into their Sakhalin project they'll just have to match what the locals here have coughed up. Of course, nobody in Beijing doubts the Nips will get their thing up and running *if* we come on board with a long-term contract. So, when we've sewn that up with Tokyo, we'll hit Canberra with an extra list of sweeteners we want from them. And if they don't agree, then we'll simply let the Declaration of Intent we've signed with them lapse.'

This gave rise to much sucking of teeth and chortling, with Winston getting excited. He continually knocked his ring against his beer glass, which caused annoying resonance in the interceptors' earphones. They were grateful that Li was an abstainer and not doing the same.

'You know,' Winston said, 'the Americans must be furious about all this.'

'Too right, and they won't be letting the locals off lightly.'

An hour passed in discussion of the implications of the eavesdropping story, with the talk interrupted periodically as waiters brought more food — and beer for the owner. Family matters of shared interest in China then came to the fore, followed by Winston's manufacturing operations on the Mainland. A number of his managers there were related to Li and had been recommended for employment by the ambassador.

'You know, I'm thinking of going ahead with those new plants,' Winston said, 'even though there's still a lot of planning to do. Of course, *Mo Gan* has been a great help on that front.'

At the listening post Khoo threw up his hands, signifying that he was stumped by this name. It sounded un-Chinese. Pronounced like 'moe gun' in English, it made no sense to him. He scribbled a quick note to Mason, asking if he knew what it meant, and adding: 'Whoever this is, they're mixed up with places like Shanghai, Xiamen and Wuhan.'

'I've got it!' Mason said.

He had immediately recognised these as the cities that Morgandale had mentioned over dinner with Winston at Doyles. And the deduction that followed came fast. While the name had no meaning as such, it was a simple and logical way for a Chinese, in any dialect, to handle a name like Bass's.

'It stands for "Morgandale" – I'll tell you more later,' Mason said, keen not to disrupt the process of listening.

Khoo gave him the thumbs up, plus a broad smile.

Isn't this lovely! Mason thought. Here we are spying on a spy to find out who he's spying for? How would I ever have lasted in the Service with someone like Bass as deputy chief?

Winston said: 'I asked *Mo Gan* about it last time I was here. He has no problem with things like that. It's amazing really. He just plucks this stuff out of the system. When I saw him the other night, for example, he'd gathered a stack of reports on China from ASIS, the CIA and the British that he thought might be useful to me. I'd said I wanted something on economic and political stability, and what he came up with was top quality stuff and remarkably cheap.'

'Yes,' Li replied, contemplatively, 'none of this costs very much, does it? All things considered.'

Winston could be heard shuffling papers on the tabletop.

'Here, look at this,' he said. 'Read these comments and see for yourself. See how China's rated in London and Washington, and in that nerve centre of the universe, Canberra. I must say, *Mo Gan* has certainly come up with some gems. Let me know if you need anything and I'll have him dig it out.'

Canberra/Sydney: Tuesday, 30 May, 7.30 p.m.

'We've lost track of Clarke!' Schneider was desperately worried, and sounded it.

Through the simple act of vanishing, when his whereabouts should have been known, Clarke had elevated himself in status from secondary to primary target.

'He's just – how can I put it? – damn well disappeared!'

Schneider was with Lambert, Pellegrini and Templeton in Canberra. He was speaking straight to camera and addressing Cantrell and the others in Sydney. The purpose of the linkup was to review the outcome of Ambassador Li's meeting with his Malaysian friend.

In the capital, Morgandale was under close surveillance. Clarke had been as well, in light of what Mason had learnt from McKinnon. But odd things were happening, and one after the other. Whether they were connected, nobody could say, but the signs were not good.

Lambert had sounded the alarm on Clarke just before six. He had also provided an earlier warning soon after lunch, reporting on Clarke's odd behaviour. When the pair returned to the office, Clarke had said he was going into another part of the building to talk to Foreign Affairs. There was nothing unusual about that. He said he might be an hour or two. Surveillance confirmed that he had not yet left the premises.

Mason, too, had reported what Nakagawa told him. He had requested a check on Roland Longfield to see where he fitted into the picture. That had quickly revealed that Longfield was indeed associated with Clarke, though to what extent was still unclear. Templeton recalled having seen them together a couple of times. A previous analysis of Clarke's network of contacts, however, had failed to throw up any relationship with Longfield, although it was known that the Indonesia desk head was closely linked to Morgandale. Clarke and Longfield, it turned out, had had numerous phone conversations, though – oddly – none of the calls had been made inside Foreign Affairs. They were between the men's private homes, and in the evening. The question therefore arose as to whether some link did indeed exist between Morgandale and Clarke – via Longfield.

Now, with Schneider in panic mode, the team feared the worst.

Levi, prompted by Mason, had acknowledged that the new concern over Clarke was well founded and that it should take precedence over the product of the Li–Winston lunch. There was now only one priority and that was to find out how Clarke had vanished in the face of careful surveillance and where he had gone. In Canberra, the Australians were the first to hazard a guess.

'I'd say the pressure's got the better of him,' Lambert said, 'and he's gone to ground to escape it. I bet you that's what it is. But how he's done it and where he's taken cover, and how long he'll stay there, who knows?'

'Right, now on that note,' Pellegrini said, 'let me outline what we've been doing here since Todd tipped us off mid-afternoon.'

Levi was listening intently, her mood reflective. She had not only conceded that Clarke was now a case in his own right, but that it was probably he who had tipped off the Chinese. What Mason had heard from McKinnon said as much.

'We've had a watch on all Foreign Affairs exits,' Pellegrini said, 'since six this evening and there's no sign of him yet. Theoretically he's still in the building, but the risk is he's somehow slipped through our cordon.'

Lambert broke in to take up the point with Mason in Sydney. 'Greg, those of us who know the ins and outs of the building can say categorically there's no way we could've missed him – bar one. That's if he's been smuggled out in the boot of a car. Of course, we can't physically search every vehicle emerging from the underground carpark, so we're relying on visuals alone. Oh, and by the way, Clarke's BMW is still where he left it this morning and his briefcase with the bug in it is still in his room.'

'Now, on the question of him being holed up inside,' Pellegrini added, 'Todd and I have had a word to a Foreign Affairs bloke we know in security – Sherif Dajani. We've told him we suspect someone might be lying low overnight and hence a discreet search has to be done. In an hour or so we'll be joining him and going over the place with a fine toothcomb. We've got infra-red heat-seeking gear, as well as an ultra-sensitive sound-seeking device, so hopefully that'll do the trick.'

Schneider and his colleagues stayed quiet. They had been struck by the realisation that the Australians had never taken their eye off the ball, even when the discovery of Morgandale's role appeared to have settled the issue once and for all. They knew Clarke better than anyone else. Only Cantrell had supported them throughout.

'Greg, a quick word on Longfield,' Templeton said. 'I think what you've heard from Nakagawa is crucial. Of course, it might be that Longfield himself has seen you around Canberra and the nasty remark he made to Needham was based solely on that. Then again, it could've come directly from Clarke. He may know that you're on to him. But whatever it is, something tells me this is the lead we've been waiting for.'

'Down here,' Pellegrini said, 'we agree with Alex. Granted, we don't actually know where

Longfield is at the moment, but we have his house under surveillance. We're also tracing back over calls he's been making, to see how his pattern of contact fits in with what Clarke's been doing. The bulk of Clarke's network is pretty much known to us now, though it hasn't had the saturation that Morgandale's bunch has recently. But that's coming on stream and soon we should've filled in all the gaps. The thing now is to cross-reference all these people to see how they interrelate.'

'Let's focus on Clarke like a bloody laser,' Mason said, 'otherwise, we'll all be left looking stupid.'

Nobody thought Mason was being unduly provocative, least of all Pellegrini, who knew that the comment was for American consumption — like his own. Even Levi seemed to have digested what they were saying.

Cantrell was paging through notes on her clipboard. 'Talking of leaving no stone unturned,' she said, 'through all this we've also been keeping an eye on the family of Gao Chun, the Chinese consul here in Sydney, who bolted the night before last. We've noticed a rash of visits by one of his colleagues — a chap who happens to be a good friend of Greg's — Zhang. He's the trade officer who handles economic briefs for Ambassador Li.'

Mason, who had worked closely with the surveillance team that made this discovery, had nothing to add at this stage. Moreover, he was still grappling with the revelation that Zhang seemed deeply involved. The thought of his Chinese mate having become an operative made him feel strange, with conflicting images of Zhang flashing through his mind. He was determined they would not blur his focus.

'Zhang and his wife,' Cantrell went on, 'have been to Gao's place three times since he left, though nobody else from the consulate's made the same effort. Gao has a daughter, twenty-two, who's doing engineering at Sydney University. There's also a widowed sister of his, who's fifty-nine and living with them here.'

Cantrell looked at her watch. It was 8.17. Mason was ready for this prearranged cue.

'You know, it might just be useful,' he said, 'if I drop round to Zhang's place tonight. There's a chance I might pick up something on what's happening on the Chinese side of all this. Since the TV news last Friday, I've had two brief chats with Zhang on the phone and in both he's actually raised the eavesdropping story himself. One was straight after the broadcast and the other was after the *Courier*'s burst the next day. But all he said was that they'd all been forbidden to comment. He joked about it in a way we both understand. "When a voice from Heaven tells you not to utter a word, you do as you're told." He said he knew I'd appreciate the position he's in and thought we might have a chance for a chat in another few days. But I could tell he was trying hard to sound laid back and relaxed. He's a happy-go-lucky type and quite irreverent when it comes to "the system", but I could sense that even he's under pressure. Anyhow, if we do get to talk, it should be interesting. He's close to Li and the hierarchy, so he'll be full bottle on what they're up to in Canberra and even back in Beijing.'

The clear consensus was that the visit should be made.

'Meanwhile,' Mason said, 'Beth will fill you in on Li's lunch, which is a story in its own right.'

When he had gone, Cantrell explained how Pellegrini had saved the day by producing Damien Khoo, an ASIO colleague based in Sydney who spoke the dialect of Chinese that Li and his friend commonly used. She then outlined what the intercept exercise had revealed. Overall, she said, the dialogue had failed to identify the Chinese Embassy's other informer, the one to whom Winston referred as Li's 'insider'. But whoever it was, one thing was certain: they and Morgandale were two different people.

Levi seemed unconvinced. 'But there's still a possibility,' she said, 'that Morgandale's the agent of *both*, and that Winston's unaware of the fact.'

'Linda, for Christ's sake!' Templeton cut in. 'Beth's read Damien's report on the intercept, and Greg – who was there too – is a Mandarin speaker *and* has a fair ear for Hokkien. They've analysed every bloody inflection and they're convinced that the two are different. They're saying Morgandale is *Mo Gan* and Clarke is the "insider". And yet somehow *you* know better. Arrgh, don't give me the shits!'

'OK, OK!' Levi snapped.

'You know, I must say,' Schneider interrupted, acting peacemaker, 'I do think we should all get behind Greg on this. From my knowledge of him his instincts are usually close to the mark.'

Stay quiet, Cantrell thought. Things are bad enough for Linda as it is. Norb's effectively told her she's been wrong all along, and so was he. Not that he's unduly worried. Not now that there's a new horse to back. But this thing's hardly over yet and Linda's not worth getting offside.

The Australians in Canberra were smiling. They were impressed by this show of support.

Cantrell, who thought the time ripe for a quick change of subject, was on the verge of speaking when Templeton chimed in again. To her it was an irresistible opportunity.

'I did it *my* way!' she crooned, in a powerful mimicking of Clarke, with a hint of Sinatra. 'I've kept you all in the dark for as long as I can. Now *you* have to find me.'

Laughter was the one thing Cantrell wished to avoid.

'Moshi moshi?' Kenichi Fujisawa said, answering his home phone: hello?

Mason was calling on his way to Zhang's flat. He would have preferred not to contact his friend in Tokyo on an open line, let alone broach with him such a sensitive issue. It was not what he would normally do, but the pair had occasionally helped each other out with vital pieces of information and had never had to go into detail. And besides, both were experienced in the art of guarded conversation, and the question had already been posed in a couriered letter. It was only the answer that Mason wanted – and fast.

Fujisawa recognised the voice immediately. '*Yappari, Greg, guzen da na. Denwa shiyo to omotta,*' he said: what a coincidence – I was about to call you myself.

Some weeks before, Ben Jameson had passed to Mason a copy of a transcript that the CIA had received from Japanese Intelligence. It had been taken from a conversation in Mandarin intercepted by the Japanese via the bug planted in Ambassador Li's office. It was then translated into English for the Americans, and Mason suspected something might have been lost in translation. It was this transcript – coupled with US material, which the traitor had apparently given to the Chinese – that had sent the CIA Director ballistic.

'Look, I'm calling on my mobile, Ken,' Mason said. 'I just happen to be crossing the Harbour Bridge, with the Opera House off to my right.'

He knew this would appeal to Fujisawa, who had a soft spot for Sydney, especially for its beaches.

The Japanese laughed.

'Greg, I've been out of the country for a week and just got back yesterday. I've listened to the tapes you mentioned and there's only one thing I'd point out. It probably won't mean much, but judge for yourself.'

When Levi had started to favour Bass Morgandale over Martin Clarke, Mason had taken the liberty of contacting Fujisawa, a fellow Mandarin speaker and analyst with the Cabinet Research Office. In his letter, he had simply stated that he'd heard from American friends in his 'old game' of serious concerns on their part about a leak in the Canberra system, probably involving the Chinese. He said there had been talk of intercepts and of someone code-named a 'singing bird'. Could Fujisawa himself check for clues to that person's identity, which transcribers might have missed?

There had been no response from Fujisawa, which was unusual. Therefore Mason decided to try him at home.

'You see, Greg, the Chinese didn't actually refer to their source as a bird. What they called him was "Chang Zhe Chan", or Singing Cicada.'

This told Mason everything. Martin's obsession with insects, he thought, is legendary. Then there's what Todd told me a few weeks back about him having that little bamboo cage on his desk.

'You see,' Fujisawa went on, 'the word "cicada" came through all right into Japanese, but in English a deliberate adjustment was made in the knowledge that singing insects don't mean much to Westerners.'

'*Domo, domo,*' Mason said: I can't thank you enough.

'Well, I'm glad it means something to you.'

'Believe me, Ken, it does.'

— — —

'*Shenme difang, wo bu zhidao,*' Zhang's wife said, cagily: I simply don't know where he's gone.

Mason sensed her embarrassment.

'I think it was some sort of emergency,' she added. 'That's all I can say.'

She was a lean and athletic woman and had an open face, though Mason had never seen it this flushed.

She's clearly not telling a lie, he thought. She just hasn't been told.

In the time he had known the couple, this had never happened and he could see that it troubled her deeply. Normally the three of them could discuss almost anything, and their trust and intimacy included Zhang's son, who was fourteen.

When Mason arrived soon after 8.45, Zhang's wife had explained that the boy was doing his homework. Now, as Mason stood in the lounge, the lad emerged from his room. Dressed in pyjamas, his hair stuck up on the crown of his head like his father's.

'I thought it was you,' he said, his face lighting up.

He rested his arm affectionately on Mason's shoulder, but quickly noted his mother's awkwardness. She had not even asked her visitor to be seated.

'*Greg Shensheng, mei you shijian, xianzai,*' she said to her son: Greg's in a hurry, he has no time to spare.

Mason had mentioned no such thing but the message was clear: Mrs Zhang was under pressure and his presence was only making it worse.

'Off you go now and finish your homework,' she said, leaving the boy in no doubt what he should do.

Mason tousled his hair, and the confused lad went back to his room.

Perfunctorily, Zhang's wife suggested they sit, but Mason took a quick look at his watch and politely refused. At the door, a frostiness came over them. Both understood that their friendship had been eclipsed by professional concerns. Nothing more could be said. But Mason had learnt much of what he wanted to know.

FOURTEEN

Sydney: Tuesday, 30 May, 9.20 p.m.

'Hell, was she embarrassed!'

Mason was addressing his colleagues in both Sydney and Canberra, with the earlier linkup still under way. Leaving Zhang's flat, he had called to say he was heading back to the safe house. When he strode in, all except Levi, who had already excused herself, were there and keen to hear what had happened.

'Let's face it, I know her pretty well,' he said of Zhang's wife, 'and I tell you she was in a real quandary. He must've left so fast there was no time to work out a cover story. In the past, whenever he's raced off on business trips, she's always had something substantial to say, like: "Oh, he's gone to Adelaide with the ambassador and he'll be back tomorrow." Something short and sweet. In fact he usually rings me himself and tells me, but this time it's different. She knew I sensed that something big had come up. The vibes said it all: "It's one of those things, Greg, that you of all people should understand. So don't force me to tell a lie. Zhang will explain when he's back." That's the kind of message it was.'

'So, what does it tell us?' Schneider asked.

'Well, beyond the fact that it's supersensitive,' Mason said, 'it also tells us that whatever's going on is highly unorthodox, urgent and most likely something that Zhang himself would prefer not to be involved in.'

'Not only that,' Cantrell said, 'but it coincides with *three* unexplained disappearances – Gao, Clarke and now Zhang. So how are they linked? OK, Gao was the first to go missing and he actually fled the country. Now these two just vanish into thin air. Well, maybe it's Zhang who's helped Clarke go to ground. Why don't we start with that supposition?'

As she finished speaking, Mason caught her eye. It was only an instant, but the look confirmed to her that she was on the right track. He's come up with something, she thought, and he'll have his reasons for keeping it to himself for the moment.

'Let's look at it from this angle,' Mason said. 'While we have no record of any contact between Clarke and Zhang, if you add Gao to the equation things start to add up. Then there's this reaction of Zhang's wife, which is awfully similar to what Alex got from that consular bloke – stonewalling. And to top it off, there were those visits by Zhang and his wife to Gao's home.

Clearly, there's a pattern in all this that speaks for itself.'

'Gao's been Clarke's case officer,' Pellegrini said. 'That's what I reckon it means, and he's been running him from Sydney. Then, when the embassy story blew in the media, Beijing got cold feet and pulled Gao out fast. Zhang took his place.'

Nobody disagreed.

'I think Zhang would go well as a minder,' Mason said. 'He's trusted by Li, he's smart, levelheaded and, from what we know, not involved in intelligence. Probably Martin's panicked and the Chinese have decided to pull him out quickly. Their first challenge, of course, would be an exit from Canberra, then to some place to lie low, if not to get right out of the country.'

'But could Zhang handle all that?' Lambert said. 'It wouldn't be easy.'

'Todd, he'd do it like a professional,' Mason replied. 'Not that he'd enjoy it, but if he were given the task he'd manage it better than most.'

'Well, let's follow that through,' Templeton cut in. 'Let's assume that the aim of the Chinese was to get him out as soon as they could. How would they do it? Would they bundle him onto the next Chinese freighter that called into port, or would they opt for an aircraft?'

'The latter, I think,' Lambert said. 'And let me tell you why. You see, I've been working on the time factor and I'm pretty sure Martin's calculated that he'd be missed by ten tomorrow morning at the very latest. We're both due at a meeting by then, but we always chat in the office first. So he knows I'd be phoning by, say, 9.45 at the latest to check where he is. I think he's cleverly bought himself time. He's stretched it from just after lunch today through until early tomorrow. That's enough to let him get away. And my guess is he'd want to go quickly, before anyone woke up to what he was doing.'

'For the Chinese too,' Pellegrini said, 'that would probably be their top priority. They'd know how hard he'd be to control if they had him locked up somewhere, waiting for the next slow boat to China.'

Cantrell, like her colleagues, was following this Australian analysis closely.

Mason and his compatriots now had free rein and their insights into Clarke's psyche were at last dictating how the group's resources should be allocated. Schneider, Cantrell and Jameson were equally determined not to let Clarke slip away. Their careers depended on it, particularly now that Levi had opted to focus on what she called mopping-up operations.

Cantrell turned to one of the FBI men. 'Eddie, can we get a readout, ASAP, on all commercial flights to China? Say from midday today for the next forty-eight hours, from whatever point in Australia. Let's look at shipping as well. Anything Chinese around at the moment, coming or going.'

'Sure thing.'

Mason excused himself, too. He said he had a quick call to make, which might help in some way.

He was back in a few minutes and found Pellegrini briefing the others on what usually happened when Canberra was alerted to a possible exit like Clarke's. He had already phoned his colleagues and activated the system.

Mason's mobile rang shrilly, cutting Pellegrini off. He waved his hand, seeking silence as he took the call.

'Hello? Uh ha, I see.' He nodded as he listened. 'I see. Adrian, mate, that's just what I wanted. Thanks a million.'

It was McKinnon from the *Courier*. His private data bank on the illicit dealings of Canberra bureaucrats and politicians was unmatched, even by Templeton.

Mason switched off his phone. 'Great!' he said. 'Here's a lead that might crack this wide open.'

Sydney: Wednesday, 31 May, 12.05 a.m.

Mason and Daniel d'Olivera, Australian Air's operations manager, sat together at a computer terminal in the Operations Centre. D'Olivera's fingers worked nimbly on the keyboard as the two men stared at the screen.

Mason's earlier call to Adrian McKinnon had borne fruit. He had asked the journalist to find out whatever he could about Longfield. McKinnon had said: 'Give me a few minutes, Greg, and I promise you I'll come back with something useful.' In the event he had done just that, and as a result a search was now under way.

'Here we go,' d'Olivera said. 'Here's an Anthony Padstow from Canberra – ANU – booked a few weeks back – off to a conference in Bali on warm-water corals. Any interest?'

'No.'

D'Olivera, who was swarthy and in his forties, had a cheerful demeanour. He was pleased to be helping. The Centre was deserted at this hour and the night duty officer was busy at a terminal in a glassed annex nearby.

The lead that McKinnon had provided was vital.

Pellegrini had immediately introduced Mason to d'Olivera, who was a longstanding professional contact. The airline executive had responded quickly after Pellegrini's call to his home, and despite the time had driven straight to his office. There he and Mason had met up a short time later.

'Here's another one,' he said, as a new name came up on the screen. 'A David Featherstone – flew up from Canberra this afternoon – connected with AA 38 through to Darwin – works in Defence – bound for Singapore – booked three weeks ago by the Department?'

'Nup.'

Mason had with him a list of names he had received from Pellegrini, compiled after McKinnon had reported that Longfield was the sole owner of a travel agency in Canberra. Managed by his niece, much of its business revolved around Indonesia, with high-level clients always handled by the diplomat himself. One of McKinnon's contacts in Canberra had also reported seeing Longfield engrossed in conversation with an ASIS officer mid-morning on Tuesday. It was that well-known Service personality, Martin Clarke.

Mason had relayed this to Pellegrini and Lambert. It was soon after their search of the Foreign Affairs building had failed to find Clarke. The joint team in Canberra had then decided to break into Longfield's travel agency and access his computer system. Recent bookings were closely examined, especially those involving travel to China and places that might serve as a stopover. An ASIO colleague of Pellegrini's, who was the Organisation's resident nerd, had helped with the task, finding himself confronted with seven travel consultants' separate desktops. It was on the fourth that the names had emerged that Mason and the manager were now checking.

'What about this one?' d'Olivera said. 'A Peter Phillips – businessman . . .'

'That's him!'

Mason had spotted the note at the foot of the screen. It had been added at the check-in counter: booked through to Bali – to be seated with W.D. Zhang.

Bookings for Phillips and his companion had been made independently, but at the same time, in Canberra and Sydney. Neither had hotel reservations listed for Bali.

'They're the ones,' Mason said.

He was obviously grateful, though he disguised a certain regret.

A glance at his watch and a quick mental deduction had told him that Clarke would now be safely out of the country. His priority, nevertheless, was to report by phone to the group what he had learnt, but this was something best not done in the manager's presence.

'Mate, I can't thank you enough,' he said.

'My pleasure, Greg. Mind you, if Joe hadn't hinted at how important this was, I'd have needed a warrant.'

Sydney Airport: Tuesday, 30 May, 5.32 p.m.

The Australian had said he would be there at 5.30 sharp, and he was – seated at a table by himself, reading a newspaper.

As arranged, Zhang walked in soon after. He casually approached Clarke, as any foreigner might who needed assistance.

'Excuse me, does the Darwin flight leave from that gate over there?'

'It certainly does.'

'Thanks.'

'Feel free, grab a seat if you want,' Clarke said, knowing that no other tables were vacant.

He removed some business magazines from a chair alongside. Among them was a large, bulky brown envelope.

Zhang made himself comfortable and pulled

some reading material out of his bag. Neither bothered to talk.

Eventually, when their flight was called, Zhang picked up the magazines – including the envelope – and tucked them into his bag.

'Let's face it, mate,' Clarke whispered, as they strode off to the gate, 'you're on a dip passport, so that stuff's much safer with you.'

The Australian Air flight departed fifteen minutes late, at 6.20. According to the pilot, they would make up time on the way. Arrival at Darwin was scheduled for 9.00, with the same aircraft leaving later for Bali. They should be at Denpasar Airport just before midnight.

Clarke and Zhang sat next to each other, neither in the mood for conversation. The Australian peered out the window alongside, taking in the receding lights of the city. It was doubtful, Zhang mused, that he'd ever see them again.

For both it had been an arduous day, if one that would free the Cicada of a load he had said he could no longer bear.

Clarke's mind drifted back to the lead-up to his exit from Canberra, with key events flashing up one after another.

'Wait till you hear what O'Sullivan's told me,' Longfield had said, excited.

Clarke had listened intently, knowing how close his friend was to the minister.

'The Americans are looking for a traitor *inside* ASIS, Martin, and they're carrying out a search of their own. And, they're also getting help from unnamed Australians. Christ, it's like that Omega Blue thing all over again!'

'True,' Clarke said, 'but God knows who the rotten bastard is.'

This was the last straw, he thought. He knew Mason had been sniffing around, as someone had put it, and this explained why. Greg and Omega Blue went hand in glove. Of course, with him being out of the Service, and with the CIA forever indebted to him for saving their skin, he'd have been the logical choice. And there was that bit of hanky-panky with his wife. Hell, he was perfect.

Now an image flashed up of Zhang putting to him an offer on behalf of Beijing. He would be given safe haven in China in exchange for everything he knew about intelligence. The lot: Australian, American, British and other secret operations, ways in which China was the focus of hostile attention, lists of operatives' names and identities, where they were posted, priority requirements they were given, the codes they used . . .

Bloody amazing, Clarke thought. He'd been about to make the same offer to them himself!

He'd agreed, of course, and also suggested that Indonesia be used as a waystation for his escape. After all, he had some powerful contacts there, who might be able to assist the Chinese with other things.

Now the business of choosing what to put in the envelope came to his mind.

It was quality information, all of it: the essence of the Service's holdings on each of the topics

Beijing had mentioned. There was data on disc, as well as hard copy.

He put the envelope into a spare satchel in his office – along with a blue passport, about which ASIS knew nothing – and left his briefcase untouched and his jacket slung over the back of his chair.

Next, he was returning from lunch with Lambert, and rushing to meet Longfield. Clarke had concocted an appropriate story for his friend: he had to leave on a delicate mission to Indonesia, but had been warned by ASIO that he was under surveillance. By whom, the spycatchers had not yet ascertained, though they had no doubt it was unfriendly. He would have to slip out of Canberra unnoticed, which would also entail safely exiting the Foreign Affairs building. Longfield had no problem with that and helped him out in the best possible way. The pair made their separate ways to the basement carpark, where Longfield unlocked his unmarked government car. Clarke got down on the floor in the back and was covered with a sleeping bag that Longfield had in the boot.

They drove out of the building and headed for Sydney. Some distance from the capital, and with no traffic in sight, Longfield pulled over and the fugitive brushed himself off and slipped into the front passenger seat. At the airport, where they arrived in good time, Longfield handed over Clarke's tickets, which had been billed to Longfield's own account at the Canberra travel agency run by his niece.

Clarke was relieved that he could travel under an assumed name, and that Longfield accepted it as being part of the job. A few years before, Clarke had acquired a passport bearing that name from a Foreign Affairs friend who provided it at a reasonable price. It was not listed on ASIS's internal register, which was designed to keep track of such things.

As Clarke checked in a small travel bag, which Longfield had packed for him with light holiday clothes, he was told: 'Mr Phillips, procedures for the Indonesian leg of your journey will be completed in Darwin. And yes, a Chinese gentleman's already checked in and he's asked for you to be seated together.'

Now, as the aircraft levelled out, Clarke was slowly unwinding. The airport had been his first major test. He had feared that ASIO might already have been alerted, along with the Federal police.

'You know,' he said, turning to Zhang and breaking the long silence, 'you're wasted in your line of work.'

'Oh, I wouldn't say that. I have a number of achievements under my belt and I've . . . '

'No, not in *that* way. I mean, your Government should've roped you into my game. Look, I was really impressed with how things went at the terminal. You were just like a professional spy.'

Zhang laughed. He had no ambition to star in that field.

'Believe me, it went like clockwork,' Clarke said. 'So you see, you're wasted in trade.'

Zhang merely smiled.

'No problems with your visa?' Clarke said.

'No, nothing. I sent a note round to my friend at the Indonesian Consulate and he returned my passport a few hours later. Not bad, eh, for a system like theirs?'

Clarke grinned. He had had more experience with that country than this Chinese would care to imagine.

Sydney: Wednesday, 31 May, 12.35 a.m.

'For Christ's sake, Beth, tell me!'

Mason's first inkling of a major development had come in his call to Cantrell. She had *casually* offered to drive round and pick him up.

What he had reported on Zhang and Clarke/Phillips, presumably already in Denpasar, had in no way dented her spirits. Now, settling into the passenger seat, he was intrigued by her smile.

'Things couldn't be gloomier,' he said, feeling awkward.

'Well, they *were*, Greg, but not any more. You see, we're back in the race.'

'We're what?'

'Yes. There's been a breakthrough. There's a CIA officer, Murchison, who works under cover in Bali on the drug game, and he's helped us out brilliantly. When we ran a check on Longfield's phone we found he'd called a number there, so we had Murchison trace it. It turned out to be a small private hotel out on Sanur.'

Mason felt enormous relief.

'So, with the link between Longfield and Martin in mind, and with Martin and Zhang disappearing, we asked Murchison to stake out the place on the off chance that Martin was heading there to lie low. We sent over mugshots of both him and Zhang. Well, a message came back a few minutes ago, just before you called. And you won't believe this, Greg, but Murchison actually saw the pair checking in. It was an hour after their aircraft touched down. And as things stand at present, they've retired for the night.'

Cantrell was grinning as she accelerated to run a red light. Mason was still digesting the news.

'One of Murchison's offsiders in Bali,' she said, 'has a squad watching the place. They've got a campervan that's rigged up to screen all incoming and outgoing calls. He's also checking on Chinese ships and aircraft in the area.'

Mason was left shaking his head.

'The plan, Greg, is for some of us to fly up to Bali quick smart, with the aim of nabbing Martin ourselves. Now, on the assumption you'd have no objection, we've arranged for you, Todd, Joe and me to leave later this morning. Once we're on site, I'll be looking after backup, while you Aussies home in on Martin. Alex is staying in Canberra to help monitor his network there – to see how it reacts to his disappearance. Then, once we've got hold of the son of a bitch, we'll whip him back here to be processed.'

'Sounds great to me,' Mason said, sighing in disbelief.

'Oh, and Ben's been on to the manager of an executive jet firm in Sydney. They'll be flying the four of us out at seven o'clock.'

Mason glanced at the time on the dashboard.

'He's from the States,' Cantrell said. 'We know him well, otherwise we wouldn't be getting the plane. He's a wizard at fixing up clearances for something like this.'

'What sort of aircraft?'

'It's a Gulfstream IV – a sleek little business job – twin-engined, with a range of about eight thousand k's. With the pilot and his offsider, and just four of us, plus no baggage to speak of, our wizard says we'll beat any commercial flight. Todd and Joe have already hit the road for Sydney and they'll be going straight to the airport. So there you have it, Greg. Any questions?'

'Questions? I'm still wrapping my mind around it!'

Cantrell laughed as she checked the rear vision mirror before heading up on to the Bridge.

'I thought you might want to pack a few things at your place,' she said, 'before we go back to the safe house for a few hours' sleep. It'll be quicker from there to the airport.'

'OK with me.'

'By the way, Greg, Norb's pissing his pants over being back in the game. Oh, and something else . . .'

'Don't tell me there's more.'

'Yes, Linda's flown the coop.'

'She's what?'

'Yep, she's dropped us like a hot potato. The story is she was recalled for an urgent job in New York, but one of the FBI guys slipped me a copy of the message she sent that triggered it off. She claimed the job here was all done, that she'd uncovered *two* major traitors – not one – *and* had shown the rest of us how to identify their networks.'

Mason was shaking his head again.

'So, Greg, she flew out a hero and left us with the trickiest bit. Shit, we'd have Martin in custody now if she hadn't stuffed things up. She left on a United flight a few hours ago. Norb was furious and Ben kicked the wall so hard he busted his foot. What really freaked her out though – at least, on the surface – was something trivial that Alex did while you were round at Zhang's place. She did this great bit of mimicry of Martin fleeing the scene, with a bit of Sinatra thrown in – "I did it *my* way" – and it went right up both nostrils. Wow, what a laugh.'

'Trust Alex,' Mason said. 'When I see her, I'll ask her to run through it again. But tell me, what else was there that freaked Linda out?'

'Well, that's where things get dirty, Greg. To be honest, I find it sickening. Anyhow, let's not dwell on that at the moment. I'll fill you in later.'

FIFTEEN

Canberra: Wednesday, 31 May, 11.45 a.m.

'Look, David, you're going to have to clean your act up. It's as simple as that. Goddammit, the President's told you himself.'

Greensborough never minced words and he was pushing the Prime Minister to the limit. O'Sullivan sat riveted. The President's call had been brief, friendly and succinct. It was the sting in the tail that had left Farnsworth reeling: 'Stay close to the ambassador, David. His instincts are reliable in predicaments like this, and he has my full authority to clear any blockages that might stand in your way.'

This was still fresh in his mind as he sensed Greensborough was about to fire another salvo.

'It's unacceptable, David, for an ally to be so *loose*. Of course, you can go it alone if you wish, but expect nothing from us if you do.'

To speak with the weight of the President was one thing. But that was not all. Greensborough also had the support of the CIA Director. Farnsworth was aware that Sherrington was deeply involved. There was no question of that. And any attempt to buck these powerful forces would see Australia cast out on its own. It would take only one American leak to the Australian press, and the local electorate would be up in arms. It would be baying for blood. 'With America offside, only ineptitude remains to defend the nation.' That sort of catch-cry would not only be heard on the floor of the House but resound across the length and breadth of the country.

'OK, Sam, I take your point.'

But Greensborough was determined to drive it home. He knew that Farnsworth was puzzled over why the meeting had been sought and was too rattled to ask.

The PM had planned to fly out of Canberra mid-morning, but had had to rearrange his schedule to accommodate the American's urgent request. An 'informal chat' at 11.30 was what he wanted, and knowing him, he would stop at nothing to get it. His apology for any disruption was perfunctory in the extreme and was as annoying as his suggestion that O'Sullivan be there as well, 'as the person responsible for ASIS'. That cynical emphasis was ominous, too.

The pair had been greeted at the embassy by Greensborough himself, along with a dour Norb Schneider, then led to the ambassador's office. The Americans had been pleasant and polite, almost to the point of condescension, with their manner reminding Farnsworth of dealings with Tokyo in the days when he had looked after Trade. Then, with the upper hand on much-needed investment in resources, the Japanese had had their own subtle way of making it known – or more correctly, rubbing it in.

'You see where we're coming from, David, don't you?'

'Oh, yes, but you must understand, *we're* doing the best we can, too.'

O'Sullivan's manifest discomfort was something the PM could well do without. That was precisely why Greensborough had invited him, and why he chose now to studiously ignore him. Schneider, meanwhile, had nothing to say, which gave the impression the ambassador was acting on instructions from Sherrington himself.

'I don't mean to be crude, David, but whatever your "best" is, it's not good enough. You see, on our side, we've just identified the traitor who tipped off the Chinese, as well as another Australian – *very* high up in your system – who's been selling them secrets.'

His pause gave ample time for the visitors to take in the news.

'Both have betrayed your country in the most despicable way. But for the time being, our priority is the one who blew the whistle on the eavesdropping job. The other is – what should I say? – perhaps more containable.'

While Farnsworth's face and hands gave little away, nothing could disguise his anxiety.

O'Sullivan squirmed, but looked straight ahead. This time he knew he had to discipline himself. His fidgeting during the meeting with Wang from Beijing had earned him a sharp rebuke. One slip now and Farnsworth might expunge him from the political world altogether – not just from cabinet.

'By the way,' Greensborough said, 'there's been an odd twist with the one who sings for a Chinese supper – something we should probably have foreseen.'

Farnsworth's expression was quizzical, while O'Sullivan's gaze remained fixed on the wall.

'You see, what's happened, David, is that he's somehow managed to give us the slip.'

The two Australians wondered what could come next. So much had occurred without their knowledge that they felt as helpless as leaves on a fast-moving stream. Inside, they were furious that no one had tipped them off to what had happened.

'Of course, the guy in question – the primary traitor – turns out to be a certain Martin Clarke, in case you didn't know. I'm told he's an assistant director in ASIS.'

'Oh, no! Not Clarke!' O'Sullivan let slip. 'He's been ...' His words were out before his mind stemmed the flow. He coughed nervously.

Farnsworth stayed quiet, looking grim, as if he had been stabbed in the back.

'Isn't that lovely?' Greensborough said, turning the knife. 'You've had a Chinese spy from the consulate in Sydney running Clarke as an agent – at least, until a few days ago. Now someone else is holding his hand. Someone who's cleverly got him out of the country. It's all in Norb's report here.'

Greensborough gestured at a folder that Schneider had earlier placed on the coffee table alongside them, but the CIA chief made no attempt to pass it across.

'You'll need to be fully prepared, David, for when we bring this guy back to Australia. There's undoubtedly a lot you can do in advance.'

Farnsworth was still unaware of where Clarke and his minder had fled.

'And when might that be?' he said, demeaned by having to ask.

'Oh, a matter of days if we're lucky. And of course Indonesia's not that far away.'

Farnsworth nodded, grateful for that much.

'What Washington wants, David, is for you and your Government to take over as soon as he hits your soil. We'd like you to be seen to be fully in charge, if you know what I mean. After all, you'll have *two* traitors to deal with, which will call for some pretty nifty footwork.'

Greensborough assumed from Farnsworth's silence that he had no idea who the other man was.

'Fancy, the deputy chief of ASIS selling secrets right under your nose,' he said. 'I'd have thought you'd have known your *Sebastian Morgandale* better than that.'

To Farnsworth and O'Sullivan, Greensborough's feigned British accent went unnoticed. Mention of

Morgandale's name had transfixed them, for he was well known to both. It was also common knowledge that he was in O'Sullivan's pocket, and with him now being revealed as a spy, that was the minister's death knell.

'Before Clarke's plane touches down you'll need to pull Morgandale in fast, as well as the rest of his cronies. Then he and Clarke will be your problem, David. We'll get right out of the act. But let me tell you, you'll have some very smart people on your side to help. We know, because we couldn't have done this without them.'

Even Farnsworth winced at this.

'Oh, and in case it's of interest, Clarke's using the name Phillips – Peter Phillips.'

Greensborough's steely gaze moved from Farnsworth to O'Sullivan, then back to the PM.

'Is there anything else you need to know?' he asked.

Gulfstream IV: Wednesday, 31 May, 11.55 a.m., Eastern Standard Time

'Delta X-Ray Yankee. Come in please.'

The pilot, a middle-aged American, adjusted his mouthpiece to respond to the call from Control at Darwin Airport.

His co-pilot, younger and an Australian, was studying a foldout map of the island of Bali. They had left the north coast of Australia an hour before, on track for Denpasar.

'Delta X-Ray Yankee. Receiving you.'

'We have a message from Sydney,' Darwin reported. 'Divert immediately to Jakarta. Divert from Denpasar.'

'Delta X-Ray Yankee. Received and understood.'

'Do you have sufficient fuel, plus reserve for Jakarta?'

'Delta X-Ray Yankee. We have sufficient to take us past Singapore.'

'Good. Sydney also advises that you now have clearance for Indonesian airspace and to land at Sukarno-Hatta International Airport. Track up south coast of Java, then head north to capital, after Jogja. Oh, and one more thing. Tell your lady on board to switch on her comms set. There's something in the pipeline.'

'Delta X-Ray Yankee. Received and understood.'

The pilot called back to Beth Cantrell through the open door of the cockpit, passing on the message.

She was sitting comfortably in a plush leather chair, chatting to Greg Mason. Lambert and Pellegrini were asleep. She reached for her shoulderbag and removed a grey laptop. Using satellite communications, the system could receive and transmit messages – written or spoken – from anywhere on the globe, and securely. Moments after she switched it on, text flashed up on the screen, which they both read. It was from CIA headquarters in Virginia.

From Langley: Relaying Schneider/Canberra
May 31, 1214 hours EST
You are being diverted to Jakarta due to developments in Bali.

Murchison and a local Indonesian operative spotted two Chinese visitors arriving at Clarke's hotel at 0930 Bali time. Operative entered premises and sighted visitors on terrace in close conversation with Clarke and Zhang. Clarke was in good spirits. Tickets, documents and currency were handed over to Zhang and Clarke.

Foursome left together for Denpasar airport and took Garuda domestic flight to Jakarta. Names of neither Zhang nor Clarke/Phillips were listed on passenger manifest, though both were on board. Flight will arrive in Jakarta less than an hour before you.

Jakarta Station is detailing full squad of local operatives to handle surveillance on and after arrival.

You will be met at airport, and immigration procedures will be taken care of away from terminal. You will stay at Agency safe house.

Current speculation here reinforces view that Chinese propose to ship Clarke out of Jakarta on freighter 'Minghua' scheduled to sail from Tanjung Priok, Thursday evening, June 1, or morning of

Friday, June 2. Destination listed as Shanghai. For Zhang and Clarke, Bali stopover was probably cleansing process to 'lose' themselves inside Indonesia.

Will revert with further information prior to your arrival at Sukarno-Hatta. Catch up on sleep. Busy days ahead.
Schneider.

'The plot thickens,' Cantrell said, 'and it takes you and me back to our old stamping ground.'

'That's just what I was thinking.'

Cantrell smiled. Her warmth was mixed with mild apprehension and Mason sensed it.

'So, Beth, tell me what it was that made you so sick about Linda. I'm dying to know.'

'You'll die when you do. But let me tell you first off, Greg, it's actually because of this that I've finally decided to part ways with the Agency. That is, after we've picked up Martin. And you're the only one who knows at the moment.'

Her expression warned Mason of the nature of what was coming.

'You see, when we heard she was leaving, Norb flashed a message to Langley complaining about her performance. A reply came straight back, telling him to leave it alone. "Just be glad she's gone," he was told. It was a bit too cavalier for my liking, so I called a friend there, who works in the Director's secretariat. Well, he held nothing back. I got the whole truth, but on the strict condition I didn't pass it on. See, when Washington first learnt there was a traitor in Australia and

Sherrington came up with his plan, the President told him to work closely with the FBI. And like it or not, they're our spycatchers. Well, naturally, the last thing Sherrington wanted was to have some high-flier from the Bureau crack *his* case. Apparently, to the FBI, he played down the sort of help he needed, even insinuating we more or less had things under control. Right now, of course, the Bureau's under a lot of pressure, what with terrorist inroads and the like, and their top people are all flat out. So they were relieved not to have to let one of *them* go.'

'So, what *did* we get?' Mason asked.

'Well, in effect, a sham. It seems Linda's not all she's cracked up to be. She's had a few wins along the way, but mainly off the back of ace teams she's worked alongside. Lately, though, she's stuffed up badly, rushing to judgement and squandering resources. That's why the Bureau let us have her.'

'So Sherrington's actively defied a presidential order?'

'Not only that, Greg, but having skilfully got Greensborough onside, he even managed to get the White House to call Farnsworth. You see, the President rarely has time to follow things through, even on intelligence, though that's an area that interests him. He simply assumes that when he's told people to work together, that's basically what they'll do. But they don't. Not always. Empire-building never plays second fiddle to the national interest. You see, I've heard that Sherrington's angling to take over the

FBI's overseas operations. That's why he wants the Agency to star on Martin's case. Which is why, I suppose, I was sent out to recruit you. Anyhow, Greg, I've done my bit and when this is over, I'm out. Right out.'

Canberra: Wednesday, 31 May, 12.25 p.m.

'Pull up a chair, Bill,' O'Sullivan said, looking at Hestercombe from behind a piled desk.

The ASIS chief could sense something ugly.

His instincts were right. Farnsworth had told his Foreign Minister – in no uncertain terms – to make sure the head of the Service pulled his weight. It was his appalling lapse in security that had allowed these disasters to occur. Now he could help clean up the mess, and fast.

'Look, I'll get straight to the point,' O'Sullivan said, 'so prepare yourself for a shock. We have *two* traitors on our hands and they're *both* in your bloody setup!'

Hestercombe went white. He was incapable of speech.

O'Sullivan glared at him unforgivingly. 'The main one, Bill – the one who tipped off the Chinese – is none other than *your* Martin Clarke. And the other is Bass Morgandale.'

My Martin? Hestercombe thought, fighting to regain balance. O'Sullivan's distancing himself already. Granted, Martin's my responsibility, and Bass is as well, but it's also no secret that O'Sullivan favours Bass. And seeks his advice.

'Bloody oath, Bill! How could you not know this was going on?'

'Well, in terms of Martin, yes, I'd cottoned on to the fact that something was wrong, some time ago, but . . . '

'Some time ago!' O'Sullivan exploded. 'Fucking hell! You had suspicions and you didn't tell me?'

'Well, I couldn't be sure. OK, he was carrying on a bit strangely, so I had a word in his ear. But then, suddenly this — I mean, it's unbelievable — it's . . . '

'Bill, your lot are supposed to be spies. Not chicken sexers or dog catchers or something like that. You're meant to be masters of human psychology.'

Given the upper hand, O'Sullivan was a bully, and Hestercombe could tell that this time the minister had his riding instructions from Farnsworth. Failure would be out of the question.

The head of ASIS sat there, humiliated. '*Two* of them,' he kept saying to himself. And *Bass*. I just can't believe it.' He looked up. 'But where did you hear this?'

'From the Yanks, Bill. That's where!'

O'Sullivan stared at him long and hard, until Hestercombe looked away.

'They've got some combined team of sleuths operating here, with *our* people in it, though we're not allowed to know who ours actually are. At least not until this mess — *your* mess — has been cleaned up.'

Hestercombe knew nothing of this either.

Canberra's own attempt to uncover the traitor had failed to throw up even one promising lead. But hearing this now almost reduced him to tears.

He's really worried, O'Sullivan thought, and suitably contrite, which is just what I want.

'You see, Bill, it can't get much worse than this, can it?'

The ASIS chief sighed deeply, but said nothing.

'See, the bloody Chinese have been running Clarke from Sydney, which means he's been going backwards and forwards right under your nose. And now, to top it off, he's given us the bloody slip. At least we have Morgandale in custody, but that's not much compensation. Apparently Clarke's shot off to Indonesia, and from there God knows where he'll go. Probably to China to start a new life. And that's a prospect, as you'd appreciate, Bill, that has the Yanks hyperventilating.' He paused. 'And this is before we even start on your other mate, Morgandale, who's also been flogging US secrets to China.'

Hestercombe was stunned. His mind was awash with implications, one crashing into the other.

'The Service hasn't done us too proud, has it Bill. Every year I get you a budget and my colleagues and I stay out of your hair. You're protected from any meaningful scrutiny and you can virtually do what you want. But in return we expect a favour once in a while.'

Hestercombe glanced at the floor. He could sense that what was coming was going to make him even more uncomfortable.

'I have just one priority at this stage, Bill, and that's Clarke. Unless we cut the head off that snake, he's going to bite us again. All of us.'

O'Sullivan sat forward and rested his elbows on the desk.

'Now, what I'm about to tell you must stay between us. Absolutely. Do you understand?'

Hestercombe nodded.

O'Sullivan was buoyed by Hestercombe's contrition. It was just what he wanted, for he and Farnsworth had resolved that without some gilding of the lily there was no way the ASIS chief would be moved to act. They had therefore fabricated a story of complete falsity.

'Right, this is the inside story. You see, the PM and I have had a long session with Greensborough and his sidekick — that living corpse, Schneider. I'm not at liberty to let you in on the detail and it's probably best you don't know anyway. But the upshot is this. The Yanks, it seems, have been using Clarke's services for quite a while on "delicate matters" that have nothing to do with Australia. In fact "dirty matters" might be a better term, but whatever, Clarke should never have allowed himself to be sucked into something like that. Certainly not without telling you. But what's done is done, and now we're left to clean up the mess.'

Hestercombe dreaded what might follow. He had been around long enough to know what politicians would do to save their skins.

'What the White House is asking for, Bill, in a roundabout way, is that we make sure — dead sure – that Clarke never gets to China. That he never gets back here. And that he *never* stands trial. Now, is that crystal clear?'

'Well, yes, but . . .'

'No buts, Bill. You and I know that the Yanks are only too capable of taking care of these things themselves, but as Greensborough's pointed out, *we* produced the son of a bitch, so *we'll* provide the solution. Believe me, if we're ever to balance the books with Washington we'll have to deliver on this. Clarke has to disappear quietly. So quietly that it's totally deniable by everybody involved.'

'Look, Michael, I don't . . .'

'For fuck's sake, Bill! I'm not asking you to knock the bastard off. I just want him, well, sidelined. Can't you understand that?'

O'Sullivan's temper was rising but he knew it would be foolish to overplay his hand. With Hestercombe, things usually took time. He was that sort of man. He had to accommodate something in his own pedestrian way.

'And that's not all, Bill. You see, the Yanks are cutting our intelligence exchange back to zilch until we clean up our act. We're out of the loop. And as you and I know, if that gets into the press, not only is the Government a gonner but *you* won't get off lightly either.'

Hestercombe seemed to be coming around.

'Bill, if Clarke were to be put in the dock, there's no doubt in my mind he'd sing his heart out. He'd broadcast his CIA links all over the place. And I hate to remind you that you'd be the next to be grilled. The *ninja* who couldn't see in the dark!'

The shock showed on Hestercombe's face.

He's fallen for it, O'Sullivan thought, as he prepared to go in for the kill.

'It boils down to this, Bill. If *you* can't do your bit, and quickly, then you'll have to be sacked.'

Hestercombe thought long and hard. 'Well then, do we know where Martin is in Indonesia?'

'Yes, in Jakarta. And he's using the name Peter Phillips.'

SIXTEEN

Jakarta: Wednesday, 31 May, 3.20 p.m., local time

Clarke and Zhang had arrived in Jakarta late in the morning, together with their Chinese Embassy escorts. A CIA team had then tracked them to the home of a Chinese–Indonesian businessman renowned for his wealth. It was his driver who had picked up the group at the airport in a sleek silver Mercedes and taken them directly to Kebayoran Baru, an upper-class residential area. The CIA team had had a readout on the businessman's address and his background before the car arrived at his home. The visitors had spent a few hours there over lunch with their host, before Clarke and Zhang re-emerged with the car and the driver. The minders had remained at the house, while the pair drove across to Blok M, a shopping complex only a kilometre away.

Meanwhile, Cantrell and Mason and the others had arrived.

They were met by the team and taken to a safe house in a suburb adjacent to where Clarke and Zhang were staying. It was owned by a US multinational and occupied by an American who ran the firm's operations in Indonesia. The residence had a spacious bungalow set in a garden at its rear. It was used regularly for CIA accommodation and debriefs and was largely shielded from the gaze of Indonesian staff working in the main house in front. With this as their base, the team were also linked to a surveillance van currently parked outside the Indonesian tycoon's mansion. By monitoring conversations inside the house, the team were aware of the proposed Blok M visit by Clarke to buy clothes, long before he and Zhang got into their car.

With the minders out of the way and the target in the company of just one other person, it was an opportunity too good to miss. It was agreed that Cantrell would take part in a hurriedly organised sting involving an unusual species of butterfly. Zhang had never met Cantrell. She had kept a low profile in Sydney and the likelihood of either Clarke or Zhang having spotted her there was remote. Speedy work on the internet by a local CIA operative had refreshed her memory of the spectacular Queen Alexandra's Birdwing, a butterfly found in the eastern part of Indonesia, where Cantrell had often travelled in years past. She recalled Clarke, who was passionate about butterflies, describing it to her excitedly: 'It's the largest in the world and when the first foreigners saw it they shot the bloody thing, thinking it was a bird!' She remembered Clarke saying he doubted that he'd ever be able to acquire a specimen.

The operation commenced with a second van dropping Cantrell off at the shopping complex and parking not far away. The American technicians in this vehicle took signals from a microphone worn by Cantrell and relayed them to the safe house, where Mason and his colleagues were listening in. The exercise began smoothly, with Cantrell tracking her quarry for only a few minutes before making contact.

'Martin! What a coincidence!'

The sound of Cantrell's voice startled Clarke, who swung around quickly. He was wearing the beach shorts and garish purple batik shirt in which he had travelled from Denpasar. Laden with upmarket shopping bags, he stood transfixed.

It was a fleeting moment of mutual doubt, which she handled well.

On duty, as she was now, Cantrell was at her most alluring. She was dressed in a pink skirt and blouse, with her collar turned up. As expected, Clarke noticed immediately. She was well acquainted with his instincts and recognised his thinly disguised smirk. They were standing on opposite sides of a clothing rack loaded with classy French jackets. Other displays crowded the menswear boutique inside Blok M.

Zhang watched from the end of the rack, feigning lack of interest. But for him, alarm bells were ringing. Alone with Clarke in a strange city, the last thing he wanted was some friend whisking his charge away. A first-time visitor to Jakarta, he was also finding the stickiness oppressive, though the cooler air in the complex offered a temporary respite.

Shenme ren? Yao shenme? he thought: who the hell's this? What does she want?

'Hey, Zhang, meet my old pal Beth,' Clarke said, smiling nervously as he introduced Cantrell. 'We go back a long way.'

Zhang came up and shook her hand.

Cantrell had noted Clarke's failure to mention her surname, but could imagine why he preferred to keep things strictly personal. Zhang, too, clearly wanted it that way.

'So, what are you doing here?' Clarke asked, still amazed. It was seven years since they had met.

'Oh, just looking for a present,' she replied, knowing that that was not what he wanted to know.

'It's a bit far to come for that.'

'Well, you see, I've left my old job and I'm operating independently. It's mainly risk analysis for the oil industry back in the States. I'm here for Exxon at the moment, but generally I'm to and fro all the time.'

Cantrell thought this a credible story, unless of course Clarke had recently checked on her CIA status. That, however, was a gamble she and Mason were willing to take. She was, after all, an Indonesia hand and if she had parted ways with the Agency she would logically take on this type of work. It was well known that US multinationals headhunted spooks, paying big money to bring their talents on board.

Clarke appeared to accept the story without question.

'And you, Martin? What brings you to Jakarta?'

'Oh, just passing through.'

Oddly, that was all he proffered, so she jumped in quickly to fill in the gap. 'I say, have I got something to tell you!'

When animated, Cantrell had always worked magic on Clarke and she watched now as his eyes lit up.

'Now, let me get this right,' she said, faking poor recall, '*Ornithoptera Alexandrae* – Queen Alexandra's Birdwing. Is that correct?'

'Yes! It certainly is, but why?'

Mention of Clarke's hobby had Zhang on edge. There was obviously a close link between Clarke and this woman, which he found menacing.

'Why? Because an Indonesian oil guy I deal with here has *three* of the things. Full specimens and in pristine condition. Can you believe it?'

Clarke was consumed by this news. 'No, I can't.'

'Well, Paul's an avid collector too, Martin. Equally as bad as you.'

Clarke laughed, partly because of the compliment, but also in recollection of times well spent with Cantrell. This was precisely the reaction she wanted. The idea of approaching Clarke in this way had been hers from the start, with Mason and the others strongly backing the idea.

Clarke was lost for words, so she jumped in again. 'Look, do you have time for a drink before you fly out? It'd be great to tell you the rest of the story.'

'Well, yes, I suppose,' he replied, glancing at Zhang. 'Actually, we're both invited for dinner tonight, but perhaps after that.'

'Yep. Sounds good to me. Say, around eleven then?'

As he nodded, she noted the glint in his eye. He had taken the bait.

'Let's say the top-floor bar at the Hilton?' she said. 'I have a room in the place.' She raised an eyebrow slightly as she spoke.

'Done! I'll be there. Right on the dot.'

'Let me give you my cell phone number,' she said, reaching into her bag for a pen. 'You never know what might come up.'

She scribbled the details on the back of a docket and Clarke seemed flustered when she handed it over, no doubt worried he might be asked to reciprocate.

'I'm afraid I don't have a number for where I'm staying.'

'No, I don't either,' Zhang chimed in, a little too hastily, when Clarke looked at him. 'A business friend's putting us up, and we're not too sure . . . '

'Oh, that doesn't matter,' Cantrell said.

As they parted, the Chinese caught her eye. It was a passing look, but even so, a tad flirtatious. She browsed through a display of Panama hats on her way to the door, then looked back before leaving. Clarke had wandered off in a different direction, but Zhang was still there. Their eyes met again and he smiled. There was warmth in his face, and puzzlement too. She gave him a wave as she left.

Cantrell was thrilled, as she knew her colleagues would be, listening in not far away.

The hope now was that, if Clarke kept his promise and turned up at the Hilton, Cantrell would lure him back to a room already booked. There he would be drugged and taken away. A CIA 'doctor' and an assistant would attend the scene and take the patient off to hospital. But before all this could occur the visitors would have to be monitored for the rest of the day. Plans had a habit of changing.

Jakarta: Wednesday, 31 May, 6.55 p.m.

Soundproofed, the van was a world of its own. A young American with a severe crewcut adjusted a dial on the eavesdropping panel. Mason, Lambert and Pellegrini gave him the thumbs up to acknowledge the improvement in reception. All four wore earphones and mouthpieces, though at this stage there was not much to hear – only dim voices at the rear of the house, where the tycoon's guests were taking refreshments.

The waiting was interminable, which was not uncommon in tech ops.

The team's driver, a Filipino–American fluent in Bahasa, kept guard out on the footpath. A rap on the van would be enough to alert those inside. Not that anything was expected to happen in this secluded street where huge umbrella-like trees met in the centre and only an odd lamp or two provided a burst of yellow-green light.

'Come on, you bastards, get back to the front of the house,' Lambert said, making the others laugh.

'Someone's got to move soon,' Pellegrini added. 'Clarke and Zhang have a dinner to go to.'

He peered out through one of the slit-windows that ran the length of the van. Looking like air ducts, they were fitted with one-way glass, which offered a clear view of the mansion across the road.

'God, what a pile,' he said, knowing that his colleagues had had no time to study it in detail. 'Not that it's my sort of mix, even with an Italian background. Touches of the European villa with bits of Indonesia tacked on. A high wall along the front, a metal security gate you'd need a bloody tank to get through, tall trees, lots of red bougainvillea. Oh, and white Corinthian columns to set it all off.'

Mason grinned. He had seen opulent Mediterranean homes in Australia far worse than this.

'So this magnate's not a contact of Clarke's?' the CIA interceptor said.

'Correct,' Mason replied. 'He's a friend of the Chinese Ambassador to Canberra – a man called Li, in case the name crops up – and of a Malaysian relative of his who often passes through Jakarta. We assume it was Li who arranged for the visitors to bed down here. Besides, Clarke would be easier to keep an eye on in a compound like this, rather than loose in a hotel. And all the better for us.'

Not long after Clarke and Zhang returned to the house from Blok M, the interceptor had picked up phone calls made by the pair. Zhang had contacted his wife in Sydney, hearing from her about the embarrassment she suffered when Mason came to their apartment. Zhang's only other call was to the Chinese Embassy in Jakarta. He had spoken to the ambassador, confirming their dinner appointment at the Residence. 'I must say, Zhang, I'm looking forward to meeting your *friend*,' the senior diplomat had said, with a stress on the word *pengyou* that suggested more than a passing interest in the Australian.

Clarke had made three calls, all to Indonesians – two in Jakarta and one in East Java. The latter was a businessman for whom Clarke had apparently been buying property in Australia. It was the other calls, however, which attracted attention. They were to top men who Clarke had 'recruited' in the army and the police during his first posting to Indonesia. Neither had been available to speak at the time, so Clarke had left his name, though not his number, and promised to call back.

'Hey, we have liftoff,' the interceptor said. 'They're moving to the front.'

Reception improved dramatically. On the roof of the van there was a raised ventilation louvre, which contained a laser device that projected a beam onto the front windows of the house. With enough glass exposed above the wall to act as a conductor, and with the help of computer enhancement, little in that part of the building was lost. This was something they had learnt before drinks were served at the rear.

'Ah, I see what you mean,' they heard the host say, evidently speaking to Clarke.

While his voice came through loud and clear, the tycoon's English was halting and interfered with the Mandarin that the others were using nearby. The Chinese minders who had escorted Zhang and Clarke from Bali were engaged in a rapid-fire exchange with their colleague from Sydney. The CIA had identified the minders as intelligence officers working under cover in the embassy. What they were discussing was cutting across the conversation with Clarke.

Via hand signals, Mason ensured that the interceptor, together with Lambert and Pellegrini, would monitor the English dialogue while he focused on the Chinese.

'*Women tongzhi shuo zheige* . . . ' one of the minders said: what our colleague intended was . . .

The speaker outlined a plan, which someone else had put forward. It seemed to relate to what was taking place in Jakarta.

'*Dui le, he, ta xiangxin* . . . ' his associate said: true, but he also thought that . . .

Another scenario was painted. No names were mentioned, nor was it possible to deduce who the two were talking about.

'Look, I agree,' Zhang cut in, 'but let's not forget the original idea, which was to leave the debrief until *after* the *Minghua* had sailed.'

Hearing this, Mason knew that the topic was Clarke, but who was the other Chinese they were referring to? There was no time to think, in light of the degree of concentration required.

'Thankfully, "Chan" is not too bad at the moment,' Zhang said. 'He's handling things better than expected.'

That confirmed it, Mason thought to himself. Martin Clarke was definitely the Singing Cicada!

'Actually, at Sydney Airport,' Zhang went on, 'I was shitting my pants.'

The familiar lilt of his friend's voice highlighted for Mason the irony of their current situation. In Australia they regularly conversed in Mandarin as often as in English, yet here was Zhang operating in his native tongue on the other side of the intelligence fence.

'*Gao de shuofa* . . .' Zhang said, quickly solving the puzzle: Gao's idea was . . .

He went on to outline a discussion he and Clarke's case officer had had prior to Gao's rushed departure from Sydney. Gao's point had been that if Clarke were to be lifted out of Australia and granted safe haven in China, his debrief should not begin until he was safely on board the freighter. Otherwise, he said, Clarke might panic and go back on the deal. The two intelligence officers in Jakarta, however, wanted to start the process straight away – and already had.

'OK, I'm not a professional,' Zhang said, 'but instinct tells me you shouldn't push him too hard. You've only just met him. I urge you not to try to meet his top contacts while he's here. I understand how tempting it is, but it's looking for trouble and we have enough of that at the moment. This American woman who's suddenly appeared on the scene has me worried. She certainly knows how to get his attention.'

'Arrgh, she's just wants a good screw,' one of the minders said.

'Possibly,' Zhang replied, 'but something tells me there's more to it than that.'

'Yeah,' the other said. 'But while he's on dry land he'd better hit her wet spot fast, 'cause there won't be anything *damp* on the boat.'

The three men burst into laughter, which completely drowned out the conversation between Clarke and his host. The others in the van looked at Mason inquisitively, not understanding a word.

'Seriously,' Zhang said, pressing his view, 'I think it's risky. Anyhow, you're the experts, not me.'

Jakarta: Wednesday, 31 May, 8.07 p.m.

General Mantiri waited patiently in the anteroom of the Istana. President Subroto's private secretary had recommended he come to the palace immediately if he wanted ten minutes with the 'boss'.

Muscular and middle-aged, the general bore the scars of a difficult life. After his childhood of poverty, the military had opened up for him vistas he had never imagined. Intellect, cunning and luck had taken him straight to the top. Neatly dressed in a suit, he was a privileged Indonesian who could move from one air-conditioned building to another in the comfort of an air-conditioned car. In Jakarta, one of the signs of power was being able to avoid the heat and never having a sweaty collar.

The wall in front of where he sat was hung with a large gilt-framed picture of a Javanese sultan. Smaller maritime scenes decorated the rest of the room. Sumptuous in a colonial way, the all-white Istana was used for ceremonial functions, with the President living elsewhere.

Suddenly there was a knock and an attendant entered, excusing himself with great deference as he held the door open. Whenever the head of BAKIN – Indonesia's Intelligence Service – visited, Javanese honorifics flew thick and fast. Moments later the President strode in. Portly and bald, he had a large, happy face and was clearly pleased to see his guest. As the door closed quietly behind them he reached out to greet his comrade of many years' standing. The two were unreserved in their display of affection.

President Subroto was hosting a dinner for governors of outlying provinces, but formal proceedings had not yet begun. He had slipped out briefly to see what it was that the BAKIN chief wanted.

'Well now, what's happened?' Subroto said, his arm still around his friend's shoulder.

'It's that *Hess-ta-comm* chap in Australia,' Mantiri replied, putting a local inflection on his counterpart's name. 'He made contact from Canberra just a short while ago.'

The President nodded.

'Look, it's all very strange. The message he sent me was strictly personal. Brief, direct, even compelling. Burn before reading – that sort of thing.'

'So, what's that lot done now?'

'Well, ASIS wants us to sideline one of its people.'

'What?' the President said, shocked.

'Yes, one of their top men – Martin Clarke – who's only too well known to us. He's in Jakarta at the moment and they want us to pick him up and hold him somewhere, *incommunicado*, for the "foreseable future".'

'But whatever for?'

'Well, don't laugh, but they believe he's been working for Beijing and he's apparently on his way up to China to create a new life. But you see, Canberra doesn't want him to leave here, let alone reach there.'

The President smiled. It was not the first time he had heard of high-level Australians like this. Jakarta had thrived on them for many a year.

'Washington's nose must be well and truly out

of joint,' he said. 'This has to be linked to that bugging fiasco.'

'Absolutely,' Mantiri replied, grinning.

The topic had run hot in political and intelligence circles in Jakarta since the recent revelations in the Australian media, all of which had been supplemented by secret reporting from Canberra. It had been the basis of many a joke.

'So, how do we accommodate *Hess-ta-comm*'s wish? How high a price do we charge?'

'Well, perversely, we don't really have to.'

'How come?'

'Because there's far more to Clarke than ASIS seems to be aware of.'

'Oh, really?'

Jakarta: Wednesday, 31 May, 8.32 p.m.

Mason and Pellegrini had just regrouped with the others at the bungalow.

When Clarke and Zhang departed for the Chinese ambassador's Residence, along with their minders, a CIA surveillance crew had followed them there. It was waiting nearby to tail them again when the dinner was over. By then Cantrell and another squad would have taken up position at the Hilton a few kilometres away. With luck, Clarke would be in their custody by midnight.

Eavesdropping was out of the question at the Residence, since the Chinese – after what had happened in Canberra – had taken exceptional measures to guard against electronic penetration. Cantrell's team, therefore, had time on its hands and was spending it at the bungalow reviewing contingency plans. Tension was high and concentration was no easy thing.

One of Cantrell's CIA colleagues strolled into the lounge room. He had with him a sheaf of transcripts from the calls that Clarke and Zhang had made on their host's phone. Cantrell, who was comfortable on a sofa studying the layout of the hotel, put that aside and flicked through the papers to see if there was anything of interest to Mason. One of the transcripts was from a call that Clarke had made just before leaving for dinner.

'Hey, Greg, listen to this. It's Martin's chat with the Army general.' She read it aloud in English as Mason, Lambert and Pellegrini gathered around.

> Pak Martin, how are you?
> All the better for hearing your voice. Say, did you get my message?
> Yes, we did, and Andi and I have discussed it at length.
> So, what do you think?
> Well, we agree there's a lot we can do together, Martin, though you must understand that we want to keep it totally separate from what we've got going now with Poulson and Imlach. We have them nicely trained, if you know what I mean, and the rewards for our side are much

greater than expected. Of course, you're in a different league entirely – oh, which reminds me, did you get my note before you left?

Yes, I did.

Well, don't forget what I said, will you? Every bit counts, you know.

Don't worry. I'm on to it at the moment, actually.

Wonderful! Anyway, Martin, we can work out the details later, when we catch up. How about tomorrow evening?

Yes, that's fine with me. Where shall we meet?

What about the lobby of the Grand Hyatt, at six?

OK, see you there, then.

'For Christ's sake,' Mason said, 'you can see what he's up to.'

Jakarta: Wednesday, 31 May, 10.20 p.m.

'I must warn you,' Ambassador Wu Jing said, 'that China's both a drinker's paradise and a nightmare. You need to know the things you can mix and the things that you can't. But I'm sure Gao will help you out when you get there.'

Clarke smiled. He seemed content. The ambassador was too.

Things were going to plan. Wu was a congenial and grandfatherly type, who looked like an aged Chairman Mao. He was seated with his guests at a round table in the Residence's dining room, with the tablecloth heavily stained from the meal. Each blotch was a record of their two-hour culinary splurge. Tall potted plants decorated the place and thick imperial-yellow drapes covered the windows.

Clarke already knew what the ambassador meant about drink. He felt flushed from the numerous toasts and was itchy around the neck, always a warning that he was in uncharted waters. He had encountered the brownish *lao jiu* rice wine and the potent vodka-like *mao tai* before, but for some reason these brands seemed stronger. Perhaps the Scotches he had started with were reacting. It worried him a little, because he still had important questions to ask.

'Excuse me,' he said, 'but I must loosen my collar.'

The others laughed politely, especially Ambassador Wu, who was one of the Foreign Ministry's most experienced operators. Fluent in English, Spanish and French, his time in Jakarta had allowed him also to get on top of Bahasa. He was a good judge of people and his friend Wang – China's intelligence chief – had asked him to meet with 'Chang Zhe Chan' before he boarded the freighter. Wang was eager to have Wu's personal assessment of the traitor, in addition to his views on how his skills might be exploited – or how 'Chan' could earn his keep after settling in to a new life in China.

The two intelligence officers minding Clarke

shared the table with Wu and his visitors. Clarke sat opposite his host and between his chaperons, while Zhang was at the ambassador's right. Wu was keen to chat with Zhang, whom he found well informed, direct and highly intelligent – exactly as Ambassador Li had described him in a cable from Canberra.

The dinner had proved an easy affair. Clarke was full of charm and appeared honoured by the gesture the ambassador had afforded him. He was at ease and his intake of alcohol had so far produced no change in behaviour. And that was something Wu and his colleagues were intent on observing. All were aware, as was Zhang, that Wang in Beijing had some notion of putting Clarke to good use.

High on her list was the possibility of giving him a new identity: that of an Australian-born Canadian citizen. He would make regular crossings of the US border and act as bagman for top Americans selling secrets to China. Unbeknown to Clarke, he would undergo a lengthy probation during which any propensity to betray the Chinese – as he had betrayed his fellow Australians – would be scrupulously assessed. He might even be subjected to mock interrogation to see if he cracked under pressure.

Wang believed that Clarke's Anglo-Saxon features, coupled with his training and experience, had significant potential if used in this way. Gao, already in Beijing, had agreed. Despite lingering question marks over the man, his aptitude as a spy could not be dismissed. China had an insatiable appetite for secret intelligence and his sorts of talents were in short supply.

It was not surprising that Zhang had been so alarmed by Beth Cantrell's appearance in Blok M. A lot was at stake.

As the evening wore on, Ambassador Wu felt he had the measure of Clarke. The others were aware of the fact. They could tell from the direction in which the conversation was now steered. It was the cue for a prearranged plan to begin.

Wu led the way, smiling at Clarke. 'If you're feeling a bit under the weather,' he said, 'there's a little something I can tell you about. In fact, I often fall back on it myself. You see, we have a special roasted wheat tea in China that happens to be one of my favourites. It's magic when your head starts to spin. Let me get you some and you can see for yourself.'

Clarke nodded appreciatively.

Wu turned to one of the minders. 'Have a word with the cook, please,' he said in English, 'and ask him to make a pot for our friend.'

The minder was back in a matter of minutes, with the cook following soon after, carrying a tray with a small, squarish pot and a matching ox-blood porcelain cup. He placed the cup in front of the guest and poured slowly. A wisp of steam climbed gracefully into the air as Clarke watched in silence.

'It might be a bit tart on the palate at first,' Wu said, as Clarke took a sip. 'If that's the right term.'

The cook, who was standing behind him, awaited the foreigner's reaction. Clarke seemed in no way averse to the flavour. When the cup was near empty, the cook filled it again.

'You're not going to join me?' Clarke asked.

'Yes, why not,' Wu replied. 'Why don't we all have a cup?' He glanced at his colleagues, all of whom welcomed the idea. '*Women dou,*' he said to the cook: a round for us too.

The cook went back to the kitchen to make a larger pot, one that would not have the powerful sleeping tablet he had slipped into Clarke's tea. By the time he returned, Clarke was beginning to feel a little drowsy.

'Look, would you mind if I had a lie down?' he asked his host, disoriented.

'Feel free,' Wu replied. 'Don't stand on ceremony with us.'

Zhang smiled at the ambassador as he helped Clarke up from his seat. So much for that American woman, he thought. She's in for a devilishly long wait at the Hilton.

Zhang's job was to see Clarke safely aboard the *Minghua* and he would allow nothing to cut across that.

Who knows? he thought. If she's that close to Clarke, she'd have to know about his hangup with boats and their engines. And with a long sea voyage coming up, she might cause him to have second thoughts.

He was pleased he had mentioned his concerns privately to Ambassador Wu.

SEVENTEEN

Jakarta: Thursday, 1 June, 7.30 a.m.

The intercept team had learnt of the excursion to Bogor from listening to the tycoon and his driver, Herman, discussing it with Zhang after he'd returned from the dinner. The minders had gone back to the embassy. Clarke had slept in the car all the way, which a surveillance squad noted as it followed behind. It was soon apparent too that the Mercedes was not heading for the Hilton and that Clarke was unlikely to call Cantrell to explain what had happened. The elaborate preparations that the team had made were wasted.

When the gates of the compound closed and the car pulled up at the door, the eavesdroppers had heard the tycoon calling out to a servant: 'Come and help Herman carry this drunkard up to his room.' Later, when Clarke was bedded down for the night, plans for the trip were finalised. The group's speech had come through clearly, with hardly a word missed. 'Don't worry,' Zhang had said, 'he'll be fine in the morning – he has to be. We're determined to get him outside the city for the day.'

Now, in the morning, Mason, Cantrell and the others were ready and waiting.

The Americans had arranged for four Indonesians on the CIA's payroll to be rigged out in military garb. The uniform of ABRI – the Army – had an authority all its own. The men were in the surveillance van detailed to follow the Mercedes on the round trip to Bogor. Their help would be vital if a clear opportunity presented itself to flag the car down and subject the Australian to a routine ID check. Invited to step inside the van, he would be overpowered with the aid of chloroform pads. The door would be closed and the vehicle would head back to Jakarta.

Mason was also in the van, together with the interceptor who would monitor the Mercedes' car phone and coordinate radio contact with two other vehicles used by the team. These were parked a few hundred metres away from the house.

Car One – a blue Mazda hatchback – was to be driven by Cantrell, accompanied by Lambert and a CIA officer of Chinese extraction. Car Two – a green Honda Accord – carried Pellegrini, with the driver also a CIA man. Both vehicles, together with the van, carried bogus plates.

It was now apparent to those listening in that Clarke and Zhang had finished breakfast with their host and his wife. Zhang excused himself and went off to his room. Clarke did the same, though he first asked if he might use the phone.

'Go right ahead,' the tycoon said. 'You know where it is.'

A moment later, Cantrell's mobile rang in Car One. 'Hello? Oh, Martin – what happened to you?'

She flicked a switch, which allowed the rest of the team to tune in.

'Beth, honey, I'm sorry for standing you up. I just couldn't get away from that dinner. We were stuck there until well after midnight. It was heady business stuff, you know, and I just couldn't get to a phone.'

'Don't worry,' Cantrell said. Her priority was to make a backup arrangement. 'These things do happen, Martin, but I must say I was disappointed. You can't imagine how much I was looking forward to last night.'

'Well, that's why I'm calling.'

'Great. So shall we do dinner tonight?'

'How does 8.30 sound?'

'Fine with me. Will we stick with the Hilton?'

'Why not? Oh, and remember, you must tell me about the bloke with the *Ornithoptera*.'

'Godammit, Martin! Am I still sharing you with an insect? But seriously, what are you up to today?'

'I'm taking my associate – the Chinese chap you met – up to Bogor. I want to show him the Gardens. It's his first time in Indonesia.'

'Well, that'll be nice.'

'Not as nice as it would be with you.'

You mealy-mouthed crook, she thought. You haven't changed one bit. Your one-liners are as slick as ever.

Cantrell and Clarke had made a number of trips to the place which, while interesting, had not been particularly memorable. Clarke had grown so querulous on one occasion that she had returned to Jakarta alone. His memory was short and selective.

'So, 8.30 then, at the Hilton,' she said.

'Done.'

The team's relief was palpable.

Mason's mind, however, drifted off to something that had kept him awake the previous night. What would happen when he and Zhang came face to face? Now he found himself ploughing that same field again.

'Bogor's not called the City of Rain for nothing,' Herman said. 'It pours here almost every day.'

Short and wiry, he took two umbrellas out of the boot. He had parked the Mercedes close to the main gate of the Gardens.

'You'll both need one,' he said, handing them over. 'Believe me, you'll know what I mean.'

Herman's English was meticulous and he used it with pride. For him this time with Clarke and Zhang was a source of great pleasure. 'As a chauffeur in Jakarta, I rarely get to feel included,' he said. It was with Clarke that he shared the greater affinity, though he found Zhang intriguing. The latter was Chinese, and Herman, as a good Indonesian, distrusted that race, though they employed him. Zhang's curiosity was boundless and Herman found himself constantly answering questions, often catching the visitor's eye in the rear vision mirror and getting an encouraging smile. He was much taken by Zhang's reasons for wanting to visit the Gardens.

Not only was this Chinese interested in plants but he also had a longstanding fascination with Sir Stamford Raffles, the Englishman whose brainchild the Gardens had been. A botanist, Raffles had spent much of his time at this hill station in Java's central mountains, away from Batavia, the disease-ridden capital. Zhang had read widely on the British Empire and had first come across Raffles as the founder of Singapore, only later learning that the British had once briefly controlled Indonesia as well.

Clarke and Zhang waited as Herman locked the car. Zhang wore his suit trousers and a white business shirt, while Clarke looked the archetypal tourist in long, baggy shorts and his bold batik shirt.

At the gate, Herman insisted on paying, which he explained was on the strict orders of his boss. Clarke and Zhang wanted him to join them inside, but he declined that too.

'Keep dry,' he said as they parted, 'and don't stray from the path.'

On the trip from the city, with the visitors clearly intent on reaching Bogor as quickly as they could, Cantrell had decided that the suveillance van and Car Two should go on ahead. As a result, when Herman pulled into the carpark Mason and Pellegrini were already there. Dressed in shorts and casual shirts, they had obscured their features with dark glasses and broad-rimmed straw hats. They were mingling now with a coachload of German tourists about to go in, and were only metres away when Herman approached the ticket window with his charges in tow.

On arrival Cantrell and Lambert parked nearby. Wearing the same sort of clothes, they too merged with the tourists.

Each team member was equipped with an earpiece, which kept everybody – inside the Gardens and out – on one common net. Cantrell, Mason and the other Australians carried sealed chloroform pads as a backup. This was in case their plan had to change and they needed to help their 'fellow tourist' – Clarke – who would suffer an asthma attack. Their present strategy, however, was to wait until later and take Clarke as he came out through the gate. The four team members on the inside would monitor his progress every inch of the way. Two would exit before him and two would follow behind. The van would pull up close to the gate as Clarke approached and the ABRI soldiers would take up position alongside it. They would casually close in on Clarke and, under the guise of wanting to check his ID, would escort him to the van.

Duress would be used if required. Once inside, the sliding door would be shut and he would be quickly sedated. The van would head for the toll road and go back to Jakarta.

The others would endeavour to deal with Zhang's inevitable protests. Mason's presence alone, the team believed, might be enough to dissuade him from calling for help.

A hundred metres inside, Zhang stopped dead in his tracks and marvelled at the extent of the place. He turned full circle to take in the lushness of the landscape and its vast expanses of green. From lawns to tall tropical trees, it unfolded in every direction. Flowerbeds and shrubs in full bloom provided splashes of colour, adding an artist's touch to the scene.

He breathed in deeply, savouring the fragrance and earthiness lacing the air. A strip of grey asphalt stretched out ahead, as straight as a die, guiding him and Clarke further into this world of serenity.

'Truly, it's a sight for sore eyes,' Zhang said. 'I can't believe there are *eighty* hectares of this.'

Clarke looked up at the comment. His mind had been elsewhere. God, it's amazing, he thought, how passionate he gets about things. I've never met a Chinese with this sort of verve.

'OK, Martin, what I'd like to see first, if you have no objection, is Raffles' memorial to his wife. He buried her here, you know.'

Clarke knew where it was. On his first visit with Cantrell she had expressed the same wish.

'It's just over there,' he said, pointing.

'Let me tell you,' Zhang said, after a moment of reflection as they walked, 'that even in the short time we've been in this place I feel as though all my worries have gone. Really, it's a very special experience and for that, Martin, I'm very grateful to you.'

Zhang's sincerity showed on his face. He believed it was the least he could do for this tormented soul, whose life was about to change radically. China, Zhang knew, would challenge Clarke to the full. And the interrogator, who Gao had already sent down from Beijing, would begin working him over as soon as the *Minghua* pulled away from the dock.

At the memorial Zhang studied the dedication that Raffles had written to his wife. The words were touching and he scribbled them down in his notebook. Just as the pair turned to go a light rain started to fall. It was more a delight than a nuisance and they relished it as they strolled further into the Gardens.

'Now, let's see,' Zhang said, 'there should be some old Dutch graves near here . . . '

His words were cut short as the skies opened up. Huge drops of rain came pelting down, splashing up from the asphalt like exploding grenades. The men put their umbrellas up, but to little effect. Shelter was the only answer. They ran up ahead to a bamboo grove whose stands hung outwards like massive green feathers. There they found the ground completely dry.

'You know, there's a saying in China,' Zhang shouted above the noise of the rain, 'that when it pours like this the heavens are . . . '

Suddenly a slender young Indonesian appeared in front of them. It was as if he had come from inside the bamboo. He stood only a few steps away, his black shirt and jeans soaked. For a moment his presence seemed benign, though his yellow-brown face was devoid of expression and his stare intense.

From behind his back he slowly raised his arm and pointed a sleek, silvery automatic pistol straight at Zhang's chest. It had a silencer attached. His other arm hung limply by his side.

It all happened so fast there was no time to react.

Zhang looked at Clarke, but he merely shrugged as if saying: 'Don't ask me!'

Mason and Pellegrini, sheltering nearby, had seen all this, though the rain skewed their vision. Cantrell and Lambert, positioned further back, had noticed their colleagues waving.

Mason ripped off his hat and dark glasses and, after a quick word to Pellegrini, dashed out to one side. He headed obliquely towards the rear of the grove. Pellegrini beckoned to the others to come forward and then the three team members advanced from the opposite flank.

Mason reached the bamboo in double quick time, rounding the thicket with the aim of tackling the gunman from the rear. Zhang remained still, although Mason knew he was aware of his presence. Clarke stood frozen.

The noise of the rain was a plus, covering any sound.

Mason had the attacker in a headlock before the Indonesian knew what had happened. As he wrestled him to the ground, Zhang lunged at the man's legs. Together they pushed him face down on top of his gun.

Clarke did nothing to help.

When Zhang had the gunman's arms locked behind his back, he lifted him so that Mason could reach underneath for the pistol. Retrieving it, Mason stood and looked Clarke in the eye. He was about to speak, but Clarke turned away. It was then that Mason's suspicions were confirmed. This was no tourist heist, nor a kidnapping. He could sense it. It was a trap.

'*Dangxin!*' he called to Zhang in Mandarin: watch out! '*Women bei zhua zhu le!*': we've been tricked!

Instantly, Zhang understood. It jelled with the way Clarke had shrugged his shoulders earlier.

Clarke now looked up and stared over Mason's shoulder.

Mason turned to discover three more gunmen. They had automatic weapons, which they cocked as they came out of the rain, ordering Zhang to get up and stand next to Mason.

The first gunman brushed himself off, then spat in Mason's face as he snatched his pistol back. No one threatened Clarke.

'What the hell have you done?' Mason called over the noise of the rain, glaring at Clarke as he spoke.

Once again, Clarke looked away. There was little doubt now about what he was involved in. He had cast his lot with Jakarta.

It's no use buying time, Mason thought, though Todd and Joe must be close by, if not the others as well. There's no way we can grab Clarke without someone getting shot, and even if we did there's no way we'd get him out of here, let alone out of the country. It's a lost cause.

'Look, I'm sorry,' Clarke said, suddenly breaking his silence. 'It's such a long story and I don't know how to . . . '

'How to explain away treachery,' Mason shouted. 'You've betrayed ASIS, Martin. You've betrayed Australia, and . . . '

'And you've betrayed China,' Zhang cut in angrily. 'As well as *me*. How could you do it, Martin? Don't you stand for anything? And all the time you knew you'd be pushing me aside, as well as Gao and all the others who've helped you.'

'Look . . .' the traitor said, reaching out.

'No!' one of the gunmen cut across him in English. 'Let's get out of here!'

It was a voice that commanded authority. He was obviously under instructions not to let the Australian renege on his deal. Clarke heeded the order. He fell in with the others and in a moment all of them had disappeared into the grove.

'I'd dearly love to, Greg, believe me,' Zhang said in Chinese. 'But I can't. Somehow it wouldn't be right.'

Mason had offered him a ride back to Jakarta, as much out of friendship as from an odd sense of professional chivalry. He explained that he had colleagues who were keen to make Zhang's acquaintance. He had not expected yes for an answer.

'I'd better stick with my driver, Greg, but thanks all the same.' Zhang was shattered, and it showed.

'Look,' Mason said, 'at least I can walk you to the gate.' He was aware that his colleagues – Lambert and Pellegrini for sure – would be watching and would leave them alone for that time.

'Well, I can't imagine the rule book banning that. So, let's go!' Zhang's smile made Mason laugh and released the pressure.

Cantrell watched them as they strode across the grass to the path. Mason had his arm around Zhang's shoulder. Neither man was bothering to talk over the sound of the rain.

Jakarta: Thursday, 1 June, 10.25 p.m.

'You got him?'

'Indeed we did,' Mantiri said, grinning.

The President had called him to his private residence to hear firsthand how the Bogor exercise had gone. The pair sat in two ornate armchairs enjoying a drink.

'Does he show any remorse at all?'

'Not really. In fact, I wonder if there's anything in his makeup now to be loyal to. Possibly money's all that's left, and the security he thinks he can buy with it. But look, none of us can figure him out. I've spoken to the people who hooked him here, years ago, and they have no idea either.'

'Well, Canberra certainly fell for his line, hmmm?'

The President had been kept abreast of major intelligence feeds that had been channelled through Clarke over the years.

'Absolutely, and it's been confirmed many times over by our other recruits down there. But as they've told us, by the time smart people in the system realise what's going on, it's too late. Too many senior people have too much to lose and types like Clarke never get weeded out.'

'So, what do we squeeze out of him now? Is he a spent force, or is there mileage in him yet?'

'Not a lot, except perhaps for a debrief, which he's agreed to start in a day or two. That might throw up something. We asked him to keep his eyes and ears open with the Chinese here, in case he picked up something on them. He says he's pretty clear now on what their priorities are in Indonesia. There might be value in that. But all in all, I don't hold out much hope for him. He claims he can help us with training. You know, tradecraft, counter-surveillance, interrogation — that kind of thing. He was on about it when he passed through here a few months back. But I doubt he'd be of much use.'

'I see,' the President said.

'No, all it'll boil down to in the end is the leverage we'll get from doing Canberra a favour.

Beyond that, we'll just settle him in and make sure he doesn't get in the way.'

'Which *we'll* have to pay for?'

'Oh, no. No, no. He's had a huge sum of money transferred from Hong Kong. Somehow he persuaded the Chinese to fill up a trust account they had for him there, before he left Australia. He's told Andi — the police fellow who helped recruit him — that he couldn't have faced coming here without his own means of support. That's what this whole Chinese caper was about — to fund his retirement here and to queer the pitch of those two former colleagues of his, Poulson and Imlach. These two set up shop here a short while ago and basically work for us. Apparently that was originally Clarke's idea. He was going to leave ASIS first and get the business up and running, then they were going to join him. Instead they opted out early and left him high and dry, but still used his contacts. That made him hopping mad. He must've felt very betrayed.'

The President wagged his head. 'You know,' he said, 'if we ever need a favour from Beijing, we could hand him over to them. What do you think?'

'Yes, that's definitely on the cards, but . . . '

'But what?' the President said, noticing Mantiri's puzzled look.

'Oh, nothing really. It's just that he's told us how devastated he was when we nabbed him in Bogor and Zhang — the Chinese chap who brought him from Sydney — found out what he was up to. That wasn't meant to happen. It seems he holds Zhang in high regard and hates the idea he betrayed him.'

The President and Mantiri looked at each other, both with their eyebrows raised.

Clarke sat alone on his bed. He was in a back room of BAKIN's guesthouse on the outskirts of Jakarta and his thoughts were on Zhang. He recalled the day they'd driven along Ocean Road at Palm Beach in Sydney, and suddenly he found himself sniffing, his nostrils filled once more with the smell of cut grass that had wafted in through the BMW's windows that day.

They were talking about the psychology of spying, he remembered, and how easy it was to get lost.

And Zhang had said: 'Well, from what I've heard, it all depends on what you are *before* you go in. That's your lifeline and your anchor. It's like a safety rope tied to your belt. And if you're not properly harnessed before intelligence grabs you, you can't expect to find much to cling to. You're in free-fall over the cliff.'

He'd been riveted by Zhang's observation. 'So, what sage in the spy world did you pick that up from?' he'd asked.

'Oh, I can't remember now, but whoever it was, they knew what they were talking about.'

If it was Gao, Clarke thought, Zhang would've remembered – and he'd have said. No, it must've been somebody else, but who?

Zhang in fact knew only too well. It was Mason.

Somebody laughed in the guest room next door. The rain was still pelting down. And he was back in the bamboo grove.

'Fucking hell,' Clarke shouted, punching his fist into the bed. 'How could I betray *Zhang*, of all people?'

He knew now that guilt was eating him up. And there was no lifeline to reach out for on the side of this abyss. He cried, hard and deep, and feared he might not be able to stop.

For the first time in his life, Martin Clarke considered the question of suicide. He was beginning to think it was the only way out.

EPILOGUE

Sydney: Saturday, 3 June, midnight

Mason and Cantrell sat on a park bench near the harbour. The night was fine: starry, crisp and still. Their grassy knoll sloped away sharply to the water and was strewn with curled leaves from Moreton Bay figs. It was the same spot – so Mason had heard from Zhang in their one Sydney meeting so far – at which Clarke had confessed he no longer felt safe in Australia and had asked if Beijing could give him safe haven.

A late ferry to Manly cut across the mirror reflections, leaving a shimmering triangle of gold in its wake. The pair sat in contented silence for a while, savouring the calm of the place. Dinner at the Sheraton with the combined team had been a pleasant affair, with welcome news from both Lambert and Templeton. Much of the future was already defined.

But Mason was still haunted by thoughts of Clarke. One moment his mind was filled with images of the man's jealousy years ago in Jakarta, and of what that had led to for poor Mustafa; then these were followed by replays of the fight over Prue.

Now images of old Alfie Trevelyan came to mind.

'Remember, Greg, if the Service isn't cleaned up, these Charlies will simply perpetuate their own existence. They'll only promote to the top those of the same ilk as themselves and the cause will be lost.'

Well, Alfie wasn't far wrong, Mason thought. As he wasn't with Martin and Bass. He picked them straight away. I must get down to Canberra to see him as soon as I can and tell him . . .

'You know, it's funny, isn't it,' Cantrell said, cutting his musing short. 'When we met back in April at Cremorne wharf, I'd actually bet Ben Jameson a hundred bucks you'd be onside by the time we arrived at the Quay.'

'Oh, really?'

'Yes, but looking back, my concept then of where you were coming from was really incredibly narrow. Even now I can't believe I couldn't see what you had on your plate. We all knew you'd do a good job – and you have – but I had no idea what I was dragging you into. OK, I knew you were battling to close off on Jakarta, but I hadn't seen the complexity of it. To me, Prue's betrayal, then Martin's, then your management letting you down, were all wrapped up in one. I hadn't realised that each had to be put to rest in its own special way.'

'Well, these things happen, Beth.'

That's the best spin to put on it, Mason thought. But it hasn't been easy.

'Come on, don't be modest with me,' she said. 'Not after what I've learnt about myself from this whole experience. You see, Greg, you've made me look long and hard at where I'm going, too, and that's why I've decided to get out.'

Mason knew she was toying with the idea of leaving the Agency and had had it confirmed in their talk on the Gulfstream. But he had not imagined she would elect to stay in Sydney. To begin with, she planned to join Mason in his resources and energy business. Lambert had also opted to abort his career and would be coming on board in a month. Templeton would see the year out in Canberra and was considering doing the same. McKinnon had assured them, via Mason, that he would 'keep the bastards honest' through an on-going stream of investigative reporting.

'First up,' Cantrell said, 'I want to get out of that safe house and find a place of my own; then we can look at where to start. Someone else can worry about how far Washington pushes Canberra to clean up its act.'

'I have no quibble with that,' he replied.

She could tell from his smile that he had already let go.

One person, he thought to himself, can only do so much. You have to move on. Martin and Bass have their backs to the wall, and I'm still alive and likely to thrive. What more could I want?

He could hear Alfie whispering in his ear, using the sort of language that became more endearing the coarser it got: 'Get your arse into gear, dickhead! Life's full of phases – some long, some short – and you've got a bloody good one heading your way. You have fine people around you, people who stand for the same things you do, so enjoy it. Don't miss one fucking minute!'

Mason felt a quiet calm he had not known for a very long while.

LANCE COLLINS
WARREN REED
PLUNGING POINT

INTELLIGENCE FAILURES, COVER-UPS AND CONSEQUENCES

Foreword by
PHILLIP KNIGHTLEY

PLUNGING POINT
INTELLIGENCE FAILURES, COVER-UPS AND CONSEQUENCES

LANCE COLLINS AND WARREN REED

IN THE AGE OF THE WAR ON TERROR, HIGH-QUALITY, RELIABLE INTELLIGENCE IS MORE CRUCIAL TO OUR NATIONAL SECURITY THAN EVER. EFFECTIVE INTELLIGENCE SAVES LIVES.

Yet from September 11, 2001 in New York to Bali, Madrid, London and the unfolding situation in Iraq, we hear endless claims and counter-claims about what went wrong and why.

As former intelligence officers with the military and ASIS, Lance Collins and Warren Reed are ideally placed to assess these claims. From the policy-makers to the agents on the ground, the authors examine the chain of command and the role of vested interests. They provide an overview for the general reader of how intelligence services work in the post-September 11 world.

Non-partisan and clearly written, *Plunging Point* outlines the historical context, the present problems and future solutions for intelligence services and their societies.

EVERY AWARE AUSTRALIAN NEEDS TO READ THIS.